The House Called Mbabati
A Novel Out of Africa

Samantha Ford

******

Dedicated to the memory of John Gordon Davis

Acknowledgements

To the late much loved and admired author John Gordon-Davis for his invaluable input into my story; his writing course in Spain will remain as one of the great experiences of my life. *www.johngordondavis.com*

My thanks to Leopards Leap, producers of a most excellent South African wine, for allowing me to use Leopards Leap as the name of Jake Henderson's house. *www.leopardsleap.co.za*

When I was growing up in Singapore I dreamed about going on safari in Africa. When that day arrived I chose the legendary Ker & Downey to plan my trip. Ker & Downey have a rich and historic link with safaris and have been in the business for over five decades. I hope my story will inspire you to travel to this beautiful continent and discover the magic for yourself. *www.kerdowney.com*

I have been on many safaris over the years and stayed in sumptuous lodges that took my breath away. Angama Mara, in Kenya, has topped everything else because it has something no other lodge has. This is where many of the scenes from the film *Out of Africa* were shot. The hair washing scene in the river, the picnic on top of the hill – unforgettable. I could almost hear the haunting, notes of Mozart's Clarinet Concerto floating up into the velvet, star studded heavens. *www.angama.com*

"A bloody good story with plenty of twists and turns and a totally unexpected ending. An excellent read indeed.

An unforgettable cast of characters within a story which twists and turns at a ferocious pace. A real page turned with a breath-taking and richly rewarding ending.

This story, with its extraordinary plot, had me guessing until the very clever ending. So clever, in fact, that I went back to the beginning of the story and read it again!

The House Called Mbabati is skilfully written and layered with mystery and intrigue. Set against the romantic backdrop of Kenya and

South Africa, the author manages to sweep the reader away into another world where the scenes are so well depicted one can almost smell the hot dry earth and the dusty pelts of the animals."

John Gordon-Davis

Chapter One

London 2007
Sophie

The thick fog swirled around her long grey cloak and dress, accentuating the whiteness of her face as she stared through the window. She had passed the shop many times, but never entered. Now, with time running out, and hoping for one final connection to her past, she had stopped.

Sophie, sitting inside at her desk, sensed someone was watching her. She looked up uneasily and saw the ghostly figure at the window.

The nun was back.

She had seen her before, but the woman had never come in. Now she was staring at her. Puzzled, she wondered what an elderly nun would find of interest in an African memorabilia shop in central London, and why she was being studied so intently. She looked back down at the papers on her desk, still conscious of the nun's eyes on her. After a minute or two, Sophie lifted her gaze and saw she hadn't moved. She had closed the shop only five minutes earlier, now she hesitated, then went to the door and unlocked it. A blast of arctic air followed in the nun's wake, causing Sophie to catch her breath as she pushed the door shut.

"We're closed, Sister, but if you'd like to have a look around, that's fine. Hard to imagine somewhere hot and sunny like Africa when you're in the middle of an English winter isn't it?

The nun inclined her head in agreement.

Sophie returned to her desk, rubbing her hands together in an attempt to warm them.

A small silver bell, stamped with a crest, glowed in the reflection of the lamp next to it. She glanced around the shop trying to see it through the eyes of the woman who was now looking around.

A pile of records was stacked up next to an assortment of old record players, some with the iconic trumpet of the 1920s. Steamer-trunks made from wood, canvas and battered tin filled one corner, the labels scratched and faded making it nearly impossible to read the destinations their once owners had travelled to. On the sides, stencilled in white, were the names of long-forgotten people who had journeyed by sea looking for romance and adventure.

Displayed on a trestle-table were various items made of silver. Candlesticks and cutlery, napkin holders with worn and illegible engravings, cruet sets in velvet presentation cases, sugar scuttles and sauce boats - objects which had graced elegant tables in places far from England. A random assortment of personal possessions, each with their own story, as lost now as their long gone owners; things that would have brought a sense of continuity to lives in an unfamiliar land, now laid out for the curious to ponder over.

On another table were telephones with cloth leads and metal mouthpieces, brass, copper and silver ashtrays and cigar boxes, and matchboxes with branding only the dead would recognize.

Hundreds of books lined the walls of the shop. Having survived the hot climate, the ants, the moths and book-worms, they stood ready for the next reader to take down. Books on hunting and hunters' stories; fauna and flora, painstakingly copied under a merciless sun for future generations; books on how to farm the hostile and unforgiving land; cookery books, medical books, and others, to help understand and survive in a new country, thousands of miles from the familiar.

The nun opened a cracked photograph album and peered myopically at the forgotten faces of nameless people. She closed it and placed it on an old writing bureau with hidden drawers and dried up ink-wells.

Sophie was proud of her shop and the memories it held. She'd been shrewd enough to advertise in local newspapers all over Africa, promising to pay good prices for pieces from the estates of the deceased. She'd contacted legal firms there offering the same deal, and this was where the bulk of her stock originated. Gradually, as the business grew and her name became synonymous with African memorabilia, her shop became a drop-off point for people selling or buying, and for travellers dropping off letters and messages. At the back she had arranged sofas and chairs where she offered coffee; it had proved to be a popular place to rendezvous. Once a month she would stay open late: this was her renowned sun-downer night which always attracted a good crowd, not only regulars who lived in London, but visitors passing through. It surprised her how so many of them knew each other, or were friends of friends from Kenya, South Africa, Tanzania or Zimbabwe.

She watched the nun move around the shop, stooping as though weighed down; her fingers trailing over a box of cutlery, a brace of

8

silver-backed brushes, a pith helmet and a fly swat with an ivory handle. She seemed lost in a world of her own. Maybe she'd been a missionary in Africa somewhere, Sophie thought, glancing out of the window. It was starting to rain; she needed get back to her flat before the night set in.

The Sister turned and walked towards her.

"So kind of you to let me look around. You have interesting things here, each one with a story, I'm sure."

Sophie smiled at her, surprised to see she wasn't elderly at all, probably only in her sixties, but having the look of someone who had suffered. Deep lines etched her face and her eyes were dull with sadness. She looked ill.

The nun's eyes moved down to Sophie's desk.

"May I?" she asked as she leaned across and picked up the bell; it chimed delicately as she turned it around. She put on the glasses that hung around her neck and stared at the crest. Drawing in her breath she reached out a hand to steady herself.

"Dear Lord, where did you get this?"

"It's pretty isn't it? I'm not quite sure where it came from."

The nun shook the bell again. Impulsively, Sophie placed her hand over the nun's. "No-one has any use for these bells anymore, they never sell. I'd be happy for you to have it."

"It's lovely, but I can't accept it. You must keep it." She looked at Sophie's hand covering her own as she returned the bell to the desk. She looked up, and the expression on her face froze as she fumbled for the cross around her neck.

A grainy black and white photograph of an old house surrounded by tall trees was tacked to the wall. Two carved eagles stood guard above an oval door. Leaded windows on all three floors looked out over elegant lawns and manicured bushes. In one of the top floor windows was a shadowy figure.

"And this photograph?" she whispered, her face ashen.

Sophie glanced behind her in surprise and laughed. "Oh, that! I had it blown up from an original. It looks mysterious, doesn't it? Kind of spooky. It was in an..." She stopped in mid-sentence, concerned at the nun's blood drained face.

"Are you alright? Here..." She indicated a cane chair with a zebra patterned cushion, "sit down for a moment. I'll get you some water."

9

Sophie watched her over her shoulder as she filled a glass in the tiny kitchen at the back of the shop. Returning she knelt down and handed it to her. "Have you seen this before?" she asked, as the nun sipped her water and stared at the photograph

"Yes… but where did you get it from?"

She frowned as she tried to remember. "A student brought in an envelope, about a year or two ago, I wasn't in the shop at the time. He told my assistant a Miss..." She tapped her forehead willing the name to come to her. "A Miss... I think it was a Miss Gray? He said Miss Gray would call in to collect it, but she never did. The envelope was open.

"I thought if I went through it I might find out who Miss Gray was, and where she lived. Or perhaps there would be some address showing where it had come from, so I could return it. There were some letters and a diary if I recall..."

The nun's expression of anxiety turned to one of fear.

"Not that I read them or anything," Sophie said hastily. "There was nothing helpful inside but I liked the photograph so I had it enlarged. I put the original back in the envelope."

The nun's eyes returned to the photograph as Sophie talked, her fingers moving distractedly over the cross around her neck.

"What did you do with the envelope, my child? Do you still have it?"

Sophie shook her head. "I honestly can't remember but I wouldn't have thrown it away. As you can see the shop is small, so once a year I do an inventory and take everything which isn't going to sell to a warehouse in Islington. I do the same with letters or parcels. If they haven't been claimed within two years, it's unlikely they will be, but I always keep them - just in case."

She was alarmed to see the woman's eyes swamped with tears.

"I'll be making a trip there in a week or so," she said hastily. "I can look through the mail and see if I can find the envelope. Do you know who Miss Gray is?"

"Yes," she whispered. "I do. I know Miss Gray."

"If you tell me which convent you're with, I'll bring it to you, and perhaps you can pass it on to her? Is she a nun too?"

The nun smiled weakly and attempted to get up. Sophie helped her to her feet.

"Thank you, God bless you. I'm with the Daughters of the Lord, not far from here."

Sophie walked her to the door and opened it. They both dipped their faces against the cold air.

"Where was the photograph taken?"

The nun turned around, her eyes lingering over Sophie's face. "In East Africa. There's a house there called Mbabati. It was abandoned many years ago."

"And what is your name, Sister?"

She hesitated for a brief second. "Elizabeth. Sister Elizabeth."

"I'm Sophie."

"Goodbye Sophie, goodbye my child."

Sophie watched her grey cloak merging into the even greyer night; turning back into the shop she locked the door behind her.

Picking up the bell she felt its coolness in her hand. She held it up to the light and studied the crest. Moving closer to the photograph until only an inch or two away, she peered at the two eagles standing guard over the door. She glanced again at the crest on the bell.

They were identical.

Chapter Two

MBABATI 2007
Luke

The bull elephant stood motionless among the trees, then lifted his heavy trunk, his old head moving from side to side. The house stared blindly back. There was no moon tonight but he knew this place. There was no fear in him; there was no reason to feel that. He looked at the blank windows and then down at the small thatched building set amongst the trees to the rear of the house. From the window a light glowed. He was not afraid of the man who lived there, for he remembered him. Satisfied the old place still stood, he melted back into the night, the rustling and crack of a branch, as he foraged, the only sound carried back on the breathless night air.

The elderly African, lying in his bed, sensed the elephant outside for he came every year. They had called him Tika. Luke had been a young man then, handsome strong and tall. The days had been full with taking care of the family, of her, and the house. The years had passed swiftly then, but now they creaked along, each day turning into a replica of the one before, the loneliness and isolation of the place biting into him.

He pulled the rabbit-skin cover over his thin bones and turned on his side, comforted by the fleeting presence of his old friend. Mbabati had been a happy house once - but now silent with its memories. He would still guard the place in the hope the package he'd sent with Matthew had reached its London destination.

Two years before Luke was visiting his cousin at a neighbouring ranch, when by chance, his cousin mentioned his employer's son, Matthew, would soon be leaving for England. Luke had known him since he was a little boy; the next morning he found him cleaning his rifle out on the veranda and asked the young man if he would help him.

"It is an important envelope for the memsahib. When she left the country, she went to this place called London. I am troubled unless I can get this package to her."

Matthew scratched his head and frowned. "What's in the package? Why's it so important?"

Luke hesitated looking down at his dust-covered feet. Afterwards, after the Bwana disappeared, he had given her the letters but she had insisted he keep them somewhere safe, along with the book for writing in, and this he had done - until now.

Getting no answer from Luke, Matthew smiled at him, his teeth white against his tanned face, his blond hair bleached by the sun. He put his rifle down on the table and leaned back in his chair. "London's a big city, but there's a place where I can leave your envelope."

Luke looked at him expectantly. "Where is this place, Mister Matthew? Will this envelope be found?"

"It's a shop. The woman who runs it, Sophie, knows everyone. She's bound to know someone who knows your memsahib. But I need to know what's in it, Customs may stop me."

"Some letters, and the writing book. I do not wish for them to get lost. I cannot read or write so I will put in the ringing bell from the dining-room table, then she will know the package is from old Luke."

"I'll take it and leave it with Sophie. Don't worry, it'll be safe."

"Perhaps you will help me again, Mister Matthew? I had to find a secret place for the letters and the writing book - a place where no-one would find them. To go to this place I will need someone to drive me. I am an old man and my legs will not carry me so far. The bus which is bringing me here will not come back for many days."

Matthew looked at the hopeful face of the elderly African. He picked up his rifle and stood up. "I need to go into town Luke, I'll take you back to Mbabati, it's not far out of the way."

He negotiated the hard packed dirt road, carefully avoiding the worst of the ruts, scanning the bush for animals as he drove. Herds of impala scattered at the sound of the Land Cruiser, leaping gracefully into the air like young ballerinas.

He pulled up at the entrance gates of Mbabati, a cloud of red dust billowed behind the vehicle before settling on the dry grey bush. Matthew wiped his sleeve over his sunglasses and turned to his passenger. "Here we are, Luke, I'll wait for you."

Luke hesitated. "It is not at the house - you must drive past and turn to the right. There is a path which leads to the hide; this is where we must go."

Matthew glanced through the gates. He saw the shuttered windows, the house locked up and abandoned. He had heard the stories which had led to the demise of the house, but he'd been too young to be bothered with ghosts from the past, and the gossip and speculation.

He started the engine waving distractedly at a fly on the windscreen. "How far away is the hide?"

Twenty minutes later, and following Luke's directions, he brought the vehicle to a halt, then looked around, bewildered. "There's nothing here but bush, old man. Are you sure this is the right place?"

He nodded his grizzled head. "It is a secret place where you can watch the animals but they cannot see you." He climbed awkwardly, and with some difficulty, from the vehicle, and within seconds he had disappeared.

Matthew jumped out of the vehicle and looked around curiously; he began to discern, from the growth of the trees and bushes around him, the suggestion of what had once been a path. It led to a small structure on short stilts sitting just off a water hole.

Thick bush covered all the sides and the roof, almost impossible to see with the naked eye. He shivered suddenly as though the temperature had dropped with its proximity to the water.

The unmoving water had a thick green scum on its surface and smelt stagnant. The silhouette of a dead tree, its withered branches pointing accusingly at the sky, added to the eerie feel of the place. There was complete stillness, as if the animals were still afraid to come here to drink. The sudden warning bark of a baboon made him jump.

He strode up to the hide, chastising himself for his overactive imagination. He pushed the slightly opened door and went inside. It was bigger than he had thought from outside and consisted of three rooms: a small living area with a rotting deck, a basic kitchen, the surface bare except for an empty bottle of champagne, lying on its side, its neck festooned with cobwebs. The only other room was built around the solid girth of a tree, its branches and leaves forming a natural ceiling.

Luke was on his knees by a rusted bed with a stained mattress, overgrown with weeds and vines, scraping the earth at the base of the tree. He looked up startled when he saw Matthew.

"Is this where you hid the letters?" Matthew asked quietly.

"Yes. No-one can find this place, unless I show them the way." He grunted with satisfaction and lifted a square biscuit tin from its hiding place. Blowing away the dust and using his sleeve to remove the remains of the dirt, he sat back on his haunches. Prising open the lid he peered inside.

14

"*Eish*," he uttered, shaking his head. "Everything is here just as it was many years ago when I buried it. The envelope is still strong; it can be used for the journey to this place called London."

Satisfied, he closed the lid then stood up stiffly and led the way out; glancing back fearfully he pulled the flimsy door shut behind them. "We can go now, Mister Matthew. Perhaps you will take me back to Mbabati? I must get the ringing bell and my task will be finished."

Matthew waited in the vehicle outside the house, loath to go inside after his experience, and his reaction, at the hide. Whatever was in the parcel, letters or diaries, he didn't want to know about. The whole thing had begun to freak him out. With the warm sun on his face he turned his thoughts to the future awaiting him in England. Let Africa and this forgotten house keep its secrets, the past didn't concern him.

Luke returned to the Land Rover carrying his package. "Will you write the name 'Miss Gray' on this for me Mister Matthew?"

Late that night Luke finally drifted off to sleep, satisfied his package would be in good hands. Tomorrow he would go into the house and dust the rooms, as he had done every day since the house had been left. He would guard the place with what was left of his life and try not to worry about what would happen after he had gone.

******

Luke's simple longing to send the package and its contents to her, to comfort her and let her know he had not forgotten her, would now inadvertently expose something the two sisters and Luke had tried so desperately to hide for over twenty years.

Chapter Three
London 2007

The priest anointed the forehead of the nun with holy oil and murmured the ancient prayers for the dying.

The Mother Superior, standing at the foot of the narrow iron bed, crossed herself and left the room.

Hearing the door close, the nun reached with a shaking hand for the sleeve of the priest. "Father," she whispered, "I have little time left. My sister… you must find my sister in Africa; tell her..."

"Tell her what, Sister Elizabeth? Where in Africa is she so I can give her your message?"

Elizabeth sighed as her hand slipped from his sleeve.

The priest scratched his head perplexed; Africa was a big place. Where on earth would he start to look for the sister he didn't even know the name of?

******

After the priest had been in to tell her of Sister Elizabeth's passing and her wish for him to find her sister, he had left.

Now the Mother Superior opened her register and ran her finger down the names until she came to a date.

Taking an iron key hanging from a nail in the wall she made her way down the dark stairs to the basement. Beneath the flickering fluorescent light, she peered at the rows of wooden boxes lining the thick stone walls. Finding the one she was looking for, she returned to her office.

The Mother Superior opened the box and went through the meagre contents. The torn envelope had been delivered by a woman called Sophie a few weeks before. She had refused to allow her to see the dying nun.

After much contemplation, she had decided against giving the envelope to Sister Elizabeth. When a woman accepted their vocation and gave themselves to God, they were expected to hand over any mementoes of their previous life, just as Elizabeth had done over twenty years ago. These items would be returned to their families in the event of their death, although Elizabeth had not given the details of

16

a next-of-kin. She had left the convent as she had entered - with no ties to anyone.

The Mother Superior had placed the envelope in the nun's box in the basement. Perhaps, she thought now, it might contain some information which would help her to locate her sister.

She lifted up the flap and removed a black and white photograph of a substantial house standing alone within sprawling gardens. Curious, the Mother Superior turned it over. *Mbabati* was written on the back in faded and smudged blue ink. There was a bundle of letters tied with white ribbon, now grubby and frayed, and a leather bound diary. Reaching for her magnifying glass she studied the faint letters on the envelopes.

The Mother Superior hesitated. She would need to find a contact of some kind. Perhaps the diary would give some insight into her family and where they lived? Reluctantly she opened it and began to read.

Three hours later, she sat back in her chair, nervously fingering her rosary. The diary had made for uncomfortable reading, the letters more so. Wedged between the pages she had found a yellowed newspaper cutting. Elizabeth had, she surmised, once been an aspiring actress. There were no entries after she had hastily left East Africa.

"May God have mercy on you, and forgive you both," she murmured, crossing herself.

Little wonder, given the sequence of events, that she had fled the country and chosen to live in England. Where was her sister now? Did she too leave East Africa in a hurry, or was she still living in the house called Mbabati, surrounded by the ghosts of their past?

If Sister Elizabeth's sister was still alive, someone would need to break the news of her death to her. After making a phone call, she wrote down the name of a priest she could contact via the Catholic Church in East Africa.

17

Chapter Four

CAPE TOWN 2007
ALEX

Alex took a sip of his coffee and watched the woman working her way from table to table, she held out a small bowl with shaking hands, disturbing the few coins within. He had seen white people in South Africa begging at the traffic lights, a shabby piece of cardboard held out asking for a job, or money, it made him feel uncomfortable. He had often wondered what had happened to this particular woman he was watching now.

Her long grey hair was roughly pulled back into a ponytail. On the occasions Alex had seen her, and being a journalist he was a keen observer of people, she had always been wearing the same clothes: a long, flowered skirt and plain blue blouse; her feet encased in broken sandals, her face drawn and lined with the years already spent.

She approached his table with a tentative smile. As always he gave her all his small change and then, on impulse, he wrapped up half of his toasted sandwich in a paper napkin and pressed it into her hand. She patted his wrist, her nails broken and split, mumbling in a language he didn't recognise.

He turned back to his newspaper, pulling his chair into the shade of an umbrella, as he did so. The heat was overwhelming, but not unusual for Cape Town in December. At this time of the year the city filled with tourists and he found the crowds and the traffic unbearable. He bit into the remaining half of his sandwich and continued reading.

Suddenly a young girl rushed into the restaurant courtyard. "Is there a doctor here?" she called out breathlessly

"What seems to be the problem? I'm not a doctor but maybe I can help?" Alex folded his newspaper and hurriedly followed her.

"A woman fell over and hit her head." She called over her shoulder as she ran towards a crowd gathering near a fountain.

Pushing his way through he saw her lying on the ground. Her bowl and his half-eaten sandwich lay next to her, the coins scattered on the ground.

"Someone call an ambulance," he shouted.

He knelt beside her and shrugging off his jacket he placed it carefully beneath her head. He felt for her pulse; it fluttered like a moth under his fingertips. She opened her eyes briefly, seeming to

18

recognise him; she looked frightened and confused, as she tried to focus on the sea of faces around her. Her eyes returned to his as she held his gaze and whispered.

He bent closer. "Tell me your name?" he asked her urgently.

"Mbabati," she whispered again.

"Barty?" Concerned with her erratic pulse he asked again. "Tell me your name. Is it Barty? Is that your name?"

"Gray. My name is Nicola Gray..."

Her eyes closed and he felt her go limp. Her pulse fluttered and slowed to a stop beneath his fingertips.

He stayed with her as the crowd dispersed, waiting for the ambulance to arrive, and when it did they loaded her body into the back. As the medic started to close the door, he turned to Alex.

"Are you coming?"

Impulsively he jumped into the vehicle. Someone would need to know who she was, he reasoned, and at least he now knew her name.

******

Alex left his contact details at the hospital and took a taxi back to the Waterfront and the restaurant where he had been eating earlier.

The same blond-haired waiter, Charlie, who had served him previously, approached his table.

"Hey, what happened to the woman you went to help?"

"She died just after I got to her," Alex told him, shrugging and lifting his hands slightly in a universal sign of helplessness.

"Ag, shame man," Charlie replied, looking genuinely saddened by the news.

"Did you know her or anything about her?" Alex asked.

"No, nothing at all, she's been around for a couple of years though. You don't see many white women begging around here."

"Where would she have lived, do you think? In some sort of shelter?"

"No idea. Unfortunately Africa isn't sympathetic to elderly white people. There's no infrastructure in place for them, unless you're rich of course."

He glanced around to see if there were any customers needing his attention. There was only one other couple sharing a bottle of wine. He turned back to Alex.

19

"You see, Africans have a different culture," he continued, "I was born in Tanzania so I know a bit about this sort of thing from my parents. Africans respect their elders and when they get old their families take them in and look after them. White people aren't like that," he shook his head sadly, "they toss their ageing folks into homes and forget about them.

"If no-one comes forward to claim her body the authorities will bury her in a pauper's grave and that'll be the end of it." He lifted his shoulders dismissively. "Can I get you anything?"

Alex ordered a coffee and whilst he waited for it he thought about Nicola Gray's last words. She had spoken to him in English; he hadn't detected any dialect. Her voice had been well modulated and educated, with only the slight hint of an accent he couldn't place.

"Barty," he murmured to himself as Charlie put his coffee on the table. Maybe it was the name of her husband.

******

The following evening Alex sat at the bar in the hotel. Over the years, as a journalist, he had specialised in human interest stories and he felt the stirrings of a story in Nicola Gray.

Peter Forbes, the hotel manager, joined him, bringing him out of his reverie. "Why are you looking so glum, Alex? No hot story to chase today. Nothing bad going on in Africa the world needs to know about?" He signalled to the barman to bring him his usual drink.

"Not glum, Peter, just disappointed in human nature."

He raised his eyebrows questioningly and Alex filled him in on the previous two days.

"I find it hard to understand how someone can end up on the streets and no-one gives a damn where they come from, or who they are."

"What did she look like?" Peter asked, taking a sip of his drink.

"A white woman, in her sixties maybe, with long grey hair and a small begging bowl..."

Peter interrupted him: "Yes, I know who you mean - I've seen her around."

"Do you know anything about her?"

"No, nothing, but she was intriguing and I'll tell you why. I'd only been managing the hotel for a couple of months, which was, let me think ... a year ago.

"One afternoon, just after lunch, I heard someone playing the piano. At first I thought it was a CD, normally we have that bloody awful background stuff, but this music was classical, haunting."

He took another sip of his drink. "We keep the piano behind a bamboo screen in the lounge; it's never used these days. I went to go have a look and I couldn't believe it! She was sitting there, all grubby and dishevelled, yet she was playing music so exquisite it made you weep. No-one else was in the lounge and even if there had been they wouldn't have been offended by the music; she was an amazing pianist. World class I would say."

"What did you do?" Alex asked intrigued.

"I couldn't bring myself to interrupt her so I just watched and listened until she finished. She closed the lid of the piano, put her hands in her lap, and just sat there as still as a statue. I wanted to say something, but before I had a chance, she turned around and saw me."

"And?"

"Nothing. She was crying though, then she picked up her bowl and buggered off."

Alex took a sip of his cold beer. "I can tell you her name - Nicola Gray."

"Nicola Gray, eh? I wonder where she learned to play like that. Someone must know something about her. With that sort of talent how on earth did she end up begging on the streets? She could have got a job anywhere - I would have employed her! I was often tempted to find out more about her, but if she saw me around she would avoid me, it was almost as if I'd seen through her and exposed something she obviously wanted to keep secret, so she kept her distance.

"Now she's dead we'll probably never find out who she was."

******

The following week Alex returned to the hospital morgue and spoke to the pathologist, Doctor Osborne, whom he had spoken with the day after Nicola's death.

"There are no government records of Ms Gray in South Africa, no next-of-kin has come forward, and there's no record of her ever entering the country. She's essentially classified as a Jane Doe except for the fact she told you her name was Nicola Gray.

"The problem is we have no way of confirming this, so we're liaising with the police to find out if she matches any missing person's reports. We ran a small article in the local newspaper asking anyone who knew her to come forward, but no-one has. That's about all I can tell you. You said she was a friend of yours?"

Alex switched on his reporter's charm. "Yes, you could say that. Nicola was a loner; she'd fallen on hard times you see..."

The pathologist ran his hand through his thin hair wearily. His morgue was full of unidentified bodies and his workload was brutal. Bulging files were stacked on his desk and on the bookcases lining the walls of his office. The man standing opposite him offered a solution for this woman called Nicola Gray.

"Will you be taking responsibility for her then, Mr Patterson - as a friend? You'll need to sign some papers before I can release her body, and I'll need to have some kind of identification from you. Ms. Gray, unusually, didn't have any whatsoever. It's a legal requirement here to carry your identity book with you."

He stifled a yawn. "I'll need your contact details, just in case something or someone turns up - not likely now though."

Alex didn't hesitate. Footing the bill for her funeral would be a small price to pay for a potentially good story. He didn't want her body lost to a pauper's grave in a nameless cemetery.

"I'll make the necessary arrangements Doc. Anything else you can tell me about her, anything else you discovered when you examined her?"

Doctor Osborne pushed aside the untidy files on his desk and consulted the notes in her own slim file. "I would say she was in her mid-sixties, maybe a few years younger.

"Apart from the fact she was obviously malnourished; the direct cause of death was the blow to her head when she fell, causing bleeding and pressure in her brain which ultimately killed her." He rubbed his eyes tiredly and looked down at his notes again. "I suspect she had a degenerative illness of some kind. Perhaps the accident was a blessing; it's unlikely she would have had the money to pay for any medication and once her disease advanced, she would have suffered - or had already been suffering. I'll get the forms you need to sign."

The hospital had given him her few personal effects and a copy of the death certificate.

******

Alex stood at the side of the grave next to the priest. The service had been perfunctory with only him and Peter in attendance. In the stillness of the afternoon heat, he watched as her coffin was lowered into the warm ground, the only tribute to her existence being the simple wooden cross with her name, *Nicola Gray.*

After the funeral he drove back to his cottage. Placing her brown hospital envelope on the veranda table, he went through to the lounge and poured himself a drink.

The cottage he'd rented was comfortable and simply furnished, and more than adequate for his few needs. Now summer was fully fledged, he spent the evenings outside. A fountain trickled into a small water feature at the rear of the garden making him feel cool just listening to it. He sat there now, his bare feet resting comfortably on the railing, and gazed out over the garden, the cloying scent of frangipani flowers hanging in the motionless hot air.

Idly he flicked open his notebook and glanced at his notes. He still had two weeks before the deadline for his latest article on life in the townships of the new South Africa. After fifteen years as a journalist for *The Telegraph*, covering war zones, he had decided that working as a freelance writer, digging up human interest stories, of which there was plenty in Africa, suited him better. The money was not as good, but his parents had left him a decent amount when they died, and he liked the freedom of being wealthy enough to work when he felt like it - and follow stories which intrigued him, like this one.

He had a freelance deal with his newspaper, hence his six month contract now. *The Telegraph* would take the articles he wanted to submit and the subject matter was left up to him.

Then he had met the lovely Sophie in London. He smiled at the memory.

Reaching for the envelope he shook the contents out onto the table. He examined the worn gold wedding ring looking for a date or name, but there was nothing. He looked at a door key with a chipped yellow tag, probably the key to wherever she had lived; she must, he reasoned, have slept somewhere.

23

He picked up a black and white photograph. A large house surrounded by tall bushes and trees, generous windows on the three floors stared blankly back at him. He turned it over. Written on the back was one word.

Mbabati.

He sat back remembering her last words to him as she lay dying. Not Barty then but Mbabati. He rolled the word around in his mouth testing the pronunciation - um baa baa tee.

He went into the lounge and picked up a magnifying glass, then stepped off the veranda and into the bright sunlight. Holding the photograph up, he scrutinized it.

The trees were big and well established; perhaps the house wasn't in Africa, maybe somewhere in India? He moved the glass across and saw two carved eagles above the entrance. A little way away from the left of the house there seemed to be a long low building. Studying it more closely he thought it might be a stable block; two round huts stood huddled under trees to the right and back of the house. Staff accommodation, he surmised.

There were long sweeping lawns, a rose garden, and what looked like a gazebo or summer house. He stared at the blank windows one by one.

Returning to his chair he took a sip of his drink. The Colonials had built their homes in the old English country style all over the world, especially in Africa and India. They'd shipped out their sofas and chairs, heavy dining-room furniture, their crystal, silver and china, and created a little bit of England in a foreign land.

Swirling the ice around in his glass he looked at the photograph again. It certainly had the colonial look but, quite frankly, the house could be anywhere - he had no idea at all.

Going to his study he opened the bottom drawer of his desk and dropped the envelope, and its contents, inside.

The journalist in him was aroused. He knew he was on to something and he couldn't let Nicola's passing go without trying to find out something about her and her possible connection to the house in the photograph, and the fact that, according to Peter, she had been an extraordinary pianist.

He picked up her small bowl, turning it over and over looking for some clue as to its origin. The base was solid wood, the top circled by a deep blue substance.

24

Still holding it he moved back to the study, turned on his laptop, and did a search for her name. There were twenty Nicola Grays delivered from the search; one in Zimbabwe, three in Johannesburg, and another in Durban. But no Nicola Grays in Cape Town. The rest were scattered around the world. Meticulously, he went through all the details he could find on all of them and came up with nothing close to a match. He did a search for 'Mbabati' and again came up with nothing more than the possibility it might be an Indonesian word. He tapped his now empty glass on the desk wondering what other angle he should try.

Feeling stumped, he glanced at his watch, picked up his phone and called Sophie in London.

As he waited patiently for her to answer, he rolled Nicola's bowl back and forwards on the table. He wondered if Sophie had already left the shop and gone home; disappointed, he realised how badly he wanted to hear her voice. He was about to ring off when she picked up, sounding out of breath.

"Hello Vintage Africa."

Alex smiled into the phone. "Sophie, my darling, I'm glad I caught you still at the shop. Are you having one of your sundowner get-togethers?"

"Alex!" He loved to hear Sophie say his name and sound so pleased to hear from him. "No, not tonight. I'm going through a box of things which has come from Zimbabwe. Nothing much of interest though.

"What's happening in Cape Town? Lovely and warm, I expect," she said wistfully.

Alex smiled again. "The place is heaving with tourists and the temperature is up in the thirties at the moment. Plus the traffic is terrible and I'm missing you. I was wondering - any chance you can find someone to run the shop? I'd love you to come here for a few weeks, I miss you."

On the other end of the phone, looking out at the rain splattered pitch black night, Sophie suddenly felt a great yearning to see him, imagining the hot sun on her skin and the feel of his arms around her. It had been a long cold winter and she was missing him badly too.

"I'd love to Alex. I'm sure I can find someone to run the shop after Christmas. Maybe one of my regulars might help out. January is a dead month anyway and..."

25

"Right then, book your ticket and give me a date - I need something to look forward to, especially as we won't be spending Christmas together."

"Are you alright, sweetheart? You sound a bit down."

"I'm fine," he sighed down the phone, "just something that happened a week or so ago that's made me think about human nature. I'm wondering why people take better care of their animals than their relatives. I'll tell you about it when I see you."

"I had a funny experience in the shop as well. A nun came in which is unusual, I don't think I've ever had a nun in here before," she said with a laugh, "and no she didn't buy anything!"

******

Sophie had initially thought Alex was a customer and when he'd been looking around, seemingly not finding what he was looking for, she had gone over to see if she could help him. "I know it looks a bit chaotic in here," she had said to his back, "but there's a certain degree of order. Are you looking for anything in particular or just browsing?"

Turning around at the sound of her voice, he replaced the set of silver pens he had been looking at.

Sophie was immediately interested to find herself looking into the face of an attractive man in his mid-forties. His full head of dark brown hair was starting to grey over his ears, and deep lines accentuated his steady grey eyes.

"Are you Sophie?" She nodded. "I'm Alex Patterson." He held out his hand and she returned his confident handshake.

"Sophie Lagrange."

"Nice to meet you Sophie. I'm a journalist and some of the guys at the Press Club were talking about Vintage Africa. How it's become a sort of hub for meeting people coming from and going to Africa.

"I'd like to write something for my paper, about you and your business here?"

Sophie grinned. "When would you like to do the interview? Any publicity is good publicity for me. I'd love to talk about my shop."

"How about now?" He never could resist a beautiful woman with a French accent and tawny blonde hair, he judged her to be in her early forties.

26

Sophie glanced around the shop where one or two people lingered; she looked at her watch.

"Tell you what, why don't you give me ten minutes to close up and deal with these last customers, and I'll meet you in the lounge of the hotel up the road.

"Browns on Albemarle?"

"Yes, I'll see you there then."

******

Sophie took a sip of her wine "People spent years building up farms and businesses, in the colonies; they had their children and lived a privileged life. White people thought it was theirs for life, but as each country gained its independence there was a shift, especially in Africa. Suddenly they were demoted to second-class citizens, hoping they'd be allowed to stay on. But you know all this."

"A tenuous existence," Alex murmured.

"Exactly, nothing was going to be like the past they'd enjoyed. Once they got into their seventies, no-one seemed to want them. Lots of them returned to the place of their birth - Europe or England."

Alex looked around the elegant bar. "No more tennis parties at the Club, no horse racing or polo, no servants, or great houses on estates set against a land teeming with wildlife. It must have been tough."

Sophie nodded in agreement. "Some stayed on in Africa, hoping their ageing retainers would look after them. But the servants were as old as they were and could hardly look after themselves, let alone their employers!"

She twirled her wine glass. "I'd have liked the colonial life; I have a hankering for the glamour of that period - the adventure. It's really how Vintage Africa was born. In a way, I feel responsible for people's old things, I try to imagine who'd owned them and what stories they could tell, and I enjoy meeting all the people who come into the shop leaving messages and dropping things off. It's like being part of a big family."

"How did you get into the business?" Alex said reluctantly tearing his eyes away from her face and down at his notes.

"I took an undergrad degree in English and a post-grad degree in African history it sparked off my passion for all things colonial.

27

"I love finding an old record player and imagining couples dancing out on the lawn under the stars with servants standing by to see to their every whim! Plus there's nothing like a bit of scandal and East Africa had plenty of that - still has to a certain extent."

"Are you hungry by any chance, Sophie? Would you like to have dinner with me?"

******

Over dinner they exchanged potted life histories. Alex told her about the apartment in Chelsea he had inherited, and how London was a good hub to work from if he was after a story.

Sophie listened, already attracted to the man sitting opposite her. "Well, maybe I can put you to some good use," she grinned at him over a forkful of pasta. "You could keep your eyes and ears open for any deceased estates, I'm always looking for stock, and in return I'll keep my ears to the ground for any interesting stories for you to go after - deal?"

Sophie continued. "Anyway, enough of work, tell me more about you. You have a slight accent, where were you born. Australia?"

"New Zealand. I'd always wanted to be a journalist and once I got my degree I hit the streets looking for work.

"Beautiful and peaceful though it is, nothing exciting ever happens there. It's all about sheep, rugby and the occasional rumble from a volcano! So I headed for London and landed a job with *The Telegraph*. What about you?"

She pushed her hair behind her ear. "I was born in France, my father died when I was eight, so my mother brought me up."

Alex was mesmerised, already planning how he could manoeuvre a second date with her. He had dated many women over the years, even married one, but the woman sitting opposite him now had his undivided attention.

"What about marriage and children, Sophie?"

"No, I don't think so. I was married for five years, but it didn't work out." She put her glass down on the table and laughed.

"And it's a bit late for children now, I missed that particular boat. My mother was disappointed I didn't stay married and have kids, but there it is. I was her only chance for grandchildren and you know what the French are like when it comes to their families. I had to buy her a dog as compensation!"

******

They'd been living together for two years when Alex received the news that the newspaper wanted him to relocate to Cape Town for a year.

"Budgets have been cut," his editor, Harry, had said when they met at the pub for lunch. "The number crunchers are looking for ways of saving boodle. These long-haul flights back and forth to Africa are costing the paper too much money. However, your articles have a huge following and we don't want to lose you. Being based in Cape Town would be a cheaper option at the moment; we'll cover your expenses there, of course."

Chapter Five

Cape Town January 2008

South African Airways announced the arrival of the early morning flight from London and Alex grinned like a child at Christmas. Sophie hurled herself into his arms hugging and kissing him.

"Oh, this was such a good idea, sweetheart," she said breathlessly. "Just walking across from the aircraft to the bus and feeling the sun on my skin felt glorious."

"God it's good to see you Sophie! Come on, let's get out of here and away from all these people."

They inched their way through the airport traffic and then out onto the motorway.

"Your first impression of Cape Town won't be a pretty one I'm afraid."

Sophie looked at the endless row of shacks lining the road on both sides. Washing was draped over fences to dry, and plastic bags and rubbish were strewn everywhere, some hanging in trees and others clinging tenaciously to bushes.

"Well, this is something you don't see on television when Cape Town comes up," she said sadly, "it looks desperate - terrible. I thought everything would have changed with the new government in place for the past fourteen years."

"Things have changed," Alex said glancing in his rear view mirror, "but it's a long process. Nothing was going to change overnight, even though the population had high hopes it would."

He pointed ahead through the windscreen and changed the subject. "There's Table Mountain - magnificent isn't it?" He indicated his intention to turn left and continued towards the affluent suburb of Constantia, joining the smooth-running traffic.

Sophie admired the majestic mountains, metal blue in the strong sunlight, the expansive gardens and lofty trees, and the expensive homes sitting snugly behind their high security walls.

Alex pulled off the motorway. "I thought we'd get you settled, have some lunch somewhere and spend the afternoon on the beach. I'm sure you could do with getting some warm sand between your toes."

He pulled up outside of the cottage and switched of the engine. Pulling her into his arms he kissed her long and hard. "Why don't you take a shower" he mumbled in between kisses, "I'll show you around afterwards..."

******

Hours later they lay in bed exhausted from their love making. He pushed the damp hair back from her face and kissed her neck.

"Ah well, beach tomorrow then?" He said. "Let's have a shower and I'll rustle up some lunch with an ice cold glass of wine to wash it down."

She stifled an unexpected yawn. "This heat takes a bit of getting used to, I'm feeling quite sleepy."

"It's not the heat my darling," he grinned at her. "We can always go back to bed after we've eaten."

******

"London will seem a bit dull after this," Sophie told Alex, lying comfortably back in his arms, her arms resting on his knees, as they sat on the beach looking out at the sun setting over the sea, turning the water a rich gold and red, the towering mountains forming a majestic backdrop behind them. "I could easily be persuaded to stay here permanently."

He pushed up his sunglasses and massaged the bridge of his nose. "It's not so enchanting when the black South-Easter's screaming through the city and the rain is slashing down. It can be grim in July and August. But it's a great city, better still if you were around. It suits you being here, you look about twenty years old."

"I wish!" She stretched her legs out in front of her, admiring her newly acquired tan, and yawned. "I'm starving. What shall we do for dinner? Would you like me to cook for you?"

"What? With all these hundreds of restaurants to choose from! No, I'm going to make the most of them and your company, eating out alone wasn't much fun. Tell you what, let's go the Waterfront tonight, I'd like you to meet a friend of mine, Peter, he manages a hotel there."

31

Sophie sighed with deep satisfaction and patted her mouth with a napkin. "Best prawns I've ever tasted!" She looked around at the bustling crowds of late night shoppers. "When's Peter going to join us?"

She had hardly finished her sentence when he walked up to their table and introduced himself.

"The hotel's packed at the moment," he said shaking his head and sinking gratefully into a chair. "I'll be glad when the seasons over and the last tourist leaves town." He ordered a beer from a hovering waiter.

"No offence," he said smiling at her. "I love my tourists but at this time of the year it buggers up my family life, I seem to be on call twenty-four hours a day."

He drank thirstily from his glass, then smacked his lips with pleasure. "So, Sophie, how are you enjoying Cape Town?"

"Fantastic, its stunning, every time we go around another corner there's something even more beautiful to see. But somehow it doesn't really feel like Africa here, it doesn't have the rough and tumble feel of, say, Nairobi."

Peter nodded in agreement. "Yes, it's a sophisticated city, more Europe in Africa, as you say. What have you got planned for tomorrow?"

"I'm taking a tour of the city on a red bus. Alex doesn't fancy it, so I'm going on my own. Anyway, I've taken up all his time since arriving and he's supposed to be writing scandalous stories about Africa!"

Alex grinned at her. "You're right; I do need a day to catch up. Besides, the last thing I need is to take a ride on a bus."

"Where's your next assignment?" Peter asked him.

"When Sophie leaves, I'm off to Zimbabwe, there's a story I'm chasing about the farmers who were kicked off their farms."

"Talking about stories," Peter asked, "any more news on the mystery woman, Nicola?"

Sophie raised her eyebrows. "Mystery woman? What mystery woman?"

Alex filled her in on the story of Nicola. When he'd finished they sat back in silence.

Peter stood up reluctantly. "Right, it's time for me to check on the hotel. Let me know if you turn anything more up on Nicola, won't you? Nice meeting you Sophie, I now understand why we haven't seen much of Alex since you arrived..." He winked at him, raised his palm and left.

******

Sophie sat on the veranda of the cottage and listened to the crickets and frogs in the garden whilst Alex mixed their drinks and brought them outside, along with Nicola's bowl.

Sophie examined it. "Well, I can tell you it's old - twenty or thirty year's maybe, and it definitely comes from Africa. In fact, it comes from Tanzania," she said smugly.

"This blue mineral is Tanzanite," she said pleased she had impressed him with her expertise. "What else was there?"

Alex returned with the envelope and tipped the contents out onto the table. She leaned forward to get a better look. Picking up the wedding ring and the key she examined them individually.

Then she turned to the photograph. Her hand flew to her mouth in disbelief. "It's not possible, Alex!"

"What's not possible?" he said sitting up in surprise at Sophie's reaction.

"This house! It's called Mbabati I've got the identical photograph on the wall of my shop." When Alex looked blank, she continued hurriedly. "Of course, you haven't seen it yet!"

Sophie told him about the nun, her package with the love letters and diary, the bell, the photograph and the abandoned house.

"I'd seen her quite a few times. She used to stand at the window of the shop and stare in, but she never came in until the last time. Sometimes she would spook me out a bit but I knew she was harmless - after all she was a nun!"

She told him about finding the parcel and dropping it off, but the Mother Superior had refused to let her in to see Sister Elizabeth.

He sat forward with his elbows on his knees and flipped the photograph over and over in his fingers, then stared intently at it again.

"The question now is this. How did two women, who lived continents apart, know the name of the house and both have a photograph of it? What's the connection Sophie?"

He sat back in the chair. "Who was your envelope addressed to, the one left in the shop by the student?"

"Miss Gray."

Alex's expression turned to one of disbelief and it was Sophie's turn to be surprised." Miss Gray? Are you quite sure?"

"Of course I'm sure! Do you think the nun, is Miss Gray?"

"Yes, I'm pretty sure she is. Why are you looking so incredulous?"

"Sophie, they have the same surname."

Chapter Six

Have you ever been to Tanzania? Alex asked her the next morning, as they were finishing their breakfast.

"No. But I did go to Kenya once, years ago though. Why do you ask? Are you thinking because the Tanzanite bowl came from Tanzania that's where the house might be?"

"It's a shot in the dark but we have to start somewhere. Both Nicola and Elizabeth had a photograph of the old house; I'm thinking they might be sisters, so maybe they were brought up there. Then at some point Elizabeth left to join a convent in England and Nicola presumably moved to Cape Town."

Sophie reached across the table for another piece of toast. "Didn't you tell me you had a chat with a waiter who was from Tanzania? Maybe we should go and speak to him?"

"Charlie? He only lived there for a few years before his parents came here. I don't think he'll be able to tell us much."

"Perhaps not, but maybe his parents lived there for a while and might remember a big fancy house out in the bush - it's a bit of a stretch but, as you said, we have to start somewhere..."

"You're right. Let's take Nicola's envelope and get down to the Waterfront."

"But, I was going to take the red bus this morning," Sophie began protesting mildly.

"Don't worry, I wouldn't dream of depriving you of your topless tour, you can jump on it at the Waterfront. Take a hat with you, it's going to be as hot as hell today, don't want you coming back with a bright red face." He held out his hand and pulled her to her feet. "Come on let's get going before it gets too hot."

They sat nursing their coffees, waiting for Charlie to come on shift. "Don't get your hopes up, Alex, the house might not even be in Tanzania at all."

"I know but most of my stories start on a tenuous hunch. There's Charlie. Let's call him over."

Charlie waved, recognising Alex. "Morning, good to see you again. More coffee? Breakfast?"

"Morning, Charlie." He introduced Sophie and continued. "Have you got a minute? I'd like to ask you a couple of things about the woman who had the accident - remember her?"

"Of course," he said, looking around at the other tables. "I'm not too busy yet, so fire away. I was hoping you'd come back."

"Why's that, do I tip you too much?"

Charlie laughed. "No, definitely not, but I heard something you might be interested in."

Alex looked at him expectantly. "What's that then?"

Charlie told him about a couple who had been having dinner at the restaurant and they were talking about the woman who had died, and he couldn't help, as he served them, overhearing some of their conversation.

"Go on," Alex encouraged him.

"They'd just returned from a holiday and were speculating whether the woman who died might be the one who had lived next door to them. They hadn't seen her since they got back. They asked me if I knew anything about her, but all I could tell them was what she looked like. As soon as I described her they knew exactly who she was!"

"Any chance you know where they live?" Sophie asked hopefully.

Charlie felt in his pocket and pulled out a piece of paper. "Here's the address, it's a double storey house next door to them, in Sea Point. You can't miss it apparently."

"Now, you wanted to ask me some questions?"

"Thanks for this," Alex said, pocketing the piece of paper. "You said your parents lived in Tanzania - you were brought up there if I remember correctly? It's a long shot, but we think Nicola came from East Africa, possibly Tanzania. Could it be worth asking your folks if they've ever heard of her, or a house called Mbabati?"

Charlie shook his head. He told them that his parents had left Tanzania over twenty years ago. He would ask them but doubted they would be able to help as it was so long ago.

Alex gave him his card.

"Sod the red bus," Sophie said under her breath as they walked away. "Let's go and find where she lived."

******

They found the address, and the double storey house, without difficulty. Stopping the car, Alex retrieved the key from the envelope.

36

They both looked up at the house, then looked at each other. "Nicola must have had money" he said, "if she lived here. Even if she didn't own it the rent would have been pretty high."

Sophie cupped her hands around her eyes and peered through a dusty side window. "It looks deserted; the furniture's covered with sheets."

Alex took a deep breath and tried the key in the lock of the front door. He exhaled, disappointed. It didn't fit.

Sophie looked up. "Hang on, there's a cottage over there, half hidden by the trees. Let's check it out."

The cottage had an air of desolation about it; the garden was overgrown, and what little grass there was looked brown, dry, and neglected.

They reached the front door and hesitated, turning to each other. "I feel a bit uncomfortable doing this, Alex. Supposing there's someone inside?" She knocked tentatively. They waited staring at a forlorn dead fern hanging down the side of a cracked flower pot.

"No-one's home here either. Are you sure this will be alright?"

"Well, it's basically breaking and entering, but we might have the key to fit the lock. We know there's no-one inside, well, no-one's answered the door..."

Looking back up the deserted path to the road, she took the key from him in a quick movement and inserted it into the lock. She twisted it, turned the handle and took a deep breath. They were in.

The cottage was little more than three rooms: a sitting-room, containing a shabby pale green sofa and a faded mismatched armchair. A table with two dining-room chairs stood next to the wall.

An old metal trunk sat next to the sofa, a heavy silver-frame lay face down on top of it.

He checked the trunk to see if there were any destination stickers on it hoping it might be a clue as to where she had travelled from, but if there had been any they had been artfully removed, leaving only a dark shadow of their shape.

Sophie wandered into the kitchen. A coffee mug stood upside down on the side of the sink. She opened a cupboard door and glanced inside at the empty shelves.

"Hey, come and have a look at this," Alex called. He handed her the heavy silver frame. "If this is Nicola, and I think it might be, she was beautiful - stunning, in fact."

37

It was a black and white photograph of a young woman seated in front of a piano, her back to the audience. She wore a dark, sleeveless gown which tumbled around the stool she was sitting on; her hands were poised over the keys, her face turned towards the photographer.

Sophie whistled softly. "Wow, she certainly was beautiful. I wonder where she was performing? It's not the Royal Albert Hall, I'd recognise it if it was. It looks more European, maybe Vienna or Paris?"

Alex nodded thinking along similar lines. "She must have been fairly well known then. We should be able to find out more about her easily enough.

"I've got journo contacts all over Europe through Associated Press. I'll ask around. Does she look like your nun at all?"

She took the frame from him and studied the photograph. "It's hard to say, Sister Elizabeth was wearing a wimple and no make-up. There's no comparison, or similarity, between her and this gorgeous creature, none whatsoever."

Alex knelt down in front of the trunk, testing the locks. "It's locked," he said, disappointed.

"I'll scout around for a key," Sophie replied, making her way into the bedroom.

A single bed stood in the corner covered with a threadbare bedspread. Here, too, the cupboards were practically empty, save for a small pile of underwear, three long floral skirts and blouses, a thin black coat and a pair of worn ankle boots.

"No keys in the bedroom or the kitchen," Sophie reported back.

"I didn't find anything in here either," Alex said, kneeling once more in front of the trunk.

"Move over, sweetheart, I think I can probably do this."

He stood up and made room for her. "I've opened a few of these in my time," she said over her shoulder. "I often get trunks and chests in the shop - invariably minus the keys - so this shouldn't be too much of a challenge."

She reached into her handbag and pulled out a small, sharp nail file. Within seconds there was a satisfying grunt from one lock, shortly followed by the other. Sophie lifted the lid.

"Well! What's inside?" he demanded, trying to peer over her shoulder.

38

"Hang on sweetheart - give me a chance to take a look. At this point, it's a pile of tissue paper and lots of black dresses. Put the light on, will you. It's so dark in here."

Alex flicked the switch hopefully. "They must have cut off the electricity. We'll have to manage without."

She pulled out the first garment and whistled. "Wow! This must have cost a fortune, look at the cut of it." She unpacked the chest, handing the clothes and expensive underwear to Alex who draped them over a chair. The dresses smelt musty and their dull scent hung in the airless room. Sophie stood up to take a better look at them.

"Evening-dresses, and all black, except for this gorgeous red one, each one from a French fashion house - Yves Saint Laurent, Dior, Chanel. They're fabulous!

"It's hard to equate the wearer of these clothes, and that photograph, with the Nicola you described to me."

Sophie turned back to the trunk and reached down to lift out a soft cotton bag. She opened it and pulled out a long, dark curly wig, she held it up for Alex to see. They started to laugh, surprised by the find. He put it to one side.

Sophie delved once again into the trunk and withdrew a square box. She opened it and looked up at Alex.

"It's full of jewellery, necklaces and bracelets, cheap stuff. Hang on, this looks interesting." She handed him a gold oval locket. "See if you can open it while I get the last things out. I wish it wasn't so flipping dark in here! It's hard to see anything."

He swung the locket by its chain; it was heavy. He examined it before catching it in his hand and pressing the catch on the side. The locket sprang open and he found himself looking at a black and white photograph of a grave with a blank headstone. Intrigued he looked more closely at it and squinted.

"Odd sort of thing to wear around your neck?" He passed it to her.

She looked at the blank headstone and shivered. "Really odd. A bit macabre when you think about it." She turned back to the contents of the trunk then stood up. "This looks like a baby blanket to me, and a big fat envelope, which I'm dying to open!" She brandished it in front of him.

A siren howled in the distance and they both looked at each other guiltily, then laughed.

39

"Let's take the envelope home with us and go through it methodically. It's dark, gloomy and bloody cold in here and I need to get out," Alex said, putting the locket into his pocket.

******

The contents of the envelope were spread over the length of the dining room table. They sipped glasses of wine as they contemplated the assortment of photographs and concert programmes.

Alex studied them. Most of them were publicity shots taken in Paris, some forty years previously, with the photographer's stamp and date on the back. He made a note on his pad; the photographer, although it was unlikely, might still be in business.

There were half a dozen programmes, all in French and all featuring the name Nicola DuPont. She was the star performer at all the concerts. It wouldn't be difficult to find out more about her now he had, what he presumed to be, her professional name. No wonder Peter had been knocked out with her playing.

Only one man featured in the collection of photographs. He was tall, slim and tanned, and standing next to a Land Rover. His hair was dark and curly and brushed the collar of his open necked shirt. He was smiling at the photographer, one foot on the bumper of the vehicle. The landscape around him was flat and empty apart from two canvas directors chairs next to a wicker picnic hamper.

He picked up another photograph at random and studied it: Nicola sitting on a packing crate facing a piano, with large windows in front of her, seeming to stretch the length of a long room. In this picture she was dressed in jodhpurs and a white shirt, her feet bare, her long blonde hair tied back at the nape of her neck. He recognised the shape of the windows immediately - Mbabati.

Sophie leaned over his shoulder and handed him a colour shot. "This looks like a photograph of a portrait. It's huge."

She was seated by her piano, the skirts of a long, strapless blue gown swirling around her feet, one slender arm draped across the top of the instrument. Her hair was piled high on her head and around her neck a triple choker of pearls.

"She was exquisite," Sophie murmured, "she reminds me of Grace Kelly with that sereneness about her, that cool classy look, don't you think? I don't know who was commissioned to paint this portrait but it's damn good, no, better than good - it's exceptional."

He rubbed his eyes. "What on earth took her from her life as a classical pianist to the wreck of a woman on the streets of Cape Town?"

"I've no idea. But it's odd she kept so many photographs of herself and only one of the chap next to the Land Rover."

"Maybe he was her husband, she wore a wedding ring remember?"

"Oh, hang on," Sophie said "there's another envelope tucked in here."

She opened the flap and shook the contents out onto the table. "Who's this?"

Alex picked up the photographs and flicked through them. All were of a woman, standing in front of a microphone, on a dimly lit stage within a dark room.

Sophie put her glasses on and looked more closely. "It's Nicola, she's wearing the wig we found in the chest." She frowned. "If she was a classical pianist, how did she end up as a singer in a night club?"

"She didn't end up in a nightclub, Sophie," he said sadly, "she ended up dead at the bottom end of Africa, completely alone."

She lowered herself onto one of the dining room chairs and sipped her wine. Alex followed suit. "Why was she wearing the wig?" he asked.

"She could have been running away or hiding from something?" Sophie suggested.

"Some kind of disguise?"

"Yes. Otherwise why bother to change her look? If this was the case she couldn't go to Europe she would have been recognized easily. Wigs or no wigs.

"However," she said warming to this new theory, "South Africa would have been a good option. After years of isolation from the rest of the world because of the apartheid era, South Africa was starved of culture. No-one famous would come here because they would have been ostracized by the rest of the world. Nicola could slip into the country and no-one would have any idea who she was. But to be quite sure, she changed her look completely; even her eyes are a different colour, probably contacts.

41

Sophie took her glasses off. "If I had been Nicola, running or hiding, I would have destroyed every single photograph, theatre programme, anything which could be linked to me but she didn't did she? She kept dozens and dozens of photographs of herself. There's not a single letter anywhere and no personal notes. No photos of children or even friends. It doesn't make sense."

"No it doesn't make sense, and the other thing that doesn't make sense... Where's her passport?" He rubbed his hands together happily. "But there *is* a story here, a bloody good one, and I intend to find out what it is. Come on, my darling, all this sleuthing has given me an appetite."

They showered and changed before heading through the leafy suburbs of Constantia to a restaurant nearby. After ordering from the impressive menu, Sophie turned her attention back to Alex.

"I need to go back to the convent and speak to Sister Elizabeth. She knows something about all of this. If Nicola is her sister, she needs to be told about her death. If she isn't Miss Gray she certainly knows who Miss Gray is. Top prize would be to get our hands on the envelope I found for her."

"Well that's highly unlikely," he said laughing. "She's not going to hand over her private letters and diary, is she?"

"No, I guess not..."

"Did you come up with anything in the concert programmes?" Alex asked, breaking the silence.

"They were quite perfunctory. Some had short introductions to Nicola, not really biographies, but listing the venues where she'd played. I made a note of them for you to send to your contact in Paris."

Alex was only half listening, preoccupied once more with his own thoughts. Realising she'd stopped talking he reached across the table and took her hand, smiling apologetically. He asked her if she could remember anything else about the letters.

She shook her head. "I've racked my brains. When I briefly skim-read a couple of them, they didn't mean much. Letters rarely do if you don't know the people involved. Obviously lovers though, they were careful, never mentioned each other's names."

He reached for a bread roll. "Were they in separate envelopes? Anything written on them - any names?"

"Yes, but impossible to read. The ink was so faint, almost illegible, as though they'd got damp at some point. I could only make

42

out two letters on one of the envelopes; a '*k*' and an '*e*', sorry I'm not being helpful here."

"Were they all between the same two people?"

She hesitated as the waiter placed their order on the table and left.

"From the few I looked at, yes." Sophie's voice trailed off. "Wait - I've just remembered something!"

He looked up mid-mouthful in anticipation. "One of them mentioned someone called Luke. Yes, something like '*Luke knows*'. It jumped off the page because, as I said, they never mentioned any names in any of the letters," she paused and twirled the pasta around her fork.

"Why on earth would Elizabeth choose to leave wherever it was she lived in the big house, if indeed she did live there, become a nun, and move to a convent in London? And," she added dramatically "how can two sisters have the same surname if one of them was married?"

Chapter Seven

Alex drummed his fingers on the table in the kitchen, impatient for Sophie's return.

He had heard from his contact in Paris. He'd scanned a photograph of Nicola and emailed it to Thierry to see if he could dig anything up for him.

I'm not sure where she lived in France, Alex had emailed, *but we're assuming Paris and she was fairly well known there. We have found some old programmes, all in French, featuring a Nicola DuPont appearing at The Palais Garnier and numerous other venues. Any information you can find for us would be more than helpful. It would appear Nicola performed in Paris during the early sixties.* Alex also included a scan of the back of the photograph with the photographer's studio stamp.

Thierry had called him an hour ago.

"Bonjour, Alex. Lucky you being in Cape Town! I have the information you require. Indeed her name was Nicola DuPont. She was extremely well known and played in many of the great capitals of the world. The French press first became aware of her when she was sixteen. She was the darling of the world of classical music. When she was in her early twenties, she appeared only briefly for a handful of performances, but not good ones. The speculation in the press was she had burned out. And then, almost overnight, she disappeared. She was never heard of again."

Alex was silent as he took this in, watching the rain cascading down the sitting room window.

"Anyway," Thierry continued, "I spoke to some older colleagues of mine and they remembered Nicola well, not only because of the calibre of her playing, but because she was exceptionally beautiful. One of them recalled she had married her agent, Max Gray. That's about all I can tell you but I hope it helps?"

"More than you know, mate. Thanks for taking the time and trouble to do this for me. I'll return the favour anytime."

"If you find out what happened to her, apart from the fact that she ended up dead in Cape Town, you will let me know? It might make for an interesting piece in the papers here in France. But, alas, she has mostly been forgotten, so it might not be of any interest."

Alex promised he would.

So Nicola had disappeared, and to what better place than an old house in East Africa?

He heard Sophie pull up in the driveway and went out to meet her with an umbrella.

"You're looking pleased with yourself," she said climbing out of the car. "Did you hear from your friend in Paris?"

As Alex filled her in, Sophie passed him the grocery bags from the boot of the car.

"What's this?" Alex asked indicating the bags as they entered the house.

"We seem to have eaten out just about every night since I got here, and as this rain looks as if it's going to hang around, I thought I'd cook dinner."

She kicked off her wet shoes and started to empty the grocery bags. "Why don't you search the web and see if you can find out anything about Max Gray."

"Okay, by the way, I think I'll fly back to England with you next week. I can rework my schedule and write the piece on Zimbabwe later."

"Brilliant idea!" She skipped around the kitchen clutching a box of cornflakes. "I was dreading saying goodbye, absolutely dreading it."

He caught hold of her, loving her happiness at his plan. "I'll come with you to the convent to see Sister Elizabeth. She might tell us where Mbabati is. You might be right about it being in Tanzania but it would be useful to have an address. You know, Africa being a big place and all," Alex said flippantly.

Sophie raised an eyebrow and threw a dishcloth at him. "I think you - with all your considerable charm - might be more successful with the Mother Superior than I was. I think you should go on your own."

"I don't think nuns are into being charmed, at least not by men or mere mortals, but I'll give it my best shot."

"Good, now off you go and let me get on." She gave him a lingering kiss then propelled him out of the kitchen.

"It's possible, you know," Sophie called from the kitchen, "the marriage didn't work out and Max went back to wherever he came from, and Nicola took off for Cape Town. He might just have locked the place up and buggered off. Might still be alive for all we know."

45

Alex half listened to her humming as she finished unpacking the shopping and started preparing their dinner. His time on the internet produced little. There was scant information on Nicola's professional life as a pianist, and nothing at all about her social or personal life. There was only a brief reference to her marriage to her agent, Max Gray. He now searched for references to Max Gray and came up trumps.

"Hey, Sophie! Come and see this."

She came through with a bottle of wine and topped up Alex's glass. Draping her arms around his neck she rested her chin on his head. "You've got five minutes. What have you found?"

"She was as mysterious in life as she is in death. No reference to any siblings. She was born in 1943 in Paris, so definitely French. There's a brief bio of her professional life as a pianist. Nicola married Max Gray in 1965, and that's all we have. But now we know exactly how old she was when she died - sixty-four.

"But look what I dug up on Max. He was born in England: he received a first class education at Eton and went on to become a lawyer. He moved to Paris in 1961. No siblings.

"Max inherited a ranch in East Africa and presumably the old house. I'm thinking when they left Paris, they went out to Tanzania to live in it."

Sophie kissed him on the side of his mouth as she reached for his glass and took a gulp of his wine. "What else did you discover sweetheart, or was that it?"

"I couldn't find any more information about either of them. I was about to turn the computer off when an obscure reference to a newspaper story about a Steinway piano being transported to East Africa, accompanied by a piano tuner and another Frenchman, caught my eye.

The article, he told her, described a rather arduous and hazardous journey of the piano by sea, train and by land through dense African bush. It was a humorous piece, poking fun at the whims and so-called necessities of East African colonial lifestyles. It seemed the piano was destined to live on an enormous estate in 'one of the old colonies'.

He swivelled around in his chair and grinned at her. "Coincidence or what?"

Sophie frowned, went over to the dining room table and returned with the photograph of Nicola at the grand piano in Mbabati. "Are you thinking there's a chance the story could be based on truth?"

"The story's dated 1964, the year we think the Gray's moved to Tanzania. There could well be a link, don't you think? A Parisian classical music doyenne, a grand piano, an estate in one of the East African colonies, Alex said, ticking each point off on a finger."

He rubbed his hands together happily. "There's a tantalizing story here somewhere and I intend to find out what it is. The only problem is we don't know where the bloody house is!"

******

"All packed, my darling?" Alex called from the veranda.

"Just about. I'll be sad to leave Cape Town, but it could be a whole lot worse if you weren't coming to London with me. What time do you want to go and visit her grave?"

Alex led her past the old headstones with their barely distinguishable names until he came to the far corner of the cemetery and found her grave, unadorned save for the white cross with her name on it.

"Here she is, Sophie. Come and say hello."

He thought of the years of fame and fortune in Paris, a seemingly perfect world for a beautiful woman to live in. Now there was this small mound with the simple cross. She'd lived alone in a sparse cottage and died in abject poverty.

He looked up at Sophie. "Hey, come on, where did the tears come from?"

Alex put his arms around her. "We need to find her family, although I'm not sure if she would have approved of us poking around in her past, she obviously wanted to keep it a secret."

He took the roses from her and placed them next to the cross, smoothing the earth around them, standing up he wiped his hands on his jeans.

Taking Sophie's hand, they walked to the wooden gates of the cemetery. Alex looked back briefly then led her to the car. "Let's go and have a glass of wine and celebrate the fabulous Nicola DuPont and who she was - not what she became."

47

They sat in the gardens of the hotel under the ancient oak trees, the soft dribble of a fountain playing in front of them. Sophie studied the Cape Dutch architecture of the old manor house slumbering in the shade of the trees, their walls blinding white and featuring the traditional dark green shutters at the windows. Old wine barrels painted green and white had the daily menus attached to their sturdy sides.

The sun glinted on her wine glass catching the glow of the liquid and turning it into a bauble of golden light. She twirled it in her fingers and tried to imagine living in the house before it became a hotel. The ladies of the Manor strolling in this garden, parasols held aloft against the brutal sun; the soft fabric of their skirts brushing against the gravel pathways, their corsets biting into their flesh making it even harder to breathe in the heat.

Farm vehicles rumbled past loaded with grape pickers calling cheerfully to each other, each vehicle laden with freshly picked grapes ready to be processed and produce the world class wines the country was famous for.

She reached over the table for Alex's hand. The moment was instantly lost as his phone vibrated on the table. Holding on to her hand, he answered it.

Charlie he mouthed at her.

Sophie looked around the gardens. A small wooden bridge straddled a thin stream as it meandered through the lush grounds. A brilliantly coloured sunbird alighted on a bush dipping its beak into a flower, the iridescent colours of his plumage dazzling in the sunlight.

She raised her eyebrow in questions as Alex finished his call. "Thanks mate, it's not much, I agree, but every little helps as they say." He placed the phone back on the table.

"Charlie's folks can't remember any scandal or stories about a house called Mbabati. The only thing they can recall was a big story about an artist who disappeared in the bush and was never seen again around the time they left the country, which was around nineteen eighty four. That was it, not much help at all."

Sophie took a sip of her wine and carefully placed her glass down on the table.

"You don't suppose it could have been the same artist who painted the portrait in the photograph do you?"

Alex tapped his nails on the table. "Far too much of a coincidence. It's more likely the portrait was commissioned in Paris and shipped out. But I'll add a missing artist and the portrait to the puzzle - you never know."

"Maybe he, or she, was eaten by a lion or something" Sophie said mischievously, then added darkly "Or murdered. Might be worth doing a quick search?"

She rolled her eyes when his phone rang again. "Do you have to answer it, sweetheart, can't we just ignore the bloody thing. It's so annoying."

He glanced at his phone. "It's Peter, unusual for him to call, I should take it, sorry my darling."

"Hey Peter - what's up?" He listened attentively, stroking the back of Sophie's hand with his finger.

"I won't need to ask her, mate, she'd love to go. Thanks for thinking of us, appreciate it. If you can email me the details I'll take it from there."

"Love to go where, sweetheart?"

"On safari!" he said laughing. "Peter has two guests who have to return to the UK unexpectedly, we've taken over their booking at the game lodge. It's nearly impossible this time of the year to book anything in South Africa, height of the season and all that. Am I forgiven for taking that particular call?"

She grinned at him happily. "When are we off?"

"Day after tomorrow." He picked up his phone, drained his wine glass, and stood up. "Come on let's go. I need to sort the flights out and organize a few things, then look for a missing artist."

******

With the flights booked and confirmed Alex searched the internet for any information on missing artists in East Africa. An hour later he joined Sophie in the sitting room where she was reading a magazine. She looked up expectantly.

"You have no idea how many artists there are in East Africa…I didn't find anything about a missing one, or a murdered one, I'm afraid, but then again I had little or nothing to go on, we don't even know if the artist was male or female." He yawned expansively and scratched his head. "Come on, my darling, time for bed, I've got loads to do tomorrow."

******

Sophie and Alex were the only two passengers on the small transit aircraft. The pilot pointed out the herds of elephant, the giraffe moving between the trees with their rocking gait, a crocodile sunbathing on the banks of a river and a huge herd of buffalo. An hour after taking off they began their descent; Sophie looked around nervously for the airport but could only see a short stretch of cleared bush, seeming to appear from nowhere, surrounded by long lion coloured grass.

The pilot banked the plane and zoomed over a herd of elephant; they shook their heads and trumpeted at the sound of the engines. Their huge bodies looked small from this height, vulnerable and toy like. Sophie turned to look at Alex and seeing he was unperturbed at the lack of a conventional landing strip, grinned back at him.

"No worries, my darling," he shouted over the noise of the engines "the pilot know what he's doing - I think."

The young bush pilot laughed and gave them the thumbs up sign before going back to his instruments.

The pilot landed the aircraft with a bump; red dust spewed up all around them as they came to a halt. After the engines were shut down there was absolute silence. A bottle green safari vehicle was waiting beneath the shade of an Acacia tree. A man looking to be in his early sixties alighted and walked towards the aircraft. His face was deeply tanned, his hair white and cropped close to his head. He smiled broadly as he watched them descend the few steps from the plane.

"Hi," he said, with his hand outstretched. "I'm Bruce Miller, manager of the lodge. Welcome to the bush. The pilot will unload your luggage and Jacob here" he inclined his head to the young African ranger who was beaming at them, "will put them in the vehicle. Let's get you out of the hot sun; I'm sure you could both use a cold drink."

Sophie dusted down her trousers and shook out her jacket. Fanning her face with her straw hat she followed Bruce to the waiting vehicle. He reached behind the seat for the cold box and handed them both a bottle of iced water.

Sophie drank deeply, wiped her mouth with the back of her hand and looked around at a panorama of unsurpassed beauty. A herd of impala grazed near the air strip, their golden pelts shimmering in the heat. Endless plains of the bush stretched out in front of her. Her head buzzed with the silence.

Bruce turned the vehicle towards the lodge. On the twenty minute drive he pointed out different birds, animals and trees. He stopped the vehicle as two giraffe crossed their path ahead pausing to nibble the top of an acacia tree before moving on.

Bruce drove through the bush, keeping a wary eye open for animals they might startle and cause to gallop in front of them. "Most of the game will be resting at this time of the day. It's too hot even for them. But they'll all be out later as the afternoon cools off. Here we are - welcome to Riverside lodge."

The lodge was striking. A well-swept path, bordered on both sides with white painted rocks, led to the main part of the camp which nestled under gnarled trees. Beneath the tall A-framed thatched roof, tables were laid for lunch and ceiling fans circled slowly stirring the thick syrupy air.

The lounge was cool and inviting, the floor covered with animal skins. Shelves of books lined the walls featuring biographies and novels by characters who once roamed the vast plains of Africa looking for game to shoot. White wicker chairs with animal print cushions and low tables were grouped around the room in small circles. Long sofas with plump cushions stood in front of a big fireplace laid with logs and ready to light. African drums served as sturdy side-tables.

An old-fashioned record player with a handle stood in one corner, its metal horn glinting in a shaft of sunlight. On the veranda, six long planter's chairs, their flat arms perfect for balancing a cool drink, stood in a row.

"I feel as though I'm standing in my shop," Sophie laughed. "How lovely to see all these old things in their rightful place, here in Africa."

Each of the ten tented suites was set on individual platforms beneath a canopy of trees; thick bushes giving each suite complete privacy. Bruce unzipped their tent and deposited the bags on the double bed.

Bruce turned to them a smile seeping into his eyes. "You should have everything you need. Come up to the main camp when you're ready. Don't forget to zip up your tent when you leave. The monkeys are curious and like nothing better than coming into a tent to check things out. If there's any fruit around," he indicated a glass bowl full of oranges, apples and grapes, "they'll take it. They can be a bit of a nuisance if they get inside. Many a guest has found a monkey in their bathroom either admiring themselves in the mirror or trying to turn the taps on."

"We'll try and remember," Sophie said solemnly and then giggled.

Bruce stepped off the veranda. "I'll let you get settled in."

They thanked him and then wandered out onto the deck. The bush rolled out in front of them, golden grasses rippled and rustled in the hot breeze. Five large Kudu antelope their graceful curling horns glinting in the sun, grazed near the river.

They unpacked their luggage admiring the luxury of their suite. A double-bed swathed with mosquito netting dominated the room. There was an en-suite bathroom and an outside shower. On the deck a low wooden table and two cream canvas chairs commanded a view over the endless carpet of bush.

******

Alex and Sophie lay in bed, beneath the billowing mosquito net as the overhead fan beat the warm air above them.

"I'm not sure if making love is better in a freezing cold climate or in a hot one. What do you think, sweetheart?"

"I don't care whether it's hot, cold or pouring with rain" he kissed her bare shoulder and ran his hand down her thigh "so long as I'm making love to you."

He yawned, pulling her head down onto his chest. "Time for a sleep I think. Then I'm going to try the outside shower before we join the others for tea and cake and the game drive. "Or," he nuzzled her neck "we could just stay here in bed until tomorrow."

"Absolutely not," Sophie protested weakly. "Come on, I'm also dying to try the outside shower. Let's shower together, we have another hour before the game drive so we could wander down to the water hole and see what's out and about. Come on, up you get."

At the water hole, a herd of Impala emerged from the tall grass. Glancing warily about, they tip-toed to the water's edge. Some kept watch, black noses lifted to the wind, their tails flicking anxiously. Others spread spindly legs and lowered their heads to drink. The sharp crack of an elephant toppling a tree in the distance startled the gazelles. They bolted from the water hole, their brown bodies vanishing into the grass with a flash of black stripes and tails.

A water buck came into view and lifting his head he sniffed the wind for danger then bent down and drank, watching his own reflection and any other which might stealthily approach. The water rippled against his steady lapping.

Sophie reached for Alex's hand. "I can't help wondering what it must have been like for Nicola living on some vast estate in the middle of the bush, especially after the kind of life she had in Paris. It's lovely out here but I wouldn't want to live here permanently. I think I'd go mad."

"Yes, I was thinking about her as well. It must have been a huge adjustment after Paris. Here comes Bruce probably ready to take us on a game drive." He shaded his eyes and watched him approach.

"The other guests have already set off on their drive. The rangers have found pug marks from a leopard, not far from camp - would you like to see if we can find the owner?"

Bruce tracked the leopard down to a dry river bed. Now they waited in the vehicle under the shade of a tree hoping the leopard would make an appearance. Sophie sat quietly, scanning the bush for a sighting. In the distance a baboon barked a warning. She felt Bruce's hand on her bare arm. He was pointing to the left of her. She felt her heart thump as the magnificent cat came silently into view padding softly on the dry sand. It ignored them as it passed in front of the vehicle and then, with effortless grace, leapt into a tree on the opposite bank.

Bruce started the engine and backed quietly out of the river bed. He headed for the hill where drinks and snacks had been prepared. Dust spun a fine red cloud and pebbles pinged against the metal chassis of the Land Cruiser as it topped the hill. A low thorn bush scraped the undercarriage releasing a pungent smell of wild sage.

He slowed the vehicle down as they approached their sun-downer spot. The last thing he wanted was a cloud of red dust settling over the white table cloth. He settled Sophie and Alex into chairs, poured her a glass of chilled wine and handed Alex a beer before sitting down and letting his eyes scan the cooling bush for anything else of interest. "Ah, here come my favourite couple."

Two giraffes sauntered nonchalantly towards an Acacia tree and began to feed, the sky growing pink behind them, and their brown-and-tan mottled hides blending perfectly with the shadows of the trees. Only their long necks rising like periscopes over the tree tops gave their position away.

Bruce smiled. "The wonderful thing about animals is they just get on with life, untroubled by world affairs, politics, money or anything else. They are born, grow up, mate and eventually die. They never ask for more than they have. Unlike humans who always want more. More houses, or a bigger one; more money, more power. Just how much does a human being need to be happy?"

Sophie nodded in agreement. Nicola certainly seemed to have had it all but look how she had ended up. Bruce was right, money and big houses were no guarantee of anything.

Alex took a handful of peanuts and sat forward in his chair. "You don't sound like a South African, Bruce. Were you born here?"

Bruce removed his sunglasses, cleaning them on his shirt. "No, I'm not a South African; I was born in Tanzania. I used to be a professional hunter but then decided to lay down the gun and take up the camera. Jobs were hard to come by in Tanzania, so I left and ended up managing various lodges in Kenya. Then I came to South Africa. It's a great country, plenty of game, plenty of lodges and far more opportunities." He put his sunglasses back on and gazed out into the bush.

They stared at each other, the snacks and sun-downers forgotten. Here was someone who had lived and worked in Tanzania for years, surely he would have known plenty of people in the expat community?

Alex shook his head slightly warning her not to ask any questions. Puzzled, she knew he would have a good reason and kept quiet.

Oblivious to their silent communication Bruce checked his watch and the sun. "Just about enough time to check out the elephants, I should think. Hop back on the vehicle."

Driving slowly through the bush Bruce pulled up next to a large herd of elephant drinking at a water hole. He put his finger to his lips warning them to be quiet. It was a breeding herd with babies hiding beneath their mothers great bellies. Occasionally, feeling brave, one or two would dart out on wobbly legs and splash in the water, squealing and waving their rubbery trunks around before turning around and running back to the protection of the adults. Sophie could hear the herd rumbling to each other; the sound coming from deep within their massive bodies reminding her of an impending thunder storm, or the distant approach of an underground train.

"They're intelligent creatures," Bruce said in a low whisper, "and they have long memories. There are a few stories of elephants being rescued and brought up by humans but eventually joining a wild herd. They come back you know, to visit their human friends. They never forget a human who has been kind to them - or not so kind to them!"

******

Returning to the lodge Alex and Sophie made their way back to their tented suite to change for dinner.

"Why didn't you want me to ask Bruce any questions?" Sophie asked drying herself after a shower. "He's exactly the right age to potentially have known Nicola, Max and their set. He might have been able to tell us something about Mbabati. I bet he knew it, or of it."

"It was tempting to bombard him with questions I agree." He buttoned up his shirt. "Let's invite him to join us for dinner, maybe tomorrow night? I can explain to him I'm a journalist, or maybe not. I haven't decided yet."

Sophie nodded as she dressed. "I'll be led by you then. At some point, he's going to ask us what we do for a living. It's the polite thing to do around the dinner table and probably more so out in the bush. You'll have to tell him what you do," she paused and lifted her head her eyes round with apprehension. "What's that noise?"

"Drums. Lodges use them to alert their guests dinner is about to be served. Come on, grab your jacket, it can get cool in the bush after dark."

They chose a table under a tree now hung with lanterns. Crystal wine glasses and silver cutlery were laid out on the crisp white tablecloth. Candles flickered in their glass holders illuminating a bowl of pink roses set in the middle of the table.

Bruce spent his evening moving between tables and chatting to the guests, before he joined a group of Americans.

55

"Have you decided how you are going to approach him with the Nicola story?" Sophie asked quietly.

"I'm going to play it by ear. Ask a few neutral questions, tell him about places I've been to in Africa, then see what happens."

A lion roared in the distance and startled them both.

Alex chuckled. "A male lion calling his pride, he's quite close to the camp. Anyway as I was saying before Leo out there started to butt in, I'm going to play it by ear."

******

The following evening they had declined to go on the evening game drive, preferring to spend their time around the watering hole watching the animals coming to drink.

The drums announcing dinner echoed across the bush. Reluctantly, they dragged themselves away from the parade of animals drinking and made their way to the dining area, delighted to see Bruce standing next to their table.

"Thanks for inviting me to join you." Bruce pulled a chair out for Sophie and they sat down. After examining the menu, taking Bruce's recommendations and ordering, Sophie told Bruce about her shop in London and how she was always on the lookout for new stock. "Or rather, old stock," she said laughing. She glanced at Alex and decided to lead the conversation.

"There must have been some grand houses in Tanzania, Bruce." Sophie said rhetorically. "With all those colonials claiming a piece of Africa for their own. I would love to know what happened to all their things when they passed on."

Bruce brushed a leaf from the table and cleared his throat. "There were quite a few colonials in Tanzania, but they didn't flock there as they did to Kenya. Kenya was definitely the destination if you wanted to put down roots and make a go of things. Tanzania was more transient. Mostly people went there on some sort of contract which supplied a furnished house."

"Did you live out in the bush or in one of the towns?" Alex asked.

"My father managed a coffee farm near Arusha. I was born and raised there. When I was twelve I was sent off to boarding school in the UK; it was the done thing then. Still is pretty much. When I

56

graduated from university I went back to Tanzania and applied for my professional hunter's licence." Alex and Sophie listened attentively.

"My parents left Tanzania and retired to the UK. At least there they could get on the National Health and receive a small pension. They weren't happy though, they missed their life in Africa. Eventually I think they just gave up," he said sadly.

"My mother passed away first and my father six months later. It was a different way of life for them and even though they made a few friends none of them was interested in the life my parents had left behind. I'd go back to East Africa in a heartbeat if I could."

Looking self-conscious, Bruce changed the topic, "So now you know all about me, I know Sophie has her shop in London which I promise to visit next time I'm there - what about you, Alex?"

Alex decided to tell the truth. "I'm a bit of a hunter myself - a hunter of stories. I used to be a full-time journalist with *The Telegraph* and then decided to freelance for them. I write a piece for them every month, human interest stories. I'm chasing one in Tanzania at the moment. It's intriguing to say the least."

Briefly, he gave Bruce a little background on the woman in Cape Town, without mentioning her name, or Sophie's mystery nun.

Bruce listened carefully as he topped up their wine, then he glanced around at his other guests and stood up.

"Excuse me for a moment. I need to check my other guests are happy."

"Alex are you going to mention any names? He might just know something!" Sophie hissed under her breath.

"I was about to when he buggered off."

A few minutes later, Bruce settled back into his chair. "Everyone seems to be happy, let's get back to your story."

"We think the woman who died in Cape Town might have come from Tanzania. She married a man who inherited an estate in East Africa. Max Gray. Did you by any chance come across either of them?"

"Gray? Yes I knew a Max Gray. I hunted with him a couple of times up on the Tanzanian border. He was an excellent shot if I recall."

They looked at each other triumphantly. Unable to contain her excitement Sophie cut to the chase. "Can you tell us anything more about Max or his wife Nicola? Maybe you can shed some light on how she ended up in South Africa?"

Bruce shook his head. "I'm afraid I don't know much. This was years and years ago. Max was a young man then, single if I remember correctly. His father had recently died and he'd inherited the family estate, he came over for the funeral. He was living in Paris I think, when his father passed away. He wanted to do a bit of hunting before returning to Paris. As I say it was a long time ago."

He smiled at them. "Although Africa is a big continent it's amazing how many expats know each other, and if they don't, someone knows someone who knows whoever you're looking for."

Sophie nodded her head. "Yes, it happens often in my shop… two complete strangers suddenly find they have a pile of friends in common in Africa somewhere."

"Can you remember the name of the estate?" Alex asked casually.

Bruce scratched his head. "Whew, you're asking some tough questions. Let me think a moment. No I really can't recall the name of the estate."

"Not to worry, mate," Alex said smiling at him. "We'll pursue the story in Tanzania even if we have to go door to door - or estate to estate."

"Well, I can tell you *one* thing. You won't find the estate or the house in Tanzania. Even though I told you we hunted together on the border Max didn't inherit anything in Tanzania - it was Kenya. That's where the family estate was."

Alex looked at him. "You've been a great help Bruce, thank you. I'm impressed you remembered his name though - long time ago."

"I probably wouldn't have remembered his name under normal circumstances. It's what happened twenty odd years later that made me remember him. He died in suspicious circumstances you see. Some say he committed suicide others had their own wild theories …." He shrugged his shoulders and took a sip of his coffee. "A couple of years before he died a fairly well known artist disappeared not far from the Gray's estate, the name of which I honestly can't remember, or the artist's name come to that - not the sort of world I move in. Well, I'm not going to repeat the gossip that went around, suffice to say the police came up with nothing."

Chapter Eight
MBABATI
Luke

Father O'Neill arrived in Nairobi from his parish an hour's drive away from the city. He collected the parcel from the young curate at the Cathedral. Tomorrow, at daybreak, he would start out on the journey to Mbabati. He had scant information as to where the house actually was, only that the nearest town was Nanyuki. He would have to hope someone would know the location of the place and point him in the right direction. It would be a long and difficult journey in his battered old car.

He looked at his watch; it was time to celebrate Mass. He was looking forward to a simple meal with his fellow priests before spending the night at the rectory.

******

Luke pulled his cloak around him against the cool night air. He poked the fire with a stick and threw another log on. Sparks flew up into the air as the flames took hold.

He looked up at the house. Each evening before he locked up he always made sure the lamp was burning in her room - just in case.

Over the years his monthly stipend had arrived faithfully at Mr Patel's shop. With this money he had been able to live comfortably and take care of the house as best he could.

He looked up suddenly, aware of a presence near him.

Tika had arrived as silently as the stars above him. Luke could make out his great bulk by the light of the moon. He smiled as he felt the elephant's trunk searching his pockets for oranges.

Finding none Tika lifted his trunk and swinging it from side to side he searched the air for a scent of the family who had once lived there.

Luke watched him. Perhaps the old elephant had come to say goodbye. Perhaps he knew she would not be coming home; she would not be coming back to Mbabati.

Tika left as silently as he had arrived, melting into the darkness. Luke turned back to his fire; now he would wait. Someone would come from Nairobi one day. He would have to unlock the big gates each morning until this person came.

******

A few days later Luke heard the vehicle coming up the drive. He shrugged on his crimson waist jacket and smoothed down his uniform in preparation for his long-awaited messenger.

He watched perplexed when he saw the man wearing a long brown garment tied with a rope around his middle, a chain and cross resting on his generous stomach. Silently he waited for him to approach.

"*Jambo* Mzee," the priest said, holding out his hands to shake Luke's in the African manner. "I'm looking for Mrs Gray. Is she at home?"

Luke shook his head. "She is not here, there is no-one here. But I have been waiting for some news. Do you have this news for me?"

Father O'Neill removed his hat and wiped the sweat off his face with the back of his sleeve. He looked at the old African, surprised he had been expecting him. "I have come many miles, perhaps I could have some water?"

"Wait here please, I will get the key."

Luke reappeared from his small thatched rooms holding an ornate iron key." Please come with me, Bwana. I will prepare food for you after your long journey, and bring you some water."

Luke opened the front door and led the priest into the dim coolness of the reception hall, and then through to a study. Pulling a dust cover off an armchair, Luke indicated his visitor should sit, then he padded from the room to see what he could find for lunch.

Father O'Neill sank gratefully into the comfortable chair; motes of dust rose from the depths of it and hung in the still air. He sneezed violently and looked around.

The focal point of the room was an arched fireplace, the grate set back inside with an iron fire guard around it; on either side books stood silently side by side. On top of each bookcase was a white marble bust on a plinth; both gazed into the room with unseeing eyes.

Framed pictures covered with sheets, hung from the walls of pale grey and green striped wallpaper, now faded with the years. Tarnished double arm wall lights graced the walls.

60

The priest shivered despite the sun shining through the window. He turned sharply, feeling as though he were being watched.

Luke returned to the room with a tray and set it down on a table next to him, then he stood by the door, his hands behind his back, and watched the white man look at the simple lunch he had prepared from his own meagre supply of food.

After blessing the food the priest ate hungrily. He had stayed overnight in a guest house halfway through his journey, and had left at sunrise. In Nanyuki he had asked for directions to the house but no-one seemed to know where it was. Frustrated, he had gone into the local supermarket where the owner had pointed him in the right direction. As soon as he had handed over the package he planned to be on his way again.

He thanked Luke for his meal, and told him he had something for him which he would get from the car.

Father O'Neill returned carrying a package. "When will Mrs Gray be back, old man? I have important news for her."

Luke eyed the package nervously and looked at the priest. "She is not here now. What do you wish me to tell her?"

"She's not here?" he said more to himself than to Luke. "Are you expecting her back some time, er, soon?" Father O'Neill tried again.

"I will give her this message from you."

The priest hesitated, not entirely sure what to do. He had come this far, and felt somehow it was his duty to see Mrs Gray personally. He reminded himself of the long return journey home and was keen to get going.

"You must tell her, her sister has died at the convent in London. The Mother Superior," Father O'Neill broke off, seeing Luke's puzzlement. "The Mother Superior is the memsahib in charge of the convent where the nuns live."

Luke had no idea what the man was talking about; but it mattered little now.

"The Memsahib Superior asked that this package be returned to the family here at Mbabati."

Seeing there was little more he could do, the priest bid Luke farewell. "Thank you for your hospitality, old man. Stay well and go in peace."

As Luke watched, the priest turned back to the house with an odd expression. He made the sign of the cross and hurried to his car

Luke waited until the vehicle retreated down the drive and disappeared between the gates. When the dust had settled he locked the gates then turned and walked slowly back to his rooms. He sat down heavily on his bed and turned the envelope over and over. With shaking hands he peeled back the flap, the tears coursing down his lined cheeks.

Yes, he had been right, but he had always known their secret.

One night, when the moon was full, and only one sister was left in the house, he had heard a noise in the grounds. Silently moving between the trees he had seen her there talking to herself and crying - she had not seen him there watching her.

It was a small mistake she had made, thinking she was alone.

He knew both of them better than he knew his own children. Miss Nicola and Miss Elizabeth. What they had done would remain in his safe keeping. He had taken a chance in sending the letters and the diary, the ones he now held once again in his hands. Many rainy seasons had passed since he had sent these things to her.

Luke walked down the path leaning heavily on his stick. The wind had picked up and threw fast moving dark clouds across the face of the moon.

He opened the iron gate and limped towards the graves. He stopped and looked around at them, then bending down he pulled a weed from the well-tended grave in front of him. Loose leaves skittered in the wind and he brushed them away. Using the threadbare sleeve of his jacket, he wiped the surface and stared at the blank marble headstone. The lamp glowed, as always, at the head of the grave.

He turned to the one on his left which had grown ugly with neglect and the passage of time. Weeds and roots had grown deep into its surface, their vicious thorny tentacles reaching for the dead man's bones, tightening their grip on him. The headstone was barely visible beneath a thick coat of lichen.

Luke spat on the grave and weakly kicked at the earth around it. This man had been responsible for everything. He deserved nothing now, only to be forgotten and covered with the wild bush, smothered for the grief and devastation he had caused the family. Luke would not care for him in death any more than he had cared for him when he was alive.

Luke spat on the grave once again, then turned and left. He walked back, stopping to look up at the house. How would it be now, should the truth be told - or left hidden like the grave?

Would she come home? Would she know her sister had died? Yes, with no written word, she would know and come back.

The wind howled amidst the trees and the rain came suddenly, swirling around the gardens and the house like a grey shroud, fat drops hammering on the rooftop like a demented ghost demanding to be let into the house.

Luke shivered as the rain ran down his face and neck. Pulling his cloak around his bony shoulders he returned to the aching emptiness of his own house.

******

Father O'Neill checked into the same guest house he had stayed in the night before. He dropped his bag in the room, then made his way down the stairs and out onto the veranda, where he ordered a double whisky.

Lowering his considerable bulk into a cane chair, which creaked in protest, he took a grateful mouthful of his drink and stared out over the bush.

Luke had invited him to stay the night, and rest after his long journey from Nairobi. But he had declined the invitation. Inexplicably he had felt uneasy as soon as he walked through the front door of the house.

Why was the name of it vaguely familiar? On the drive back this afternoon it had come to him. There had been a lot of gossip and speculation about what had happened, true or otherwise. Even now he found it difficult to remember the details.

What he had never forgotten, however, was the distraught woman and her confession to him before she left the country all those years ago. But now there was no doubt in his mind. The name of the woman - the woman who made the shocking confession to him - was Elizabeth. She had lived at Mbabati.

He crossed himself quickly and, with a trembling hand, reached for his whisky.

Chapter Nine
London

Alex held the umbrella over Sophie as she fumbled around in her bag for the keys to the shop.

She turned the lock and used her shoulder to push the door open and shivered. "It's freezing in here; I'll get the heating going."

Alex closed the door against the volume of cars hissing and splashing past, and propped the umbrella in the hollowed out foot of an elephant and grimaced. Sophie laughed. "I know it's hideous, isn't it? When hunting was alive and well it wasn't unusual to use elephant feet as umbrella stands, bins, or magazine holders."

She shrugged off her coat and draped it over a chair. "I didn't know what else to use it for, and I couldn't throw it away. What on earth would the rubbish removal men have thought! I'll make some coffee."

Alex kept his coat on, and rubbed his hands together to keep warm. The heat of a South African summer seemed a million miles away.

They'd arrived in London early in the morning, deposited their luggage in the apartment and headed for the shop. Alex was anxious to see the blown-up photograph of the old house and the silver bell with the crest.

He walked over to Sophie's desk and stared up at the photograph and shivered. "You're right," he called out to her, "the house does look spooky, but a great backdrop for your desk." He moved closer to examine it hoping to find some sort of date.

The low buildings slightly to the left of the house looked like stables, close to what appeared to be a large paddock. The walls of the house were covered in thick ivy and the large leaded windows on all three floors were framed by wooden shutters.

Sophie put down his mug of coffee, circling her own with her hands. "The gardens were beautiful. They must have had an army of gardeners to keep them looking so good."

He sipped his coffee. "It certainly has an English country house feel - but that's what they did. Created a bit of England in what was a hostile land, right down to the formal layout of an English garden. Imagine hacking all the bush back to create it and finding the right flowers, trees and bushes to grow there, and survive. Quite an achievement when you think about it."

Alex turned and glanced around the shop. "Let's hope your assistant didn't sell the bell. Where do you think it might be in amongst all this lot?"

Sophie put down her coffee mug. "I put it in my desk for safekeeping. Here it is."

Taking the proffered bell he studied the crest before looking once more at the photo. "You're right; the crest over the door is identical to this, so it must have been inside the envelope with the letters and diary." He passed it back to her.

Alex picked up the magnifying glass on her desk and worked his way across the grainy detail of the photograph. He caught his breath.

"Soph, is it just me or does there seem to be a kind of figure here?" he said at last, pointing to the top left-hand window of the house.

They stood next to each other up close to the photograph and then walked around to the other side of the desk to look at the image from a distance.

"Bloody hell," Alex said under his breath.

"It's a woman." She shivered suddenly, rubbing her arms. "Actually it looks more like a flipping ghost."

Alex checked his watch. "I'll let you get on with things here, I'm going to call in at the newspaper and see what's happening. I'll come back here when I'm done."

"Don't forget I have my sundowner evening tonight?"

The shop door opened and a middle-aged couple came in. Alex kissed Sophie, put on his coat, and headed for the still open door.

******

"I wasn't expecting to see you in London, Alex." His editor deposited two pints of beer and two pork pies on the table in the pub. "I thought you were off to Zimbabwe to cover a story for us."

"I was Harry, but I think I've a bigger and more interesting one to follow with a connection here in London, and another one in Kenya." He took a mouthful of warm beer and brought Harry up to date with what had happened in Cape Town.

Harry bit into his pie. "So you've got a nun in England, Max Gray who inherited an estate in Kenya, and a famous pianist who ended up begging on the streets of Cape Town," he raised a questioning eyebrow. "You've got a rumour Max may, or may not, have killed himself, might have been murdered in fact..." He took a second bite and chewed thoughtfully.

"You've got good instincts, Alex. You've a journalist's nose for a story but it sounds like you're being fed stories from a variety of sources which aren't reliable. You must have heard of the most famous murder in East Africa, in Kenya - Josslyn Hay, Earl of Errol? His body was discovered with a bullet in his head. He was an adept seducer of wives, wrecking a good few marriages in Nairobi."

"Remind me, I forget the details," Alex said reluctantly.

He told him about Sir Delves Broughton, with whose wife Errol had been sleeping, he was arrested and tried for his murder but was acquitted. No one was ever convicted of Errol's murder, and the question of who did it became a big rumour-fuelled mystery.

"Why are you telling me this, what's the link?" Alex interrupted.

"Sir Delves Broughton committed suicide in a hotel room in Brighton or somewhere. I doubt even an intrepid investigative journalist like you will be able to dig up any more dirt on who killed Lord Errol."

Alex smiled. "Well, we certainly have similar components: an English aristocrat, East Africa, and a suicide. There wasn't an artist involved in any of this, was there?"

Harry shook his head. "There was another murder in Nairobi in early two thousand. He was an artist, a Polish name I can't recall at the moment because it was tricky to pronounce, he died in a similar way to Lord Errol. The circumstances were intriguingly similar."

Alex slumped in his seat.

"Cheer up, lad," Harry said chuckling. "You know how people forget things, or get facts wrong over time. Sounds to me as if the information you have are two stories muddled up because of the similar circumstances."

Alex leaned forward unperturbed. "Two women, living continents apart, have a definite link to an abandoned house. We may have got the wrong end of the stick about the suicide and all of that but there's still a riches-to-rags story here and I'm going after it."

Harry nodded, drinking from his pint glass. "Look into it," was all he said.

Alex drained his beer and stood up to leave.

"The paper won't be able to fund a trip to Kenya." Harry called to Alex's retreating back. "Maybe the old nun will be able to answer all your questions and you can get back on the Zimbabwe piece."

Alex half turned and held his arm up in farewell. The front door of the pub banged shut behind him.

******

Matthew, now in his third year at Edinburgh University, stepped off the train at King's Cross.

He checked the time on the station clock; he had three hours to kill before meeting up with his girlfriend for a drink. He wound his scarf around his neck and decided to go to Vintage Africa and check if any of his old Kenyan chums were around. Friday evening was always a good time to catch up on a bit of gossip from home. He knew his friends in London often dropped in there.

He had been to the shop twice before, once to drop off Luke's parcel for Miss Gray and the second time for one of the sundowner evenings. He'd wanted to meet the owner but both times she'd not been there. He sprinted for the bus, making it just before it departed.

It was raining hard when he got off, and he'd forgotten his umbrella. He dodged in and out of doorways until he entered the more familiar streets of Mayfair and saw the familiar awning of Vintage Africa. There was quite a crowd inside and he could hear the rumble of voices and the bursts of laughter erupting from the coffee area at the back. Grateful for some shelter from the rain, he pushed the door open and entered.

*****

Alex was making his way across the crowded room looking for Sophie. He spotted her handing over a letter to an elderly man. A young man, dressed like a student, stood with his back to her desk examining some books waiting patiently for her attention.

Sophie spotted Alex and waved him over. "How was your day? Everyone pleased to see you?" She gestured around the shop. "Quite a

67

gathering this evening, it's always busier when it rains," she stifled a yawn, "after the long flight I'm starting to feel a bit knackered!"

"Excuse me, are you Sophie?" She turned at the sound of her name and smiled at the young man on her left. "Yes, that's me."

He held out his hand. "I'm Matthew, great to finally meet you. You and your shop are a legend in Africa."

Sophie laughed, delighted, and introduced Alex. Matthew unwound his scarf. "I dropped a package off here about two years ago?"

She smiled at him. "Yes?"

"Well, as I was in the area I thought I'd check to see if the lady collected it. It was given to me by someone at home, who was anxious it should get to her. I'm going back for the summer holidays, and I wanted to be able to tell *mzee*, the old man, it had been delivered safely. I hope he's still alive - he was pretty old the last time I saw him."

"Well I do keep a running record of letters and parcels," Sophie said, walking back to her desk and feeling in the drawer for her ledger. "Yes, I know a ledger is a bit old fashioned," she said, laughing at his look of disbelief. "But it's sort of in keeping with the shop. Now what name am I looking for?"

"Miss Gray. I'm sure she's picked it up by now. I just wanted to reassure the old man she did."

She and Alex looked at each other, wide-eyed. "Unfortunately Customs stopped me at Heathrow and the packet was opened. There were some letters and a leather book, a diary maybe. Oh yes, and a silver bell."

Once again, Sophie felt under her desk. "It wouldn't be this one by any chance, would it?"

"Yes, that's it! It should have gone with the other stuff, but that's probably my fault. When I made the trip from Scotland to deliver it here I didn't have anything to seal it up with so I used an elastic band. Not secure I agree," he said sheepishly, "but it was all I could find on me. Did she eventually collect it?"

Sophie looked at Alex who was listening to the conversation avidly. "No - well not personally. A nun came into the shop a few months ago she said she knew Miss Gray and if I could locate the package she'd give it to her. I didn't realise until much later the bell had come in the same packet.

"You can let the gentleman know Miss Gray did eventually receive it. I'll make sure she gets her bell back, we can pop over to the convent and drop it off."

"That would be great. Thanks." Matthew's eyes moved to the photograph behind her desk, and widened with astonishment.

"Hey, I know that place!" He started to laugh. "This is really weird! That's the ranch next to my parents. Well, where we used to live before they sold it. That's where the old gentleman who wanted the parcel delivered lives. This is amazing."

Sophie sat down on the edge of her desk feeling her heart beating a rapid tattoo in her chest.

"What's his name?" Alex asked as nonchalantly as he could.

"The old man you mean? His name's Luke." Matthew replied.

Luke.

Trying to keep his excitement at bay, Alex asked him if he could tell him the address of the house.

"We don't exactly have addresses there. The ranches are spread around the country. Ours, like the Grays', was over two hours' drive north from a town called Nanyuki." He looked at his watch. "Must dash, I'm meeting someone. I'll pass the good news on to Luke."

"I think I might be doing that myself." Alex muttered under his breath.

Chapter Ten

S ophie chopped the tomatoes and added them to the sauce. "I'll have to get back into cooking mode. All those lovely dinners out in Cape Town have spoiled me. I could do with one of those little bells to summon up some help right now…"

Alex sat in the kitchen watching her as he sipped a beer, ignoring the subtle jibe.

"I'm thinking of going over to the convent tomorrow, see if I can speak to your nun."

Sophie turned to look at him as she licked a spoon. "Well for goodness sake don't mention you're a journalist or the Mother Superior will slam the door in your face! They're touchy about their private world. You'll have to have her permission first."

She turned back to the simmering pot. "She was rather short with me; actually, she was terrifying, considering I only wanted to see one of her nuns to deliver something. I mean, it's not the sort of convent where the nuns have taken a vow of silence!" Sophie filled up a pot with water and covered it with a lid.

Alex laced his fingers behind his head and leaned back on the kitchen chair. "What a stroke of luck with Matthew. The old retainer Luke must have been Elizabeth's lover."

Sophie looked up startled. "What makes you so sure?"

"The letters 'k' and 'e' on the lovers' envelopes. It's obvious. Anyway let's not jump to any more conclusions, I'll speak to Sister Elizabeth and take it from there."

"I agree," Sophie said, spooning the sauce over the pasta. "Funny the nun didn't mention she recognised the bell when I tried to give it to her…"

******

Alex checked the address Sophie had given him and looked up at the moody Gothic building in front of him. This was the right place: The Daughters of the Lord.

He straightened his tie and smoothed down his hair before reaching for the bell in the recess of the old wall.

A disembodied voice came through the speaker. "Yes?"

"I wonder if I might speak to the Mother Superior? My name is Alex Patterson."

"Do you have an appointment?

"Actually no, but I've come all the way from Cape Town in South Africa to see her."

"Please wait, I'll ask the Mother Superior if she'll agree to see you."

He jumped when he heard the buzz of the gate letting him in a few moments later. He made his way to the front of the convent and saw the door was open. A young nun stood waiting for him.

He followed her down the dark corridor, her habit whispering on the floor as she walked. She stopped at a deeply pitted door and knocked.

"Good luck," she said grinning at him, "her bark is worse than her bite." She opened and then closed the door after him.

He suddenly felt nervous. Should he shake hands with her? Bow? Wait to be asked to be seated?

"Sit! Mr Patterson." A voice barked at him.

He looked at the unsmiling elderly woman across the wide desk. She was indeed formidable - terrifying in fact - no wonder Sophie had been nervous.

"What may I help you with? I'm sure you haven't come all the way from South Africa to see the inside of an old convent?"

He thanked her for seeing him at such short notice, then his voice trailed off. How was he supposed to address her?

"You may call me Reverend Mother," she said sharply, as if reading his mind.

"Reverend Mother, I wonder if it would be possible to see Sister Elizabeth? I think I briefly met her sister Nicola, in Cape Town, but it was an unfortunate meeting." He hesitated; the Reverend Mother was looking at him stonily.

"Go on Mr Patterson."

He told her Nicola had died, on the second of December, and that he thought someone should let her sister know.

The Reverend Mother stood up and went to the window turning her back to Alex.

"What exactly is your profession, Mr Patterson?"

"I'm a journalist, Reverend Mother." He swallowed hard.

The elderly nun smoothed down her skirts whilst she marshalled her thoughts. This was one story she did *not* want told. It would implicate the convent and bring unwanted, and invasive, publicity, and, without doubt, the police.

Turning from the window she looked at him. "As far as I was aware Mr Patterson, Sister Elizabeth did not mention a sister to any of us here."

Alex frowned. "You're using the past tense, Reverend Mother."

"Sister Elizabeth passed away last year. I cannot recall the exact date. So I'm afraid your visit has been a waste of your time - and indeed mine." She moved towards the door.

"Please give me a little more of your time," Alex asked quietly, not moving. "There's more to this than just the death of Nicola in Cape Town. There's a house in Kenya called Mbabati where I believe Nicola and Elizabeth may have lived at some stage. It's possible there are other relatives who need to be informed - a Christian thing to do, I'm sure you'll agree?" he finished smoothly.

The Reverend Mother smiled faintly at his boldness. "How did you know we had Sister Elizabeth here under our care?"

"A friend of mine met her in her shop. A package was brought there for a Miss Gray, Sister Elizabeth said she knew her - look, it's a long story..." he said lamely.

The Reverend Mother reached for her cross. He already knew far too much. Rapidly she thought of the best way to handle the situation. She returned to her chair, her mind made up.

She took a deep breath, then let it out slowly. "I am, of course, under no obligation to disclose any part of Sister Elizabeth's life to you but you have come a long way. The package for Miss Gray was put in Elizabeth's personal box. Our sisters have no need for earthly possessions."

She paused and chose her next words carefully.

"When a woman enters this convent we ask nothing of her, not even her name."

Alex interrupted her. "But why put the package in Sister Elizabeth's personal box? You must have had some idea then that Sister Elizabeth and Miss Gray was one and the same person?"

Flustered with trying to cover the truth, the Reverend Mother floundered, closing her eyes briefly as she tried to make a decision.

Perhaps if she gave him just a little information he would go away, but being a journalist after a story such as this, she had her doubts.

She sighed heavily. "Sister Elizabeth was ill and I felt, at the time, the contents of the parcel might upset her further and what good would it have done?"

"So you opened it?" Alex asked bluntly.

The Mother Superior ignored his question and ploughed on. "When one of our sisters dies we do everything we can to locate family members to inform them of their death.

"After Sister Elizabeth's died I went through her box and the package to try and locate family members. There were a few letters which I hoped might help me find her family - I had no choice other than to read them.

"Yes," she said heavily, "before you ask, from what I read, Elizabeth did have a sister and her name was Nicola. But please let me be quite clear, Elizabeth at no point in her time here mentioned this." Alex kept quiet.

The Reverend Mother cleared her throat. "I contacted the Catholic mission in Nairobi and told them I would arrange for Elizabeth's personal effects to be sent there. This I did, but only in January - Christmas is a busy time for churches," she said tartly.

"However, it would appear the good Father's journey would have been made in vain if Nicola was already dead." She crossed herself automatically.

Alex nodded in affirmation.

"So as far as you are aware," he said, "Elizabeth's personal possessions, including the package have been returned to the house in Kenya?"

She told him that Father O'Neill confirmed he had left the package with someone at the house who said the owner was out.

"Wait, there's someone living at the house?" Alex asked, leaning forward.

"This is what Father O'Neill indicated, yes."

"Any idea who it might be?"

"Well, I was under the impression it was Nicola before you came here today, but I've obviously had to revise my assumption," the Mother Superior replied curtly, standing up and indicating the interview was over.

"Is there anything else you can tell me? I'm going to the house in Kenya to follow this up, I think there's an interesting story here."

"No, Mr Patterson. There's nothing more I can help you with."

"Was she happy here, do you think? Sister Elizabeth?"

The nun sighed irritably. "She was a troubled soul but we gave her the solace and security she needed," she said brusquely. "I believe in the end she had accepted her life and was content."

"May I see her grave Reverend Mother?"

"That will not be possible - she was cremated."

Alex knew there was little more he was going to get out of her. But he gave it one last shot.

"I don't suppose for a minute you'd tell me when Sister Elizabeth entered your convent, Reverend Mother?" he said, giving her what he hoped was a beguiling smile.

She shook her head abruptly. "I'll show you out."

******

She closed the door behind him and leant against it, the cross around her neck vibrating as her heart thudded in her chest. If the media got hold of the story of the two sisters they would descend on the convent in their hundreds, something to be avoided at all costs.

She bent her head and prayed both sisters would be forgiven for what they had done, and could finally rest in peace. She also prayed she would never see Alex Patterson or Sophie again.

******

Alex walked thoughtfully back to Sophie's shop and reported on his meeting with the Mother Superior.

"She knows far more about those sisters than she's letting on. I think she read something in either the letters or the diary, and she's worried about it."

"I told you she was a battle-axe."

Sophie looked up as a couple came into the shop; she smiled at them and then turned back to Alex. "Why don't you book your ticket to Nairobi? You can track down the Catholic priest, which shouldn't be too difficult, and once you have the location, you can head out to Mbabati and check it out."

74

"Hang on, aren't you coming with me?"

Sophie fiddled with a pair of scissors on her desk. "I'd love to come with you, I really would, but I've been away for three weeks, and I can't ask Sally to mind the shop again."

She put her hand over his and squeezed it apologetically. "Anyway I think you'll be more successful on your own. People are more likely to open up to one person rather than a couple?"

He nodded begrudgingly, visibly disappointed.

Sophie laughed. "I've never seen you look so disappointed to be off chasing a story. Go on, sweetheart, book your ticket! I'll put some of the photographs we have together for you and her bowl - it'll prove to Luke that you did meet Nicola, just in case he has any suspicions."

Reaching into the drawer she lifted the bowl out and rolled it across the table towards him. In the strong light of the angle poise lamp she spotted something she had missed before. Snatching it back she held it up to the light and ran her fingers across the base, examining it closely.

There was a small square in the wooden base, a slightly lighter brown than the rest of the bowl. Putting on her glasses she ran her thumb over it then pressed. A miniature drawer reflexed and opened smoothly.

"A hidden drawer..." Alex threw down his notebook and came around to her chair." Yes, and there's something here, wrapped in some kind of waxy paper."

She carefully opened it. "It's a man's signet ring, feel the weight of it," she said, dropping it into his outstretched palm. "If Nicola was so down and out why didn't she sell it?"

Alex shook his head. "It's quite worn, probably been passed down from father to son for a couple of generations." He held it up to the light. "Like most signet rings it has a family crest, but that doesn't help much unless we know which family, and we don't." Alex handed it back to her.

She placed it back in the recess. "Maybe whoever is living at the house might recognise it - maybe it belonged to Nicola's husband Max."

"If it belonged to Max I'd stake my money on the fact the crest would be identical to the one on the bell, and, my darling, it's not."

He stood up and looked around the empty shop. "Come on, close up and I'll take you down to the pub for a drink."

Chapter Eleven
Kenya

Kenya Airways started its descent into Nairobi. Alex wiped the window with his sleeve and looked at the pink dawn sky and the city sprawling beneath him. The aircraft thundered down the runway and then sedately made its way to the terminal building, coming to a standstill with a lingering hiss.

He walked from the aircraft to the terminal building, breathing in the warmth of the morning. The arrivals hall was packed with sign boards and noisy people and he was pleased to see his name held up with a smiling face beneath it.

"Norfolk Hotel Mr Patterson?"

Approaching the outskirts of the city Alex looked around with interest. There was rush-hour commuter traffic everywhere, coming from all directions and without any semblance of order. Traffic lights grappled with the mass of vehicles. Motor bikes, trucks, old and new cars all jostled for position on any vacant piece of road. Pedestrians dashed in between the vehicles, their eyes darting from side to side. On the pavements, people wove colourfully between each other; businessmen and women in smart suits carrying briefcases, and mothers with babies strapped to their backs. Mopeds zipped past, weaving expertly in and out of the traffic chaos.

Music blared from the brightly painted commuter buses, the honking of horns and squealing brakes adding to the cacophony of noise. Black belching smoke from elderly trucks hung in the air, whilst gleaming Mercedes with tinted windows slid past them.

The car took a left turn and headed away from the heavy traffic; a few minutes later they arrived at the Norfolk Hotel. The driver helped Alex with his luggage, thanked him for his generous tip, and climbed back into his car.

Alex checked in and followed the porter across the lush green courtyard to his suite. This would be his base until he located the priest. This afternoon he would take a taxi to the Catholic Church and try to find Father O'Neill.

"You should find the estate easily enough once you get to Nanyuki," the young priest told him. "Better give yourself four or five hours. Father O'Neill said there were signposts for a game lodge called Leopard's Leap, once you get to the main town, follow those. If you stop at the lodge someone will give you directions to the Mbabati estate. I'm sorry you missed Father O'Neill - he's away on a retreat in Uganda.

"There aren't any good roads here in Kenya," he continued. "I'd definitely hire a four-wheel-drive vehicle."

Feeling exhausted and sticky with heat and dust, Alex returned to the calm oasis of The Norfolk. That evening he dined on the famous Lord Delamere Terrace of the hotel, watching the pedestrian traffic. Tour operators were dropping their camera laden clients off for an overnight stay before leaving on safari; the place was buzzing with activity.

After dinner he wandered around the hotel studying the black and white photographs of past guests which decorated the walls. All the familiar names were there: Roosevelt, Blixen, Hemingway and many of the film stars of a bygone time who had flocked to Kenya on safari, or to star in films being shot there. It was a delightful glimpse into the history of early Nairobi. The hotel had hardly changed in its one hundred and ten year history.

Nicola would have had to come into Nairobi on her way to the estate; maybe she and Max had stayed at the Norfolk and eaten on the same terrace as he had that evening.

It was an odd thought to be standing where they may well have stood.

******

After breakfast the next morning, the four-wheel-drive vehicle he had hired was waiting for him in the car park. He drove out of Nairobi, keeping his wits about him as he negotiated the heavy traffic.

Once he had cleared the outskirts of town he was able to relax and look at the scenery. Open savannah and golden grasslands stretched for miles around him. He passed forests and fruit sellers, villages with their cultivated fields of cabbages, maize and potatoes, sprawling markets and donkey carts loaded down with produce.

Two tall Masaai warriors watched him imperiously as he passed, their red-gold ochre smeared bodies, elaborately plaited hair and brightly beaded thick necklaces and ankle bracelets, adding a searing splash of colour on the dusty landscape. He lifted his hand in greeting and in return they raised their spears courteously.

He was making good time thanks to the directions given to him by the young priest. The difficult part of the journey was yet to come. Once he had located the lodge he would only be around two hours away from the house. He glanced at the silver bell on the passenger seat and put his foot down. He felt excitement spritzing through his veins. It was moments like these when he loved his job the most.

Three hours later Alex slowed down as he reached the outskirts of Nanyuki. It was a busy market town and he drove cautiously, passing a dusty park in the centre of it, and rows of small shops selling colourful materials, drinks and food. In the hub of town there were small busy supermarkets and garages, hotels and restaurants.

He spotted the sign for Leopard's Leap and an hour later pulled up in a cloud of red dust in front of the thatched lodge. A security guard walked towards him with a clipboard. "You are checking in, sir?" he asked politely, looking at Alex's dust-covered vehicle.

"No, I'm looking for directions to an estate called Mbabati. Do you know where it is?"

"Yes. But no-one lives there anymore, sir," he said puzzled.

Alex smiled at him. "Perhaps you would direct me?"

He pointed down the road behind Alex and into the distance. "It's about two hours from here. Follow this road until you come to a village and a supermarket, or *duka* as they call them here, called Patel's. You pass this place until you come to a fork in the road. Take the right turning. .You are staying at Mbabati, sir?

"I'm not sure. I might have to come back and check in here, have you got availability?"

He looked down at his clipboard. "Yes, we have three rooms available tonight." He stared at Alex again. "You are family of Mbabati perhaps?"

Alex shook his head and reversed, not wanting to answer any more questions. He made steady progress, enjoying the drive as he followed the directions. Occasionally he passed a village with its round huts and thatched roofs, goats, chickens and plots of vegetables. Alongside one village a donkey, pulling a cart laden with

78

watermelons, stubbornly refused to make way for him. He slowed down and went off-road covering the donkey and driver with a cloud of dust. He lifted his hand in apology before joining the rough bush road again.

He slowed down again as he approached a flat building on the left side of the road, which the guard had told him about. Patel's was easy to locate with its bright red Coca-Cola sign, a single petrol pump and a large sign reading *Patel's Supermarket*.

Alex went in, his eyes adjusting to the shadowy interior. The shop seemed to stock just about everything from food to bales of cloth, to shoes and sacks of grain. A slender, middle-aged Indian man greeted him.

"May I help?" he asked politely.

Alex asked him if he had any bottled water. Years of travelling in Africa had taught him bottled was safer than any tap.

"Yes indeed I have bottled water. The water in this area is very good, sir, quite safe to drink," he said as if reading Alex's thoughts. "But, if you are preferring it in the bottle," he shrugged. "How many would you like?"

Mr Patel put the pack of bottles on the counter. "You are travelling far sir? Perhaps you are in need of fuel. There is no-where else to fill up for many miles."

"Yes, I think I will then, although I don't think I've far to go; just visiting a house not far from here."

Alex thanked him and went back to his car. Whilst Mr Patel filled his tank he looked at his watch and squinted up at the sun; he'd made good time and still had a few hours left before sunset.

Going back inside he paid for the water and fuel, then returned to his vehicle, aware Mr Patel had come out of the shop again and was watching him intently as he drove away.

He concentrated on finding the fork in the road and when he did he turned right. His vehicle bucked and rattled over the deeply rutted and pot-holed road making his teeth chatter. He clung grimly to the steering wheel, keeping his eyes on the road, waiting for his first glimpse of the house he had come so far to find.

Alex slowed down, his stomach tight with excitement. The rough dirt road had brought him to the entrance of the estate. The tall scroll-topped iron entrance gates, set in cement pillars, were held together with a rusting chain and padlock. An old rose bush clung stubbornly to one of the pillars, oblivious of the passing years. A brass plate set deep in one of the pillars, and green with verdigris, was engraved with the name of the house - Mbabati.

Alex switched off the engine and stared at the silent tree-lined driveway. He got out and stretched, noticing the dust from the road settling behind him. He took off his sunglasses, wiping the half-moons of dust from under his eyes, and sipped from his bottle of water. Wiping his mouth with his sleeve, he tried to work out what he should do next. He picked the bell up off the passenger seat and put it in his pocket.

Alex walked up to the gates and shook them; the padlock stood firm and unyielding. Impenetrable thorn bushes grew either side of the gates. He walked along one side but saw no means of access. Crossing to the other side of the heavy gates he spotted a half-hidden oval wooden door and tried the handle, it appeared to be locked. He pressed the handle down again and using his shoulder leaned heavily against it. With a deep growl the rotting door opened reluctantly - he stepped through.

The stillness and silence of the place made his ears ring; he walked along the tree-lined drive and suddenly there it was.

Mbabati.

The three storey, honey-coloured mansion, stood facing him. There were the two eagles carved in stone above the entrance. Some tiles had come loose and crowded at angles in the gutter, leaving holes in the red roof which stretched and dipped across the house. The arched windows were closed and shuttered giving the house a blind and desolate look, as though it had closed its eyes against the present. Thick ivy crowded much of the walls and covered some of the windows on the second and top floor, gripping relentlessly onto the shutters.

The pathway leading to the grand entrance with its portico was a mess of broken flagstones. The garden either side was tangled and wild with neglect, as if the bush was determined to claim back its own and consume the once elegant grounds. Wild grasses and weeds distorted the edges of the stone steps leading up to the carved doors.

In what once would have been a formal rose garden, untidy chickens pecked busily at the ground. A dark brown goat was tethered to a rusted garden bench and bleated forlornly at his approach.

To the left of the house he could see the roof of the low stable buildings had collapsed; ivy and brambles were crawling up its dusty sides. To the right and to the back of the house were two round mud structures with a thatched roof. Here there were more chickens and another dark brown goat who stared at him with unblinking yellow eyes.

He stood gazing at the house. Impulsively he drew the bell from his pocket and shook it lightly.

Suddenly the door to the round house was flung open. An old man squinted into the blinding sun as he hastily put on his jacket. His dark skin was pulled taut over a thin face lined with deep wrinkles. A cloud of startled doves rose from the ground, their wings beating rapidly.

"You have come back!" he called, shuffling in a slow gait towards Alex. "I heard the bell calling me as it always used to."

He broke off and his wide smile froze when he saw the white man standing looking at him in astonishment.

"You have come from her, Bwana?" Luke said tentatively, buttoning his jacket lopsidedly.

Alex held out his hand. "Are you Luke?" he asked, not answering the question.

"I am Luke." He shook Alex's hand, smiling broadly with relief. "Is she coming, but not with you?"

Alex hesitated, reluctant to quash the happiness in Luke's old face. Instead, he held the bell out to him. "I think this belongs here, to the house. I've brought it from London."

Luke blinked rapidly as he took the familiar object. "I will return this to the dining room where it has always lived."

Alex grappled with how to begin. He introduced himself and told him how he had travelled from Cape Town then London and now here to Kenya, to find him.

Luke looked bewildered with this news. "Why are you looking for old Luke in this place called Cape Town and London, Bwana Alex? I have been here always."

Alex smiled at the truth of this, then he told him how he had met Nicola.

Luke sucked in his breath. "Miss Nicola," he murmured.

"I went to London to see Eliz - er, Miss Elizabeth," he corrected himself hastily.

Luke looked puzzled and then suspicious. He frowned. "The man of God, the priest, in Nairobi came here. He has said Miss Elizabeth is dead in London."

Luke looked down at the bell in his hand. "Miss Elizabeth, she gave you this? You saw her?"

"No, I didn't see her. I was too late."

"Too late for what, Bwana Alex?"

This was going to be difficult. "Perhaps we could go inside?" Alex suggested politely, wiping the sweat from his brow with his bare arm. "It's pretty hot out here."

"*Eish*, Bwana Alex, I am forgetting myself with all this talk. You will be tired after your journey. You have come many miles to find old Luke; you will be hungry and thirsty." Alex nodded, relieved. "Your car is at the gates?" He nodded again. "It is safe there," Luke said disappearing into his thatched house and reappearing moments later with the front door key.

He followed Luke up the stone steps to the entrance. Luke unlocked the door and led him into the hallway.

Alex looked around, adjusting his eyes from the brightness outside, seeing only briefly what the priest had seen. Luke ushered him into the study.

After all the weeks of speculation about Mbabati and the two sisters, Alex could scarcely believe he was now in the house itself.

"Bwana Alex, you would like something to drink?"

Alex brought himself back from his reverie. Not wishing to offend him, and hoping Mr Patel was right, he asked for a glass of water.

Luke returned reverently carrying a tarnished silver jug and a tall glass, and put them down on the table. Alex helped himself, knowing Luke was watching and waiting for him to say something.

He drank greedily then placed the glass back on the tray. "You asked me how I came to have the bell, Luke. I think you sent it with some letters with Matthew?"

Luke's head jerked up. "This parcel it was opened?" he said fearfully. "But, how is it you have this bell? It was for Miss *Gray*," he said, stressing the last word. "Matthew was telling me of a shop in

82

London. It is like a post office where people from Africa can come for parcels and letters. Matthew said he would leave it there and that it would be safe.

"The man from God, this priest," he stumbled over his words, "he said Miss Elizabeth was staying in a place where many memsahibs are praying to God."

"A convent," Alex said. He explained briefly how he had come to have the bell in his possession.

The next part was not going to be easy. He took a breath and told Luke about Nicola dying, her burial and finding out about Mbabati. When he had finished, silence filled the room.

"When you saw her in Cape Town, when she was poor and looking for money, did she speak of me? Did she speak of Luke?" He asked, his eyes bright with impending tears.

Alex prayed he would be forgiven for what he was about to say; he wanted to bring some comfort to him. "She told me she trusted you to look after all she loved. In fact," Alex said, rummaging through his bag, "I brought you her bowl, the one she used for collecting the money people gave her." He handed it to him.

Luke frowned. "This bowl cannot come from... but how did you know the memsahibs were sisters? And how did you find Mbabati?"

Alex told him. He watched as Luke wrestled with the news he had brought him. After a moment or two he seemed to come to some kind of resolve, and asked Alex if he planned to return to Nairobi that evening.

"Well, it'll be dark in an hour or so and I need somewhere to stay tonight. I'll go back to Leopard's Leap."

"It is far," Luke said, clicking his tongue. "But there are many rooms in this house. You are welcome to stay here at Mbabati for some days, if you would like to?"

Alex smiled with relief, and asked him if he was prepared for a guest.

Luke shook his head regretfully.

"Look, it's easy for me to go to the shop I passed on my way here, Luke. I can bring back some food and maybe some general supplies? Is there anything you need?"

"I will go and make a list for you and prepare a bedroom."

Luke watched as Alex made his way back down the driveway. He turned and shuffled back towards the house, the ragged hems of his trousers dragging in the dust.

Bwana Alex had made a mistake, perhaps not spoken the truth. But now he must prepare a room for his unexpected guest.

He made his way up the stairs, the bowl heavy in his pocket. He collected bedding from the linen closet and entered the dark and cool bedroom he had selected; Luke pulled back the curtains and struggled with the wooden shutters, his arms objecting to the effort. With a final push the shutters flew open, squealing in protest.

Satisfied, he set about making up the bed; then he checked the bathroom. A flat red spider scuttled across the basin and vanished down the side of the cupboard. As in the bedroom, he pushed back the shutters and let in the hazy afternoon light.

Before descending the staircase he looked up briefly, and shook his head. No-one had been to the top floor since she had left. The door to the room had been boarded up with planks of wood; it was impossible to get in. It was forbidden to go there.

Luke only wanted to remember how it had been when Miss Nicola would play the piano after dinner. The music would drift out through the open windows, over the gardens and into the navy blue night. He would lie on his bed and wonder how such a big piece of furniture, this piano, could produce such beautiful music.

He sighed, it was better to forget these things, he told himself, continuing on his way down the staircase.

******

Mr Patel hid his surprise well when Alex returned to the shop; he saw him frowning at the list and smiled.

"Perhaps, sir, I may be of assistance. Luke does not read or write, but over the years I have come to understand his lists."

He looked up startled. "How do you know Luke?"

Mr Patel lifted his shoulders and raised his hands. "It was not difficult. You said you were going to a house close by to here - there is only one house."

Alex followed him around the shop as he consulted the list and piled the tins, packets, frozen foods, meat, and vegetables on the counter.

"How can he make a shopping list if he can't write, or am I missing something here?"

Mr Patel smiled politely without looking up. "He copies the letters from the packet of whatever he needs but there are many items he remembers how to write. Now, I think we have everything he has requested."

So, Alex thought to himself, it was impossible for Luke to have written any of the love letters.

Loading up the vehicle with his shopping Alex returned to the house, pleased to see the previously locked gates now wide open. He and Luke deposited the shopping in the kitchen. Alex looked around. It was old-fashioned but spotless. Cream terracotta tiles covered the floor. A sizeable gas cooker sat in one corner and dozens of copper pots of varying sizes hung from a beam. A glass-fronted dresser was stacked with crockery and serving dishes. Cavernous sinks were positioned beneath the windows. Tall wooden cupboards stood in another corner, and past an open door Alex could see a walk-in pantry. In the middle of the room was a worn solid oak table for preparing food

Luke made his way past the swing doors of the kitchen, indicating Alex should follow him. The doors brought them out into the dim hallway. Luke pointed to the first floor. "Your room is ready for you; it is the room with the open door."

He thanked him and made his way up the staircase, Luke returned to the kitchen to unpack the shopping. Alex looked around the bedroom and whistled softly through his teeth. No expense had been spared with the rather old fashioned furnishings.

He dropped his bag onto the bed and stuck his head into the bathroom, looking hopefully for a shower. He was not disappointed. He stripped off his clothes and turned the tap, waiting for the gurgle and rumbling of the pipes to clear and the water to appear. Brown water belched forth and he stepped nimbly to one side. After a few moments it ran clear and he stepped beneath the ice cold water.

Drying himself he pulled on a clean shirt and dressed, keen to explore downstairs. As he left the room he flicked the light switch - ah, hence the cold shower. No electricity. He paused before descending the stairs and looked up briefly, where Luke had stood earlier, remembering the story of the journey of a piano in the custody of the Frenchmen. If the piano was here, as he hoped it was, it might well be up there on the top floor.

He walked down the grand staircase looking up at a massive chandelier in the centre of the lofty ceiling. With the last of the sun shining through the open front doors he could see everything clearly.

The floor of the entrance hall was paved with black and white tiles, the classic staircase of all great country houses rising up from its centre, curving left and right to the bedrooms, then continuing up to the top floor. The fading sun streamed through stained-glass windows throwing a kaleidoscope of shimmering colours onto the walls.

Alex stopped abruptly when he reached the last step. Hanging on the wall, was the life size portrait which he recognised instantly.

The canvas was extraordinary; the photograph hadn't done it justice. With exceptional skill the artist had painted Nicola as though she were about to step out of the frame. The blue of her dress shimmered with life and her bare arms looked so real he wanted to stretch out his hand and touch them.

"Hello Nicola," he whispered, smiling at her, "remember me?"

He studied the portrait for some time and then went closer to see if he could spot the signature of the artist. He jumped when he heard Luke coming through the swing doors from the kitchen. He was wearing a long white *kenzo* with a scarlet and gold embroidered waistcoat and a red fez on his head.

"For special occasions," Luke said modestly with a shy smile. "This is my uniform. In the old days we would be wearing these clothes every night for serving the dinner." Alex nodded in appreciation and turned back to the painting.

"This is an excellent piece of work, Luke. Who's the artist?"

"This is Miss Nicola!" Luke said proudly, "with her piano."

"Yes, I thought so, but who painted her picture?"

Luke looked down at his bare feet and then back up at Alex. "He was Miss Nicola's friend, but he too is gone now. Let me show you to the dining-room. You have brought beer from the shop - shall I bring you one, Bwana Alex?" Alex nodded and followed Luke into a room leading off from the entrance hall.

Alex looked around the magnificent space with its dark wood panelling and pale tiled floor. A fireplace dominated one end of the room with large baskets on each side for holding firewood. Luke had prepared and lit a fire in anticipation of the coolness of the evening to come.

A long dining table stretched down the room easily able to seat thirty guests. Dining-room chairs, somewhat dusty, with faded pale grey and green striped seats stood like silent sentries. Three tarnished silver candelabra graced the surface of the table at regular intervals. Alex was amused to see the bell, dwarfed by its environment, next to the place set for one.

The walls were hung with framed hunting prints and scenes of what looked to him, as he peered closer, like the English countryside. To one side of the room was a side-table with six domed, but tarnished, silver serving dishes. In a corner of the room a bar was set out with an ice bucket and a dozen crystal wine glasses, dull with dust, but still managing to glitter in the glow of the yellowing candles in their glass containers which Luke had lit. Bottles of liquor, not all of them full, were grouped on a heavily stained tray. Sumptuous dark green velvet curtains were already pulled across the windows.

He accepted a warm beer from Luke and wandered around the room, the bottle in his hand.

"Bwana Alex?" He turned and saw Luke had followed him with a tray. "Here is a glass for drinking the beer."

Alex smiled sheepishly. "Yes, of course, I'm forgetting where I am. Thanks. I'm going to sit outside for a while, before it gets too dark.

Sitting on the top step of the sweeping veranda, Alex looked around. The straggling lawns showed patches of brown grass and what might have been a rose garden at some point was tangled and overgrown with weeds.

He sipped his beer, surprised at how cool the evening air had become now the sun had set. A bat flew low and fast over his head and he instinctively ducked. In the distance he heard the grunts and calls of the animals in the bush, and the chatter and chirrup of birds coming home to roost. The high pitched whine of a mosquito had him brushing his hand in front of his face to fend it off before it bit him. He still couldn't believe where he was.

Hearing the sound of the bell he grinned, getting up he made his way back into the shadows of the house.

With a flourish Luke lifted the domed tarnished lid of the dish and placed his dinner in front of him.

"Perhaps you wish for some wine from the cellar?"

"The cellar?" Alex echoed.

He smiled proudly. "There is a fine wine cellar here, with many bottles. They came from England and from the place called France."

"You know about wine, Luke?"

"Yes, I know of wine," he said shyly. "You are having steak tonight; it is a bottle of red wine for this, which I have chosen for you."

Alex shook his head with amazement. "How do you know which wine is which?" diplomatically not mentioning he knew Luke couldn't read.

"Bwana Max taught me to read the pictures. There were many pictures to learn for the wine cellar." Smiling broadly he left the room.

He had expected the inside of the house to be derelict and crumbling with neglect. Instead it felt as though the owners had stepped out and would be back shortly. Certainly most of the surfaces were dusty, the silver in need of a robust polish, but a sense of time within the house felt as though it had been paused.

It was obvious the house would not have internet access; he would have to work out how he was going to get in touch with Sophie. Leopard's Leap would surely have access and he might be able to use their facilities.

With a sense of occasion Alex spread his linen napkin over his knees and watched as Luke poured a small amount of wine into a hastily cleaned glass. He stood back proudly and waited.

Alex savoured the wine. After what he assumed was years of being in the cellar it was surprisingly palatable. "Good choice, Luke, I'm impressed." Luke beamed at him and filled his glass, one arm held stiffly behind his back.

The clinks of his cutlery and the crackle of the fire were the only sounds in the silent room. He watched the flames in the fireplace scatter orange flecks of light along the dining table towards him. Luke had cooked the steak to perfection; crisp golden potatoes in a cheese sauce and a green salad accompanied it.

Alex ate hungrily, his mind full of visions of how life must have been for Nicola. He speared the last piece of steak. Feeling a little embarrassed he picked up the bell and shook it tentatively.

Luke appeared immediately and cleared away the plates, returning with a pot of coffee.

"This I would normally serve in the sitting room, Bwana Alex, but I have no time to prepare and dust it. This I will do tomorrow.

"There is no power in the house. This was gone a long time ago. We have lamps for you to use. I will leave this one here," he said, placing a lit hurricane lamp on the table next to Alex.

"Thank you for coming to find me, Bwana Alex. I am glad Miss Nicola did not die alone. A funeral costs much money and you did not know her, but still you paid. This is a good thing you have done."

"Before you go, Luke?"

"Yes, Bwana, is there something else you need?"

"The top floor of the house - what's up there?"

Luke swiped at a cobweb festooned between the candlesticks which had escaped his notice earlier. "It is the music room. But it is not possible to go in there. The room is closed, with many pieces of wood and the door is locked."

Intrigued with this piece of information he continued with another question. "Miss Elizabeth? Did she live here at Mbabati?"

"Miss Elizabeth lived in America. She did not live here until there was much sadness in the house. After this happened, she stayed. Goodnight, Bwana Alex." Hastily he left the room.

Alex sipped his coffee, begrudgingly admiring Luke's ability to avoid giving direct answers. Over the years interviewing Africans, he had learned there was an unspoken order of things to ask and talk about before approaching the real purpose of a meeting. Family members and their health had to be enquired after, the state of the crops, the weather, amongst other topics. He needed to gain the trust of Luke if he was to find out what had happened in the house.

He glanced at his watch, it was after nine. It had been a long and emotional day and an early night would not go amiss. He blew out the candles, checked the fire, and made his way out into the entrance hall, the lantern in hand.

The kitchen was quiet and silence radiated around the house. Alex held the lamp aloft and looked up at Nicola. Her eyes seemed to follow him, a slight smile playing on her lips in the flickering light of the flame.

"What made you run, Nicola?" he whispered to her. He mounted the staircase and at the top turned to look back.

She was still watching him.

Chapter Twelve

A light tap on the door woke Alex the next morning. Luke entered and placed a coffee tray next to the bed. "*Jambo*. You slept well?"

The scent of fresh coffee helped Alex rouse himself from his sleepiness. He looked around almost surprised to find himself at Mbabati. He yawned, sat up, and smiled at Luke, taking the cup from him.

"Indeed I did." A thought suddenly occurred to him. "Tell me, Luke, how do you heat the water here? What do you do for electricity?"

"There is a machine in the garden, it is called a generator. It is possible to use this for electricity and to heat the water but now no fuel to do this. For keeping the food you bought cold, we will be needing this machine."

"Okay, I can sort that out. What do you do for money, Luke? How do you buy your food?"

"Miss Nicola sends money to Mr Patel each month for my wages. He also brings me the food from the shop."

"I'll go and get some fuel, Luke. Let's see if we can get the generator working." He asked him if there was anything else he needed.

"Perhaps more gas for cooking? It is running low."

"No problem." He swung his legs out of bed dreading another ice cold shower.

✶✶✶✶✶✶

Before heading for Leopard's Leap Alex made a detour towards the lake he could see in the far distance. Parking his jeep under the shade of a tree he walked out onto the dilapidated jetty, noticing the rotting rowing boat tied alongside, its rope frayed and bleached white by the sun. The water was still and, despite wearing sunglasses, he screwed up his eyes against the glare reflecting off its surface. A mother and her ducklings waddled purposefully out of the papyrus grass and slid into the water, causing only the slightest ripple on its surface.

The haunting cry of a fish eagle made Alex look up. The bird circled high above the water then suddenly dropped like a rock, swinging back up gracefully, a fat silver fish grasped in its talons.

His eyes were drawn to a disturbance in the water; the large head of a hippo broke the surface of the lake, it twitched its ears briefly before silently sinking back into its depths.

He stood up feeling the heat on the back of his neck. A swarm of insects buzzed around his face, he jerked his neck and brushed them away. It was time to get out of the sun and continue on his journey.

He parked under an awning on the driveway of Leopard's Leap. A young game ranger came out the front door when he heard Alex's car.

"Good morning, sir. Are you checking in?"

Alex shook his head. "No. I'm staying at a house near here, but there's no internet access and I need to send an email. Any chance I can use yours, if you have it? I'm happy to pay."

The ranger hesitated, scanning the horizon as if he might see a house somewhere. "We do have internet access but it's slow, I'm afraid. Come in out of the heat and I'll show you where the computer is."

Alex followed him into the lodge, past a central courtyard open to the sun, and under a tall archway into the cool of the lounge. Groups of chairs surrounded low cane tables. A long bar took up one wall of the room; green palms in long white pots were strategically placed around the room. Ceiling fans spun lazily above his head. In the corner sat the computer.

"May I get you a drink of something?"

"A beer would be great, thanks mate."

Alex waited, sipping his beer. It was taking forever. An hour later he had brought Sophie up to date with everything so far.

He hit the send button waiting patiently for it to go. When it finally did he wandered out onto the veranda. A woman in her mid-forties wearing khaki shorts and a pink shirt was sitting in a cane chair sorting through some papers spread out in front of her. He cleared his throat and she looked up with a smile.

"Did you get your email sent?"

Alex smiled back at her. "It took a while, but yes, it's on its way, thanks."

91

He walked over to where she sat, his hand extended, "Alex Patterson."

"Hi Alex, I'm Penny. Where are you staying then, most people have the internet these days?"

"A place called Mbabati, do you know it?"

"Do I know it? Of course! Everyone knows it, but it was abandoned years ago." She shuddered. "Are you a relative of the family?" Penny gestured to the chair opposite her. "Have a seat."

"I suppose you could say I'm more of a friend of a friend than a relative." He told her he was here on business and had promised to check up on the place and see the old man who had been looking after it.

Penny lit a cigarette and inhaled deeply. "No-one's been near the place for years, let alone inside. Isn't it falling apart?"

"It's in a pretty good state considering," Alex paused, "any idea how long it's been empty?"

"No, haven't a clue. My parents bought this place about sixteen years ago - they'd always wanted a game lodge, Mbabati was already closed up by then."

She told him how they had been interested in purchasing Mbabati but it had been impossible for them to find out where the owner was to ask if she wanted to sell. But, even if she had wanted to, she told him, it would have been impossible to get any staff to work there. The locals thought the place was haunted.

"I know it's ridiculous but these rural Africans are a superstitious lot."

"So your parents bought here instead," Alex prompted.

"Yes. Leopard's Leap was originally a private house. It took years to wind up the estate after the owner died. He had assets in quite a few countries so it was complicated."

"I'm curious, Penny. You said everyone in Kenya knows about Mbabati. How come?"

"Did you know it had a link to this house?" Alex shook his head and Penny continued.

"It was owned by an artist called Jake Henderson. Where we have our sitting room now used to be his studio. Have you heard of him?" Alex shook his head a second time, wary of stopping Penny's flow with words of his own.

She licked her lips and he could tell she was relishing the opportunity to share a bit of gossip. "Apparently Jake was having an affair with the lady who lived at Mbabati. Then one day he went out riding and vanished off the face of the earth.

"The police were involved, of course, but they never found his body, the horse he had ridden, or his rifle." Penny paused to light another cigarette. Alex felt the excitement crawling up his spine. The two faded initials on the envelopes containing the love letters; the '*k*' and the '*e*' had obviously been '*Jake*.' Finally, he thought, some of the story is coming together.

"The money was on the husband having killed Jake and he somehow hid his body. But I always wondered," Penny said leaning forward and narrowing her eyes for dramatic effect, "what happened to the horse? It never returned to the stables here." She let this sit with Alex before carrying on; he had the distinct impression she'd told this story many a time.

"There was no proof of anything and eventually the case was closed. Some years later, we had a severe drought. The Grays' had a lake on their property and what was found at the bottom, when the water level dropped, forced the police to re-open the case."

"Do you know what they found?"

"Nope. We never found out."

"What about Nicola's sister?" Alex asked.

Penny glanced at him curiously. "How did you know she had a sister?"

"I told you - I'm a friend of a friend so I know a little, not much, but a little."

She stubbed out her cigarette and flicked the butt into a thick bush. "Nicola's sister lived in America but used to come here now and again.

"By all accounts she was a bit wild, a real party animal. She used to dance on the tables apparently. Rumour had it she came out here to dry out. I think she was a model or showgirl at one point, but I would imagine her bad habits put paid to that. Maybe she was having an affair with Jake as well - who knows what really went on in that house."

"What about Max?"

"He committed suicide. Nicola stayed on at Mbabati for about a year and then left. No-one ever saw her again. Has the old man been there the whole time?"

Alex nodded.

"Let me think a minute. Gosh, he must have been on his own for about twenty years."

Alex sat quietly, the information swirling around his head.

She smiled at him, misunderstanding his silence. "Sorry for the gossip! But it's rife here in Kenya and always good fodder around the dinner table." She looked up suddenly and cocked her head to one side. "Excuse me, I hear a vehicle out front. My guests have arrived. "

Alex watched her retreating figure, then called out to her. "Penny, did they have any kids?"

She looked back over her shoulder. "One of them did, but I'm not sure which one."

Alex headed back to the computer. He needed to send another email to Sophie and share his latest news with her. He hesitated; maybe he would be pushing his luck to use it again and be sitting there when the new guests wandered into the lounge, maybe wanting to use it themselves.

He walked back out to his car, passing the new arrivals and nodding to them. So Elizabeth had been a wild sort of girl who loved to party. He shook his head as he backed out of the drive. Extraordinary.

******

Penny poured herself a cup of coffee and thought about Alex Patterson's visit the day before.

She found it strange after years of no-one visiting the old house, as far as she knew, that someone should just pop up asking a lot of questions and, even more odd, be actually staying at the house.

He had said he was a friend of the family, but how could it be? He could only be in his early forties so it was highly unlikely he would have known the Gray family, so why all the questions? If he was a friend of the family he would know a bit more about them surely. Unless, she mused, Alex had met Nicola Gray at some point, over the past twenty years. If this was the case John would be extremely interested.

94

Penny picked up her mobile phone. "Good morning. May I speak to Chief Inspector Groves please?"

Chapter Thirteen

Early that afternoon Alex arrived back at the house, the vehicle laden with household supplies and a jerry can of diesel fuel for the generator.

Luke led him down the pathway at the side of the house to a shed surrounded by bushes.

"We did not use this generator all the time," Luke said, pushing back the heavy undergrowth and reaching for the handle of the shed. "Each morning I would put on this machine to heat the water in the house. Miss Nicola liked just to have candles in the evening. People need hot water for showers and baths; they do not like cold water."

Ain't that the truth, he thought to himself.

Alex filled the fuel tank, the sweat running down his back, darkening his shirt, Luke cranked the engine; it turned over once and died. They looked at each other.

"Here, let me have a go, Luke. It might take a few tries before it starts up."

After a few more attempts the generator growled into life with a steady throb, Alex looked at it with disbelief. "Who would have thought after all these years this machine would still work - incredible!"

Luke looked pleased. "I have looked after this machine, in case Miss Nicola came back. This is why it is working so well now."

"Well done, Luke, I'm looking forward to a hot shower tonight," Alex said relishing the thought as they made their way back to the house. "I think I'll sit outside for a while and have a beer."

"I will go and unpack your car, Bwana Alex." He wiped his hands on his worn trousers and bustled off.

Alex thought he detected more of a spring in Luke's step; certainly he wasn't using his walking stick when he left the house as he had done before. Clearly he was enjoying having someone around after his years of isolation

Alex wiped the sweat off his face. The back of the house was as impressive as the front. A deep covered veranda stretched across the length of it. Cane chairs and sofas, covered with dust and leaves, were grouped in half circles surrounding white square wooden tables. Two Grecian urns had once stood at the top of the steps leading down into

96

the garden; now they lay cracked on their sides, dry earth spilling out of them.

Dust-covered bougainvillea climbed the length of the supporting square pillars creating a riot of colour; cream, magenta, pink and crimson. Two sagging wicker baskets, dark with damp and mould, and covered with spiders' webs, stood either side of the empty fireplace at the far end of the veranda.

To the left of what had been another walled rose garden, close to the entrance of the kitchen, were several low greenhouses which, he presumed, must have been the kitchen gardens. Towering trees lined both sides of a curved pathway leading to a rusting gazebo. A three-tiered fountain with a cherub at is apex stood dry and empty and full of crisp leaves.

Yes, Alex thought to himself, you would need an army of gardeners to keep these grounds in shape. Luke would never have managed them alone. But, despite the years of neglect, there was still a faded elegance about the place.

At the end of the parched lawns he could make out broken wooden fencing surrounding the deserted paddocks. In the distance he could see the lake, the sun turning its surface to silver. The lake, he assumed, supplied the house and grounds with water. He was curious to know what had caused the police to re-open their investigation having found whatever it was at the bottom of it.

An oasis of green grass caught his eye and he walked towards it. A low stone wall covered with red hibiscus bushes surrounded a small square area. A rusted iron gate opened with an indignant squeal as he entered. He was surprised to find himself looking at eight gravestones.

He bent down to take a closer look. Four of the graves were obviously beloved family dogs. Two, much older graves, had the names Robert Gray and Olivia Gray inscribed on their respective headstones, Max's parents. The seventh grave, with a rusty lamp at its head, had nothing written on the headstone at all.

He remembered the photograph in Nicola's locket. The grave was well tended, along with the six others, but rather odd that it was anonymous with nothing to indicate who might be lying there.

There was only one grave which appeared untended and forgotten. Alex moved towards it. It was notably neglected, covered with weeds and vicious looking roots with razor sharp thorns. Curious,

Alex picked up a stick and scratched at the headstone trying to scrape off some of the lichen.

Max Gray. No dates and no loving message.

******

After an enjoyable hot shower Alex changed into trousers and a long-sleeved shirt, hoping they would protect him from the mosquitoes, and made his way down the stairs and into the kitchen.

Luke told him he had prepared the sitting room and would bring him a beer.

Intrigued Alex entered the room. A fire crackled in an enormous fireplace, an ornately-carved mirror reflecting the whole room. Covering the entire floor was a pale green and cream carpet.

Four bookcases reached from floor to ceiling bulging with books; a smaller one stood next to the fireplace. The majority seemed to be books relating to the law, books with solid sober, black and red, spines. Max had been a lawyer, Alex remembered.

Deep chairs and sofas were placed around the room. A stately Grandfather clock stood silent against the wall, its pendulum still. A basket of old magazines stood next to one of the settees. Alex picked one up searching for a date. December 1988. He flicked through the once glossy pages depicting snowy scenes, festive food and gifts, and wondered how a Christmas in Kenya, at the height of summer, could have any relevance to the photographs in the magazine. He placed it back in the basket.

Beneath one of the four windows in the room stood a now highly polished table with clusters of photographs in silver frames. Next to it was a gramophone player with records neatly piled on a carved wooden and brass box. He picked up one of the silver frames. The photograph was of a young Nicola with a lion cub in her lap. There was a photo of Nicola and Max on their wedding day. Nicola dressed in a long ivory gown looking woodenly at the camera. One by one he put them back on the table.

The room was hung with wildlife paintings - oils of elephants, lions and plains game. Interspersed between them were half a dozen animal trophies glaring down at him as he moved around the room; thick cobwebs stretched between their horns, like bridal veils.

98

To the left of the door, were more photographs, all framed and hung haphazardly. Sipping the beer Luke had brought him, Alex took a closer look. In all the photographs, Nicola was wearing sunglasses and various hats against the heat and glare of the sun. There was another photograph of Max, his boot on the neck of a dead buffalo, a shotgun bent over his arm.

He had been a good-looking man with a tall strong physique; his teeth were white and even against his tanned face, his eyes light as he smiled into the camera with pride at his kill.

He had had film star looks, a gorgeous and talented wife, privilege and wealth and a breathtakingly beautiful home. Why would he commit suicide?

He recalled the photograph they had found in Nicola's trunk. There had only been one featuring a man and it definitely wasn't Max.

He returned to the cluster of silver framed photographs on the table next to the record player. Racehorses with their African grooms dominated most of them. Two black Labradors, their tongues hanging out, were sitting next to a mound of dead birds. Another photograph of a young elephant with a blanket covering its back made him smile. Only in Africa, he thought. Leaning against the wall was another large frame but this one was empty; briefly, he thought of the blank headstone in the graveyard.

Luke appeared at the door. "Dinner is served, Bwana Alex. The fish is from our lake. A fisherman from the village brought it here this morning, for selling, even though it is from our own lake... I have chosen white wine to go with this stolen fish."

Alex followed him, noticing the gun rack to the right of the door; the four shotguns silent in the glass case.

******

Alex picked up the hurricane lamp and made his way down the path towards Luke's small house. He was sitting next to a fire looking up at the stars.

Alex had the impression he had been expecting him. Luke prodded the fire with a stick and sparks flew up into the night. He indicated Alex should sit on a sturdy log to the left of him.

The whoop and giggle of a hyena echoed around the bush, swiftly followed by another. Luke lifted his head and looked in the direction of the sounds. "There are many hyena out there, but they will not come near the house."

For the next ten minutes they talked about the rains, the crops, politics and the country in general. Choosing the right moment he asked after Luke's family.

Luke threw another log on the fire and told him his wife had been dead for many years but had given him two sons. Both were grown up now and living in Nairobi with their own wives and children, and he had not seen them for some years.

Luke cleared his throat noisily and changed the subject. "Something is troubling me. Why did Miss Nicola go to Cape Town where she knew no-one and had no money? And why did Miss Elizabeth go to be in the convent for praying to God? Why did they not come home to this house, where there is money and food for the table, and where Luke would have taken care of them as he has always done?"

Alex lifted empty hands. "To know the answers to those questions Luke, I think I have to find out what happened to them before they left, or after they left, the house." He slapped at his wrist as he felt the sting of a mosquito, he wiped the thin sliver of blood on his trouser leg.

Luke made a sound like a soft grunt from the back of his throat, "Eh."

Alex looked out into the night. "For me to understand, I need to ask you some questions about Nicola, Elizabeth, Max and," Alex hesitated, "and Jake."

Luke plucked at the edge of his frayed blanket nervously. "But you are a stranger, I cannot tell you these things now, I must think on this." He was quiet for a minute or two.

"Before Miss Nicola left this house she asked me to do something for her. She said if I should hear of her death, I must open the music room and set her spirit free. I was much afraid of this request. Tomorrow I will take you there. Perhaps you will help me to open the doors. It is something I cannot do alone, there is much wood to be removed."

Alex nodded, his heart speeding up with anticipation. "I'll help you, but there's something I'd like you to help *me* with. Miss Nicola's bowl?"

The old man reached inside his blanket and held it out. Alex turned the bowl around until he found the hidden compartment. He pressed it and retrieved the signet ring. Luke raised his eyebrows in surprise.

"Have you seen this before?"

Luke took the ring and examined it. "This is the ring of Bwana Jake, for wearing on the small finger." He handed it back to Alex and poked at the fire. "Bwana Jake made the picture of Miss Nicola, he came to this house many times."

"Did he wear it all the time?" Alex asked, undeterred.

Luke sighed heavily and nodded.

"I've heard he went riding one day and didn't return. So what's his ring doing here?"

"It is true Bwana Jake wore this ring all the time. But I do not know how it is in this bowl. Perhaps when he went on his horse he did not wear this ring?"

Alex put the ring in the drawer and gave the bowl back. Not wanting to be disrespectful he phrased his answer with care. "It's possible, but somehow I don't think so."

He stood up and patted Luke's bony shoulder, then made his way back to the dark house, the light of the lamp casting shadows across his path.

If Jake had worn the ring on his finger all the time, it was unlikely he would take it off when he went riding. Someone must have seen him after his so-called disappearance.

That someone could only have been Nicola.

Chapter Fourteen

Alex lay in bed listening to the storm outside, the howling wind had woken him. He checked his watch, surprised to find it was early morning. With the dark sky outside he had presumed it was much earlier.

He looked up startled as one of the shutters came loose from its mooring and crashed against the window.

He shivered as he looked out over the gardens, the trees and bushes bending violently in the wind. Leaves danced briefly on the lawns before being sucked up into a gust of wind and then discarded on the pathways. The old Victorian gas lights, scattered around the gardens, trembled with the force of the wind. An ear-splitting crash of thunder made him jump again. He looked up at the bloated clouds with their dark underbellies, then suddenly the rain came, hammering on the roof and bouncing off the dry ground, like glass marbles, bringing with it the smell of rain and wet earth.

Alex heard the generator kick to life followed by its soothing thump-thump. He saw Luke walking as fast as he could across the grounds towards the front of the house.

Wrapping a towel around his waist he watched the storm, then turned at the firm knock on the door.

Luke shuffled into the room, a little out of breath, and placed a tray of coffee on the table next to the bed.

"*Jambo*, Bwana Alex," he said raising his voice to be heard above the noise of the storm. "There is no sun coming today, only rain and wind, it is the beginning of the long rains which come this time of the year.

Luke told him he would prepare breakfast and then after this he would find some things from the shed to open the music room.

After showering Alex dressed, pulling a sweater over his shirt against the chilly morning. Before descending the stairs, he glanced up at the top floor. Perhaps he should take a look and see what tools might be necessary to open the music room.

When he reached the top he stopped, hardly able to believe his eyes. The oval carved doors were crisscrossed with thick planks of wood crudely held in place with heavy rusted nails and punctured with tiny holes made by woodworm.

Alex tentatively pulled at one of the planks but it held firm. Puzzled he wondered who had gone to these lengths to seal up a room and why. If someone had wanted to seal up a room for posterity why not make a neat job of it? This looked like the work of someone in some kind of frenzy; surely a woman would never have had the strength to lift and nail together these planks; they were solid and no doubt heavy. It wasn't going to be as easy as he'd thought to dismantle them and gain access to the room.

Hearing Luke ringing the bell announcing his breakfast was ready, he made his way down the staircase, pausing at the bottom.

She was looking at him.

"Morning Nicola," he said cheerfully, "you'll be happy to know we'll be opening up your music room today." He could feel her eyes on his back as he went into the dining-room.

******

Alex paused, the sweat dripping down his face and arms. "One more plank to go, Luke, phew, this is heavy going! At some point you're going to have to tell me who did this and why."

He handed Luke the last nail and wrenched the final plank from the door. He staggered back and leaned against the balustrade, catching his breath. "Have you got the key?" he panted. Luke reached into his pocket, looking apprehensive, and handed it to him.

Alex put the key in the lock and turned it; he pushed gently at first and then put his weight behind one big shove. With an agonizing groan the doors slowly opened. He sucked in his breath and stared. Despite the gloom he immediately saw the ghostly outline of a piano standing in the centre of the room. A sheet of paper, unsettled by the unexpected draught from the open door, fluttered from the piano and settled in the thick dust on the floor.

Alex shivered, either from the bitter cold of the room or the atmosphere, he wasn't entirely sure. Pulling his jumper back on he walked into the room, his shoes leaving soft prints behind him; bending down, he picked up the sheet of music and replaced it carefully on top of the piano above the closed lid.

He gave a low whistle; a Steinway Concert Grand - the Rolls Royce of all pianos; not that he had expected anything less given

103

Nicola's reputation as a world class pianist. He looked around, aware of Luke motionless behind him standing at the threshold of the room.

"Let's see if we can get these shutters open, Luke, and get some light in here."

"I have the lamp here. There is no power for this room, Miss Nicola liked only candles." Luke said from the door, turning up the wick and looking around him fearfully. The light pooled weakly around the room.

The room was thick with stale air, and dust covered every surface. Bookcases, stretching from the floor to the ceiling were crammed with books, their titles obliterated by curtains of dense cobwebs. At the far end of the room was a fireplace surrounded by a half circle of deep sofas and chairs. On a table was a vase, its flowers mummified by the dust.

Luke held the lamp aloft, his eyes darting around the once familiar room. Alex moved towards one of the windows to let some natural light in. He wrestled with the catch on the window, swiping away the cobwebs latching onto his face. He grunted as he tried to push it open. It finally gave a few inches, giving him enough room to navigate his arm and hand and grab the latch on the shutters. This lifted easily but he struggled to get the heavy shutters open more than an inch. Through the aperture he'd made he saw thick cords of vines stubbornly clinging to them. Giving up he moved to the next window and tried again.

With a screech which cut through the room, the vines begrudgingly gave up their tenacious hold on the shutters, and the grey morning light spilled in. A bat, startled by the unexpected light, flew blindly across the room. Alex ducked, waving his hands in front of his face as more cobwebs, disturbed by the air now circulating, swayed back and forth. He felt something cross his foot; his scalp crawled as he looked down with trepidation, hoping it wasn't a snake. A mouse scuttled into the fireplace and disappeared.

Luke, who at last had moved into the room, stood next to the piano and spoke softly. "There is much dusting and cleaning needed here. " I will go to the kitchen for cleaning things."

Alex asked him if there was any casual labour in the village they could use. It would take them days to clean the place themselves.

Luke frowned. "Perhaps Mr Patel will know where to find some people? But I am not sure they will come..."

Alex looked at him remembering Penny's remark about the locals thinking the place was haunted. When Luke said nothing more he asked him if there was a saw, or anything else he could use to try and open the shutters.

Luke scurried from the room with alacrity, clearly anxious to leave. Alex followed him down the stairs and out into the grounds. They reached a low building half hidden behind a line of fruit trees.

After a brief struggle with the iron door they went inside, their shoes crunching on dried mouse droppings. Luke flicked the light switch on.

Four horse-boxes were lined up against the far wall, two dark green Land Rovers, their tyres flat and cracked, were parked next to them. A sand-coloured safari vehicle with no roof stood covered in dust and leaves, next to it an open-top American jeep, the framework, for what was left of the torn canvas roof, bent and buckled.

Along the length of another wall was a workbench with tools hanging on pegs on a board. Petrol cans, lawnmowers, rakes and other gardening equipment were stacked in the corner.

A grey car with white-walled tyres stood parked in another corner. Alex walked over to it and whistled in admiration. An old Jaguar, its interior upholstered in light fawn leather, with a handsome walnut dashboard, and a large white steering wheel.

"This car was belonging to the father of Bwana Max," Luke said fondly, running his hand over its dusty surface." He turned back to the workbench, reaching up he unhooked a saw from the wall and examined it.

Alex turned reluctantly from his study of the car and joined him. He ran his finger gingerly along the rusted blade. "This should do the trick."

"You have finished here now?"

Alex nodded, wondering why none of the vehicles were up on blocks, the normal procedure for cars if they were to be left for any long period of time; it would appear then, that Nicola *had* planned on returning at some point. But he was beginning to realise that nothing was normal here.

They returned to the music room. Losing track of time Alex hacked and sawed the vines clinging to the exteriors of the shutters on all of the windows until they finally gave up their obstinate hold. With all the windows and shutters now open the room was plainly visible. Luke had sat on his haunches leaning against a wall, unmoving. He now raised himself up stiffly.

"Bwana Alex? It is past the lunchtime. I will go to the kitchen and prepare some food for you."

"Okay. I'll go to the shop after lunch and see if Mr Patel can find us a couple of cleaners."

Luke looked pleased. "Eh, it will be like the old days when we had staff for the house. But what of the piano. It was forbidden to touch this. Who will clean it?"

"I think it'll be your job, Luke." As they turned to leave Alex spotted a cupboard beside the fireplace, its door slightly ajar. "What's in there?"

"It is the small machine which can make music like this one," Luke said pointing at the piano.

Intrigued Alex opened the cupboard and found himself looking at an old cassette player. Brushing away a spider and its web, he wiped his hand on his jeans and pulled it out. He opened the battery compartment where four bloated batteries had leaked their acid over the years. If there was a tape player, he reasoned, there must be tapes somewhere.

A wooden box, slightly gnawed at one corner, held twenty or thirty tapes in transparent boxes all neatly labelled. He pulled one out and held it up for Luke to see.

"This is for putting in the box, Bwana Alex. This will make the music like Miss Nicola. She would play this music and the same music would come out of the box."

Alex grinned. Finally, he would be able to hear her play from her own recordings. He wrapped one of the dead batteries in his handkerchief and put it in his pocket. If there was one place in the world which would still stock batteries of this size, he would put his money on Mr Patel's shop.

Sanjay Patel's eyebrows rose at seeing him again. Alex felt the curiosity emanating from him.

"Good afternoon Mr Patel. I have another shopping list," he said, pulling it from his pocket. "This time it's for cleaning materials. I need something to clean a piano with, any ideas?"

Sanjay's eyebrows crawled even further upwards. "It will be possible to find something, yes."

Alex dug in his pocket. "Would you by any chance have any batteries this size?"

Intrigued, Sanjay found everything Alex had asked for, including the batteries. "Will you be staying at Mbabati for some time?" he asked casually.

Alex was surprised he had managed to contain his curiosity for as long as he had. "I'm not sure at the moment. Do you know the house?"

"Indeed I do. I go each month to deliver Luke's wages. In fact his wages for this month are right here." He pulled open a drawer and handed Alex an envelope. "Perhaps you'll give this to him?" After a pause, Sanjay asked, "Are you a relative maybe?"

Alex shook his head. "No," he introduced himself, "more a friend of the family."

Sanjay lifted a box of groceries onto the counter top. "This is for Luke as well, Mr Patterson.

"I heard about the passing of Miss Elizabeth. Luke told me about her the last time I saw him. She was the sister of the owner."

"Did you know the family?"

He told Alex his father would have known them. He had been studying in India when he passed away. His brother inherited the shop in Nanyuki and he inherited this one. Mbabati was already closed by the time he had arrived.

Alex asked him how long he had been delivering the money and food to Luke.

"A long time," Sanjay said. "I had been here a few weeks when the first envelope arrived, I took it out there and this was when I first met him."

"Where do the envelopes come from, Mr Patel?"

He told Alex they came from his brother in Nanuyki. The money was paid into his brother's account, for Luke, and he brought it out each month when he came to check on the family business.

107

Alex turned the envelope over in his hand. "But who pays the money into your brother's account?"

Sanjay looked at Alex suspiciously. "This is family business, sir," he smiled tightly. "Perhaps I can assist with carrying these things to the car?"

At some point, Alex determined, he would have to track his brother down in Nanyuki.

"One other thing I need your help with, Mr Patel," Alex said as they carried a box each to the vehicle. He asked him where he could get a couple of cleaners.

"I have three strong sons who work in my shop and they're always keen to earn extra money. You won't get any Africans to work in the house. They're scared to go there. I can drop them off tomorrow, what time would suit?"

He pulled up in front of the house, Luke was waiting for him. Together they carried the shopping inside. "This box is for you, Luke, and," he patted his pocket and pulled out the envelope, "here's your envelope from Mr Patel. Does your money ever come with a letter?"

Luke shook his head. "Just money. No letter."

Alex left him crooning to himself in the kitchen as he continued to unpack the shopping.

Chapter Fifteen

Luke had opened the front gates for the arrival of Sanjay and his sons. He now stood on the front steps waiting for them. At seven on the dot, a rusting Peugeot crawled up the drive and ground to a halt in front of the house.

"Good Morning Luke," Sanjay said, getting out of the vehicle. They shook hands and he introduced him to his sons.

Sanjay looked curiously towards the open door of the house before climbing back into his vehicle and driving off.

Luke led the three young men into the kitchen and gave them coffee. He told them what he needed done. But the piano was not to be touched, he would do this himself.

They nodded, their eyes round with amazement at the size of the house. Armed with buckets, dusters, cleaning materials and mops, they headed for the top floor.

Diplomatically Alex left Luke to supervise the workforce, only venturing up when they took their lunch-break in the kitchen.

The transformation of the room was already impressive. The wooden floors had been swept and polished, the books and shelves dusted. The fireplace had been swept and laid and the copious cobwebs had been cleared. The floor-length sheer curtains, after a thorough dust and shake, had emerged as pale pink although they had, in places, lost their battle with feasting moths.

Nicola's piano was a masterpiece of craftsmanship. Luke's hard work had revealed the deep sheen of the mahogany wood glowing in the shafts of the sun.

He had looked up the price of a Steinway when he was in London and been staggered to learn they cost around a hundred and fifty thousand pounds. The brown leather padded piano stool, which Nicola had sat on to play, displayed hairline cracks where the leather had dried and aged. He lifted the lid. The inside of the box was stacked with sheet music and music books. He pulled one out - Chopin's Nocturne No.1, Alex placed it on the music stand and sat down on the stool, trying to imagine her sitting there playing.

Luke appeared at his elbow, startling him. "This is how it looked when Miss Nicola was here." He ran his duster reverently over the already highly polished surface, clearly proud of his work. "You can play this machine, this piano?" he asked.

"Sadly no." He stood up. "I'll leave you and your lads to finish up here. Are you pleased with what they've done so far?"

Luke raised his eyebrows and sniffed. "Not as good as the staff I was training here. But they are good enough."

Alex turned to leave and nodded to the three smiling young men at the door. "Great job, guys!"

He made his way down to the second floor where, for the first time, curiosity got the better of him. He opened each bedroom door and glanced inside. Although they smelled musty, he saw Luke had kept them fairly dust free. He came to the last room and pushed open the door.

A large, carved four-poster bed festooned with yellowing mosquito nets stood with its headboard against the wall. Floor-to-ceiling mirrored cupboards filled one entire wall. He opened one of the doors. Nicola's gowns, including the one she had worn for her portrait, were hung neatly in a row, their dust rimmed skirts brushing the floor of the cupboard.

On the dressing table was a cluster of dried up perfume bottles and two tarnished silver backed brushes. Alex inhaled deeply feeling her presence. Carefully, he closed the cupboard and walked into the bathroom. A free-standing bath with gold clawed feet stood in front of sheer glass windows with an elevated view over the gardens and the bush beyond. Shaking his head he returned to the entrance of the room and closed the door behind him. How on earth had Nicola ended up in such a bad way? Why hadn't she just come back home where all this had been waiting for her?

******

The boys had left and Alex took a glass of beer into the grounds. After the rain the garden was still and quiet, disturbed only by the night insects and frogs and the occasional forlorn bleating of Luke's goat. He looked up at the clear velvet black sky crowded with brilliant stars, then sat on a rusting iron bench and looked back at the house.

The lamps were now lit in different rooms across the three floors: the music room, his bedroom and the sitting and dining rooms. He thought back to the first time he'd seen the house, in the grainy black and white photograph with Nicola's pathetic possessions. It had looked sinister then but now, with the lights shining from the rooms, and the moon outlining the elegant shape of the house, it looked warm and lived in.

Hearing the dinner bell he went back inside. "Tonight it is chicken with mushroom sauce. This chicken is from my own garden."

Alex looked up at him innocently. "By the way I eat just about anything except for goats..."

Luke laughed uproariously. "I will not kill my goat for your dinner; I am liking this goat for her milk."

Alex relaxed. "I'm glad to hear that. You must be tired after all your work today."

"Yes, but I am happy to see Miss Nicola's room as it was. She will be happy now and her spirit will be free."

When Luke returned to clear the plates away Alex asked him another question. "Tell me, why are there no photographs of Miss Elizabeth in the house. If she came to stay here someone must have taken a photograph of her?"

Luke froze but didn't look up from the plates. "There *are* photographs of Miss Elizabeth, but you cannot see them," he said firmly, lifting the tray and leaving the room.

Puzzled, Alex tried to understand what Luke had just said. He sighed with frustration. He most certainly was the keeper of secrets. Maybe he'd packed them all away somewhere.

When Luke returned to say goodnight, he pulled a photograph from his pocket, the one he had found in Nicola's box in Cape Town, and asked him if he knew who the man was, if he knew his name.

He held it at arm's length, narrowing his eyes. "Yes, this is Bwana Jake. He came for many years here and then one day he was gone. The police came here to look for him." He handed the photograph back, shaking his grizzled head sadly.

When Luke didn't say anything further, he continued, "I saw the family graveyard, Luke. You take good care of all the graves, but not Max's?"

Luke clicked his tongue but said nothing.

He asked him why there was a grave with nothing written on the headstone.

Luke shrugged his shoulders dismissively. "This was the way it had to be."

Alex was alarmed to see the old man's eyes brimming with potential tears and swiftly changed the subject.

111

He thought about his next question before asking it, he decided to throw in a punch. He asked him if Max had killed himself in the music room.

Luke looked at him, clearly shocked. "He did not kill himself..." He paused briefly to compose himself. "He did not kill himself in the house. Why would you think this thing?"

"Because the music room door was so heavily boarded up, I thought this might be why."

"No," Luke said shaking his head forcibly, "by this time, when he took his life, Bwana Max had already put the wood on the door. He killed himself in the hide - it is out in the bush by a watering hole."

Alex asked him if he would show it to him.

He shook his head. "It is dangerous to go there. For many years only snakes and small animals live there. It is rotting with the rain and no-one to take care of it. You would not like it there."

Alex saw he was beginning to cause Luke distress and put a stop to his barrage of questions. "The music room looks great. Miss Nicola would be proud of what you've done for her today. In fact, the whole house has been well looked after, Luke. You've done a good job over the years."

"Not everything so well," Luke said shaking his head and walking from the room.

******

Frustrated with all the unanswered questions, Alex drained his wine glass and picked up the lamp Luke had left for him. He headed once more to the music room.

He was about to place the lamp on the piano then pulled it back as though he had been scalded by it. Christ, Nicola would kill him if he did that. Laughing he put it on the table and lit some of the candles in and around the room.

After opening all the windows he sat on the piano box, then bent down to the cupboard and retrieved the cassette player. Pulling the new batteries from his jacket pocket, he inserted them into the machine. He opened the wooden box and randomly selected one of the tapes. Inserting it into the machine he pushed the play button and watched as the tape jerked to life.

The room filled with music as she started to play, Alex felt his throat tighten unexpectedly. The combination of a magnificent piano, the perfect acoustics in the room and a truly talented pianist was exquisite. He turned up the volume and went over to the fireplace. Lighting the fire, he sat down and leaned back in one of the armchairs, closing his eyes as the music washed over him.

******

Luke prowled the garden with his troubled thoughts. He turned back to the house when he heard the windows opening. He lowered his tired body onto a nearby bench and watched Alex moving around the room.

Suddenly, notes from the piano floated out of the windows and into the gardens like motes of dust being expelled from the room. Luke leaned forward and rested his chin on his stick. He closed his eyes, the memories flooding his mind; the tears trickled down his face as he listened to the familiar sound of her playing.

Tika lifted his massive head, his ears moved slowly as he picked up the sound coming from the house. With soft footsteps, he moved ponderously through the bush heading for his old home. He passed the deserted stables where he had been weaned as a young calf and made his way across the gardens. Tika raised his trunk, searching the night air for the scent of her. He turned his head looking for Luke.

Luke, sensing Tika's presence, opened his eyes. "You have come again, old friend," he called softly, "but she is not here, she is not coming back. You must go to your own family now and forget this place."

Tika snorted at him, blowing air through his trunk, he searched Luke's pocket and happily found an orange.

"I knew you would come when you heard her playing…what will happen to old Luke now, eh, Tika?"

Tika flapped his ears and their soft rustling caused Luke to nod his head. "Yes, perhaps it is time after all," he said finally.

The elephant stood near Luke, his stomach rumbling. When the piece of music finished and the silence of the bush returned, Tika delicately touched Luke's head and face with his trunk, then turned to leave. Luke watched him, hearing the occasional soft tearing of branches as he went back out into the night.

113

He stood up stiffly and walked back to his house. "*Eish*, what will happen to old Luke?" he asked again into the darkness, but could only hear the silence ringing in his ears.

Chapter Sixteen

Alex stowed his bag into the passenger seat of the Land Cruiser and turned to Luke." I have to find the person who's been sending you money, Luke. It's possible Miss Nicola left instructions for you and the house."

Luke looked into the distance. "Perhaps it is the man with the briefcase who will know about this?"

Alex frowned. "What man with a briefcase?"

"An African man is visiting here every year for making sure I am not dead. He looks around all the rooms - but not the music room. No-one else has come here in all these years, only the African man with the briefcase." His voice trailed off when he saw the frustration on Alex's face.

"What's his name?"

He shook his head and shrugged." You will be coming back here soon?" Alex nodded. "Then I will keep the house open for you and await your return. Where will you find this person you are looking for?"

"I'm not sure, but I know where I'm going to start looking."

With a final wave he turned out of the gates and headed for Patel's supermarket. Alex walked in and they greeted each other. "What can I do for you today Mr Patterson?"

"I need your help, and so does Luke, "he said abruptly.

Sanjay stared at him as though he had expected this. "What *is* your relationship with the Gray family Mr Patterson?"

Uncertain of how much of a gossip Sanjay might be, he gave an edited account of Nicola's death in Cape Town and his involvement with it.

"I need to speak with your brother in Nanyuki," he finished.

Sanjay hesitated for a moment as though trying to make up his mind. He sucked his breath in noisily.

"My brother's name is Rashid Patel. He has a small supermarket, a *duka*, on the main road. It's not difficult to find. He will be able to help you."

Alex set course for Nanyuki following the same route he'd taken ten days ago.

After parking his car, he walked along the main road until he saw the sign for Rashid's Supermarket, which seemed identical to his brother's, complete with the iconic Coca Cola sign swinging outside. He found Rashid unpacking boxes at the back of the shop.

"Mr Patel? Rashid?"

Rashid wiped his hands on his trousers and looked at Alex. "May I help you with something?"

Alex found himself looking at a rounder version of Sanjay, but with the same gentle brown eyes and polite demeanour. He spent the next few minutes giving a similar overview he had given Sanjay.

"Mr Patel, Rashid, I need to meet with whoever deposits Luke's money into your account each month. I need a name?"

Rashid shook his head vigorously. "Of course, sir. Things must be done in an orderly manner. The money comes from a firm of attorneys in Nairobi called Hallard and Shapiro. I'll get the address for you, please wait."

Rashid returned and handed Alex a small piece of paper with the address and phone number of Hallard and Shapiro.

"Perhaps you will be kind enough to let me know the outcome of your meeting? If I should still expect this money into my account or if other arrangements are to be made?"

Assuring Rashid he would, Alex thanked him and left.

******

By the time Alex finally arrived in Nairobi, and worked his way through the heavy traffic to the Norfolk Hotel, it was four thirty in the afternoon. After checking in, he went to his room and sat on the edge of the bed. He wasn't sure of the best way to approach the task in hand; impetuously he picked up the phone.

"Good Afternoon," said a bored female voice, "Hallard and Shapiro Attorneys, how may I help you?"

Alex cleared his throat. "My name's Alex Patterson, may I speak to someone who deals with Mrs Nicola Gray's affairs please?" There was a pause and Alex heard the click of nails on a keyboard.

"That will be Mr Shapiro, sir, the senior partner. Please hold."

After a brief pause a surprised male voice came on the line. "Martin Shapiro here."

Alex paused; he hadn't expected to be put through so rapidly and certainly with no questions asked, he didn't want to tell this chap of Nicola's death over the phone.

"Mr Shapiro, thanks for taking my call. I wonder if I could possibly meet with you? It's in connection with Mrs Gray, I met her in Cape Town in December and she asked me to pass on some information to you."

"In Cape Town, you say? I had no idea. Excellent news indeed, I trust she's well?" Not waiting for an answer he continued. "Yes, why not come and see me at..." His voice trailed off and Alex imagined the man on the other end of the telephone consulting his diary, "How about eleven-thirty tomorrow?"

Alex agreed, hung up, and threw himself back on the pillows on his bed in relief. It had been a lot easier than he'd thought it would be.

He had a shower, and then made his way to the business centre of the hotel, hoping the internet in Nairobi would be faster than it was out in the bush. He logged in and was more than pleased to see an email from Sophie:

Sweetheart I've been going crazy here with curiosity and, of course, I'm missing you madly. What wouldn't I give to be there with you! Mbabati sounds exactly as I imagined it. I'm sure by now you've won over Luke and explored all the rooms in the house. What was on the top floor? Was the piano there?

What else have you discovered? Any bodies buried under the floorboards?

Alex smiled as he continued to read her email. He hit the reply button and brought her up to date with all that had happened since the last email to her - the difficulty he was having getting information from Luke, the magnificent piano covered in twenty years of dust, the curious graveyard and, finally, Luke's recognition of the ring and the photograph confirming its owner was Jake Henderson.

Chapter Seventeen

Martin Shapiro shook Alex's hand and gestured for him to sit down. He was a tall, silver-haired man in his late sixties, dressed in an elegant pin-striped suit. "I'm pleased you've taken the time to find me, Mr Patterson. I haven't heard from Mrs Gray for some years and I'm curious, to say the least.

"May I ask who you are, first and foremost, and enquire as to your relationship with Nicola?"

Alex began to give a full account of his involvement. Whilst he talked, Martin sat quite still and listened intently. His elbows rested on his desk, his hands loosely clasped together.

When Alex had finished, a silence fell between them. He could hear the Nairobi traffic in a muted uproar outside the window. Finally, Martin broke the silence.

"You said she gave you a message for me before she died?"

Alex recalled he had said this the previous day when he had called to secure the meeting. He felt uncomfortable, but tried to reassure himself that he had stretched the truth in the pursuit of good. "She asked me to make sure Luke's looked after."

Martin looked surprised. "Obviously we've followed the instructions she gave us before she left."

Martin glanced up at the clock on the wall. "In light of all you've told me, I suggest we have lunch tomorrow. I need to contact a colleague of mine in Cape Town. Even though you've shown me a copy of her death certificate, I still need to check its authenticity, and a few other details.

"I'll also need to contact someone at the Convent of the Daughters of the Lord in London." He'd not taken any notes and Alex was impressed by his memory. "I believe you're staying at The Norfolk?" Martin continued. He looked up at Alex innocently from beneath his bushy eyebrows, pleased to see his surprise.

"I did my homework. I've heard nothing from my client in over twenty years, when suddenly I get a call out of the blue from someone purporting to have a message for me - and the call coming from a journalist no less."

He stood up and held out his hand. "I'll see you tomorrow on the terrace of the Norfolk at one o'clock."

Feeling distinctly as though he had been dismissed, Alex stood up, shook the lawyer's hand, and made his way out of the plush office suite.

******

"Let's dispense with the formalities, shall we?" Martin said the next day after ordering lunch. "Call me Martin, please. It was a surprise to hear from you, and certainly the news you brought did come as a shock. I hope you'll forgive me if I was somewhat guarded but my responsibility is to my client first and foremost and I needed, as I told you yesterday, to check up on the veracity of your information."

He rubbed his forehead distractedly. "The two mysteries are that Nicola died penniless and Elizabeth died in a convent. Not what I thought would happen to either of them..."

Alex relaxed at Martin's more personal tone. "Yes, I know. In terms of Elizabeth it does sound unlikely, given her propensity for parties and the good life."

Seeing Martin look quizzical, he explained. "I heard some of the gossip, and the scandal, when I arrived here."

"Yes, I'm quite sure you've been asking some questions ..." Martin continued. "How odd Nicola died penniless when her own trust fund was considerable. With one telephone call I could have transferred any amount of money to her in Cape Town. It's difficult to understand why she didn't get in touch, when she was obviously in serious financial difficulties."

He took another sip of his beer, watching the steady flow of traffic passing the hotel terrace. "I'm grateful to you, Alex. It might have been years before anyone informed the firm about the sisters' deaths."

"Especially Nicola's," Alex said swiftly. "Not a single person came forward to claim her - she would have died in obscurity."

Their food arrived and whilst they ate Alex took the opportunity to justify his particular interest in Mbabati.

"There are some fascinating stories coming out of Africa. Eccentric Englishmen and women building stately homes in the middle of the African bush, a bit like Mbabati. That's why I'm following the story of Nicola. She seems to have been the victim of

119

some kind of tragedy both here and in Cape Town." He looked steadily at Martin across the table.

"Did you ever meet Elizabeth?"

Martin smiled broadly, surprising Alex. "Yes indeed I did. She was the younger sister, I met her soon after Max's death. She was here on holiday when it happened."

They finished their lunch in silence, both of them absorbed in their own thoughts and unanswered questions. After their plates were cleared away they ordered coffee.

"There's one thing - amongst countless others - I just don't understand," Alex said. "Why did Elizabeth have Nicola and Max's surname? She was a DuPont by birth, as was Nicola. And it was such a renowned surname in France."

"Renowned?" Martin asked, his eyebrows shooting upwards with interest.

"Nicola was a world famous classical pianist. Up there with the best of them."

"She was? Good Lord!" He slapped the table with his hand, genuinely surprised. The waiter hovered behind them, unsure of whether to interrupt and put their coffees down. Martin waved him to do so.

"I knew she played the piano, of course, but I had no idea she was famous. I can't believe Max didn't mention it!" He was silent for a moment, digesting this new information.

Alex waited.

Martin seemed to be mulling something over. "Well, there's your answer! If Nicola was so famous and her career collapsed under such a mysterious cloud, as you've told me, it's highly likely Elizabeth DuPont used the name Gray so she wouldn't be hounded by the French Press to find out where her sister had vanished to. They were close, those two."

Martin stirred sugar into his coffee, appraising Alex across the table. "I can see why your interest in this family has been piqued. Are you planning on publishing this story?"

Alex blew on his coffee and took a tentative sip.

"Yes. But at the moment, I don't *have* the full story. I'd like you to trust me with it. I think I've earned it, don't you?" Alex said raising his eyebrow and grinning.

"Yes, I suppose you have. You've certainly put a lot of work, and money, into things to date." He looked at the journalist, weighing him up before he made his decision.

He pushed his empty coffee cup to one side and sat back in his chair, waving a persistent fly away from the sugar bowl.

"The rumours and gossip went around Kenya like wildfire; everyone had their own opinion as to what really happened. Our firm have always protected the Gray family - and Nicola in particular when the police re-opened the case. I'll tell you the facts of the story as far as I know them."

Alex felt the familiar fizz of excitement but tried not to let it show.

The lawyer leaned forward, steepling his fingers under his chin. "I'll need you to sign a document agreeing to let me see anything written about the family before it's published?"

Alex agreed. He wanted to hear the full story and Martin was about to tell him, but on his terms.

"I can't comment on the story of the artist who disappeared," Martin continued, "or the suicide of Max Gray, although I do have my own theories as to what might have happened."

He patted the inside pocket of his jacket and pulled out an envelope. Unfolding the document he spread it in front of Alex and handed him his pen.

"Please initial each page and sign off at the bottom of the last one."

Martin leaned back in his chair again as Alex perused the document. He looked at the passing traffic remembering the first time he had met Elizabeth. "Ah yes, Elizabeth," he mused aloud to no-one in particular, "quite extraordinary. I don't think I'll ever forget the first time I met her..."

******

Alex spent the night at the Norfolk Hotel. The next morning he drove back to Mbabati. He spent the five-hour journey running through Martin's story and the information he now had. As he tied things together in his mind he noted the nagging points only Luke could answer; he was the only one who could fill in the missing pieces.

121

Martin Shapiro's story had been more than a revelation; it had been shocking - unbelievable.

Why hadn't Luke told him about the sisters? Or the grave in the garden, with the blank headstone? Why hadn't he told him whose final resting place it really was?

Luke also knew something else.

He knew the woman buried in a grave in Cape Town was not Nicola Gray.

Chapter Eighteen

PARIS 1965
ELIZABETH

Max and I had been lovers for a few months before I introduced him to my sister. He'd wanted to meet her for some time and being a top agent he was always looking for new and extraordinary talent to represent; up until then Mother had managed Nicola's career.

Growing up in Paris, we lived a gilded and privileged life, and when my father decided to return to the States where he was born, and divorce my horrified mother in the process (she was a Catholic) our life didn't change at all. My father had been a shadowy sort of figure and we were both too young to remember much about him.

Many years later Mother decided to marry her long-time lover and leave France, to go and live in Argentina. Max smoothly took her place as Nicola's agent.

Nicola and I had strikingly different personalities. I was the wild one in the sixties, when we were in our twenties, the Beatles had taken the world by storm, mini-skirts and big hair was all the rage, my life was full of fun, boyfriends, and endless parties, where we all smoked and drank far too much.

My older sister, by contrast, filled her life with practicing and playing, as she'd done since she was six years old, and Max put her under a lot of pressure as he planned and shaped her future to be the best she could be. To say she was gifted would be somewhat of an understatement. She was a gentle soul, my sister, and she rarely raised her voice or argued with anyone. Music was her whole life, and at that perfect point in her life she had no reason to be frightened of anyone or anything.

I soon bored of Max who had turned from being a gorgeous amusing escort, and adept lover, to a somewhat serious agent obsessed with making as much money as he could out of my sister. My greatest ambition was to be as famous an actress as Nicola was a pianist, and to go and live in California, which I eventually did.

I wasn't surprised to find out Nicola had moved into Max's apartment and they too had become lovers - it was inevitable; they spent so much time together, and when I left for the States, and with Mother living in Argentina, she must have felt as though she'd been abandoned. I didn't tell her about Max and I - it wasn't really important to me, just a bit of a fling.

Then Nicola fell pregnant...

Max was beside himself with rage, no doubt seeing all that lovely money flying out of the window; he insisted she have an abortion. Both of us were Catholic so, as far as Nicola was concerned, it was out of the question.

Max had her performance schedule booked up for years in advance and he knew an unmarried mother wouldn't cut it in the world they moved in. Her sparkling talent and unblemished personal life would be in ruins.

Nicola was very much in love with Max and thought when she told him she was pregnant he would be thrilled and marry her immediately, thereby negating any bad publicity. But he was adamant that he wouldn't be forced into marriage. He told her; have an abortion or I'll leave you.

She found herself in an impossible situation. At the age of twenty-two she had the world at her feet; if she left Max, and had the baby, her career would be well and truly over. No other agent would take her on in her condition, and even if she disappeared for a while she would still have to explain to a new agent where she had been for the past six months. The scandal would sink her even if nothing else did. In the end she had to give in to his demands otherwise she would lose her career, her lover, and her agent. But she refused to have an abortion.

Nicola continued to play for her adoring fans until she began to show slightly, and at this point Max spirited her away to a private clinic in Geneva, assuring her that her career was safe in his hands, and that he would re-schedule her booked performances as best as he could.

I'd come back from California and went to see her in Geneva. I suppose I told her even more lies than Max had.

Hour after hour she talked about the baby and how desperately she wanted to keep it, and she cried a lot. I tried to convince her, using all Max's arguments, that this was the only solution as an unmarried mother.

So Nicola had her baby and it was adopted.

What Nicola didn't know was that her career was already over. Max's mad idea, had brought it to a shattering end. There were many stories in the newspapers about Nicola, all discreetly kept from her whilst she was in the clinic.

Nicola went into a heavy depression when she returned to Paris, hardly going out of their apartment; she cut herself off from the outside world, so deep was her grief at losing her child. I don't think she thought, or cared, about what was going on in the world outside. Just as well - all things considered.

Then one day, some months later, she told him she was ready to go back to work and wanted to see how he had re-scheduled her performances for the coming months.

This is when he had to tell her it was all over. He told her she had stayed out of the public eye for too long. Orchestra managers were a fickle lot, he said, and had looked for someone to replace her. They had found another extraordinary pianist called Sue Ling. He blamed Nicola for insisting on having the baby and told her the whole sorry affair was her own fault.

Well, you can imagine, she was stunned and shocked, unable to believe what he was saying. She knew she was an exceptional performer and begged and pleaded with him to find her work, any work. Max knew she didn't have a hope in hell of ever performing again, and he knew that his own days as a top, and highly respected, agent were finished.

Then his father died and he inherited that damn house.

Chapter Nineteen

PARIS
Nicola

Max had flown out to Kenya the following day. Nicola, trying to gather herself and not succumb to her anger, misery and the sense of loss that threatened to overwhelm her, decided to brave the cold February weather and go out for a coffee. The phone had remained ominously quiet and although she'd been tempted to call some of her many contacts in the music world, and beg for another chance, her courage had failed her. This was Max's job and he would be incandescent with rage if she bypassed him as her agent, and approached anyone herself.

The café was busy with Parisians taking shelter from the wind and rain. Limp wet umbrellas and coats leaked onto the floor between tables, and the windows were steamed up with the press of people all talking and warming themselves with hot drinks. Navigating her way through she found a table at the back.

The elderly waiter, Michel, whom she had known from years of coming to the café since she was a child, arrived to take her order and sighed with the pleasure at seeing her again.

"Mademoiselle DuPont, welcome back!"

Seeing her quiet and somewhat subdued, Michel bent down conspiratorially and asked, "A hot chocolate for you, Mademoiselle? *Comme d'habitude?*"

She smiled, cheered by his friendly greeting.

Michel bustled off and Nicola, suddenly conscious of being watched, glanced sharply to her right. A middle-aged couple were studying her and quickly averted their gaze when she looked at them; she assumed they must recognise her and hope flared inside her. Max might be wrong, maybe her public had not moved on as quickly as he had said.

Her thoughts were interrupted by Michel placing her cup and saucer on the table with a flourish.

"*Et voila, your chocolat*, Mademoiselle." He hesitated and then asked her quietly, "I trust you have recovered?"

Nicola looked at him in surprise. "Recovered?"

"It happens sometimes," Michel continued, nodding his head sagely. "Things do not always go as well as expected. Perhaps you

126

were tired, and pushing yourself too hard? I'm sure you will make a triumphant and glorious comeback!"

Somewhere at the front of the cafe a glass broke on the floor. Michel lifted his shoulders, excused himself and fetched a broom and dustpan from behind the coat rack.

Nicola blew on her drink trying to work out what Michel had meant.

The couple next to her stood to go; they inclined their heads sombrely in passing. Nicola glanced at their table and saw they'd left a newspaper. Wanting to silence her thoughts, she reached over for it; she hadn't read a newspaper for weeks. As had been her habit she turned to the music reviews. The young Chinese pianist Max had told her about, Sue Ling, had received a standing ovation for her two-hour performance the night before. The reporter had compared her to Nicola.

Nicola DuPont who, at the height of her career dazzled audiences all over the world, was one of the finest pianists France has ever produced and yet, despite her last disappointing performances, the Rachmaninoff piece in particular, she will always be remembered for her brilliance on stage. It appears Mademoiselle Sue Ling is our startling and excellent consolation prize, filling the void left by Mademoiselle DuPont, as the new darling of the stage.

Nicola slowly folded the paper. She thought back to her final performances. Perhaps they had not been good - certainly she had been pre-occupied and distraught with the thought of having to give up her baby. The ever present tears rose again in her eyes.

Finishing her hot chocolate, she left payment in coins on the table, then stood up and walked unsteadily out of the café.

******

Nicola was unaware of the open glances she received when leaving. There were many who recognised her and remembered the articles in the newspapers. So poor had been her performance the theories and rumours abounded - had she been drunk? Under the influence of drugs? Had she been ill? No-one could say. They only knew she hadn't been seen in Paris for months afterwards, and assumed she was in recuperation for an illness or addiction of some kind.

******

When Nicola returned to the empty apartment, a dark and flat depression threatened to swamp her. She thought back to the article she'd read in the paper. "Dear God," she whispered to herself, "I must have played badly; I've just blocked everything out."

She felt panic rise up inside her as she went into Max's study. Sitting down in his oversized chair she picked up the phone and dialled her sister's number. The connection was full of hissing, as though of a dissatisfied audience. The phone rang for a long while and as she was about to hang up, it was answered. The sound of a party in full swing thundered into the emptiness of the apartment.

"Hello!" Elizabeth shouted.

"Lizzy?"

"Nicky! I'm having a party, sorry it's so noisy. Can you hear me?"

Nicola closed her eyes. "Yes, just about. I need to talk to you, it's important."

"Alright, hold on a second, I've an extension in my bedroom."

Nicola tapped her fingers against the desk; it occurred to her they would no longer serve her as they once had. She squeezed her eyes shut as her fingers stilled, and gripped the edge of the desk.

Elizabeth picked up her extension. "What's happening?"

Nicola's words poured out as she filled Elizabeth in. On the other end, Elizabeth closed her eyes, her knuckles white as she tightened her grip on the phone. The hopelessness and despair in her sister's voice sliced through her.

"I'm sorry, Nicky, you have no idea how sorry I am. Where's Max?"

Nicola told her about the conversation she and Max had had preceding the telephone call about his father and his subsequent hasty departure.

"Maybe Kenya would be the solution, Nicky"

"What do you mean?"

She heard the click of a lighter and Elizabeth exhaling on a cigarette.

128

"A new life - somewhere different."

"Why would I want to go anywhere with him! He's made it blatantly obvious he doesn't want to marry me. In fact he doesn't need me for anything at all now does he?"

Elizabeth cringed at the anguish she heard in her voice.

"Do you think my career is finished?" Nicola asked her directly, her voice breaking. "Is this because I took the time off to have my baby?"

"Max never wanted it. He told you it would damage your career."

Elizabeth continued. "If he feels you missed your chance by being off-stage for such a long time, well, he knows the market. If he can't swing you another performance," she hesitated, "then no-one can. You had some kind of breakdown and, to be honest, your last performances were not good, not good at all. I'm sorry to be so brutal. You need to move on. You need a new start."

"I want my baby back," she screamed down the phone.

"It's not possible, Nicky, you know that!"

******

Nicola put the phone down and gazed at the Parisian lights. Dusk had drawn night in and the rain still lashed against the window panes blurring the lights outside. A strong wind was blowing, lifting leaves up into air before settling and sticking on the wet pavements. She realised she was sitting in the dark but made no move to illuminate the room. She looked at the empty apartment and then at her empty arms, feeling and seeing the child she had held so briefly. The sound of her raw grief ricocheted around the room.

******

A month later, Max returned to Paris. He was exhausted after weeks of sorting out his father's affairs. The estate was not in as good a shape as he had anticipated. It would need a heavy financial injection.

Any thoughts of selling it had been quashed by the terms of his father's Will. On the flight back he had spent hours with his calculator working out how he could keep things going - all roads led to one person and one person only - Nicola.

With the considerable amount of money she had earned over the years and what he had earned as her agent, there would be more than enough to get the estate back on its feet again.

An added incentive for his bigger plan was the fact that Nicola would inherit a considerable trust when her mother died, and there was only one way he could get his hands on that.

He'd have to marry her.

On his trips into Nairobi to meet with Martin Shapiro, the family lawyer, he'd spent many hours at his club enjoying the company of his old friends; and now he was the son and heir to Mbabati plenty of women had made it clear to him they were available should he be interested. And interested he was.

Nicola was the key to everything now. If he played his cards right he could have it all.

******

Nicola poured him a large whisky and took it into the sitting room where he was asleep in an armchair by the fire. She sat down and looked at him; despite everything she knew she still loved him.

With his high cheek bones, generous full mouth, and mop of dark hair he could have stepped out of the pages of a fashion magazine. Yes, he was an attractive man and he was all she had left now.

During the month he had been away she'd had plenty of time to think about her future now her career was over. If Max decided he didn't want her she would have no-one. The thought of being totally alone made her stomach somersault with fright.

Max opened his eyes and smiled at her, reaching for the glass of whisky she had placed next to his chair.

"How was the trip? What was it like being back again?"

"Good; I enjoyed it more than I thought I would. The estate needs a bit of work to make it viable again, but the house is in good shape."

"So will you sell it?"

"No, that's not going to be possible. The terms of my father's Will are quite clear. The estate must stay in the family. No argument there." He sighed deeply, watching her reaction to his words.

"Why don't you put a manager in to run it?"

He scratched the stubble on his face and yawned, then took a generous mouthful of his drink.

"I thought long and hard about our future on the flight back. I think we could be happy in Kenya. It's a great country and being back made me realize how good the lifestyle is: lots of servants, plenty of sunshine and a slower pace of life. So that's my future - Mbabati… and I hope it will be yours as well."

She looked at him in surprise. "Mine?"

"Yes. I want to marry you, Nicola."

Hope soared through her. He did still want her; he wasn't going to abandon her.

Then he reeled her in. "The house must be passed to the next generation, which is obviously me, and after that to any children we may have. Giving up the baby was hard for you, Nicola, and I know you don't believe it," he lied, "but it was hard for me too. However a decision had to be made."

He took another mouthful of his drink. "By the way, have there been any calls from anyone?"

She shook her head looking overwhelmed by his proposal but badly needing an answer to her next question. "There's something I need to ask you. I read something in the paper, in the music reviews; it was an article comparing me with the pianist Sue Ling."

He looked at her - this was going to be easier than he thought. He knew this particular subject would come up at some point, and he was prepared with his answer.

"The article said that my last few performances were disappointing. I've thought long and hard and tried to recall them, but I just can't - there seems to be some sort of blank which I don't understand. Did I play badly?"

He leaned over and took both her clenched hands in his. "Yes, I'm afraid you did. I didn't say anything because you were in such a state about the baby. I'm sorry darling, I didn't know how to tell you."

She stared at him numbly. "I don't understand..."

He carried on smoothly. "There's nothing left in France for either of us. I've no choice but to go back and run the estate, and I want you to come with me. I want you by my side, as my wife, and mother to our children."

With nothing else to lose, and with the solid promise of a future and a family, she reluctantly accepted his unexpected proposal of marriage.

Chapter Twenty
KENYA

In October that year they travelled to Kenya by ship from Marseille. Knowing Nicola's irrational fear of flying he'd had no choice but to join her on the long sea voyage. Trains and ships had always transported her to her international performances, and the logistics had sometimes been a nightmare for him to arrange. Despite trying to cajole her into at least trying to overcome her fear by trying a short flight, she stubbornly refused.

Nicola spent her time in their first class suite or out on their private deck, taking her meals in her suite and only seeing her fellow passengers on the rare occasion she chose to walk around the deck. Wearing sunglasses and a hat no-one had recognized her.

Max spent his days at sea mixing with the other first class passengers in the various bars and lounges. He'd spent many pleasant hours in the suite of a particularly attractive married woman, whiling away the time as the ship steamed towards East Africa. Nicola seemed to have little interest in making love, although she acquiesced when he became insistent, so why not enjoy other women, he reasoned.

After the ship docked in the sea port of Mombasa, they cleared customs and boarded the ferry for the short trip to the mainland, and the overnight train to Nairobi.

Nicola looked at the train with apprehension as the porters stowed their luggage.

Seeing the look on her face, he laughed. "I know it looks a bit of a wreck, it's rather old I agree, but its good fun. I've been on it many times coming here for school holidays. Did I mention we have a holiday cottage here in Mombasa?" She shook her head.

"The train is noisy and hot," he continued, "but you get a good look at the countryside, and the animals, as we head into Nairobi."

Early next morning, being careful not to wake Max, she lifted the slatted shutter and took her first real look at the countryside. There seemed to be nothing but endless miles of dry scrubland, scrawny flat brown trees and bushes dotting the landscape, and the occasional small village with round huts and thatched roofs.

Women, already working in the fields straightened up, easing their aching backs, to wave at the train and the blur of faces.

Nicola slumped back on her bunk. What a stark contrast to the elegant streets of Paris.

******

Winston, Max's father's elderly retainer, a tall thin man, dressed in a white shirt and khaki trousers, had been waiting on the platform as the train came to a noisy hissing halt. Max greeted him in Swahili and introduced Nicola.

Winston inclined his head gravely. "*Jambo* Memsahib, welcome to Kenya." Summoning a porter to carry their luggage he led them out to an old, but highly polished grey Jaguar.

"This is the old man's car, not sure how old it is but it seems to have been around for as long as I can remember.

He opened the door for her. "We've a long drive ahead but the Jag should make it a comfortable one."

Although the journey had been hot and dusty, Nicola had been enchanted with the changing scenery; now on the final leg, the landscape had changed from farmlands, small villages and shops to the wide open space of the bush, the wavering honey gold grasses softening the dry brown landscape.

Winston took a right-hand fork in the dirt road, the dust billowing behind the car coating the bushes and trees scattered either side of the brutally rough road. He pulled up in front of two large ornately curved iron gates, giving two sharp beeps on the horn.

"Ah, here comes Luke, Winston's son."

Nicola smiled at the handsome, strongly built young African, who was grinning widely as he unlocked the padlock and swung the gates wide open. "*Jambo* Memsahib!" he called out as they drove past him. He closed the gates and sprinted after the car.

She gasped as the house came into full view. "Oh, it's beautiful!"

Max introduced her to a breathless Luke who smiled at her shyly, before turning to the car to unload their luggage.

Two black Labradors bounded down the steps in a frenzy of excitement. Max introduced them as Maggie and Monty pointing to each dog as they barked a greeting and circled her, their tails rotating like windmills. Taking her arm, Max led her into the cool of the entrance hall. She looked around waiting for her eyes to adjust after the bright sunshine outside.

"Why, it's so - it's so grand, Max!" Nicola looked up the magnificent staircase, feeling behind her for his hand. "Come on, show me around!"

Proudly he showed her the sitting room, the dining room, the wine cellar and finally the kitchen where the chef, Cookie, was busy preparing dinner for them.

Leaving the kitchen she turned to him. "What's his real name - not Cookie surely?"

"Actually I don't know, he's always been Cookie to me. Come on, I'll show you upstairs.

Nicola looked around the spacious master bedroom with its floor-to-ceiling cupboards and mirrors, the highly polished wooden floor and four-poster bed draped in icily white mosquito netting. The walls, with their embossed wallpapers in shades of lemon and pale green, gave the room a soft ambience. The view over the gardens, and the bush beyond, which she could see from the bathroom suite with its floor-to-ceiling glass windows, made her catch her breath.

Any doubts Nicola might have had about moving to Kenya had dissipated. For the first time in months she felt hopeful. It would be the perfect place to bring up a young family.

******

Later they wandered into the gardens, drinks in hand, as the sun sank swiftly into the horizon. She turned to look back at the house. Light shone out of all the windows, competing with the radiance of the stars beginning to appear above.

"You've shown me all over the house but not the top floor - what's up there?"

Max put his arm around her shoulder, and kissed her cheek lightly. "I'll show you after dinner."

Nicola started to protest then stopped when the faint sound of a bell carried across the stillness of the evening.

"Dinner's ready. Come on, it's getting cool out here."

Silver candelabra shone on the dining room table picking up the gleam of the dark wood; crystal wine glasses and silver bowls filled with roses decorated their places. Winston, wearing a red and gold waistcoat, stood next to the serving dishes waiting for them to be seated. Luke, wearing an identical waistcoat, opened a bottle of wine and stood holding it carefully.

Winston cleared his throat. "Tonight, memsahib, we have the loin of the impala with roast potatoes, cauliflower, peas and green beans."

"Impala? Um, I'll have a little of everything, thank you, Winston."

Winston turned back towards the serving dishes. Luke stood to attention next to Max's chair, ready to pour the wine.

Their serving duties completed, they left the room with barely a rustle.

"Such style, *cheri*, I'm impressed," Nicola complimented. "It's like being in a grand chateau out in the French countryside!"

Max speared a piece of impala and chewed it appreciatively. "I shot this impala myself - what do you think?"

Nicola nibbled a piece tentatively savouring the gamey flavour. "It tastes like venison. Is it a type of deer?"

"Yes, exactly, an impala is an African antelope."

She took a sip of her wine. "Where does all the food come from? I didn't see any shops on our drive here. Just a funny little store with a Coca Cola sign."

Max twirled his glass and took a sip. "That's the grocery store." Seeing her blank expression he hastened to add, "Mr Patel stocks just about everything from car batteries to tinned ham. But most of our supplies come from Nairobi. We get a delivery once a month."

"Shopping only once a month?" she said incredulously.

Max chuckled at the look on her face. "Cookie and Winston give me a list of what they need and I give it to Mr Patel. He provides whatever he can and the rest he orders from Nairobi, the same with the post. Our mail is collected and delivered along with the shopping and newspapers."

"French newspapers?" she said, her voice lifting hopefully.

"No, *The Times* from London." There was no way Max wanted her to read anything more about herself in any French newspaper.

Nicola tried to hide her disappointment, and changed the subject. "It's odd to hear the name Patel out here. It's Indian, isn't it?"

He nodded and explained how the Indians were integral to the smooth running of remote estates like theirs and how their families had been in Kenya for generations running the small supermarkets, or *dukas*, as they were known as.

"Where does this lovely wine come from?" she asked, taking a delicate sip from her glass.

"I order cases from our merchant in London, and the ever efficient Mr Patel arranges the rest."

Max picked up a small silver bell and rang it vigorously.

Winston and Luke arrived within minutes and began clearing away their plates. She watched in amusement as they left with the trays. "The bell seems an important element in running the house."

He smiled sheepishly. "It probably does seem a bit odd to you. It's a big house and ringing the bell is better than yelling out to the kitchen. I can't remember a meal here without it. You'll get used to it.

"Come on, I'll show you the top floor."

She walked through the carved doors and stopped. "But there's nothing in here." Nicola said looking around blankly. "It's practically empty, not even carpets on the floor."

He took her hand. "I thought you might like to choose some furniture from the rest of the house - a few chairs and tables perhaps, to put around the fireplace at the end there."

"But why sit up here when the sitting room is so comfortable?"

He told her this was going to be her room, and the ship that they had travelled on had brought her a surprise. A late wedding present which was due to arrive in the next few days.

She looked at him, perplexed. "Will you tell me what it is? I can't wait for days, I'm far too curious."

"It's something to make up for what you lost." He paused. "It's a Steinway."

She almost knocked him over as she threw herself into his arms. "What a wonderful thing to do, *cheri*." She looked up at him. "But to transport a Steinway is a professional job," Nicola said worriedly. "How will it get here?"

"It's being escorted by a man from the Steinway factory, he'll assemble it right here in this room - the music room. Yes, I know what you're going to say next. Along with the man from Steinway is a top piano tuner, they travelled on the ship with us."

Nicola put her hands to her cheeks in stunned surprise. She looked around the room already imagining how it might look.

137

He put his arm around her and led her out. "I think I know how you can show your appreciation..."

******

Max lay on his back in bed, Nicola sleeping trustingly beside him. It had been easy to persuade her to transfer her money into his account. He'd told her some convoluted story about the red tape of moving to Kenya, and, as he was a permanent resident, it would be easier to combine their accounts.

The purchase of the piano, transporting it to Kenya and hiring the two men had made quite a hole in their finances.

He hoped she would adjust to such an isolated life, and being out here meant she would be unlikely to discover the part he had played in the destruction of her hard earned professional life.

Chapter Twenty-One

L uke watched fascinated as the two white men gesticulated and shouted in a strange language to the Africans helping to unload the back of the truck. What piece of furniture was this, that it needed so many clothes to keep it safe and hidden? The memsahib could not keep still in her excitement as she walked around the big truck.

Max beckoned him over. "Show the men to the top floor of the house Luke. Nicola, you'd better go as well and tell them where you'd like the piano positioned."

Nicola watched anxiously as the two men, and four of the garden and house staff, manoeuvered the piano pieces into the house, negotiating the staircase with care. The Africans wiped the sweat from their faces, grinning widely, curious to know what they had carried into the room.

Nicola shooed them all away and turned to the two Frenchmen.

"Mademoiselle DuPont...," the piano tuner, Pierre, stuttered in astonishment, recognising her instantly now she had taken off her hat and sunglasses.

Nicola smiled at them. "You must be tired after your journey," she said in French. "Luke," she gestured towards him, "has prepared rooms for you. He'll show you where they are and bring some refreshments. You'll join us for dinner, *messieurs*?"

They stared at her speechlessly then followed Luke, completely overwhelmed at seeing her in such an unlikely place.

Nicola looked longingly at the shrouded piano parts then went to find Max. He was standing outside looking out over the garden. She told him she'd invited Pierre and Maurice to join them for dinner that evening, and how she was looking forward to talking about the world of music, and who was doing what in Paris.

Max frowned. Any regrets expressed by the Frenchmen that she no longer played for the public could prove to be a disaster for him.

"I think they'd be more comfortable eating together out on the veranda." He said shortly. "Besides, I've never been one to mix business with pleasure; they've got a job to do."

She smiled at him brightly, hiding her disappointment. "It's not important... I must go to the kitchen and see what Cookie's preparing for dinner; I've given him a French dish to try."

Nicola was sitting on a chair next to the window watching the two men remove the cladding from her piano. With an exasperated gesture, the smaller Frenchman, Maurice, threw up his hands in despair and turned to look at her.

"Madame," he said in French, "the journey with this fine piano was arduous enough, in fact nerve-wracking for both of us. But to be in the presence of a pianist, a pianist whom all of France loved, and to find you out here," he gestured expansively out of the window, "makes us a little nervous, *non*? Perhaps Madame would allow us to continue with our work and we will call her when we are ready?"

******

Nicola was in the sitting room composing a letter to Elizabeth. For two days she'd curbed her impatience to go up to the music room and see how the men were progressing.

The ceiling fan cut its way through the languid heat of the day, the dogs were asleep at her feet. At a knock on the door, Nicola looked up.

Pierre cleared his throat nervously. "Madame, your piano awaits you."

Nicola sprang out of her chair and squeezed her hands with excitement. Pierre stood aside, as she ran up the stairs with the dogs barking at her heels.

She walked into the room and gasped. The magnificent piano sat in the centre of the long room, a triumph of craftsmanship. She sat down on the soft leather-padded stool, ran her fingers across the cool keys and began to play.

******

Pierre and Maurice stood by the door hardly daring to breathe for fear of interrupting their private performance. Nicola DuPont was as impressive as the instrument she was playing so exquisitely.

Pierre fumbled for his handkerchief, tears filling his eyes. Such perfection; he wiped his eyes and listened. How could it be Nicola DuPont had been shouted and booed off the stage by her fellow countrymen?

140

Her playing now was as glorious as ever - France had lost one of its greatest treasures to the middle of the African bush. Alas, he was sworn to secrecy or he would have gone straight to the press when he got home, and told them where she was living now. He shook his head and dabbed his eyes.

Tomorrow they would be returning to Nairobi, their task here completed.

Chapter Twenty-Two

Luke under the watchful eye of Winston, served them their coffee outside. The fire at the end of the veranda crackled and hissed, shooting sparks up into the chimney.

He asked Luke to tell the grooms to have the horses' ready the next morning, as he wanted to give the memsahib a tour of the factory, and show her the hide.

Luke looked at him hopefully. "You wish for Luke to come with you?"

Max nodded absently, telling him they would leave after breakfast.

He looked at his wife. After only a few months in Kenya, Nicola seemed to have settled well, gradually taking over the running of the house, and supervising the staff.

"What would we do without Luke?" she said watching them both return to the kitchen.

"He's likeable I admit. We both grew up here and used to play together, before I went to school in England, he taught me how to use a rifle when I was a kid."

"Where did he go to school?"

Max leant forward to light a cigarette and then sat back, putting his feet on the coffee table to get more comfortable.

"He didn't. The nearest school was miles away and Luke's whole life has been centred here. When I inherited Mbabati, our relationship changed a bit, I've gone from being 'Max' to 'Bwana Max'."

She sipped her coffee and looked out over the grounds; the strategically placed hurricane lamps threw shadows over the trees and bushes. A thin plume of acrid smelling smoke rose from a green coil propped up in a saucer in the centre of the table. This, she had learned, was to keep the mosquitoes at bay, she didn't care for the smell of it, but it was better than being bitten.

She put her cup down and stretched. "I'm looking forward to our ride tomorrow; I'm glad you didn't sell all the horses."

Max blew on the end of his cigarette. "It was a difficult decision to make. Pa bred horses here for over twenty years but it's risky and the investment too high - what with horse sickness and all the other things that can go wrong out here in the bush. I plan to make the estate easier to control and concentrate on growing the sisal."

"Sisal? What's it used for?" she asked curiously.

"Lots of things: rope, twine, mattresses, carpets, furniture, that sort of stuff. A local chief runs the business; he chooses the workers and I pay the chief. It makes the estate easier to manage that way. I'll show you tomorrow. We can stop at the lake then have lunch at the hide."

"The hide? It sounds rather odd?"

He laughed. "Yes, I suppose it does - wait and see."

"Is it safe to ride out in the bush? What about the wild animals?"

So far he'd only taken her to the lake, and the area around the estate in the Land Rover and her concern was understandable.

"The animals won't bother the horses. The only thing that can spook a horse now and again are giraffe, probably because they're so tall. Now how about playing something for me before we go to bed?"

Nicola played for over an hour, lost to the world she had once loved. Now she folded her hands in her lap and looked at her husband.

"I'd like to have children; start a family, if that's alright with you?"

Max looked towards the window and yawned. "Time for bed I think.

"And children, Max?" Nicola repeated stubbornly.

"This house has to be passed to the next generation," he said irritably. "It's one of the terms of the bloody Will. So I suppose we'll have to have children."

"Well, try and sound a bit more enthusiastic!" she said, stung by his response.

Max avoided her eyes. The long days he spent at the sisal factory were tedious and he hated the endless hours he had to spend there, but it was their only source of income now. When she was more settled he'd take a trip into town and see if any of the old crowd were around.

Chapter Twenty-Three

The horses were saddled and waiting, their tails twitching with irritation at the flies.

Luke had arranged for a picnic hamper to be delivered to the hide. He handed Max his rifle, and mounted his horse.

Half an hour later they arrived at the low building of the factory, its corrugated tin roof quivering and creaking with the heat of the sun.

Long strips of fibre were hanging in the sun to dry for as far as the eye could see; machines inside pounded away at the freshly harvested leaves crushing and beating them into a pulp. African women sang harmoniously as they worked, and dipped their heads in greeting when they saw the boss and his new wife.

Nicola wiped the perspiration from her neck with a cotton handkerchief and readjusted her hat; the heat was still something she was trying to adjust to; even in March it didn't seem any cooler.

After fifteen minutes inside the sweltering noisy factory, she tugged at Max's arm. "It's too hot in here for me and I can't hear anything you're saying. Can we leave this for another day - a cooler day? I think I might faint if I spend another minute in here."

Leaving the factory they rode down to the lake. They dismounted and handed the reins to Luke who led the horses away to the shade of a nearby tree.

"Sorry about the tour of the factory, the smell, the noise and the heat was too much for me. I could dive straight into the water," she said longingly.

"Not advisable, my dear, there are hippo in there and the odd crocodile. You're safe enough to dangle your toes in the water from the end of the jetty though."

Nicola pulled off her boots and sat down gingerly, lowering her feet into the cool depths of the water, she sighed with relief. She pulled her hat down lower and adjusted her sunglasses against the glare of the shimmering water.

"Are you coming for a paddle?"

He hunkered down next to her. "I don't feel the heat like you do. Don't forget I was brought up here." He took off his hat and wiped the sweat off his face with his sleeve.

She looked down to the side of the jetty and noticed a wooden rowing boat rocking slightly in the water. "Oh, how lovely, shall we go out on the lake, it might be cooler out there?"

"Too dangerous I'm afraid, we rarely ever use it. One of the staff was out fishing from it, some years ago now - a hippo came up from nowhere, tipped the boat over and killed him. They're dangerous beasts, more dangerous than any other actually."

He stood up. "Come on, it's too hot to sit around here; I don't want you spoiling that beautiful skin of yours, anyway I'm starving, time for lunch I think. Here, put your boots back on and let's go see what Cookie has prepared for us."

******

Max reined in his horse. "Here we are."

Nicola looked around, fanning her face with her hat, and frowning. "Well, there isn't anything here except for the waterhole." Max helped her dismount and threw the reins at Luke.

"The trick to being in the bush is to not look for the obvious. Look through the bush, Nicola, not at it."

She closed her eyes against the glare of sunlight and water and then opened them again. Beneath the bushes and leaves she now saw a small wooden structure with a narrow pathway leading to a flimsy door.

She smiled. "I can see it now. It's well hidden; it reminds me of some kind of den." She followed him up the narrow pathway and into the cool shadows of the hide.

It was simple inside: just three rooms, an area for sitting, with four green canvas chairs and a wooden table; a tiny kitchen, and a bedroom with a double bed and a mosquito net suspended above it. Half of the bedroom was covered with a roof of corrugated iron; the other half contained a large tree, its heavy thick branches providing a natural extension to the roof. She walked towards the tree and put her hand against its rough surface. He came up behind her.

"This was my mother's idea. She hated anyone chopping down trees. So, when Pa found the perfect spot for the hide she refused to let him cut it down, he had to build around it. There aren't many people who have slept in a bedroom with a tree right in the middle of it."

"It's wonderful," Nicola agreed. "I love the outside bathroom, how marvellous to take a shower under the stars." She hesitated for a moment, then asked him where the water came from.

"Hidden in the bush outside the bedroom there's a water tank; it's filled by the rain and supplies the water."

Out on the simple deck Winston had delivered the picnic hamper. Nicola looked around with interest. A table with hurricane lamps each end and two more green canvas chairs was the only furniture, the trees and bushes providing a natural canopy and shade from the sun. Thick bushes at the front, waist high, kept them partially hidden from the animals drinking at the waterhole, its muddy edges churned and rutted with hoof prints. Straggling green grey bushes and numerous thin trees were interspersed around the water providing a little shelter for the thirsty animals.

They nibbled on chicken legs and cherry tomatoes and sipped ice cold glasses of home-made lemonade. A stately male water buck appeared from nowhere and dipped his head towards the water then suddenly lifted his dripping muzzle and stood still, his ears twitching as though he was aware of them.

Nicola stopped chewing and remained stock still. She heard Max laughing quietly beside her and realised the animals couldn't see her.

He handed her a box containing cucumber and salmon sandwiches with their crusts removed. "Who taught Cookie how to do all this?" she whispered, holding up a sandwich, "It's so very English."

"Mother," Max murmured, "she liked things done the way they were done at her parent's country heap in Surrey."

She held a finger to her lips as an enormous rhino ambled out of the bush and headed towards the water." Have you ever made love beneath a tree?" he whispered in her ear.

Nicola giggled. "Of course not, but what about Luke?"

"Bugger Luke, he's probably had his lunch and sleeping under a bush. Come on, all this fresh air has given me an appetite bigger than the one I had for lunch."

Luke heard the familiar sounds and grinned. Maybe there would soon be babies in the house he could spoil. He leaned back against the tree, closed his eyes, and dozed off.

Nicola's memories of the hide, and what happened there years later, would stay with her for the rest of her life, slithering through the

146

cracks in her dreams and jerking her awake with her own terrified screams - still feeling the silkiness of his hair between her fingers.

Chapter Twenty-Four

Max began his meal silently then put down his knife and fork with a loud clatter. Nicola glanced up at him. "Don't you like the veal?"

"It's fine. Sorry, I've a lot on my mind at the moment." He turned to Winston and Luke who stood side by side by the door. "Thank you, Winston, thank you Luke," he said pointedly. They nodded and left. She put down her own knife and fork, looking at him uneasily.

"What's wrong? I've hardly seen you the last few weeks."

He looked down at his plate and spoke evenly. "I'll have to let go of two of the house staff, to lower expenses."

Nicola frowned with consternation and leaned forward in her seat. "Not Luke or Winston, surely?"

"No, the other two. I hate to do it because work is impossible to find around here and I can't use them in the factory. I think you'll be able to manage. You'll need to give more responsibility to Luke. Speak to Winston about it, will you?" He stood up abruptly, threw down his napkin and left the dining-room.

Luke hurried into the room looking anxiously at Max's empty chair and the half-finished plate of food. "Bwana Max is not liking the French cooking, memsahib?"

"I'm not sure. He's gone into the sitting room - take the wine through and serve him coffee in there. I'll take mine upstairs."

Luke watched Nicola leave the room before placing the wine bottle in the bucket and taking it to the sitting room.

Max was leaning against the fireplace, his head in his hand, staring moodily into the fire. As silently as possible, Luke set down the bucket and left the room to prepare a tray of coffee. Bwana Max had a quick temper and when he was like this it was better to leave him alone. Even as a child he had been moody and unpredictable.

Luke found Nicola in the music room playing. He placed the coffee tray on a side table and checked the fire. "Memsahib?"

She paused and smiled at him. "Luke, I've been here over two years now and I think it's time you called me Miss Nicola. I don't like to be called memsahib. It doesn't sound right to me."

"Yes, Miss... Nicola," he said shyly, and padded from the room on bare feet.

When Nicola went down to breakfast, Max had already left the house. Puzzled he hadn't said goodbye, as he normally did, she rang the bell and waited for Winston.

"Did Bwana Max have breakfast?"

Winston shook his head. "No, just coffee."

Max had been in an odd mood for the past week or so, he had been quiet and preoccupied and inclined to snap at the servants and her. But he had never left the house before without telling her his plans for the day.

She shrugged. "Please tell Luke I'd like to go riding after breakfast, Winston."

They rode out into the bush, Luke, with the rifle, following closely behind her. The wind in her hair felt good and lifted her spirits. Max's latest mood had cast a pall over the entire house and she wondered if perhaps it was more than their financial situation bothering him. Maybe he was regretting his inheritance and missing his old social and business life. God knows there were many things she craved for and missed herself.

Max had taken her to the club in Nanyuki once a month but it was something she didn't enjoy. The hours standing, or sitting, at the bar, whilst he and his friends talked about life in Kenya, and who was doing what, none of it was of any interest to her.

On one or two occasions he had lost his temper as they drove back to the house, haranguing her for not being more involved with his friends and taking an interest in the conversation. Wisely she remained silent; she had come to learn that after a few drinks he could be bad tempered.

After her ride, she showered and changed into a simple white linen dress. Tying her hair back into a pony tail, she went out onto the veranda and had a light lunch. The long afternoon stretched ahead of her and she decided to drive to Mr Patel's to see if there was any post or newspapers.

Mr Patel bending down under the counter, produced two letters. "One from America, Mrs Gray. Your sister, I think? Another from South America, perhaps your mother?"

She took the letters from him and put them in her bag. A small child looked at her shyly from behind a sack of grain. She went over and bent down to ruffle his dark hair. "Hello, what's your name?"

Mr Patel smiled proudly. "He is my son, his name is Sanjay."

She ran her finger down the silkiness of the child's face. "He's lovely…well, goodbye Mr Patel and thank you for the letters."

Back in the Land Rover she hesitated, drumming her fingers on the dashboard. It was too early to go back to the house. She decided to go to the club; she would read her letters there.

Sitting on the patio Nicola ordered afternoon tea. The gardens were filled with flourishing bougainvillea bushes in cream, magenta, apricot and red. Lush bushes of Yesterday, Today and Tomorrow, with their blue, white and purple flowers exuding a heady perfume, had been positioned throughout the gardens. High arching water sprays clicked rhythmically back and forth giving a sense of coolness. From the tennis courts she could hear the thwack of balls against rackets and the occasional cry from the players. Nicola opened and read Elizabeth's letter.

Sorry for the long delay in responding, Nicky, I seem to spend all my time looking for work. I've had one or two tiny walk-on parts this year and hopefully they'll lead to better things. My social life is still as hectic as ever. You have to get out and be seen in this town, so this means endless cocktail parties, opening nights and dinners. I don't seem to spend an evening at home.

You sound from your last letter as though you've adapted to life in the jungle. Are you still playing in your music room? How lovely to have Luke and Winston and the other staff pandering to your every whim. It must be heaven not to have to lift a finger to do anything, but I don't think I could stand not to have a social life. I know you love the house and had fun redecorating and making it yours, but don't you yearn for some company apart from Max? Yes I do remember his black moods; he can be ugly when he's had a few drinks. Has he taken you down to the beach cottage yet?

That night, Nicola sat alone in the dining-room. She asked Luke if Max had told anyone where he was going to be today.

He shook his head avoiding her eyes.

Nicola pushed the food around on her plate. If he had suddenly decided to go somewhere, he might at least have mentioned it, she thought crossly.

The sound of tyres crunching on the driveway brought her to her feet and out into the entrance hall. Max stormed into the hallway.

150

"For goodness sake," she said angrily, "where have you been? Why didn't you tell someone where you were going?"

He threw his hat and keys on the table. "I don't have to explain where I've been or what I've been doing." Max raised his voice and Nicola flinched. "You seem to forget this is *my* house. I don't answer to anyone!"

"Luke?" Max yelled out. Luke scurried in from the kitchen. "Bring me a brandy!" He walked past her without another word or glance.

Nicola followed him into the sitting room and sat gingerly on the edge of the sofa, trying to think of something to say to diffuse his mood. He threw another log on the fire and stabbed it savagely with the poker.

"I was worried about you."

"I'll do the worrying around here." He flung himself down onto a chair and ran a hand over his face. "God, I miss my other life, I sometimes wonder what I'm doing here, checking the bloody estate day after interminable day." He reached into his pocket and pulled out a rolled cigarette. He lit it and inhaled deeply.

She waved her hand in front of her nose. "Have you changed your brand of cigarette? They smell different."

Max rolled his eyes. "God you can be so naive, Nicola. The *dukas* in town don't just sell potatoes." He took another drag. "A lot of expats in this country sometimes need something to take their minds off the bloody rains, or the bloody drought or the sameness of every bloody day!" He blew on the end of the joint making it flare up briefly.

Nicola picked at the hem of her dress, feeling her temper rise. "You think I don't miss my life?" She turned her face away from him. "I miss my child..."

He didn't give her the chance to finish her sentence. "Oh for God's sake! Maybe it would help if you loosened up a bit - here, have a drag, you might even enjoy it." He held the joint out to her.

She waved it away angrily. "Where did you go today?"

"The bloody club!"

Nicola stood up, smoothing down her skirt. "I don't like you when you're in this sort of mood, I'm going to bed. I'd prefer it if you slept in one of the guest rooms tonight."

151

She turned to look back at him. "By the way, I was at the club this afternoon - funny how I missed seeing you sitting at the bar." His laughter followed her as she ran up the stairs.

******

The next morning Max was sitting reading the newspaper when she came into the dining room. He shook the paper and folded it.

"Sorry about yesterday," he said absently, "I think it would do us good to go to Nairobi for a couple of days."

Nicola eyed him warily as she sat down, gauging his mood.

"You could do a bit of shopping. There's a dinner dance at the Muthaiga club next weekend, we could go to that?"

Nicola nodded tentatively. She'd hardly met anyone, apart from his friends at the club. The thought of going into Nairobi and doing something different was appealing and he was obviously keen to go.

Chapter Twenty-Five

Nicola glanced at her watch. Nearly midnight, they had been at the party for three hours and still no sign of any food. The noise, the music, the heat and the smoke-filled rooms were giving her a headache.

She wandered out onto the veranda at the back of the house and looked up at the stars. Thinking back she realized she had never had a social life, focusing instead on her career. Her life had been too different, too regimented, and she wasn't comfortable with crowds of people around her especially when she didn't know any of them.

Her thoughts were interrupted by two young women, shrieking with laughter, who had stepped outside. They both lit up and blew grey plumes of smoke into the darkness.

"I see Annabel has got her claws into Max again, she pipped me to the post there. Have you met his wife?" The tall blond woman shook her head.

"She's a gorgeous looking creature. I love the dress she's wearing, very chic indeed. She reminds me of the film star who married the Prince, Grace someone..."

Nicola froze and shrank back into the shadows of the house.

"She'll need to keep a tight leash on Max though; I wonder if she has money?" The dark haired woman said, coughing wetly.

"Max always was attracted to women with money. The estate he owns is high maintenance. I heard his father ploughed tons into it."

"Have you slept with him, Felicity?"

Felicity threw back her head and laughed. "Oh God! You should be asking who *hasn't* slept with him!" Finishing her cigarette she dropped it on the ground and squashed it with her heel.

"He's been through just about all the women in town, well the good looking young ones. Come on, let's go back and join the crowd; it's getting chilly out here."

"What a shame he's married," Felicity said, wistfully picking up her now empty glass.

"Knowing Max it won't make much difference," her companion said opening the door and releasing loud music, voices and laughter into the garden. The door slammed shut behind them.

Nicola stared at the closed door, appalled by what she had overheard. Max was a good-looking man and she knew women were attracted to him. So what if he had had affairs in Nairobi before he met her? The words hung in the air. Had he married her for her money? She shivered. Yes, it was getting chilly, she should go back in.

Edging around the crowd she made her way to an empty window seat. She turned around at the sound of her name.

"Hi Nicola, I'm Jill."

Nicola looked at the thin dark-haired woman in front of her and smiled tentatively. Jill swirled the ice cubes around in her drink. "Your rather attractive husband pointed you out to me and asked me to come and say hello. I must say we were all surprised, to hear he'd got married - never thought he would, not our Max. Anyway here I am as instructed. How are you settling down in Kenya?"

"It's different but interesting. I'm gradually getting used to things..." Her voice trailed off as she scanned the room looking for her husband.

She turned back to Jill. "Have you lived here long?"

"All my life, like most of us here," she said gesticulating around the room. "We've all known each other forever it seems. Of course some married in. It's always good to have fresh blood..." Seeing Nicola's perplexed expression, Jill added hastily, "so to speak. Where are you from? You sound French."

"I am French; I come from Paris. Africa is something else altogether." She smiled at Jill warmly, grateful to have someone to talk to.

Jill finished her drink with one long swallow. "What did you do before you married Max?"

Nicola hesitated for a moment, there was no point now. "Nothing much."

"Ah ha! You're Old Money, are you? It's what we all thought. You must have plenty of it if you didn't have to work."

Nicola said nothing and kept her eyes fixed on the empty glass in her hand.

Jill sighed theatrically, "I haven't seen you around Nairobi at all, not at any of the parties. How on earth do you fill your days out in the bush? It must be awfully dull."

Nicola glanced around the room desperately looking for Max and a way to escape from the conversation. Seeing only unknown faces and cool glances returning her own, Nicola replied shortly. "It's not dull; it's a big estate and takes up a lot of my time."

154

Jill gave her a long hard look and excused herself. She went to join a small group of men and women who had been watching her talk to Nicola.

"What's she like then - the ice maiden Max married, the blushing bride?" whispered one of her friends.

"A bit insipid if you ask me, boring as hell, not much in the way of conversation. I don't think she's going to fit in with our crowd."

"Don't be such a bitch Jill," a flushed young man interjected, "give her a chance! I personally think she's too good for our so-called crowd. I think a classy looking woman like that, and an extremely beautiful one, would have better things to do than hang out at clubs and bars with the likes of us. Who's for another drink?"

******

Nicola took a sip of her warm wine and looked around for her husband. At a table in the corner Max was sitting, deep in conversation, with an attractive red-head, his arm draped around her shoulders. Their faces were inches from each other and the red-head was giggling at something he had said. Nicola frowned and walked across the room towards him, aware of the eyes of several of the guests watching her with anticipation and interest.

"Perhaps you'd like to introduce me, Max?" Nicola said calmly.

He lifted his face and reluctantly dropped his arm from around the red-head's shoulders. He scowled at Nicola, trying to focus on her. "This is an old friend of mine, Annabel. Annabel, this is my wife."

Annabel held out her hand. "Delighted I'm sure. Sorry I'm a bit sozzled otherwise I'd stand up and be polite."

Someone tittered behind her but Nicola stood her ground, glancing pointedly at Annabel's hand still resting on his arm. "I want to go back to the hotel, Max."

He made a small gesture with the tips of his fingers, as though brushing dust off an imaginary shoulder. "Go and make some friends, for heaven's sake. It's why we're here."

"I want to go back to the hotel."

"It's too early, the party hasn't kicked off yet and I can assure you when it does, I'll be right here. Afterwards a bunch of us are going to a club."

Without another word he turned back to Annabel, dismissing her, much to the amusement of some other guests who had witnessed the exchange. Now they waited to see what would happen next.

She reached into her bag. "A club you say darling," she said sweetly, "well, in that case you will, as always, need money; you never seem to have any of your own. I do hope this will be enough, if not... well, you know where to find me."

Slapping some notes down on the table she walked out of the room, leaving the shrieking laughter and noise behind her.

"Well, well," Jill whispered to her friend, "she certainly put Max in his place. Not so insipid after all, he'd better watch out with this one."

She stood on the steps of the house. Where was she going to find a taxi?

"Mrs Gray?"

Nicola turned around.

"I'm Martin Shapiro," the tall distinguished looking man introduced himself, "your husband's lawyer. Forgive me, I couldn't help but overhear your conversation with Max. Most unfortunate," he smiled at her, "but nicely handled if I may say so. Perhaps you'd allow me to drive you somewhere? Where are you staying?"

She felt relief flood through her. "The Norfolk," she extended her hand, "I'm Nicola."

"Try not to judge us all by tonight, Nicola," he said glancing over his shoulder as he led her to his car. "Nairobi can be a bit wild sometimes. It's just everyone's way of letting off steam. Life can be tough in Kenya but I can assure you there are some exceptionally nice people here. "You just seemed to have met some of the wilder ones tonight. Here's my car," he said, opening the door for her.

Nicola slid into the passenger seat and Martin left her to her thoughts as they drove to the Norfolk Hotel in silence.

He pulled up outside the entrance. "I hope you'll come out to Mbabati sometime, Mr Shapiro. As the family lawyer, I'd like to get to know you."

"Well, you can start by calling me Martin." He opened the passenger door for her. "I'm happy to visit any time you like. Here's my card," Martin said, pulling one from his jacket pocket and handing it to her. "I'll leave it up to you. Goodnight."

Nicola walked into the silent gardens of the hotel, not ready to return to her room. If this weekend was a barometer of life in Nairobi then she preferred the isolation of the bush. The evening had been a disaster and Max's behaviour inexcusable. He had dismissed her as though she were a servant, and in front of all his friends.

She smiled at the memory of his face contorted with fury as she threw the money down. She'd had the last laugh.

She made her way to the reception and asked for another room.

Chapter Twenty Six

During her third year in Kenya Elizabeth had come to stay. "I've no work at the moment, Nicky," Elizabeth had said during the crackling phone call, "I thought I'd come and visit you in your African jungle. I need a change of scenery and my liver would be grateful for a break from the booze."

Nicola was overjoyed with the news and now waited at the top of the steps watching Winston park the car. Elizabeth climbed out of the Jaguar and stared up at the house. "Wow! Look at this place, it's fabulous!"

Nicola ran down the steps and threw herself into her sister's open arms. "Lizzy! Oh God I've missed you." They laughed tearfully as they stood hugging each other.

Wiping the tears from her eyes Nicola took her sister's hand and led her up to the front door. "Welcome to my house in the jungle, as you call it."

"I'm dying for a shower after the long flight and the ghastly journey from the airport. Your driver drove like a snail; I thought we'd never get anywhere, just miles and miles of bloody bush with wild animals leaping about all over the place."

Nicola studied her sister. Her short dark hair was still cut in the same pixie style she had worn in Paris and she had acquired a slight American accent. Apart from this she looked the same as she had always done.

******

Elizabeth was turning the pages of one of the magazines she had brought out for Nicola, waving away the occasional fly with irritation. Throwing the magazine down on the cushion beside her she slumped back in her chair, exhaling noisily.

"Phew! Is it always so hot here?"

"It cools off when the rains come which should be in the next couple of weeks."

"Don't you ever have any parties out here, Nicola?"

She laughed, "No."

"Don't you get fed up with being surrounded by...," Elizabeth gestured around her vaguely, "by absolutely nothing? I mean, the dogs are all very well and the servants are charming, the monkeys are amusing for a while, and even Max can be entertaining when he makes an effort - if he's sober, which isn't often. Haven't you got any friends nearby? Oh hello Max, I didn't see you there."

He flopped down in the chair next to Elizabeth, a drink already in his hand despite the early hour of the day.

"She doesn't have any friends and she doesn't like mine. Isn't that right, Nicola?" he asked raising his glass and an eyebrow to his wife. "But," he said turning to Elizabeth, "I'm up for a party if you are?"

Her face lit up with excitement and Max caught on to her enthusiasm. "I'll invite a few couples out. They can stay overnight, there're plenty of bedrooms."

She tucked her feet under her and leaned forward. "A party would be fun! I'm intrigued to meet some of the local set. What do you think, Nicky?"

Nicola put her glass down on the coffee table between them, she looked at her sister's expectant face and relented. Elizabeth had a low threshold for boredom and she wanted her to enjoy her stay with them. "If it's what you want, why not!"

Elizabeth cornered Max after a dinner spent planning the party. "Any chance you could arrange some light entertainment for me for the party? You remember what I like from our Parisian partying days?"

He grinned salaciously. "I wondered if you'd kept up your bad habits. Tell me what you want and I'll fix it. Maybe you could slip a little something into Nicola's drink - loosen her up a bit."

"Leave her alone, Max," she snapped, her mood changing. "You won't change my sister. She's never been into parties or drugs. Her whole life was based on her excellence in mastering the piano and making a career out of it. Thanks to you she doesn't have that anymore." She dropped her voice to a whisper, "It makes me shudder when I think of what happened."

******

"Weekend party coming up, girls," Max announced cheerfully coming in for breakfast. "I've just had Simon on the phone confirming five couples are arriving Saturday lunchtime," he winked at Elizabeth, "they come bearing gifts."

He turned to his wife: "I'll leave you to organise the guest bedrooms and menus," he said dismissively.

"I'll sort out the entertainment. See you both tonight." He rammed his hat on his head and left the room, whistling through his teeth and looking decidedly pleased with himself.

Nicola sat back in her chair, pushing her half eaten breakfast away from her. "Let's go for a ride, Lizzy. I can feel a headache coming on at the very thought of the weekend. I'm not sure I can cope with it."

Luke shadowed them as they walked their horses through the bush, the gun slung across his horse's saddle.

"Where are we going? I'm roasting."

"I'm going to show you the hide. It's a lovely peaceful place - nice and cool - where we can watch the animals and birds, but they won't see us." They came to the waterhole clearing. "I come here now and again when I want to be alone. Come and have a look."

Elizabeth looked around the rooms, perplexed. "Why on earth would anyone want to sit in this cave-like place and watch anything? It gives me the creeps. Half an hour here would be enough for me."

Elizabeth squashed a line of red ants with her riding boot. "I don't know how you stand living here in the bush. A week or two is fine, but permanently, well, I would go off my head. It's far too isolated. I mean the house is lovely but that's about it."

Nicola walked onto the deck and picked up a pair of binoculars. "Don't get me wrong, Lizzie, I do like people and enjoy company as much as anyone, it's just I don't like Max's friends. They talk too much about nothing in particular, except who's having an affair with whom, and they drink far too much. I'd rather sit here on my own quite frankly."

She turned to her sister and grinned, "In fact that's not a bad idea."

Elizabeth looked at her as though she were mad. "How's he going to explain your absence to his friends?"

Nicola laughed. "You love parties and meeting new people, Lizzie, you can act as hostess! Tell them I've gone to Mombasa or Timbuktu. Tell them anything you like."

"He isn't going to like it."

"I don't care whether he does or he doesn't. I think he'll be delighted to have the house and his guests to himself. He's always telling me how dull and reclusive I am. Well fuck him."

"*Nicola*! I've never heard you swear, especially *that* word! Good lord the next thing you'll be asking me for a cigarette!"

"I would like one actually, thanks," she held out her hand amused at the expression on her sister's face.

For the first time since Elizabeth's arrival, Nicola told her some of the details of her rapidly failing marriage.

"So basically I've decided how I want my life to be. I like my house, I like the country, I love my piano and I like having servants. My plan is to have at least four children who will keep me busy and occupied for years to come."

Elizabeth spluttered on her cigarette and snorted. "And how do you propose to produce four miracle children when you have separate bedrooms and don't have sex?"

"Ah well, that's where you're wrong you see. When I feel like sex I whistle him up, he's always desperate for it. I'll get pregnant eventually."

"Don't be too clever Nicky, Max can be ugly when he wants to be, as I'm sure you now know..."

******

Elizabeth could hear Max shouting at Nicola in her bedroom at the far end of the corridor. She smiled to herself. If Nicola wanted to spend the weekend in her hidden cave in the bush with a bunch of smelly animals, bugs and the house servant, then this was what she would do.

That afternoon Max and Elizabeth had gone to Mr Patel's for some last minute shopping and to collect the mail. They were driving back to the house, when Max casually dropped his hand on her bare knee. "I don't suppose you'd like to try out your sister's bed tonight?"

She smacked his hand away. "What happened in Paris might be inexcusable, but I'm not going to compound things by sleeping with her husband."

"God, you sound just like her," he sighed heavily. "What's a bit of fun between relatives? All cats are grey in the dark, you know; just pretend I'm someone else," he said putting a cigarette in his mouth and lighting it.

"I would find that impossible as I don't particularly like you, Max. I tolerate you for Nicola's sake. If you're bored with her and if all cats are grey in the dark, why don't you pretend she's someone else whilst at least being a decent husband?"

He shrugged and narrowed his eyes. "I could imagine it's you I suppose, you were a good screw if I recall."

They drove in hostile silence for some time.

"I'm sorry I ever introduced you to her." Elizabeth said bitterly.

******

Luke sat outside the hide by a small fire, his cloak wrapped around him against the chill of the night. He watched Nicola, her head bent as she wrote by the light of the hurricane lamp. He had prepared a simple supper of fish and salad, happy not to have Cookie peering over his shoulder to make sure he was preparing it correctly. It was peaceful away from the house, with just the occasional grunt of an animal in the distance.

Luke stood up as Nicola ducked through the small door of the hide and came over to his fire, sitting in the canvas chair he had placed there for her.

A hyena giggled with laughter close to the hide and she shuddered. "I hate that noise. It doesn't sound like an animal at all. Is it close by?"

"It is close but do not be afraid. He is waiting for something to be killed. He will not come near this place with the fire and the lamps, and my gun."

Nicola shuddered. "They frighten me. Do they ever attack humans?"

"They will eat anything killed and left behind by another animal and sometimes they will kill for themselves. But, I think if they were to eat a human, he would have to be dead first."

She shuddered again and hastily changed the subject. "I'd like to learn to shoot Luke, would you teach me?"

162

Elizabeth rubbed her blood shot eyes tiredly and looked around the sitting room. There was no sign of the party which had gone on long into the night before. Winston and Cookie must have been up at dawn to clear up the chaos in the house.

Max's appearance in her bedroom in the early hours of the morning had incensed her. The damn man could not handle rejection. For a fraction of a second she had been tempted to give in to his advances, remembering how adept he had been between the sheets in Paris. He had been furious when she had told him to bugger off and go back to his own room.

They certainly were a wild bunch, Max's friends. She had done her fair share of drinking and smoking, so much so she hadn't needed much encouragement to kick of her shoes and dance on the long table in the dining room, her audience clapping and shouting for more.

All the guests had left after a long liquid lunch and she had been relieved to see the back of them.

Elizabeth stretched out on the chaise outside and fell into a light sleep, only rousing when she heard the crunch of tyres on the gravel drive.

"I guess the party went well?" Nicola said archly, narrowing her eyes and studying her sister.

Elizabeth opened and then closed one eye. "Why are you rubbing your shoulder like that. Have you hurt yourself?"

Nicola smiled brightly. "Luke's teaching me to shoot; I thought it might come in useful one day. I loved it, but now my shoulder aches."

Elizabeth rubbed her eyes and yawned. "What else did you learn down there in your cave?"

"It's not a cave, Lizzy, it's a hide!" she said crossly. "Luke taught me the sounds of the night: hyena, lion, owls, bats and things, it was interesting."

Elizabeth looked at her sister. She loved her dearly, no two sisters could be closer, but she could see how Max could be frustrated with her lack of interest in anything other than the house, the gardens, and her piano - and now she was into animals and bats. The sooner she became pregnant the better.

"Would he teach me to shoot? It might come in handy to know one end of a gun from another in case I get a role in a cowboy movie," she laughed.

"I'm sure he'd be happy to teach you. I'll have a word with him later; at least it'll give you something to do."

******

Max scowled at Elizabeth as they sat down for dinner that evening. Unfolding his napkin he picked up his glass of wine. "So, Luke tells me you want to learn how to use a rifle. I'm sure it's going to be really useful in California," he said sarcastically.

Elizabeth looked at him slyly. "You never know when a predator might be around; it's always a good idea to have something to defend yourself with, don't you think Nicola?"

Nicola watched them and wondered what had happened between them both at the party; there had been some kind of confrontation judging by their bickering.

After a subdued dinner, they retired early. Sometime during the night Elizabeth had awoken startled. Turning over she made a mental note to ask her newly informed sister what kind of an animal would make the sound she had just heard.

The next morning, Elizabeth waited for her sister to join her for breakfast, as had become their routine. After ten more minutes she decided to check on her.

Knocking softly at her door, she pushed it open. "Nicky?" she whispered, "Are you okay?"

Nicola stirred slightly and mumbled, "Be down in a minute. Sorry, must have overslept."

Elizabeth watched her sister help herself from the silver dishes on the sideboard. "Why are you wearing long sleeves? It's going to be roasting hot today. You'll fry in that outfit."

Nicola returned to the table and smiled weakly. "I think I caught too much sun at the hide, I want to keep out of it today."

Elizabeth stabbed at the egg on her plate. "By the way, I heard an odd noise in the night and wanted to test you on your newly acquired knowledge of nocturnal sounds."

Nicola bit her lip, avoiding her sister's eyes.

"It was a kind of yelp," Elizabeth started and then stopped, horrified as tears slid down her sister's cheeks.

Elizabeth sprang out of her chair and went to her. "What is it?"

164

Nicola said nothing, as she lifted her hands to her face her sleeves dropped and Elizabeth saw the bruises.

"What's he done to you? What has the bastard done to you?" Elizabeth demanded with venom in her voice.

"He raped me," she whispered between sobs, burying her head on her sister's shoulder

Chapter Twenty-Seven

Max leaned back in his chair and closed his eyes. His relationship with Nicola had deteriorated to such an extent they barely spoke to each other. He recalled the night he had lost his temper and forced himself on her - the revulsion he saw in her eyes had made him more violent with her, stinging as he was from being rejected by Elizabeth.

He leaned forward and drained his glass, refilling it immediately. Upstairs he could hear her playing and his mind went back over the years to when they lived in Paris. The thought of spending the rest of his life living in the house with a wife who wouldn't speak to him had given him cause to reconsider his options. With another poor sisal crop the bills were mounting up.

Something he needed and wanted was her inheritance. He'd have to try and make her pregnant. That would sort things out.

He would eventually get the money and she would get the child she so desperately wanted, leaving him free to pick up where he would have to leave off now. If this meant giving up his mistress, it would be the price he would have to pay. There were plenty more girls in town who he could get involved with at a later date.

Satisfied with his decision, he topped up his drink, downed it in one and made his way to the music room.

She looked up with surprise and stopped playing.

"Yes?" Her face was a mask of indifference.

"Look Nicola," he said with what he hoped was a conciliatory tone. "I know our marriage is in trouble, and I admit I've been the contributing factor in most cases."

She looked at him stonily, saying nothing.

He cleared his throat and gave her a tentative smile. "I want to have another go at it." He took another step towards her and rested his elbows on the piano. She pulled back from him as he leaned towards her. Then he played his trump card.

"I want to make our marriage work. I think we should start a family."

She rubbed her forehead tiredly with the back of her hand. "What guarantees will I have? I know for a fact you *don't* want children."

He stood up straight and patted his pocket taking out his cigarettes, aware of her hostile eyes watching his every move. He lit one and went back to the window. "I give you my word," he said simply, "it's all I can give you.

"It'll be Christmas soon, we could go to the beach cottage in Watamu. Let's get away from here for a couple of weeks and have another go at things?" He gave her what he hoped was a warm and winning smile.

"I'm prepared to try again..." she said cautiously, and he saw the flare of hope in her eyes. "I'd love to have children."

******

The cottage sat right on the beach under a canopy of rattling palm trees. Its whitewashed rectangular structure, thatched roof and open patio led down to the beach; she found its simplicity refreshing after the formality of Mbabati.

Max, true to his word, was gentle and considerate towards her, and had cut his drinking back to a few glasses of wine in the evening, so much so that the sense of humour she had almost forgotten he had, returned.

Finding herself with the man she had fallen in love with in Paris, she tentatively began to hope a future with him was still a possibility, she longed to be pregnant, to feel the weight of a child in her arms again.

On their return from the coast, Luke was pleased to see they now shared the master bedroom again.

******

Driving around the estate, Luke was the first to notice the thick canopy of vultures dipping and circling in the distance, Max drove towards them to investigate.

The female elephant lay dead in the hot dust next to a dried-up waterhole with both of her tusks missing, her calf standing forlornly beneath the tree a short distance away. Their herd had moved on, unable to help the mother or persuade the calf to leave her.

"Bloody poachers! Come on Luke, let's leave him to his fate, nothing we can do here."

167

Luke looked at the frightened calf. "This baby will need much milk, Bwana Max, for he is very weak."

"I don't bloody care what it needs, what am I supposed to do?"

Luke scratched his head. "I'm thinking this calf should be saved. Miss Nicola could do this..."

Max nodded. He was right, it would give her something to look after and nurture and she would be impressed with his compassion and concern for the calf.

"Good idea Luke," he said smoothly. "I'll go and round up some of the men from the factory; we'll need one of the bigger trucks to transport him in."

He climbed back into his vehicle. "Shoot anything that tries to take him!" he shouted over the noise of the engine. "The vultures can wait. They can have the mother after we've removed the baby."

******

Nicola watched the men off-load the terrified calf, her hand over her mouth with concern.

"What happened?"

"Bloody poachers shot his mother," he said shortly.

"He's so sweet, where are you going to put him?"

"I thought the stables. He'll have a better chance of survival if he's not left alone. I'll need your help."

She nodded, eager to get involved.

"Ask Cookie to bring out all the powdered milk he has in stock. This is going to be one thirsty boy." He turned to Luke and told him to get the stable boys to prepare one of the stalls, with plenty of bedding and blankets.

Once the calf was safely installed in the stables, Luke prepared the powdered milk in a gallon drum.

"He must be on his feet when he feeds, not lying down," Luke told the grooms sternly. "You must be his mother now. Send someone to find some maize plants and ask Cookie if he has any oranges."

Nicola stroked the calf's head, surprised by its docility, murmuring words of encouragement to him. Here, finally, was someone who needed her and her spirits lifted, how unexpected it was of Max to want to save its life.

Over lunch they talked about the calf. "It'll be touch and go," he said, chewing thoughtfully. "Luke seems to know what he's doing. As long as the calf can keep the milk down and digest it, he has a chance of survival."

"What shall we call him?" she asked.

"Why don't you choose a name? I'm going to bring Amber in and see if we can get them to bond."

She raised her eyebrows incredulously. "Has it been done before?"

He pushed his plate aside. "I'm not sure, but elephants have been known to bond with all sorts of different species, so no reason why he shouldn't bond with a horse."

The horses snickered at the unfamiliar scent in the stables. Nicola bent down and stroked the calf's head again. "Your name is going to be Tika," she said.

"Tika?" echoed Max. "What does that mean?"

She smiled at him. "I made it up."

The calf lifted his rubbery trunk and touched Nicola's face and neck, then wobbled over to the curious horse watching him. Amber showed the whites of her eyes and lowered her head, sniffing the new arrival tentatively.

******

Tika had been with them for eight months and followed Amber around the paddock, his comfort blanket draped over his back. Each day Nicola and Luke would walk with him, the dogs joining them.

Nicola held Tika's trunk as they walked along, and asked Luke what they would do when the elephant grew up.

"This elephant must go back to his own family one day, Miss Nicola. He cannot be living here when he is very big."

Later, sitting out on the veranda, she posed the same question to Max. "How can we get Tika to join another herd? I think he's forgotten he's an elephant."

He looked up from cleaning his gun. He told her he'd noticed a breeding herd down to the south of the estate, which might well be his mother's original herd. With a bit of luck they may accept him back, he told her, but Tika needed to be fully independent by then, and realize his natural family had four legs and not two.

169

He squinted down the barrel of the gun; satisfied, he placed it on the table. "Tika must be the first elephant in history to be brought up on Beethovan."

Nicola smiled at the unexpected compliment. It was true; when she played in the afternoon Tika would stand outside the house looking up at the top floor waving his trunk around as if he was the conductor of an orchestra. When he grew bored he'd run off, squeaking and squealing, his blanket flapping around his legs, looking for Amber and the grooms.

With the arrival of Tika, Max had been totally focused on the elephant's survival and well-being. He rarely went into Nairobi now and the weekend parties had ceased. He seemed calmer and happier, and to her joy she found herself pregnant again.

******

It was a Sunday evening and they had retired to the sitting room to read the papers which had arrived with the mail at Mr Patel's shop.

Max folded his paper and reached for his brandy. "I bumped into Jake Henderson a couple of weeks ago; he's back at his ranch." He swirled the brandy around his glass.

Nicola looked up from her magazine. "Jake - who's he?"

"Our closest neighbour. He's a bit reclusive, one of those brooding artist types."

"He sounds interesting," said Nicola. "Did he grow up here?"

"No, his parents were American, they sent him to an aunt in the States to be educated when he was about eight. He must be around thirty-two now."

"Are his parents still living here then?"

He told her how Jake's parents had decided to leave Kenya and retire to the States. Ezekiel, Luke's cousin was left to look after the place, and then Jake had decided he wanted to return to Kenya to live and work.

She interrupted him, "Is he a painter, or a sculptor?"

"He's a painter, I think. I'm not sure. We should invite him over for dinner sometime. His ranch is about an hour's drive from here. I should be able to find a phone number for him."

He looked up at the grandfather clock and putting his hands on his knees he levered himself up, telling her he was going to check on Tika and would she like to come with him.

"I might play for an hour. They say babies in the womb love music. Then I think I'll have an early night."

"Good idea." He kissed her on the forehead and whistled for the dogs to join him. "Babies in the womb love music? What a load of crap," he muttered to himself as he walked towards the stables to check on his other investment - Tika.

He had made one trip to Nanyuki to collect his share of the sale of the ivory. Pity about the bloody calf. He hadn't noticed it down by the water hole when he raised his rifle and shot its mother.

Meanwhile with Nicola pregnant he had ensured his financial future. Whistling happily through his teeth he let himself into the stables.

Chapter Twenty-Eight

Nicola looked at her watch. There was time before lunch to drop in and introduce herself to Jake Henderson. She turned her Land Rover and headed for the house called Leopard's Leap.

It was spread out on two levels with a deep green veranda surrounding it. Lush green plants in tall white pots were scattered along its expanse. Pulling up outside of the front entrance she turned off the engine and hesitated. Perhaps this wouldn't be a good time to call unannounced, the artist might be working and she'd be interrupting him, she knew how irritating that could be.

Before she could change her mind the front door opened and she looked up with a nervous smile, seeing a tall dark haired man with a broad smile on his tanned face coming towards her.

"I'm sorry to just drop in like this," she said getting out of the vehicle as he held her door open. She introduced herself and wiped her hand on her trouser leg. "Sorry I'm a little dusty from the drive!"

She held out her hand and he took it firmly in his own. "I'm delighted to meet you. Come inside."

He led her into an open courtyard with rooms leading off to the left and the right under a covered walkway. In the centre was a small dribbling fountain. Curtains of bougainvillea in purple and white cascaded down the four alcove walls, blending effortlessly with potted palm trees.

"Goodness!" she said smiling, "how very Italian this is, it's lovely."

"Yes, it was built by an Italian; it's extraordinary how people want to bring a little bit of their home country into Africa - a bit like Mbabati with its Englishness. I've never understood it myself," he indicated to the alcove on the left of the courtyard.

"Let's sit in there, it's supposed to be the sitting room but I've made it my studio, the light's better. Ah, perfect timing Ezekiel. Please bring some of your excellent lemonade for Mrs Gray." Nicola smiled a greeting at the cheerful round faced Kenyan.

Nicola studied the light airy room with interest. A long trestle table, spattered with paint, stretched the length of one wall, its surface covered with containers holding brushes and tubes of paint. Boxes and clay pots jostled for position alongside a variety of petrified pieces of twisted branches, bird feathers, long yellow grasses and twigs.

Propped up on the table was a portrait of the local Maasai dressed in their traditional flame red cloaks, shuka's, and intricate bead necklaces added a glorious dash of colour to his work. Jake watched her, saying nothing.

Slightly unnerved by his silence, she turned and looked at him. He was sitting near the window, his long legs stretched out in front of him, his hands laced behind his head. His dark hair touched his shoulders and hung over his forehead shading his dark blue eyes; his high cheekbones and full lips reminded her of an Irish actor she had seen a photograph of in a magazine somewhere. His open necked shirt revealed the clean etched lines of his collar bones under his tanned skin. Realizing she was staring at him she hastily dropped her gaze.

"May I?" she said, gesturing with her glass, indicating she'd like to look at some of his work displayed around the room.

He smiled slowly, mesmerised by the beautiful woman standing in his studio. "Of course."

Huge canvases lined the walls, some hung, the others propped against the wall. He painted with passion using brilliant colours; the subjects ranged from fiery sunsets, vast bush landscapes and studies of the abundant wildlife.

"These are stunning, Jake," she murmured unable to keep the admiration out of her voice "They must sell well?"

He told her they did, and that he had galleries representing him in New York City and in Europe. He gestured around the room. "They keep me busy. I try to get to them all, during the course of the year. Their clientele always like to meet the artist."

"How lovely to travel to all those great cities," she said wistfully. "Which one is your favourite?"

He sat forward and scratched his cheek thoughtfully. "I like the architecture and culture of Europe, but this is my favourite place - the bush. I'm thinking of spending a lot more time here. I'd like to spend more time painting, and less time sitting on a plane or in a hotel room."

"I imagine painting must be a solitary profession, especially out here?" she said turning back to study a painting of a single male elephant; the backdrop was Mount Kenya, the heavy skies bruised dark blue and purple.

"I enjoy my own company, and I work better alone; besides, now I've met my next door neighbour I know where to go if I ever get lonely."

She looked up quickly, completely thrown by his remark. He stood up and leaned against the window watching her, his soft smile diluting any offence his words might have caused. The sun glinted off the heavy signet ring on his small finger. She frowned, unnerved by her unexpected attraction to this man. She turned back to the canvases and pretended to study the painting of the solitary elephant again.

Jake came and stood next to her. "So," he said softly, "what do you do, Nicola, to fill your hours whilst Max is out and about on the estate? You don't strike me as the sort of woman who's content to stay home and watch the servants cook and clean?"

She was acutely aware of his proximity and closed her eyes trying to compose herself. She cleared her throat nervously.

"I like to ride, and I love my house, but my greatest passion is my piano. I spend a lot of time playing even though my only audiences are the monkeys, the birds, the dogs and Tika."

He raised an eyebrow in question and she laughed up at him. "Tika's an orphaned elephant we've adopted. He follows me around like a puppy - a big one."

"You have a slight accent - French I think?"

She walked over to the window and looked out over the wild garden and the bush beyond. "Yes." She gave an audible sigh. "I miss Paris, the beautiful shops and restaurants, the old buildings and the river, but this is my home now..."

"Max told me a little about you. I bumped into him at the club a few weeks ago. At some point I'd like to capture you on canvas, if you'd allow me to."

"I, um, I don't think it will be possible to capture me on canvas as you put it. I'm sure an artist of your calibre would charge a fortune, and the estate gobbles up every penny we make. Anyway I really must go. Sorry I didn't call first; your telephone doesn't seem to be working."

Jake was watching her, his expression amused, as she put her now empty glass back on the tray.

"Am I making you nervous, Nicola, or do you always talk so fast?"

She didn't know how to answer. Perhaps her pregnancy was making her light headed.

"Would you like to come for dinner sometime?"

"How about next Thursday?" he said without hesitation.

"Lovely, I'll look… I mean we'll look forward to it. Will you stay the night? It's quite a drive back in the dark?"

"No thanks, I enjoy driving through the bush at night; gives me time to think."

"I really must be going," she said again, her thoughts all over the place.

Flustered, she made her way past the courtyard and out to her vehicle, Jake following her. She turned to him as she fumbled in her pocket for her keys. "Well, it was nice to meet you, Jake..." Her voice trailed off as he took her hands in his and kissed her on both cheeks, she dropped the keys in surprise. He smiled as he bent down to retrieve them, and opened the Land Rover door for her.

"Goodbye Nicola, see you on Thursday...something I'm more than looking forward to."

******

Jake sipped his glass of wine and took another mouthful of the excellent roasted guinea fowl, as he watched her discreetly. Nicola was one of the most beautiful women he had ever seen, with her green eyes and blonde hair swept up on top of her head; she was wearing a soft, apricot-coloured dress which made her skin glow. He had fallen for her the moment he had met her.

Realizing he was staring at her, he turned and found Max watching him.

"You seem distracted Jake. I was asking you how long you planned to stay in Kenya?"

"Quite a while, I need to produce a lot more work to fill the galleries, it should keep me busy."

Max sat back in his chair, looking bored as he twirled his now empty wine glass. "Nicola, my dear, perhaps you'll play for us now? Luke can bring the coffee up to the music room."

"I'm sure Jake would rather talk than listen to me play," she said. "He might hate classical music. Not everyone loves it you know."

175

Jake smiled at her encouragingly and held her eyes with his own, a fraction longer than was necessary. "I'd love to hear you play." He stood up and came to her, pulling her chair out. "Shall we?"

In the music room the candles glowed and the fire warmed the cool night air. The coffee had been served and as Nicola prepared to play she was aware the ever faithful Luke had melted back into the shadows of the room to watch and listen to her.

Max lit a cigarette and warmed his brandy by the fire. "Come and sit, Jake, we can chat while she plays."

He shook his head. "I'd like to listen if you don't mind?"

She made herself comfortable, feeling unaccountably nervous she lifted her arms and lowered her hands to the keyboard, acutely aware of Jake's presence.

He listened, mesmerized, unaware of Max's close scrutiny. Nicola was a superb pianist, and with such talent and beauty he wondered how she had ended up in Kenya, married to a man who scarcely knew how to hold his temper.

He had heard stories about his host, and none of them had been flattering - he was a womaniser of some note. Jake was an astute judge of people and animals, he had studied them for years with his work, he had noticed how tense and nervous Nicola was during dinner; as skittish as an antelope sensing danger nearby. Max had treated her as though she was invisible.

Over the years he had had affairs with beautiful women, but all of them paled into insignificance compared to the woman who sat at the piano playing so exquisitely. A woman, if he was not mistaken, in the early stages of pregnancy.

Chapter Twenty-Nine

Max watched her walking unhurriedly through the gardens wearing a wide brimmed hat and a long white dress. He supposed most men would find their pregnant wife attractive; he hadn't found this with her first pregnancy and he certainly didn't now. She wasn't going to be happy with his news.

Her mother's sudden death three months ago had devastated her, but the thought of her baby had gone some way to help her cope with her grief. He had managed to sound sympathetic and caring but in reality he was more interested in the impending trust fund she would inherit.

Nicola sank gratefully into a chair. "I feel as big as a hippo and just as ungainly, I can feel the baby moving around," she said happily, stroking her stomach. "Only a few more weeks to go..."

"I'm going hunting on Thursday," he said abruptly. "I'll be gone a week."

She looked at him incredulously. "You didn't mention you were planning a hunting trip. Surely you could have put it off until the baby's born!"

"Afraid not. A bunch of guys from the club said they'd had a cancellation and want me to make up the numbers. I need a break so I'm going."

"You can't leave me here on my own," she said, her voice rising angrily, "what happens if the baby comes early?"

"Stop making such a fuss for God's sake! It's not due for another month yet."

"You don't care about me or the baby, do you?" she said bitterly. "It's all about *you* and what *you* want isn't it?"

"You're being ridiculous, Nicola. I suggest you go and lie down for a while instead of sitting here and working yourself into a state. I can't stand hysterical women."

She stood up awkwardly. "Well, go on your damn hunting trip, no doubt you'll make a detour to go and visit your mistress in Nairobi!"

He watched her limp away and suppressed a laugh. If nothing else she was astute. How the hell had she worked out he was back with his mistress?

He shouted for Luke who came hurrying from the kitchen. "Bwana Max?"

"Get my guns cleaned and ready for Thursday. I'm going on a hunting trip."

Luke looked at him. "You are leaving Miss Nicola here alone?" he asked with disbelief.

"For Christ's sake Luke, don't you start! You're her bloody shadow, how can she be alone? I'll be back before the damn baby is born. Bring the drinks tray to the study."

******

Luke woke when he heard her screaming; struggling into his trousers and shirt he ran across the garden and into the house. He knocked on the bedroom door before entering.

"Luke, the baby's coming! You must get someone to help me!"

Luke took her hand in both of his. "I will get someone from the village, Miss Nicola. There is a woman who has delivered many babies, she will help you. I will get Cookie to sit with you. I will go as fast as I can."

He ran to the garage and leapt into the Land Rover. He had travelled many times with Bwana Max and had studied his driving, it would not be too difficult. After a shaky start the vehicle jerked and bucked down the driveway before catapulting out onto the bush road.

Half an hour later he returned with the midwife from his village. Tika was standing on the lawn watching the house.

The old African woman entered the house and stopped dead, her eyes wide with wonder. Suddenly a scream pierced the air and she hurriedly followed Luke up the stairs.

The midwife leant over the bed and put her hand on Nicola's forehead. "You must not be frightened, memsahib, I have delivered many, many babies. You must follow what I say and all will be well."

She dismissed Luke with instructions to bring hot water and towels.

Luke paced around in the kitchen, each scream putting his teeth on edge. He cursed Max for going hunting and leaving his wife alone at a time like this. He stopped his pacing and ran from the kitchen into the sitting room. He'd driven the Land Rover and was sure he could

178

work the phone. It seemed you picked up the instrument and waited for a voice, then asked for who you wanted to talk to.

******

Although it was two in the morning Jake was still awake and working. Within two minutes he was racing out of the driveway and on his way to her.

He pulled up in front of the house, leaving the vehicle door swinging open as he raced up the front steps where Luke was waiting for him. "How is she, Luke?"

"The woman from the village has been with her for some time now. We are not allowed to enter the room, only allowed to bring hot water and towels. You must not go in there, Bwana Jake, she is fierce this midwife and will not allow men in the business of childbirth..." His voice trailed off as he heard the lusty cry of a baby, followed by the squeals and grunts of Tika who had also heard it.

Jake shook Luke's hand. "I'm not sure what I can do here. Her bloody husband should be with her, not me."

"This is true Bwana Jake."

The old midwife stood at the top of the staircase and looked down at them, and then she beamed. "Miss Nicola has a fine baby girl. Not as fat as I would like but she is healthy."

Luke clapped his hands softly. "May I do anything, Mama," he asked her, using the African title of respect for an older woman.

She told him to come and help tidy the bedroom and take the towels and water away. Then she looked at Jake standing helplessly at the foot of the stairs, his arms held loosely at his sides.

"Are you the husband?" her tone was suspicious.

"No, Mama," he answered quietly, "but, by God, I wish I was," he added under his breath.

Luke crept into the bedroom and gathered the towels, looking over his shoulder to make sure the midwife was not around. He padded over to the bed and looked down at Nicola and her baby.

"You have a fine girl baby, very beautiful." He whispered. "You must sleep now. Luke is here to look after you both."

"Luke!" the old African midwife hissed, having come back into the room unnoticed, "It is not your place to be here. Make some tea for the mother and bring it quickly."

179

Luke scuttled out of the room smiling broadly.

******

Jake sat on the bottom step wondering what he could do to help. When Luke appeared with a tea tray he leapt up and deftly took it from him. He knocked on the bedroom door and found himself face to face with the midwife.

"I'd like to see her, Mama, I'm a friend and came from my ranch to help."

She grinned at him, showing her gums. "Come in, Bwana, but do not wake her."

Jake sat gingerly on the edge of the bed and stroked her arm. "You have a gorgeous daughter, Nicola. Well done."

At the sound of his voice, she opened her eyes. "Jake… what are you doing here?"

"Luke phoned me. I wanted to make sure you were alright." He touched the baby's cheek with his finger. "Not only are you a brilliant pianist but you make beautiful children, she's gorgeous. What are you going to call her?"

Nicola gazed at her child fiercely, "Catherine. And no-one will *ever* take her away from me."

"Well of course no-one will take her away from you. She's your daughter," he said laughing with surprise. He leaned forward and kissed her on the forehead and then, without thinking, he kissed her softly on the lips.

"I'd better go before Mama comes charging up the stairs to see if I'm still here. She's terrifying!"

"I'm glad you came..." She closed her eyes, drifting off to sleep holding the baby in the crook of her arm, still feeling the touch and the taste of his lips on hers.

******

Jake lay on his bed in the guestroom. He had only seen her a few times since the dinner here at the house, the night he had first heard her play. Max had invited him for lunch a few times after that, but ensured Jake had spent no time alone with his pregnant wife.

180

"Why bother with pregnant women when Nairobi is full of bright young things," he had said pointedly as he walked him to his vehicle. "I can give you a couple of phone numbers if you like - and recommendations. I've tried and tested a good few of them."

Disgusted, Jake had driven away. From the moment he'd met her he'd felt a bond with her, but now with the baby perhaps she'd be able to repair her marriage and be happy. As for himself, he was looking forward to some female company of his own.

He was going to spend four months visiting the galleries that represented him, then a few weeks in the South of France with an old girlfriend who lived in Nice.

Just after dawn the next morning, he drove reluctantly back to his house trying to block out the memory of the softness of her lips and the taste of her.

Chapter Thirty

Catherine was just over a year old and already starting to walk. After she was born Max had suggested they find a nanny for her but Nicola refused. She wanted to look after her baby herself and Luke was more than happy to take over when she needed a break.

Nicola watched her daughter squealing with laughter as Luke held her up to see Tika who rumbled happily as he touched her with his trunk before searching Luke's pockets for oranges.

The birth of her child had ended her deteriorating relationship with Max. He had not bonded with Catherine in any way and now resented all the time Nicola spent with her. He had moved into another bedroom, citing her interrupted sleep to feed the baby as the reason.

They conversed politely during meals but apart from this she saw little of him. Her thoughts often turned to Jake but she was determined to suppress her feelings for him.

Elizabeth had not come back to Kenya, much as she had wanted to see the baby. After her last visit, and the blistering row they had had when she had confronted him about his despicable behaviour with Nicola, Max had made it clear to her that she wasn't welcome in his house again.

Chapter Thirty-One

New York
Jake

From the window of Susan's apartment on Fifth Avenue, Jake looked down on the snow-covered sidewalks of New York City and thought about his next exhibition in Palm Springs, his last before he returned to Kenya.

"Jake, honey, come and sit, or do something useful like putting a record on."

"Sorry, I was miles away, Susan. What would you like to hear?"

Susan Cohen was his New York agent and owned a gallery on Madison Avenue. She was one of the toughest women he had ever met in the City, but she was an excellent agent. Unlike most women here in Manhattan she had a complete disregard for how she looked; her passion was the world of art. In her mid-thirties her hair was cropped short and already shot with grey, her ample figure invariably covered in a black polo neck sweater and black trousers; her only concession to colour was a slash of bright red lipstick and scarlet nail polish.

"After that heavenly, but outrageously expensive dinner you treated me to, I'm in the mood for something classical. You'll find the records on the left-hand side of the cupboard. I'll go put the coffee on."

Jake shuffled through the records and, overwhelmed by the choice, he gave up. "Tell you what," he said joining her in the kitchen, "you find something and I'll bring the coffee."

"I want you to try your hand at portraits, Jake, expand your repertoire," Susan said over her shoulder when he returned from the kitchen. "I still need your wildlife work, which sells well here. But portraits seem to be coming back into fashion and there' a demand for them. Maybe try some of those Maasai warriors with their gorgeous red robes, or cute African kids with their big brown adorable eyes?"

The record Susan had chosen clattered onto the turntable as she sat down and reached for her coffee. Yes, he thought, half listening to the music softly playing in the background, he could certainly do some portraits.

Susan stood up again and walked over to the record player, turning up the volume. "This gal sure can play Beethoven. This piece is one of my favourites and commonly known as The Emperor, makes me want to weep, it's so beautiful." She sat down again and closed her eyes as she listened.

Jake felt a shiver run through him, and in his mind's eye he saw her, surrounded by candlelight, seated at her piano. He too closed his eyes as the music filled the room. He knew whose portrait he wanted to paint when he got back to Kenya.

The last note hung in the air and then there was silence. "It's the only record I have of hers. I've looked everywhere for more but no luck."

Jake opened his eyes, and asked her who the pianist was.

"I'll get the sleeve and you can read what little is known about her."

Jake stared at Nicola as she looked serenely back at him. "I don't believe it!" he muttered to himself, feeling a jolt go through him.

"Don't believe what? Have you heard her play before?" Not waiting for a reply she continued, "I saw her perform at Carnegie Hall here in the city. She was magnificent; I'll never forget that performance, you could have heard a pin drop when she finished, then the whole place erupted." She grinned at him. "You know how rowdy and boisterous we Americans can be!"

She leaned back in her chair remembering the only article she had ever read about Nicola DuPont. "There's a bit of mystery about her though. She lived in Paris and her last few performances there were so bad she was booed off the stage.

"Rumour has it she married an African and went to live in the jungle somewhere, she was never heard of again."

"May I borrow this?" Jake said holding up the record cover.

As he walked along Fifth Avenue, the record tucked under his arm, his mind was racing. Nicola had told him she had played the piano from childhood and he'd listened spellbound as she played for him that night at Mbabati. Yet, nothing had been said about a career as a concert pianist.

The only thing he wanted to do now was get the exhibition in Palm Springs over with and be on his way back to Kenya. He badly wanted to see her again.

Chapter Thirty-Two

Nicola parked under the shade of a tree and turned off the engine. Holding Catherine, she walked towards the club breathing a sigh of relief as she entered its cool entrance. She found a table in the corner and with Catherine sitting on her lap she ordered some sandwiches.

Engrossed in the paper, she didn't see him enter the room or his approach to her.

"Hello Nicola," he said quietly, his voice interrupting her concentration.

"Jake!" Nicola felt her cheeks getting hot. "When did you get back?"

"A couple of days ago." He bent down and stroked Catherine's cheek. "Hello gorgeous, you've grown a bit." Catherine rewarded him with a smile and latched onto his finger with her hand.

He sat down still attached to Catherine. "You look as beautiful as ever. Are you still playing your piano?"

"Of course, although sometimes I think the animals, birds and monkeys would prefer something a bit racier than Chopin. Ezekiel told Luke you had gone to America. Why don't you come for dinner and tell us about your trip?"

"Only if you promise to play for me again. May I?" He lifted his camera and took a photograph of them both. He indicated the camera. "My new baby. Have you still got your young elephant, Tika?"

Nicola nodded. She told him about the resident herd of elephants who seemed interested in him, and how they hoped he would join them at some stage and go back to the wild.

"How's Max?" he asked, his voice flat with disinterest.

Nicola looked down, avoiding his eyes. "I don't see much of him." She stood up. "I'll call and fix a date for dinner."

Jake kissed her on the cheek and as she made to move away he said quietly. "I missed you - you've no idea how much."

"I missed you too," she whispered unthinkingly. Flustered, she lifted Catherine up, grabbed her bag and left the room, unnerved once again by the way she reacted when he touched her.

Tika lifted his trunk and caught the scent of the herd of elephant grazing across the dry river bed. The two grooms sat patiently under a tree waiting to see who would make the first move.

Tika turned back from watching the herd and approached them, he wrapped his trunk around first one and then the other. They spoke to him softly in Swahili encouraging him.

Tika made his way towards the river bed, his now ragged, and faded, blanket flapping around his legs. He looked back once, before crossing over to join his new family. The matriarch of the herd explored him with her trunk and, as if making up her mind, snatched the blanket from his back and threw it in the air.

The herd moved off leaving puffs of dust behind them. When it settled all that was left was the blanket and the sound of guinea fowl as they called to each other. Rising from their shady spot the grooms collected the tattered blanket and headed back to the stables.

******

Luke, holding Catherine's hand, made his way to the stables. Catherine skipped along next to him calling for Tika. Luke lifted her up and showed her the empty stable.

Puzzled, Catherine looked into Luke's face. "Tika?"

"He has gone to his own family now, little one, just as you are with yours. But he will come back to visit us when he is ready."

Catherine's eyes filled with tears. "No more Tika, Luke?"

He hugged her. "No more Tika, little one, but we still have Monty and Maggie. Look, here they come now."

Holding the inconsolable child in his arms, Luke walked back to the house to let Miss Nicola know Tika had finally gone to be with his own kind.

******

Nicola heard the sound of Jake's Land Rover in the drive and her stomach tightened as it always did when he visited.

He'd come to the house frequently since his return, always with his camera at the ready, somehow timing his visits when Max was busy with the workers in the drying sheds, or away on one of his

186

regular trips to Nairobi. Catherine's little face always lit up when she saw him.

Nicola lifted Catherine off her lap where they'd been colouring a picture together, and the child ran to the front door. "Jake, Jake. Tika gone!" Catherine said when he appeared in the hallway.

He swept her up in his arms and kissed the top of her head. "Yes, gorgeous, so I've been told, that's why I've come to see you. I have something special for you."

Luke showed Jake into the sitting room and Nicola stood up smiling. "Hello Jake. I feel as though I've lost another child." Jake kissed her on both cheeks, then touched her lips with his own.

Puzzled, he looked at her. "Another child?"

Rattled by her mistake she asked Luke to bring tea for them and juice for Catherine. The child trailed after Luke as though he might somehow have hidden Tika in the kitchen.

Jake opened the envelope he had been carrying, placing some photographs on the table in front of him. Catherine, after searching the kitchen, came back to the sitting room and climbed onto his lap.

She squeaked with delight when she saw the photograph he had taken of her holding onto Tika's trunk and laughing up at him.

"This photograph is just for you, gorgeous. We can put it in a frame and you can have it next to your bed, so when you miss Tika you can look at him and talk to him as if he's still here."

Catherine turned and squashed her nose against his cheek. He hugged her and keeping his arms around her, showed Nicola the other photographs he had taken. "I like this one of the house, with you standing in the shadow of the window. I think it gives the house, and you, a mysterious feel…"

For the next hour they discussed the photographs, and his plans to produce a book. Catherine fell asleep in his arms.

"Are you alright, Nicola?" he whispered, reaching for her hand. "You seem preoccupied."

She nodded and removed her hand from his when she heard Luke's footsteps. "Can you stay for dinner? Max has gone to Nairobi for a few days."

"I'd like that. I want to speak to him about starting on your portrait. Have you mentioned it to him yet?"

"Yes I have, he thinks it's a great idea. He wants to chat to you about it when he gets back, whenever that might be..."

Chapter Thirty-Three

Do you have any long gowns Nicola? Jake asked, not looking up from the drawing he was helping Catherine with.

"Yes, many in fact, I used to..." She stopped herself mid-sentence. "Why?"

"I'd like to paint you sitting at your piano wearing something long and elegant, pale blue if possible?" He looked up at her, in his mind's eye he could already see the finished piece.

She went upstairs to her bedroom and rifled through her dresses, knowing exactly which one she would choose. Changing into it she returned to the sitting room.

Jake whistled softly when he saw her. "Perfect." The blue strapless gown with a full skirt billowed around her as she sat. She smiled at the open admiration in his eyes.

"Mummy you look like a princess! You look so pretty."

"Yes, gorgeous, indeed she does, your daddy is a lucky man."

Max had been enthusiastic about the project. "If times get hard we can always sell it, eh Nicola. Him being famous and all that."

She had cringed at his crudeness in front of Jake.

Now Jake turned to Nicola, telling her he was ready to start work. She bent down and hugged her daughter. "Luke will look after you whilst Mummy is busy darling. Be a good girl now." Catherine, holding his hand, happily followed Luke into the kitchen.

Following her up the staircase to the music room, Jake closed the door firmly behind him.

He positioned her at the piano and arranged the skirts of her dress around the seat.

Only the soft tick of the clock disturbed the peace of the room as he worked. Twice he adjusted the position of her arm, his touch sending a frisson of now familiar pleasure through her.

Each day he made the journey to the house and worked on the portrait. Nicola eagerly looked forward to the hours they would spend together. When Jake felt he had captured the very essence of her he moved the unfinished work to his own house, and worked from the photographs he had taken. The time he'd spent sketching her had given him a legitimate excuse to look at her for hours.

He was in love with her.

During these sessions, Nicola learnt more about Jake's life - his childhood at Leopard's Leap, his years at school in America, his passion for painting, and his Irish-American parents who had finally gone back to the States.

"Now it's your turn, why don't you tell me about you, before you came to Kenya?"

She shook her head. Puzzled at her reticence, but now understanding it, he bent to the canvas and they finished the session in comfortable silence.

******

Jake stepped back to evaluate his work. He was more than satisfied with what he had produced. He'd managed to capture not only her beauty and coolness but also a sense of mystery about her - much like the woman herself he thought.

The following day in Nairobi, sitting on the terrace of the Norfolk Hotel, his mind was preoccupied with thoughts of Nicola and the portrait, and how it would look when hung in the entrance hall of Mbabati. As he reached for his beer he spotted Max sitting at a table at the far end of the terrace, his arm around a woman with short blonde hair. At the same moment Max noticed him and beckoned to him. Reluctantly he knew he would have to go over.

"Jake! Unusual to see you in town. Meet a friend of mine, this is Sara."

"I've completed your *wife's* portrait, Max," he said pointedly, ignoring the woman at his side. "I plan to take it out to your house tomorrow and hang it. Will you be around?"

"Doubt it, old boy. But you go ahead and send me the bill." He turned his attention back to Sara, as Jake walked angrily away.

As Max drained his glass he made a mental note. He'd have to call in and see his contacts on the way back to Mbabati. To pay for the bloody portrait he'd have to shoot another elephant and make the money from the sale of the tusks. Pity Tika was still too young to be taken out - but he'd be a good investment somewhere down the line.

189

Nicola and Catherine sat on the stairs watching Luke, Cookie and Jake struggle to get the huge portrait up on the wall.

Jake adjusted the frame slightly and stood back, his shirt sticking to his back with the effort and the heat. He lifted his camera and took several quick shots.

Catherine clapped her hands and bounced down the stairs. "Look Mummy, it's you!"

Jake lifted her up to get a closer look. "Yes, it's Mummy and very beautiful she is too. Like it Nicola?"

He turned to look at Nicola who was gazing at the portrait, her lips slightly parted.

"Very much - you've immortalized me! Let's have a glass of champagne and celebrate."

They sat on the stairs, close together, admiring the portrait as they sipped their champagne. Catherine was in the kitchen with Luke busy drawing her own version of the portrait.

"Well, let's hope Max is pleased with it, Jake, he should be back sometime soon."

"Actually, I saw him at the Norfolk yesterday..." he admitted.

"Oh, did you ask him when he would be back - or was he with one of his women friends?" she asked carelessly.

He looked at her and she saw in his eyes the answer to her question.

"You need to think about your life, Nicola, and how you're going to spend the rest of it," he said more abruptly than he meant to.

She looked away from him. "I can't divorce him, I'm too much of a Catholic to do that. God I wish I could see my sister," she said tearfully. "Elizabeth hasn't even seen Catherine yet and she's nearly three. She and Max had a huge fight before she left and he's banned her from the house, he won't even let me speak to her."

He put his arm around her. "Why don't you come to my place and call her from there, you can talk for as long as you want."

Wordlessly she put her arms around his neck and kissed him.

Chapter Thirty-Four

I'm going to Paris for a couple of months, Max announced without warning as he folded his newspaper and threw it down on the sitting room table. "I need to get out of bloody Africa for a while."

Nicola looked up surprised and pleased. "Oh, I'd love to go back to Paris!"

"Well you can't," he said emphatically, "I've things to attend to and I can't afford to take you and the kid as well. Anyway with your ridiculous fear of flying it would take weeks to get to Europe."

"Don't you think I'd like to get out of your bloody Africa? To see my own country again? Don't you think I've at least earned that right?" she demanded, her voice rising angrily with disappointment.

"Frankly," he snapped, "you've earned absolutely nothing." He stood up. "And don't get any clever ideas about running away when I've gone. One wrong move and I'll take Catherine away from you as well. Is that clear?"

He strode out of the sitting room and once inside his study he slammed the door. He sat down heavily in his chair and looked at the marble busts on their plinth, on either side of the fireplace; they stared blindly back at him. In a temper he threw his brandy balloon at one of them. It hit the implacable marble cheek and shattered on impact leaving a brown tearful streak down its cheek. Minutes later there was a knock at the door.

"Bwana Max?"

"Bugger off, Luke," he bellowed. "I didn't call you. Is there no place in this bloody house where a man can be on his own for five minutes without someone banging on the sodding door!"

******

The following week Nicola rode to the hide. Sitting alone with her diary open in front of her, she saw a herd of elephant appear from the dense bush and make their way towards the waterhole. A young male lifted his trunk and sniffed the air. She caught her breath - it was Tika.

He had picked up her scent, she was sure, but he couldn't see her. He had grown impressively in the three years since she'd last seen

191

him. Catherine would be happy to know he'd stayed with the herd he had chosen to adopt. She watched him until, satiated, he joined the herd and moved on again.

Nicola stood up at the sound of a horse approaching the entrance of the hide, surprised at the intrusion. It was Jake.

"Hello Nicola, I thought I'd find you here in your secret place, Luke said you'd be here." he said looking down at her. "I had a bit of a job trying to remember where it was. God it's good to see you."

She watched him dismount, absurdly happy to see him again. Over the past three years the demand for his work had increased to such an extent he'd spent less time in Kenya and more time abroad. Whenever he returned he made a point of seeing her at the earliest possible opportunity.

I'm in love with him, she admitted to herself, as he dismounted and walked towards her, completely and utterly in love with him.

"Hello Jake, yes here I am, hiding away from the world, or maybe the world is hiding away from me! Come in, I'm sure you could use a drink, God its hot today isn't it?"

She poured him a glass of cold beer. "I've just seen Tika! He looks incredible. When did you get back from London?"

"Yesterday."

Without thinking he pulled her into his arms. "I missed you. I thought about you constantly. I couldn't wait to get back."

He pushed the hair back from her face and kissed her hungrily on the lips. "I missed you too," she said, tightening her arms around him and returning his kiss.

Reluctantly she disentangled herself from his arms and sat down, her legs trembling at the force of emotion she was feeling. "We both know what we want Jake, but it's too dangerous. It would mean risking everything. He would take Catherine away from me and that's something I can't even begin to think about. She's all I have, I just can't do it. I can't…"

He stood looking down at her, knowing they had reached the crossroads.

He knelt down in front of her and put his hands on her shoulders. "I'll never hurt you or force you to do anything you don't want to do. All I know is that I want you, I want to be with you, but I can wait - I won't let you put Catherine at risk, or yourself. If this is all I can have of you then it'll have to be enough. One day Catherine will be all grown up - I'll wait for you for as long as it takes."

He stood up and looked out over the bush wondering how many years it might be, how many years he had committed himself to.

"How's Max? Not that I really care much," he said indifferently, fighting his desire to kiss her again.

"He's going to Europe. He won't take us with him."

"Good news as far as I'm concerned." He grinned at her and took a deep swallow of his drink. "Why don't you invite your sister out while he's away? It's the perfect opportunity…

She launched herself from the chair and into his arms, covering his face with kisses. "Whoa, steady on," he said laughing, "just an idea - but a good one obviously!"

"Oh Jake," she said looking at him, her eyes shining with anticipation, "it's a brilliant idea, something I've dreamed about for months. But…"

"But what?"

"If Max found out he'd be furious, he won't have Elizabeth in the house…"

"It's time you put your foot down Nicola, to hell with him. Have a word with Luke, Cookie and Winston, they're far more loyal to you than to Max, he doesn't have to know anything about her visit. If he should find out what's the worst thing he can do, that he hasn't already done to you? Go on invite her out, it might be the only opportunity you'll ever get."

She twisted her hands in her lap. "But if he should find out…."

"Alright, how about this for another idea. She can stay with me, that way Max hasn't got a leg to stand on - would that make it easier for you?"

She looked at him and narrowed her eyes. "I think I would prefer to take the chance and have her at Mbabati - you're way too attractive and she's an outrageous flirt - I don't want to tempt fate. I wouldn't sleep at nights knowing she was with you and I wasn't. No she can stay with me where I can keep an eye on her."

He threw back his head and laughed before pulling her into his arms again. "Don't trust me eh? I kind of like it that you want to keep me all to yourself…"

He closed his eyes. If this was all he could have then it would have to be enough.

193

Chapter Thirty-Five

Nicola breathed a sigh of relief as she saw Max's retreating Land Rover turn out of the drive.

Elizabeth had leapt at the chance to get away from California and spend time with her sister and niece.

"It's perfect timing, Nicky," she told her over the phone. "I've no work at the moment. Will you collect me from the airport?"

"Jake will collect you, Lizzie."

"Jake? Is he a new member of staff?"

Nicola looked over at Jake. "He's a friend, you'll like him, probably too much knowing you!"

Jake watched Nicola's animated face as she talked to her sister on his phone. When she rang off he took her into his arms, breathing in the scent of her hair as he held her. Lifting her chin he kissed her and was rewarded with a long and lingering kiss in return.

******

"How will I recognize her?" he asked.

"Don't worry, you will. The last time I saw her she had short spiky dark hair, but that could have changed. She's an actress, as I told you, so goodness knows what she'll look like. You heard me describe you, I'm sure you'll find each other," she said grinning.

"You're up to something…"

"Absolutely nothing," Nicola smiled sweetly, "trust me, you'll know it's her - she knows how to make an entrance especially when there's an attractive man waiting for her. She'll make a bee line for you!"

******

The Land Rover approached the front door of Mbabati and Jake braked; a pall of dust settled over the vehicle. Elizabeth pulled the scarf from her head, took off her sunglasses and dusted down the front of her white linen jacket. "It would have been nice to have a roof to go with this Land Rover, Jake," she said dryly.

The front door flew open and Nicola raced towards her, the dogs barking behind her. They hugged and kissed each other, both talking at the same time. Catherine watched as she held Luke's hand.

"That's my aunt, Luke! Do you think she's brought me a little present from America?" Luke squeezed her hand reassuringly.

Nicola shooed the dogs away and beckoned for her daughter who, overcome with all the excitement and her first meeting with her aunt, promptly burst into tears.

Jake mounted the steps two at a time and took her hand. "Come on, gorgeous, don't be shy. Say hello."

"Why honey, you're as brown as a nut and you look just like your mother when she was a little girl, give me your hand and you can show me where I'm going to sleep." Her eyes big with wonder and her cheeks still wet with tears, Catherine slipped her hand into Elizabeth's and led her into the entrance hall. Jake, Nicola and Luke followed.

Elizabeth slowed to a standstill in front of the portrait. "Fantastic!" she murmured. "Who did this, Nicky?"

Nicola raised her eyebrow indicating Jake.

Elizabeth hugged him impulsively. "It's more than fantastic - it's extraordinary." She turned back to the portrait and studied it. Shaking her head, she looked down. "Now where's the little brown girl who's going to show me my room?"

That evening they dined together, Catherine was now glued to Elizabeth's side and followed her everywhere. In honour of her aunt she had even put on a dress instead of wearing her normal shorts and tee shirt. No shoes though.

Elizabeth leaned over and hugged her niece. "I think I'm going to call you Cat, not Catherine. With your little brown body and green eyes you remind me of a Burmese cat. Yes, that's what I'm going to call you - Cat."

Catherine giggled. "Cat," she repeated and grinned at her mother. "I like my new name Mummy, do you?" Nicola nodded bemused. "Yes darling, it certainly suits you."

Jake looked around the table. How different tonight was from the other times he'd dined here under the watchful, and often resentful, gaze of Max. Tonight the room was filled with laughter and conversation as the two sisters, and Cat, switched between English and French. Catherine's eyes darted from one to the other grinning and laughing happily. Luke beamed with pleasure as he passed the food around and filled their glasses.

"Shall I bring coffee to the music room, Miss Nicola?"

"Thanks Luke. Catherine can stay up as long as she likes tonight, as a special treat." She rang the bell vigorously and silence descended around the table. "Shall we go upstairs? My sister is on fine form tonight and I think she should entertain us. What do you say Lizzy?"

"I'm a bit jetlagged but I'll give it a shot!"

Jake raised an eyebrow questioningly. "You play as well, Elizabeth?"

"Yeah. But not the tedious, and boring, classical stuff my sister so enjoys."

"I can play contemporary music too Lizzie," Nicola protested weakly.

Luke stood by the door tapping his foot and swaying in time to the music. Jake sat with Nicola talking softly, as Elizabeth sang and played, moving from French folk songs, to Fitzgerald, Billie Holiday and Piaf. Cat sat next to her aunt on the piano stool, her eyes shining with happiness.

"Play some more, Aunt Elizabeth," she implored as Elizabeth stopped and reached for her glass of wine and a cigarette.

"I'm going to take a break, sweetheart. Maybe your Mom will play something for us. I think I'm going to go and sit with gorgeous Jake, and get to know him. He could provide just the sort of entertainment I'm looking for in the next few weeks!"

Nicola seated herself at the piano waving her arms at the trail of smoke Elizabeth had left lingering in her wake As she played she was aware of her sister flirting outrageously and felt a stab of unexpected jealousy. With a grin she switched from Chopin to Scott Joplin and saw the surprise on Jake's face as his head jerked up in astonishment, a smile spreading across his face.

"You never cease to surprise me Nicola..." He stood up and walked towards the piano. "Whatever will you do next I wonder, and, God, I pray it will include me," he whispered in her ear.

Elizabeth decided she wasn't making any headway with Jake who obviously had eyes only for her sister. She walked over to the window, lighting another cigarette.

"Hey! There's a bloody great elephant standing on the lawn!" she spluttered.

"It's Tika, its Tika. He's come back!" Catherine said excitedly, leaning out of the window.

Tika stood still, his great ears moving slowly back and forwards. Cat jumped up and down with excitement. "Can I go and see him, Mummy? Can I?"

Nicola hesitated. "Well, he's a wild elephant now, darling, I'm not sure..."

Luke materialized out of the shadows. "I will take Cat, Miss Nicola, he will remember her and will not harm her. Come, little one, we must find some oranges for him."

From the window in the music room they watched Cat feeding oranges to the gentle giant on the lawn.

Nicola smiled at Jake and her sister. "Well now I know it's true - elephants never forget."

******

The sisters walked through the gardens. It was Elizabeth's last night in Kenya.

"What a difference it makes when Max isn't around to taint everything with his foul moods," Elizabeth said. "It's been great, and Cat is adorable. I love her to bits. As for Jake, well, he's just too gorgeous for words with that faint Irish accent, those deep blue eyes and oh so sexy smile.

"He's in love with you, you know, his eyes follow you everywhere. You should take a leaf out of your husband's book and have an affair with him, if you aren't already?" she said slyly.

"Of course I'm not going to have an affair!" she said, rather too hastily, Elizabeth thought. "It's out of the question. Max is bad tempered and unpredictable enough as it is - God knows what he'd do if he thought I was having an affair.

"But I *am* in love with Jake, Lizzie, and it's impossibly hard to deal with."

Elizabeth put her arm around her sister. "I've been thinking about something. Why don't we plan to meet up this time next year at your place down at the coast? You said Max never wants to go there - maybe Jake could join us?" she said, trying to look innocent.

Nicola smiled with pleasure at the thought. "Perhaps Lizzie, perhaps."

Nicola pulled up outside Jake's house. Ezekiel came hurrying out to help transfer Elizabeth's luggage to Jake's vehicle as he'd offered to take her back to the airport. The two sisters said their tearful goodbyes.

Elizabeth knelt down in front of Cat and hugged her. "When you're a big girl, Cat, you can come to America and visit me."

Cat nodded, the tears spilling unchecked down her face. "I'll come and see you next holidays, we'll go to Mombasa, but it has to be our special secret, just your Mom, me and you little Cat - okay."

Cat rubbed her fists in her eyes. She hugged Elizabeth again then went to stand next to her mother.

Nicola held her daughter's hand and they waved at the vehicle until it turned out of the drive.

Ezekiel asked her if she would stay for tea, before heading back, she said they would.

Nicola glanced at a magazine as she sipped from her cup, Cat reached out and picked up a record propped up against a pile of books.

"Look, Mummy, Jake has a picture of you." She held it up.

Nicola put her cup down clumsily, spilling tea as the cup rattled in the saucer. "It's not a photo, darling, it's a record. Let me see."

"What's your photograph doing on a record?" her daughter demanded, puzzled.

Nicola stared at it. Jake had never mentioned he had a record of hers. As far as she was concerned he knew nothing about her life at all, but this record proved otherwise. He must have known all along about her past and chosen to say nothing.

"Put this back exactly where you found it, darling, and don't say anything to your father about seeing it. It has to be our secret."

"But why has a record got your photograph on it?" her daughter demanded again.

"It's a long story, darling. I'll tell you one day, but not now."

******

She heard his vehicle approaching the hide and closed her diary. Luke was watching over Cat back at the house, where she had to finish an English exercise Nicola had set her.

She looked at Jake warily, as he lowered himself into a chair on the deck, unsure of what to say.

"I called at the house and Luke told me you were here. I wanted to let you know Elizabeth caught her flight yesterday with no problem. Are you alright?"

"So you know who I am?" she said softly.

"Sure, I know who you are. Nicola Gray, Cat's mother, my beautiful neighbour..." he said jokingly.

"You know what I mean Jake."

He reached over and took both her hands in his. "Yes, I know who you are. I was waiting for you to tell me yourself, it's obviously a private matter."

She stood up wrapping her arms around herself as she looked into the distance.

Oh God he wanted her. He had read, and heard, about love at first sight but never believed it existed, until he had met her eight years ago. He loved Nicola with an intensity which sometimes overwhelmed him, his desire for her was like a swollen dam holding back an avalanche of water, and sometimes he thought he would go crazy with his longing to make love to her.

"My agent in New York lent me the record and told me a little about you. She's a big fan of yours. What made you give it all up?"

She sat down next to him again and took his hand. "I didn't give it up, Jake. In a way it gave me up. It's true I was well-known, Max was my agent then."

Barely able to hold back her tears she told him what had followed. Her baby being adopted, and the demise of her career. "I can't remember anything at all. Absolutely nothing," she finished tearfully.

He listened, twisting his ring around his finger, wondering if Max had anything to do with this.

"Perhaps you did have a breakdown."

He cupped her wet face in his hands and kissed her. "You're still a magnificent pianist; no-one can take that away from you. I love you, Nicola, and I think you love me, and you know how much I love Cat."

She nodded, her eyes still wet. He took a deep breath, his mind made up. "I want you to come and live with me. I know you won't divorce him, but we can still live together. I'll take you anywhere you want to go. New York, London, Milan - anywhere." He told her how his agent had told him how collectable her records were and how difficult to find.

"You could make a come-back Nicola, with me by your side."

He took both her hands in his and squeezed them as he continued. "Come and live with me," he repeated.

She ran the back of her hand down his cheek. "You're an easy man to love, Jake... It's just not possible, but God it's what I want to do."

"I've already told you I'm not going to give up on you - I'll wait for as long as it takes. I know you think he'll take Catherine away from you, but he might have a fight on his hands, everyone knows about his numerous affairs, a judge would throw a custody battle out of court. But I know you don't want to put her through anything like that."

Seeing how upset she was he changed the subject. "I found something in Nairobi I think you'll like. I'll get it."

She looked at the exquisite wooden bowl in her hands. "It's beautiful, Jake! What's this blue stone called?"

"Tanzanite, it's only found in Tanzania. There's a hidden compartment built into it. I thought of you when I saw it... I guess you'll have to keep it away from Max; maybe you should keep it here. Does he ever come to the hide?"

Nicola turned the bowl around in her hands relishing the first gift he had ever given her. "No, I've sort of taken ownership of it myself. Max hasn't been here for years. I don't want to leave this here. I'm going to keep it in my bedroom."

He smiled at her, pleased. "Come up with a good story then. He's bound to ask."

She stood up, tucking her shirt into her trousers. "We've had separate bedrooms since Cat was born."

"Man's a bloody fool," Jake muttered under his breath, although he was delighted with that particular bit of news.

Chapter Thirty-Six

Max had called Nicola once in the eight weeks he'd been away. "I thought you'd like to know I went to hear the Chinese pianist, Sue Ling play." The silence which he heard at the end of the phone made him smile maliciously.

"She was brilliant and fully deserved the ten minute standing ovation she got." Max paused. "It reminded me of the good old days when you were right up there with the best."

Nicola remained silent, hardened to his cruel barbs. "Oh well, no point in looking back," he summed up.

She asked when he planned on returning home, hoping it wouldn't be anytime soon.

"I haven't decided yet," Max said distractedly. "Mbabati's like an albatross around my neck, like you and the kid. I'm sure neither of you are pining for me, I'll come back when I feel like it, a couple more weeks maybe."

"Don't rush back, Max," she said angrily, "stay as long as you damn well like.

"By the way, in case you're interested, your dogs are both dead. Tick fever." She slammed down the phone with a satisfying clatter.

Nicola stood in Max's study and stared stonily out of the window. Heavy storm clouds, bloated with rain, rolled across the bush beyond the grounds of the house; thunder rumbled ominously as lightning streaked across the darkening sky.

******

The trees lining the driveway began to bend and sway as they were buffeted by the strong winds building strength as they swept through the gardens. Nicola heard the first heavy drops of rain splatter against the window in front of her.

She watched the earth suck the moisture greedily; within minutes she couldn't see the gardens or the trees as the rain turned into a deluge of furious water, pounding the earth into submission. Rivulets appeared and, gathering momentum, turned into small rivers snaking through the grounds.

Luke tapped and entered the study with two hurricane lamps. "There is a big storm, I am hoping it will not break the roses and vegetables."

"I'm not going to stay in here, Luke," she said, walking back to the sitting room.

"Make sure the grooms stay with the horses until the storm has passed."

Standing by the window, watching the elements gather force, she saw a flash of light from the road. "There's someone at the gates, Luke, go and see who it is!"

Nicola watched him pulling on his raincoat as he ran down the steps and along the drive. The wind sucked at his coat as he struggled with the gates.

She saw Jake's Land Rover, its wipers working furiously against the deluge, pull up outside. Ducking his head against the rain he ran up the front steps, carrying a box, Luke close behind him.

"What on earth are you doing out on a night like this?"

He ran his fingers through his wet hair and wiped his eyes. "I decided to drive over before the storm hit, but it came sooner than I thought." They took off their coats and Luke went to hang them up in the kitchen; he returned with a towel.

"I thought you and Cat might like some company; I know she doesn't like violent storms, and I've bought her a present." He indicated the sodden box he had put down on the floor. He rubbed his hair vigorously with the towel.

She told him Cat was staying at a friend's house for the weekend. She had been inconsolable when the dogs died - Nicola had thought a break away from the house might help.

Jake bent down and opened up the box on the floor and out tumbled two golden Labrador puppies. Nicola scooped one up and held it close. "Oh, they're adorable, Cat will be thrilled!" She nuzzled the puppy's nose then reached for the other one, who licked her face enthusiastically.

Luke stood grinning broadly. "I will feed them and show them where they will be sleeping Miss Nicola." Clasping one puppy under each arm he took the two wriggling bundles into the kitchen.

Jake followed Nicola into the sitting room and watched as she mixed him a drink.

He took the proffered glass. "I had some ideas for the cover of my book," he said, tapping his signet ring on the glass, a habit she had become used to.

They began to discuss his ideas whilst Luke prepared a simple supper. As the evening and the storm progressed, they had to raise their voices to be heard above the raging storm outside. "It's certainly a wild night," Jake said, standing up and peering out of the window. "The lightning's fantastic. I've tried capturing storms on canvas and it's damn difficult to get the mood and the light right."

Nicola jumped as a sharp crack of thunder broke over the house. "I think I'll let Cookie and Luke off early tonight. If this gets any worse they won't be able to make it back to their own quarters. You ought to think about staying as well, it'll be murder trying to drive back in this." Nicola left the room and returned shortly afterwards. Jake was staring out at the storm still tapping his ring against his glass.

"All fixed, Cookie will leave supper in the oven; we'll have the place to ourselves for a change." She straightened the cushions on the sofa distractedly.

"Would you do something for me, Nicola, after we've eaten?" he said returning to his seat.

They looked at each other for several minutes, not saying anything.

"I'll do anything for you…"

He grinned at her. "Will you play for me, and wear your blue dress?"

******

After dinner they made their way to the music room. The closed windows and shutters muffled the rage of the storm outside. Nicola lifted the lid of the piano and arranged herself on the padded stool.

"What's on your mind, Nicola, you seem sort of different tonight."

She told him about her conversation with Max. "I've had enough Jake."

He held his breath, saying nothing.

"He's a bully," Nicola continued, "and he's cruel. Now my personal wealth has gone, he's not interested in me anymore. Thank God he never managed to get his hands on my trust fund."

She ran her fingers lightly over the keyboard. "In a strange way, I feel liberated after his call. He's emptied me. Shostakovich, I think."

"Sorry?" Jake said perplexed.

"The second movement of his *Concerto Number Two*, it's a haunting piece and suits my mood tonight," she said as she began to play.

The candlelight flickered between them, turning her skin to gold. He watched as his portrait came to life and the beauty of her music brought a lump to his throat. Tonight her playing was full of passion and confidence and as it washed over him he knew this was the woman he would love for the rest of his life. He closed his eyes. Whatever the price might be he was prepared to pay it, he didn't want to live the rest of his life without her in it.

******

Nicola played for over an hour and when she stopped, silence pervaded the room. Jake opened his eyes slowly. She was kneeling in front of him. He reached up and released her hair from its clasp, the light from the fire turned her hair a red gold as it tumbled around her shoulders, her large green eyes looked into his and he sucked in his breath.

She stood up and held out her hand to him. "Come with me..."

Her bedroom was dark, only illuminated when streaks of lightning raked the night sky. He pulled her close to him and buried his face in her hair.

"I love you, Jake," Nicola said simply, putting her hands on either side of his face. "I've loved you since the first day in your studio, when you made me so nervous."

Slowly she placed her lips to his and kissed him. Where he had thought she might be tender and gentle, he found her passionate and hungry. He responded and kissed her in return. Their clothes were swiftly removed, barriers to their intense desire to feel one another's skin. He pushed her away from him briefly, as lightning lit the room. He drew in his breath as it formed a silver halo around her.

"God you're beautiful, Nicola, and this incredible unbelievable moment, is something I've dreamed about for years."

Their lovemaking was as intense and as wild as the storm sweeping around the old house, and he was astonished by her physical intensity. Their cries were drowned out by the rain on the roof, and then, as suddenly as it had started, the storm was over.

They lay together, panting softly. Jake roused himself and kissed her eyelids. When he made to move out of her, she held him in place and he smiled at her, overwhelmed, hardly able to believe he was finally making love to her.

They were softer and gentler with each other the second time and only fell asleep in each other's arms as a chorus of birds heralded the dawn of a new day.

******

The next morning they lingered over breakfast. "I'll never let you go now," Jake whispered to her across the table.

She reached over and put her finger to his lips. "I don't want you to let me go...

"I can hardly sit still I'm so happy. Let's go for a gallop after breakfast, if we can't go back to bed I need to do something…although," she added laughing, "I'm a little tender here and there."

She rang the bell and asked Luke to have the horses saddled up and prepare a picnic then deliver it to the hide.

Luke left the room looking forward to having the puppies to himself for the day. His smile broadened as he walked to the kitchen - he knew they'd spent the night together.

The sun was high and hot as they rode; the heat was already evaporating the puddles and drying the freshly washed bushes and grasses. Slowing to a walk, Nicola lifted her face to the sun, reaching for his hand. He lifted it to his lips and kissed her palm, shaking his head.

"I feel drunk with happiness this morning; I can't even string a full sentence together. See what you've done to me, my love, I'm a basket case".

Later, they lay in the rustic bed in the hide, gazing up at the tree, exhausted by their lovemaking. Nicola turned in his arms and looked up at him. "I could stay here forever with you. I didn't think it was possible to love like this."

She sat up and stretched lazily. "We should stay here tonight, my love. The horses can graze safely and there's a small *boma* we can put

205

them in to keep them safe from lion. I don't want to go back to the house. I want to stay here with you."

He reached for her and pulled her down into his arms, holding her tightly to him. "Lying with you, watching the stars through the branches and leaves, and falling asleep with you in my arms is something I've dreamed about for years. But what about Luke, he'll worry if we don't return tonight?"

Nicola grinned at him. "Luke's been watching us for years. He won't wonder where we are - he knows exactly what's going on. Let's be decadent and have a glass of wine and something to eat, I'm starving. Luke has delivered the hamper, there's enough food for two days and nights...," she said dreamily anticipating the precious hours ahead.

"Not yet, my love, the hamper can wait - but I can't. Come here…"

******

The following evening, Nicola sat between Jake's legs his chin resting on her head, as they watched the animals congregating at the waterhole. The setting sun turned the water to gold as it rippled with the steady lapping of a herd of impala.

The high pitched giggle of a hyena made her shudder. Reaching for a blanket hanging on the back of the chair, he put it around her shoulders and wrapped his arms around her again. "Horrible sound, isn't it?" He rubbed her head with his chin, breathing in the scent of her freshly washed hair. "You're safe with me - you always will be, and somehow we'll find a way of being together."

Nicola sighed and turned around to look up at him. "Yes," she said softly, "we will." She was quiet for a few moments. "I'll do whatever you want me to do.

"No-one ever comes to the hide, we could meet here for a few hours each week whilst we work out how - and what - we're going to tell him."

Jake tasted her lips and mouth with his own before he answered. "It's not ideal but if you're sure he'll never come here..."

He stroked the inside of her wrist softly with his forefinger. "I want to marry you Nicola DuPont."

206

Lifting her in his arms he carried her to the bedroom desperate to be inside her again, to feel the softness of her breasts against his chest, and to make her his own for a few more precious hours.

Chapter Thirty-Seven

Jake cut through Central Park on his way to Susan's offices on Fifth Avenue.

Arriving at the gallery, Susan, wearing her usual black, was delighted to see him. "Time for a large Martini, don't you think?" she said picking up her handbag and walking back towards the door before he had a chance to answer. Susan filled him in on gossip about mutual friends and acquaintances as they made their way to The Waldorf; she didn't stop talking until the drinks arrived at their table. She took a long sip and smacked her lips with satisfaction.

"Best Martinis in town," she breathed, and with her usual hurried and rapid gestures took a handful of peanuts from the bowl on the table, then sat back sizing him up. "You're looking good, Jake. What are you working on at the moment?"

Before giving him the chance to respond to either of her questions, she suddenly leant forward. "You didn't forget to bring back my record did you, honey?"

Jake looked at her and smiled. "I've got it here," he said tapping his briefcase. "There's a shipment on its way to you - enough to fill a few walls. But, I've had another idea I want to talk to you about."

Susan eyes narrowed slightly as she listened. "Some years ago I completed a large canvas," Jake continued, "it's the best thing I've ever done."

"What's the subject matter?" Susan asked surprised. "You've never mentioned this?"

"A beautiful woman," he started clumsily.

"Of course," she said, looking smug, "that's why you look so good. Who's the broad, then? Methinks you might be in love. What's her name?"

Jake pulled the record from his briefcase and held it up. Susan reached across and took it from him. "Thanks," she said tucking it safely beside her, "Who'd you paint?" she asked again.

Jake hesitated, desperate to talk to someone about her; to tell someone how much he loved her. "Her name, Susan, is Nicola DuPont."

Susan snorted and took another sip of her drink. "Yeah, yeah, Jake. So you painted her picture from the record cover - that's not very original and it ain't gonna sell in this city, my friend. We need the

208

African stuff we talked about - the portraits." She narrowed her eyes again. "There's something you're not telling me. So shoot - and enough already with the puppy dog face."

"Remember you told me the story about Nicola DuPont and how she had disappeared at the height of her career?" She put her drink down, reaching for another handful of peanuts. She looked at him chewing expectantly.

"Nah, don't tell me. You found her hiding in the middle of the jungle, right?"

"Pretty much."

"You're kidding!" She searched his face, the peanuts in her hand forgotten. "Okay, so you're not kidding. This is a big story, Jake. A huge story. it will make your painting of her valuable beyond words. When can I see it? Is it with the shipment coming over?"

He told her it was a private commission and not for sale. Seeing the disappointment in her face, Jake laughed. "But, I've got a photograph for you."

Susan studied the photograph, unthinkingly emptying her hands of the peanuts onto the table. She swallowed hard. "Even from this I can see it's excellent. Who else knows where she is?"

"Her sister - and her husband."

"Ah, I see. You're in love with a married woman - that never works." She handed the photograph back.

Jake took a sip of his drink, and told her he wanted to produce a limited edition of a book entitled *The Lost Child*, just twenty copies. He reached for his briefcase and withdrew a thick envelope. Pushing their drinks aside he handed her the first photograph of Cat standing on the end of the pier at the lake, her arms outstretched and the sun sparkling on the surface. One by one, he showed them to her.

"These are extraordinary. You've captured the rawness of Africa, and softened it with the beauty and innocence of a child. Is this Nicola's kid?"

He nodded.

"Seeing Nicola DuPont like this gives her another dimension from the cool, aloof blonde on the record cover. Journalists would kill for these - and pay huge sums of money.

"So what's the story, Jake?"

With relief he told her everything from the beginning when he and Nicola first met and what they planned to do.

"She wants to return to playing professionally," he added. "She still has exceptional talent. Do you think you can handle the book for me, Susan?"

"A love story like this? Honey, you bet I'll handle it for you! I'll get the movie rights as well. Hey, don't look so worried. Not a word shall pass from between these lips until you give the go ahead. I know someone in the City who would love a project like this and he's young enough not to have a clue who he's looking at when he handles the photographs. We'll use him. What about the words - the copy?"

"No copy. I want the pictures to tell the story, but I do want music." He reached for the pile of photographs and shuffled through them until he came to one of Luke.

"This is Luke, he has a noble face and his look of disdain would work well with Beethoven's The Emperor. Anyone who knows and appreciates classical music will understand the message, but, as I said, it's not for the public. I want to give a copy to Nicola, one to Cat and another to Elizabeth. I'm not sure about the rest of them. I'll decide about that once Nicola and I are together and she's confident enough to face the world again. I'm going to marry her."

Susan looked across at him. "Yes, I see. I love this. I don't think it's been done before. Wow!"

Warming to his subject, Jake continued. "I want the book to have an air of mystery. Most of the shots of Nicola have been taken in shadow, so she can't be identified. I think this shot would work well on the back cover."

She was speechless. "Is this a wild elephant I'm looking at here? Is the kid about to be attacked?"

He grinned at her incredulous face. "The elephant, they call him Tika, was brought up by the family. He's completely wild now, but comes to the house to visit."

"You're kidding me, right? He comes to visit the family, like, he walks into the garden and knocks on the door with his long nose? Does he come for Thanksgiving?"

Jake laughed. "Not quite. I like this pic because it shows the might and wildness of the elephant against the vulnerability of the child, but highlights the trust they have in each other."

Susan studied the photographs again. "I need another Martini, Jake, my mind is exploding with ideas. Are you sure you only want an edition of twenty? It has the potential of becoming an international bestseller, it could make millions."

"Just twenty, Susan, and I retain all rights," Jake said firmly.

She nodded, her eyes glittering with excitement.

"When the book's finished, I want you to hold the copies here. You can send Elizabeth's to her, she won't show it to anyone. She's fiercely protective of her sister and won't want the media to find Nicola any more than Nicola wants to be found. I'll have to be careful about Cat and Nicola's copies… if her husband gets wind of the book he'll probably kill me."

"Well, if it should happen, and he knocks you off, what would you want me to do about it?" Susan said laughing.

She stopped when she saw the look on his face. "I'm going to draw up a document before I leave New York. I want you to keep it with your lawyer. Should anything happen to me, you're to do nothing about the book. I can't put Nicola in any danger by leaving her the rights to publish it. I'm leaving those to her daughter."

"Sure, honey. I know you live in deepest darkest, but let's not be so morbid." She leant over and patted Jake's knee. "Leave the document with me and I'll take care of things. Why the title? Why *The Lost Child*?"

Jake hesitated. "When Nicola was quite young, she lost a baby," he began as their second round of drinks arrived. Susan was looking at the photographs again and looked up thirstily as her drink was handed to her. "Miscarriage? Probably for the best if she was at the height of her career. Can't have kids around in that kind of world. Now let's talk about the book."

Chapter Thirty-Eight

Over the years she had become accustomed to her father's indifference towards her, and his changing moods which drifted below the surface, exploding unexpectedly. She avoided him as much as possible.

But she loved Jake.

"So, Cat," Jake had said during their last lunch before she left for boarding school in England, "are you looking forward to your new adventure?"

She grinned at him across the table. "I'll miss home and Mummy, of course, and Suzy and Sam..." The dogs thumped their tails on the floor at the sound of their names; she glanced at her father and added hastily, "And you, Daddy. I'll miss Luke and Cookie because without them looking after me I'll have to do everything myself." She frowned. "I've never had to do that before."

Jake looked at her as she chatted away. She had grown up to be a beautiful young girl and, at the age of fifteen, was turning into the image of her mother. Over the years she had become the daughter he now knew he would never have, and he loved her dearly.

"Catherine!" Her father's voice boomed down the length of the table, making them all jump. "For fuck's sake, stop chattering and eat your lunch. You're giving me a bloody headache."

Jake narrowed his eyes. "Steady on, Max, it's not necessary to speak to Cat like that."

"It's my damn house and I'll use any damn language I choose." He threw down his napkin and stomped out of the room, the door shuddered in its frame behind him.

Tears filled Cat's eyes and her mouth wobbled as she lifted her knife and fork. "Sorry, Mummy," she whispered. "I didn't mean to put him in a bad mood, really I didn't."

Jake and Nicola looked at each other helplessly. Jake leaned over the table and squeezed Cat's hand. "Tell you what, gorgeous, I'll be in England during the spring and if the school allows, I'll take you out for dinner. Would you like that?"

Cat's face brightened immediately. "I'd love to! I'm going to miss you Jake."

He stood up from the table. "I think I should go." He bent down to kiss Nicola's cheek. "I love you," he whispered in her ear.

He walked over to where Cat sat and she stood up and hugged him tightly. "You will look after Mummy when I've gone, won't you, Jake?"

He promised he would.

******

Running the brush through her hair Nicola gazed at her reflection. It was almost impossible to believe she had been in Kenya for twenty years. Without her beloved child and Jake life would have been intolerable, but now Cat was leaving, she couldn't bear to think how it would feel without her. With a final glance in the mirror she left the room.

Luke was waiting for her at the foot of the staircase, with a rifle in his hand.

"Your horse is ready, Miss Nicola, and I have cleaned the gun for you. Cat is reading in her bedroom with the dogs."

"Where is Bwana Max?"

"He is working in his study, then he is going to the drying sheds. He will be back after the sun has gone down," he assured her.

Nicola urged her horse on, anxious to reach the hide. Jake was waiting for her and she dismounted quickly, unbuttoning her shirt in anticipation. They fell onto the bed pulling at each other's clothes greedily. Without a word Jake ran his hands over her naked, and now familiar body, kissing her roughly, unable to control his longing to be inside her. Gently pushing her legs open he felt the softness and wetness of her.

"Take me now Jake, take me now," she urged.

With a groan he rolled on top of her and plunged himself inside of her feeling her rise to meet his thrusting body; pacing himself as well as he could he waited for her to orgasm before finally letting go of his own in an explosion that rocked his very being.

The love and passion they had for each other had not abated over the years and, if anything, there was more urgency to their lovemaking. Now she lay with her head on his chest and waited for her heartbeat to slow down. He stroked her damp hair and looked up into the tree branches, glimpsing the blue sky between the leaves.

"Make love to me again," she whispered, "I want you so much - I need to feel you again."

This time their lovemaking was more languid as they lost themselves in each other, their hands seeking and stroking, their lips salty with the now familiar taste of each other.

Afterwards Jake buried his head in the slope of her damp neck breathing in the scent of her, waiting for the beat of his own heart to slow down before he spoke.

"I don't know how much longer I can go on with this, my love. I want to kill Max when he speaks to you and Cat the way he does. You've no idea how difficult it is for me to sit there, wanting and loving you, not knowing when you'll finally leave him."

She turned the ring around on his finger and kissed it. "We've come this far, *cheri*, we must keep going until it's safe for me to leave." She looked stealthily at her watch, the one movement Jake hated most.

They dressed with practiced haste; she looked around carefully, anxious there should be no sign of their assignation. Max hadn't been to the hide for years, but she couldn't take any chances.

As he always did, Jake led his horse away from the hide, tethered him and retraced his steps to brush away the second set of hoof prints as well as his own. They embraced tightly and Jake watched her gallop away across the plains, her hair flying out behind her. He turned his horse and rode slowly away, taking the long route back to Leopard's Leap.

Max stepped out of a thicket of brush on the other side of the waterhole; still holding the binoculars in one hand, he brushed himself off grimly.

Some weeks previously, doing a loop of the estate, he'd decided to check the hide and recognised the two horses tethered outside. He'd dismounted quietly and approached on foot, hearing laughter and low voices as he came to the bedroom window. The bushes outside gave him some cover as he watched his naked wife lying in Jake's arms.

Blind with rage he had stumbled back to his horse and waited on the other side of the waterhole with his binoculars trained on the door of the hide.

He watched them cover their tracks and embrace before mounting their horses. For hours afterwards, he stayed out in the hot sun attempting to figure out how long Jake had been sleeping with his wife.

Returning to Mbabati, he'd poured himself a large drink and planned his next move. If he confronted her she'd tell him the truth; he didn't want to give her an easy way out.

If she moved in with Jake Henderson he'd be the laughing stock of Nairobi, and he wasn't about to let that happen.

In the following weeks he had studied Nicola's routine; every Thursday she took off for the afternoon and he had tracked her until he was sure the hide was the only place she met Jake. They followed the same careless pattern each week.

******

Max pushed his plate away violently. It teetered briefly on the edge of the table before crashing to the floor. Nicola looked up startled. "Is something wrong?"

Luke hurried into the dining-room and, seeing the broken plate and food on the floor, returned to the kitchen for a dustpan and brush.

"What sort of food do you call this?" he asked sarcastically.

She looked at him with surprise. "It's a traditional French casserole. We've had it before?"

"I seem to have lost my appetite. Luke, for God's sake stop grovelling around on the floor and bring me a bloody drink!"

Nicola stood in the sitting room watching Max pace the gardens, drinking straight from the bottle Luke had given him. Feeling uneasy, she made her way to the music room.

******

Max stood at his father's grave, the bottle of brandy held loosely in his hand. "Why did you land me with this albatross, Pa? Wasn't it enough you struggled with it for forty years? Why did you have to wish the same thing on me? I mean, look at it!" He gestured towards the house with the bottle. "I have a daughter who moves around the place like a terrified ghost and a wife who's taken a lover," he spat bitterly. "I curse the day you died and left this bloody house to me!"

He walked unsteadily back to the house and hearing Nicola playing, hauled his baulk up to the music room. He kicked the door open.

"Well, well, so you're still up are you? I thought you might be tired after your exhausting day and all the physical exertion?"

Shaken by his entrance Nicola continued to play, her nervousness causing her to miss some notes.

He brought his fist down hard on the piano. "Not only have you betrayed me but you've betrayed our daughter. If she is my daughter, that is."

Nicola stood up unnerved. "Of course she's your daughter! Please don't doubt that."

"Get out, Nicola, get out of my sight! I can't bear to look at you. I never want to hear you play this bloody piano again." He slammed the lid of the piano down violently.

She fled from the music room, running down the stairs to her bedroom. She sat on the bed, her mind reeling and her heart staggering with fear.

He knew about Jake.

She heard his heavy footsteps as he came down the hallway. Holding her breath, she waited for the sound of his bedroom door closing.

Instead, her bedroom door was kicked open. Max entered, pulling at his shirt and tie.

"Please God, no Max, please don't do this."

He pushed her onto the bed, his lead weight paralysing her. He tore at her dress and, unable to control his temper, wrenched the pearls from her neck; the beads scattered and bounced across the floor.

"You bitch! You're my wife!" Spittle settled in the corners of his mouth. "I'll do as I want with you!" He hit her hard across the mouth then wound his hands through her hair, anchoring her to the bed. Helplessly, she lay pinned beneath him, unable to move, as he brutally raped her.

When he had finished he looked down, his eyes glazed and dispassionate. Her lips were swollen and bloody, and dark bruises were appearing on her neck where he'd torn the necklace from her throat. He looked at the blood streaked across her upper thighs as he reached to pull up his trousers.

"If you betray me in any way again, I'll break your fingers in half. In fact, if I ever hear you play again I'll do just that. Get it?"

She whimpered, cowed dumb by his violence. The door shuddered in its frame behind him.

Hidden behind the heavy curtains in her mother's room, Cat's heart pounded fearfully. She had been covering her ears with her hands, when she heard the slam of the door; she crept to the side of her mother's bed. Horrified, Cat looked at her bruised neck and bloodied face.

"Don't be frightened, Mummy. I'll help you get into bed - I'll get Luke. He'll know what to do. Don't cry, Mummy, please don't cry." Tears streamed down her face as she helped her mother into bed; then she ran to find Luke.

Cat held a bowl of warm water whilst Luke gently wiped the blood from Nicola's mouth, her eyes wide and unseeing in her expressionless face. "*Eish*, this is a bad thing, Miss Nicola," Luke murmured, "a bad thing to happen."

Luke glanced at Cat, seeing the silent tears.

"Bring me a fresh cloth from the bathroom, little one, everything will be alright."

As Cat stood up and walked towards the door, she heard Luke whisper to Nicola, "Shall I call for Bwana Jake? He will come and help you. Bwana Max is drunk tonight and he is sleeping deeply now. It will be safe."

She shook her head, tears seeping into her hair. Cat returned from the bathroom with a fresh towel.

"I'll pick up all the pearls from your broken necklace Mummy, we can mend it and make it as good as new," she babbled with terror. She lay down next to her mother and put her arms around her. "We'll make you better Mummy, Luke and I will look after you. Don't cry Mummy, please don't cry."

******

Nicola parked her car at the airport terminal and turned off the engine. "Well, this is it, Cat darling," she said trying to sound cheerful, "time to say goodbye, and see you off on your big adventure." Her voice wobbled unexpectedly. "How empty the house will be without the sound of your voice and those footsteps running down the stairs." She swallowed hard. "Now come on, I don't want you to miss your flight." She adjusted the soft scarf she was wearing to hide the fading bruises around her neck, and helped Cat with her luggage.

Having checked in, they stood holding each other, dreading the final parting. Amongst the crowds Cat saw Jake heading towards them.

Cat flew into his arms trying to suppress her sobs. "Hey, come on, girls. I can't have both of you in tears." He reached over and squeezed Nicola's hand, disentangling himself from Cat's fierce embrace.

"I know we've already said goodbye, gorgeous, but I wanted to come and see you off. I thought it might help if I was here."

Nicola blew her nose and tried to hold herself together.

"They're calling your flight, darling." Nicola wrapped her arms around her child and hugged her again. She buried her face in her daughter's hair, her eyes stinging with hot tears. "I'll think of you every single day," she said her voice breaking, "and count the hours until you come home again, my darling child."

Jake watched them, his own eyes getting hot. Picking up her hand luggage Cat walked towards the departure lounge and with a tearful wave was soon lost amongst the crowd of passengers.

It was the last time Jake would see her.

Already beginning to feel the weight of her loss, Nicola stared at the empty space where her daughter had stood seconds before, turning she walked blindly out of the terminal building.

Taking the car keys from her shaking hands, Jake opened the door for her and helped her in. "It's tough I know, my love, but she'll be home for the holidays before you know it, and I'll see her in a few months' time to check how she's settling down."

He looked at his watch. "You'd better start back. I still have some things to do in town." He squeezed her shoulder and she put her hand over his, looking up at him.

"He knows about us," she said dully, "somehow he found out. We had an ugly scene at the house. It's too dangerous for us to meet for a while, I'm frightened of what he might do next, Jake."

He looked down at her. "I can't just give you up. I won't give you up." He glanced up as a plane took off. "God, I wish we could walk back into the terminal and jump on the first plane to anywhere."

Nicola also glanced upwards. Her movement revealing the bruises under her scarf.

"What?" he began, the colour draining from his face. He smashed his fist on the roof of the car. "I swear to God I'm going to kill that bastard…"

He bent down to her side again, his voice urgent. "You have to leave him, Nicola. Come home with me *now* and to hell with what people think and say, I don't give a damn!"

She laid her head on the steering wheel, exhausted. The situation felt completely out of control and she didn't have the energy to do anything. She lifted her head and looked at him, her eyes filled with despair. "Oh, God! What are we going to do?"

He put his arm around her. "I'll never let you go, Nicola. I don't care what it takes or what I have to do, but I'm going to do something, and it's going to be soon. If you won't come with me now, try and hold everything together until next Thursday. Don't do anything until then. Keep out of his way and make sure Luke is always around. Lock your bedroom door at night."

Chapter Thirty-Nine

So Nicola, Max said shaking his newspaper noisily, "what are your plans for the day?"

Nicola looked up nervously. "I haven't got any particular plans. I might go for a ride after lunch."

He folded the newspaper and threw it down on the table next to him. "I want you to do something for me. I have to order more wine and I need to know what we have in stock. It shouldn't take more than a couple of hours. I have to check the perimeter fences this afternoon, so I won't have time."

"Why don't I do it tomorrow?"

"Sorry, has to be done today, not much to ask is it? The order must be in tomorrow if we want the shipment before Christmas."

He watched her struggling to come up with an excuse with malicious relish. He had thought his plan through with great care.

"Alright," Nicola said eventually, sighing resignedly.

Max waited patiently until it was shortly after two o'clock. He sat in his Land Rover, beneath the shade of a heavily leaved tree from where he could see the hide clearly. He saw the dust before he saw the man. He took a long pull from his hip flask and waited for Jake to enter the hide, then drove quietly up to it, parking a short distance away; he ordered Suzy and Sam to stay in the vehicle.

******

Jake heard the vehicle approach and smiled in anticipation. He walked to the entrance of the hide and stepped outside, impatient to see her. His smile froze when he saw Max.

He took a deep breath, relief flooding his body at the opportunity now presenting itself.

"Well Jake, what a surprise to find you here on your own. I know I said you could use the hide whenever you felt like it but when did my generosity extend to sleeping with my wife. No, let me re-phrase that - fucking my wife?"

Jake hesitated. There was no point in denying anything. He shaded his eyes from the sun and faced his lover's husband.

"I love her. We didn't plan this, it just happened."

Max looked at him coolly but Jake saw the colours of anger, jealousy and rage flit across his face.

"It's been going on for a while, some years in fact."

Max closed his eyes briefly. "I'm asking you to leave my wife alone. Give her up. Even if she doesn't love me anymore, our marriage is important to me."

"Sorry," Jake said shaking his head, "I can't, and won't, give her up. She wants to leave you and live with me. We've waited years for Cat to be old enough to understand and accept the situation. I love Cat like my own daughter - I'll look after them." He cleared his throat. "I'm asking you to let them both go. I love Nicola." He turned towards his horse and began to untether it.

"You want it all do you, Jake? Well, I'm not going along with it. She belongs to me and so does Catherine. You'll never have either of them!"

******

The shot rang out across the still afternoon and Jake's horse reared up in terror. A flock of startled birds took flight, their cries joining the thud of hooves as the impala drinking at the waterhole bolted into the bush.

Max walked over to Jake and nudged his body with his boot, flipping him over onto his back.

He looked at him dispassionately, then crouched down beside him. Silently and meticulously he stripped Jake of his clothes whilst a hush spread over the hot bush. When he'd finished he whistled for the dogs who jumped from the Land Rover and ran eagerly towards him. Once more Max raised his rifle and fired twice in quick succession.

He was well aware how sound could carry across the bush. By the following day, it would be impossible, to distinguish the dogs' bodies from Jake's - after the hyenas had done their job.

He stuffed Jake's clothes in his horse's saddlebag and took a final look at him before untethering his frightened horse and tying it to the Land Rover; then he drove slowly to the lake.

Max sat and watched a fish eagle swoop down to catch a fish, effortlessly lifting it from the water in its talons. He took a long pull from his flask, wiping his mouth with the back of his hand. He saw it had a slight tremor and took another pull to steady his nerves.

He looked back towards the hide, noticing a cloud of vultures already beginning to circle above the kill. He walked to the end of the wooden jetty and untied the small rowing boat. Max rowed a short distance from the shore and with some difficulty, threw the saddle as far as he could into the depths of the lake, before rowing back to the jetty.

Satisfied with events so far he now led Jake's horse into a clearing and shot it.

Tomorrow he'd return to the hide and remove anything the hyena, and vultures might have left, which he doubted would be much, a few bone fragments maybe.

The vultures gathered in number all afternoon, ready to play their part in the final dance of death.

******

Max sat next to the crackling fire reading, his hand shook as he reached for his drink. Nicola sat opposite him staring unseeingly at her book.

She glanced up and watched him through half closed eyes as he refilled his glass once again. His silence was starting to unnerve her.

She closed her book and stood up. "I finished the list of wine we need to order. I left it on your desk in the study." He kept his eyes on his book ignoring her.

"Have you seen the dogs, they didn't appear for their dinner and Luke hasn't seen them either?"

Max looked up and scowled at her; she flinched at the hatred she saw in his face.

"I shot them."

Her hands flew to her cheeks in horror. "What!"

"Stop being so dramatic!" he said shortly. "They were attacked by baboon and injured, so I put them out of their misery."

"Where did you shoot them?" Nicola asked eventually.

"In the head," he said, innocently watching her. "Oh I see you meant *where* did I shoot them - at the hide."

The hyenas gorged greedily on the kill, occasionally lifting a hideous, blood soaked, muzzle to sniff the night air for other hungry predators. The vultures hopped and danced in the shadows waiting impatiently for them to finish feeding.

Chapter Forty

The following Thursday Max watched Nicola as she walked purposefully down to the stables. He saw her galloping across the property in the direction of the hide and smiled to himself. Her ultimate punishment was yet to come.

Nicola slowed down as she approached the hide feeling her horse becoming agitated; she glanced up and saw a single vulture circling high above on the thermals.

Her horse snorted and pranced with fright. Nicola patted his neck and spoke comfortingly to him wondering if there was a predator in the bushes which the horse could sense. Her nerves and senses on high alert, she went inside and looked around. Jake's watch was lying on the table.

She picked it up. He'd been there the previous Thursday waiting for her. It had become a habit to remove his watch as soon as he arrived, as if he could somehow slow down the few precious hours they spent together. Puzzled he'd forgotten it, she pocketed it and went back outside to wait for him.

Her horse whinnied and pawed at the ground and she went over to calm him down. "What's wrong Coco? What's bothering you? Is it the dogs you can smell?" She glanced around trying to see any traces of Max's execution. Noticing prints in the soft earth, she walked slowly around, studying them.

Nicola bent down to take a closer look, noticing two smudged sets of boot prints and an area of disturbed ground surrounded by animal tracks. She ran a hand over the darkened earth but apart from two small pieces of what looked like sharp bone, there was nothing.

She stood up, not understanding the markings. As she straightened, she noticed something dark fluttering on a thorn of a bush. She reached out her hand and pulled a tangled clump of dark fur from its grip.

Her screams echoed around the waterhole as she realised what she was holding. Expecting the wiry stiffness of fur, she felt instead the silkiness of Jake's dark hair. She bent over and began to retch until there was nothing left in her curdled stomach.

Max sat in his study and lit a cigarette. He knew she'd find nothing out there after he had disposed of what little was left.

He heard the heavy front door open and knew Nicola had returned. Despite being certain he had covered his tracks, he felt a thrill of danger and a rush of superior knowledge.

That evening she was late for dinner and when she arrived, she looked terrible. Her eyes were swollen with crying, her hair loose and untidy, and she hadn't changed out of her riding clothes. She sat immobile at the other end of the table, staring at nothing. Max found he was enjoying himself too much to keep quiet.

"How was your ride, my dear? Did you have a good hack through the bush? Go to the hide perhaps?" Nicola made no indication of having heard him.

After a few minutes of silence, he couldn't resist asking, "Did you see anything interesting today? Luke," he said gesturing vaguely at Luke who stood in the corner, as always, "tells me he saw vultures down at the hide a few days ago. Must have been after the dogs. Wish I'd shot those bloody baboons whilst I was at it, but they were too quick." He reached for his glass of whisky and downed it.

He continued cheerfully. "I might go over to Jake's tomorrow; his phone doesn't seem to be working. I thought we might go hunting next week."

Nicola kept her eyes fixed rigidly on a single spot. Slowly and deliberately, she rose from the table and walked out of the dining room.

******

Nicola lay tightly curled on her bed attempting, through her shock and horror, to make sense of what she had seen and found. She needed to get hold of Jake. If she could speak with him, just hear his voice on the other end of the phone, she would know she was imagining what she had seen. Phoning him now, if the line was still not down, would be too dangerous.

She felt again the softness of the hair she had held in her hand, and squeezed her eyes shut against the memory.

Nicola walked unsteadily into her bathroom. She splashed cold water on her face and stared at her reflection in the mirror.

The clump of hair she had picked up could have belonged to an animal, she told herself. How gruesome of her to assume it was Jake's. Max was going to drive to Leopard's Leap tomorrow. She knew Jake wouldn't go hunting with him, but at least he could reassure her Jake was safely at home.

******

The following day, Max drove to Leopard's Leap. He had one more thing to do, to fully cover his tracks.

"*Jambo*, Ezekiel, is the boss in?" he called out when Ezekiel opened the door of the house.

"No Bwana Max. He left here some days ago. He is not with you at Mbabati?"

"No, we haven't seen him for a couple weeks. Well, never mind, I'll catch up with him another time. When he gets back, ask him to call me will you? He wanted to go hunting with me; I thought we might go next week."

Max reversed his vehicle and drove off. He was enjoying himself.

Ezekiel hurried back into the house and after hesitating a moment, he reached for the telephone.

******

A police vehicle pulled up outside the front steps of Mbabati. Luke met Max coming out of his study; the sound of the vehicle approaching had brought them both to the front door. He flicked his hand at Luke who retreated to the kitchen, then took a deep breath and walked out to meet the disembarking policeman.

Inspector Groves was tall and well-built with straw blond hair bleached almost white by the sun; his eyes were covered by a pair of sunglasses.

"Good Morning, Officer," Max said amiably, shaking the man's hand. The second policeman remained seated behind the wheel of the car.

"Morning, sir. Inspector John Groves from the Nanyuki police station. We're here in connection with a missing person. Jake Henderson?"

226

Max creased his forehead in a frown of concern. "Missing?" he repeated with wonder and then, as though catching himself. "He's an old friend of ours. What do you mean exactly when you say he's missing?" He sipped nonchalantly at the cup of coffee he was holding.

"Mr Henderson's house servant called us after your visit yesterday morning; he was concerned he wasn't with you at Mbabati. We've subsequently checked all the surrounding estates and farms but no-one's seen him."

"But that's ridiculous," Max said raising his voice. "He must have told Ezekiel where he was going?"

"Mr Henderson left his house on horseback several days ago. His stable boy believes he was coming here. We'd like permission to search your estate for any sign of him."

"Of course, Inspector. Go right ahead."

"Have you seen his horse by any chance, sir? It hasn't turned up here on your estate?"

"No. If something had happened to Jake, his horse would have found its way home, they invariably return to their own stable."

"You'd think so, but there's been no sign of it. Thank you, Mr Gray." He saluted smartly and climbed back into the police vehicle. Max leant down beside the open car window and gave directions on how to navigate around the estate. Best to be helpful, he thought.

After the dust from their departing vehicle had settled, he walked thoughtfully around the grounds. He was sure he hadn't overlooked any incriminating evidence.

He returned to the house, making his way upstairs to the music room, he knew he would find her there even though she wasn't allowed to play anymore.

Nicola sat immobile by one of the windows, gazing unseeingly into the distance. She didn't turn when he entered the room. He cleared his throat and stood in front of her.

"That was the police. Jake's gone missing."

Her head snapped around. "You told me yesterday Ezekiel said Jake was staying at another ranch?" Nicola felt panic surge through her.

"Well, it appears no-one's seen him for at least a week. He went out riding and hasn't been seen since."

He patted her shoulder. "Any idea where he might have gone? You must tell me if you know anything to help the police in their search."

Shocked, she stared at him, and he saw the fear in her eyes.

"The police are combing the estate looking for signs of him. They'll question you and ask when you saw him last." His eyes narrowed spitefully. "So, you'd better come up with something."

******

The next morning, Nicola was standing by the open doors in their sitting room when Luke ushered in Inspector John Groves.

"Good morning, Mrs Gray. Thank you for seeing me at short notice." Nicola gestured for him to sit down, before she lowered herself into the chair opposite him.

"I'm here to ask a few questions about Jake Henderson. Your husband said he was a frequent visitor here?"

Nicola nodded with effort. "Yes, he's been here often. He's our nearest neighbour."

John Groves studied the woman sitting opposite him; he had heard gossip at the Club that Jake, whom he had met on a few occasions, was involved in some kind of a relationship with Nicola Gray. He'd been curious to meet her and now he watched as she nervously twisted her wedding ring.

"When did you last see him, Mrs Gray?"

"About three weeks ago," Nicola said, closing her eyes briefly. "It was at the airport. I was seeing my daughter, Catherine, off to school in England and we bumped into him."

"Do you know what he was doing at the airport? Did he mention he was planning to go away for a few days?"

"No, he came to say good-bye to my daughter. He's fond of her," she said lamely.

"So he wasn't planning a trip of any kind, nothing you were aware of?"

"I don't recall him saying anything about going anywhere."

"Did he come to Mbabati after you had met him at the airport? Perhaps to see your husband?"

228

Nicola stood up unsteadily." As far as I know he didn't come here. It's possible Luke might know if he did. She held on to the head rest of the armchair. John noticed her knuckles were white.

"Thank you." John said, also rising to his feet. "I appreciate your co-operation. I'll have a quick word with Luke?"

Luke glanced up in surprise as the Inspector entered the kitchen; he stopped what he was doing and wiped his hands on his apron. "Yes sir, may I help you?"

"You've heard Mr Henderson has gone missing?"

"Yes, everyone has heard this, sir."

"When did you last see him, Luke? Was it here at the house?"

"Yes sir, it was here. He came for lunch to say goodbye to Miss Cat before she went to school in England."

"Can you remember when that was?"

"It was maybe four Sundays ago. This was the last time I saw him."

"Thank you, Luke."

He saw the Inspector out and hurried back to the kitchen to finish making his trifle.

******

John drove back to the police station, wondering how difficult it was going to be to get a warrant to search the Gray's house; he and his men had already searched neighbouring estates and come up with nothing.

Three days later, he returned to Mbabati, a search warrant in his hands.

Max was having his breakfast when Luke showed him into the dining-room. He stood up, his chair toppling over behind him, his lips pressed together with annoyance.

"Yes Inspector?"

"I have a warrant here to search your house," John began, lifting the folded official document.

"Search the house?" Max blustered angrily. "What the devil for?"

John explained that they had searched the grounds of all the estates in the area and that it was their intention now to widen the search to include the properties themselves. He apologized for any inconvenience.

"It's bloody inconvenient, actually. What do you expect to find? Jake Henderson's body underneath the floorboards, or in our laundry cupboard?"

He threw his napkin onto the table and strode out of the room. "This is unacceptable," he shouted over his shoulder. John shrugged, placing the warrant on the dining room table.

For four hours the police officers meticulously searched the house. When John entered the music room and saw the magnificent piano, he whistled softly through his teeth. It must have cost a small fortune to buy it and have it shipped out to Kenya. On his police salary he couldn't even afford a mouth-organ. He warned his men to be extra careful, but thorough, when they searched the room.

Knocking firmly on the sitting room door, John entered without waiting for a response. Luke had told him the Grays were waiting for him in there. Nicola was staring blankly into the empty fireplace. Her husband sat opposite her with a face like thunder. He launched himself upright and stood when he saw John enter.

"Have you finished invading our home yet, Inspector?" he asked sarcastically.

"We're done here, I'll see myself out. Good afternoon to you both."

John walked swiftly out of the house. Max Gray's uncalled-for anger at being shown the search warrant surprised him. His wife was visibly distraught and he began to suspect the rumours about her relationship with the missing man had been based on an element of truth. From what he could observe, the Grays didn't have what he would term 'an intimate relationship'. For a start they had separate bedrooms.

******

Max walked towards the stables, tapping his riding crop agitatedly against his boots. Damn police. At least, so far as he could tell, they hadn't discovered the hide or they would have been crawling all over the place. He was positive Nicola wouldn't have mentioned it as the last thing she would want was for the Inspector to find out about her grubby little affair with Henderson.

Nicola saw the tail lights of Max's Land Rover recede down the drive. Every Thursday, she'd returned to the hide hoping Jake might suddenly arrive, throw his arms around her and tell her he'd been commissioned to paint a portrait in New York and had to leave in a hurry. She stopped her train of thought, unable to spend another hour in the house, and made her way to the kitchen.

"Luke, I'm going into Nanyuki to see if there's any news, I want you to come with me. On the way back we can go to Bwana Jake's house, maybe Ezekiel has heard something."

Nicola drove in complete silence. After some time, Luke cleared his throat and coughed politely. "This is a bad business, Miss Nicola."

When she said nothing, he continued.

"I fear for the life of Bwana Jake, it has been many days now since he has gone. It is the same many days since Bwana Max shot the two dogs," he said finally.

Nicola glanced at him sharply, pushing her sunglasses up on her head. "What do you mean, Luke! What are you trying to say?"

Luke stared straight ahead. "There were many shots on that day, Miss Nicola. More than just two for killing the dogs."

She looked back at the road. "Bwana Max said there were baboons and they attacked the dogs. He might have been trying to shoot at them."

Luke continued to look straight ahead. "Bwana Jake is dead. Too many days have passed."

"You don't know for sure, Luke! Perhaps he had to leave the country on business. You don't know he's dead!" Nicola's voice rose with panic.

Luke looked steadfastly through the windscreen, avoiding her eyes. "Bwana Jake rode away from his house on his horse," he said calmly. "Where is this horse now? A horse, when the rider has gone, will always go back to his stable. This horse has not returned. I fear this horse is also dead. Bwana Jake would not go to the airport on a horse."

"Stop it! Stop talking like that! I can't bear to think about what you're trying to say," Nicola shouted.

She braked suddenly, sending a cloud of dust into the air around them; she turned to Luke, breathing hard. "You said you heard many shots," she said eventually. "What time did you hear these shots?"

"It was after lunch when you were working in the wine cellar. I was in the vegetable garden and Bwana Max had left in his vehicle. It was maybe around two o'clock when I heard them: three shots at first and not long after, another one."

"Do you have any idea what direction the shots came from?"

"It is difficult to know this but as there were vultures later in the sky above the hide, I am thinking the shots came from there."

Nicola put her hands to her face to stop them shaking. Then sitting up straight she put the car into gear and drove on, unable to deal with the possible truth of Luke's remarks.

At the club, Nicola ordered lunch and found a quiet corner where she went through the local paper. It had run a short story on his disappearance, and suggested it was more than likely he had left the country on one of his many business trips. She picked at her lunch listlessly; she was aware of the covert looks she was getting from the curious crowd at the bar.

Reversing out of the car park they headed for Leopard's Leap. Ezekiel let them in and, after making tea for Nicola, he and his cousin retired to the kitchen.

She walked around Jake's studio, her fingers touching his things as if it might bring a sense of him back to her.

"Where are you, my love? Please come back to me," she whispered. The room remained still and silent.

She walked into his bedroom and looked at the large board of photographs he'd propped against the wall. There were dozens of them: photographs of her, of Cat, Mbabati, and numerous wildlife and bush shots.

She lay down on the bed and buried her head in his pillow. The scent of him caught her off guard and, overwhelmed by everything, she gave into her despair. He was dead. She felt it now, the emptiness. Otherwise he would have found some way of contacting her.

The bed shook with her sobs and when there was nothing left inside of her, she lay on her back and stared at the ceiling, her eyes burning and red; her mind full of fragrant memories of their love affair.

She thought about telling the police Inspector about her suspicions; then realised she had no concrete evidence. The little information she and Luke had patched together was circumstantial at best.

The inspector would want to question Max, and she would have to admit to her affair. The scandal would catapult through the community and Cat would be embroiled in it when she returned for the holidays.

What on earth would she tell her beloved daughter? How could she comfort her when she couldn't even find any herself?

There was a soft knock and Luke opened the door. "We should go now, before it gets dark. Bwana Max will be angry if he knows you have been here."

Nicola continued to stare at the ceiling. "Will you go to the police with your story, Luke? Tell them what you think might have happened?"

"*Eish*, no, Miss Nicola," Luke said, clicking his tongue. "No good will come of this. It is over and we must go home now."

As they pulled up outside Mbabati Luke withdrew a bundle of letters from his pocket.

"Ezekiel gave these to me, he said they belong to you. He kept them somewhere safe when the police searched the house for Bwana Jake.

She took them speechlessly as the name on the envelope blurred in front of her.

Chapter Forty-One

Cat still hoped that one day Jake would turn up at the school gates and take her out for the promised dinner. But, two years down the line, she had resigned herself to the fact she would never see him again - how was it possible that he could have just vanished with no trace?

Cat closed her books with an irritable slam and wandered over to the window, looking out at the cold grey afternoon; the sky was the colour of wet cement, the tree outside stubbornly clinging to a last single leaf despite the strong wind blowing. Tomorrow she would be flying back to Kenya for the holidays, back to the warm sapphire skies of Africa.

******

The aircraft taxied to a halt at the international airport in Nairobi. Nicola saw Cat striding through the arrivals hall. She smiled as she watched heads turning to look at her daughter. How good it would be to have the house filled with her laughter and chatter again. The last two years with Max had been difficult, to say the least. The silence yawned down the long table during meals making them seem interminable. Without Luke's cheerful and constant presence around the house, she would have gone mad with loneliness.

She threw her arms around her daughter, inhaling her life and energy. It had been six long months since they had seen each other. "Darling!" Her voice wobbled precariously.

Cat hugged her mother. "How are things at home?" she asked, noticing how thin and tired she looked, the lines like a spider's web beginning to imbed on her face.

She linked arms with her daughter as they headed for the car park. "We've been having the most awful drought; you'll have to take quick showers now - strictly no baths - so we can conserve what little water we have left." They walked to her car, stowed the luggage and climbed in.

"The lake's never been at such a low level," she continued, "and the gardens have suffered with no rain." Seeing her daughter's frustrated expression, she added hastily, "Luke's looking forward to seeing you; he's been planning to make your favourite treats for weeks now."

"I didn't really mean how the house and garden was," Cat said, as Nicola steered the car out of the car park and began their journey home. "I meant Daddy. How are things with both of you? Has he relented yet and let you play your piano?"

Nicola shook her head and patted Cat's hand. "No, he hasn't, but we somehow rub along together. I try to keep busy, try to keep out of his way, but I miss my music, you have no idea," her voice trailed off. "I miss Jake too. I still expect to see him bounding up the steps to the house."

She looked sideways at her daughter and saw her eyes fill with tears, and changed the subject.

Cat was relieved when they finally arrived at Mbabati and saw Luke rushing out of the kitchen door, a wide smile on his face, to greet her. He gave her a fierce hug and welcomed her home.

Max watched his wife and daughter across the dining room table gauging the moment was now right for the next part of his plan.

"Nicola?"

Her heart squeezed with apprehension; something unpleasant was going to happen.

"Yes?" she replied woodenly.

"Why don't you play something for us after dinner? Let's celebrate the homecoming of our daughter."

Nicola looked at him, then glanced at Cat; she hadn't played the piano for over two years.

"I'd love to," she murmured, her fingers flexing in her lap in anticipation

"The piano cost a fortune; I think it's time you took it up again." He smiled slyly at his daughter, who looked at him with trepidation.

Upstairs, Nicola arranged her long skirt over the stool and lifted the lid of the piano. Max and Cat had settled themselves by the fireplace. Cat looked at her father. The uncertainty Nicola saw on her daughter's face was a mirror to her own, and her hands trembled as she flexed them and held them over the keys.

"Before you start," Max said interrupting, "I'd like to hear one of my favourite pieces." Her hands froze over the keys as she looked at his flushed face, seeing he was already well lubricated.

235

"What would you like?"

"The piece by Grieg you used to play so well." He said rubbing his hands together in anticipation.

"I can't remember how to play the whole thing; I'll need my music." She looked through her music books until she found it. She sat down again; placing the music book on the stand, she opened it.

Taped to the first page was Jake's signet ring. Her stomach muscles clenched and the taste of bile rose sourly in her throat, seeping through her mouth as she stared at it in disbelief.

"Play on, my dear," Max said encouragingly. "Your music brings back lots of memories. Memories are so provocative, aren't they?"

Nicola lifted her hands from her lap and pulled the ring free from the tape, placing it on her lap. Her hands shook as she played the opening bars; the blood had drained from her face and the notes swam and blurred in front of her eyes.

"Are you alright, Mummy?" Cat asked her anxiously, "Grieg sounds a bit wobbly tonight."

"Just a little out of practice," Nicola said. She forced herself to play the entire piece, when she had finished, she closed the lid of the piano, and rose unsteadily to her feet, Jake's ring biting into her clenched fist.

She looked at Cat's concerned face. Putting her hand to her forehead she forced herself to smile. "All the driving has given me a headache. Goodnight, darling, I'll see you tomorrow." Nicola walked over to her daughter and kissed her forehead. Ignoring her husband, she fled from the room.

Nicola's legs shook as she descended the staircase. He had put the ring there. It had been him who had suggested she play this evening and that particular piece of music. He wouldn't have known she might not remember the entire piece but it was a good guess.

Jake had always worn the ring and never taken it off - not when he slept, bathed or made love.

She sat down on the edge of her bed, her mind recoiling from what she was beginning to know was the truth. The place she kept returning to.

Jake would not have given Max his ring voluntarily.

She ran to the bathroom and threw up, the blood in her veins turning icy. Soaking a small towel in cold water, she patted it over her face. Feeling her legs giving way beneath her, she slid to the floor. Leaning back against the wall she wrung the towel between her hands, then lowering her head to her knees she became still.

******

The next morning, Cat wandered into her mother's bedroom and sat on the bed. "It's such a beautiful day and a hot one - I think I'll go for a drive around the estate." Cat smiled at her, concerned with the unsteadiness of her hands as she drank her coffee.

"Is everything alright with you, Mummy?"

"Darling, I'm absolutely fine," Nicola said, squeezing her daughter's hand attempting to assuage her anxiety.

Cat took a deep breath, unsure of her next question, but she needed an answer to it.

"Mummy, I know things are *not* alright. I've known it for years. Since the night," she paused, "when Father did what he did to you." She stopped, seeing her mother's expression turn to one of horror. Cat rushed the words out: "I heard everything he said, I saw what he did to you. What did you do that was so terrible? You have to tell me!"

Nicola held up her hand, trying to compose herself. She remembered Luke being in the room, helping her afterwards, but had no memory of her daughter being there.

"Hush, Cat, it was all a long time ago. But what on earth were you doing in my bedroom anyway?"

"I just wanted to snuggle up to you in bed, like I used to when I was little - it was going to be a surprise." She shook her head at the memory of that night.

"The fight you had with father. Did it have something to do with Jake?" Cat asked, tears balancing precariously on her clumped lower lashes. "I miss him too, you know. Is it because of him you go down to the hide and cry?"

"Now, Cat, enough," she said as steadily as she could manage. "There's nothing for you to worry about, all that's in the past now. Why don't you go for your drive? Perhaps Luke would like to go with you."

After Cat had left the bedroom, Nicola searched for Jake's ring beneath her pillow.

"I'm sorry, my love, so terribly, terribly sorry." She picked up the bowl he had given her, her first and only present from him, and slipped his ring into the hidden compartment. It was a perfect fit.

It would be twenty long years later when Sophie and Alex discovered it in its secret hiding place.

Chapter Forty-Two

Cat and Luke drove down to the drying sheds to say hello to the workers she had known all her life, she was relieved her father was not around when they arrived. She greeted them in Swahili and exchanged pleasantries with them, before turning to Luke.

"It's so hot Luke!" she said wiping the back of her hand across her forehead and pulling her long hair up into a clip. "Let's go down to the lake and see what the situation is there? Maybe there'll be enough water for me to paddle; my feet are swelling up with the heat."

She parked the jeep under a tree and surveyed the lake. "It's almost unrecognizable like this. Not enough water to come up to my ankles; even the boat's marooned in the mud. Do you think the rains will come soon?"

Luke looked up into the sky and squinted. "It will be soon, little one, you can see the clouds are coming, and when they come there will be strong rain and storms; maybe in a few days it will be here."

The jetty stood stranded in the bed of the dried-up lake. Cat sat at the end of it swinging her legs in the hope she could cool them off a bit. Luke stood next to her surveying the muddy surface. Suddenly her eye was caught by the sun glinting on something half submerged in the mud. She stood up, shielding her eyes with her hand to get a better look.

"There's something out there," she said pointing with her other hand. "It might be a dead hippo. Can you see it?" He followed the direction of her hand, adjusting his eyes to the fierce glare of the blinding sun. "Shall we see what it is Luke? It looks big and bulky."

Together they walked through the thick, gluey mud and shallow puddles of water, keeping a careful eye open for slumbering crocodiles. Cat prodded the mound with a stick wiping some of the mud away. "It looks like a saddle! See if you can pull it out."

The mud of the lake sucked stubbornly at the saddle before suddenly releasing it, together they carried it dripping and muddy back to the shore. "This is a strange thing, little one. None of the grooms have reported a missing saddle."

He opened one of the saddlebags and found a bridle, and in the other a bundle of clothes. He shook out a sodden shirt, its faint check still recognizable. He reached into the bag again and withdrew a man's

239

belt, holding it up for her to see, followed by a sodden pair of safari boots.

"What is all this, Luke? Who do these clothes belong to?"

He looked into her frightened eyes and chose his words with care. "I have seen this shirt and this belt before. These clothes belong to Bwana Jake... this must be his saddle."

Cat held her hands over her ears trying to register what she was looking at. "You think this is *his* saddle! But what's it doing in the lake? Do you think he had an accident and drowned here?"

He shook his head unable to answer her questions. "Why would he take all his clothes off?" She started to cry hysterically. "We'll have to report this to the police, Luke, and tell them what we've found. Oh God, you don't think he was swimming and taken by a crocodile do you?"

"We must take these things back to the house," he said calmly, ignoring her questions, visibly shocked by what he had found in the saddlebags. "Your mother will tell us what to do with these things." He shook his head remembering the shots that hot still afternoon. It made sense now and his suspicions had been confirmed.

Cat drove erratically back to the house and parked in the driveway, leaving the engine running in her haste, then ran up the stairs to the house, shouting for her mother. Nicola appeared at the top of the stairs, alarmed by the sound of her daughter's hysterical voice. "What is it, Cat? What's the matter?"

"We found something in the lake, a saddle. Luke thinks it might be Jake's!"

Nicola's knees started to buckle beneath her and she reached out a flailing hand to the balustrade. Taking a deep breath she tried to suppress the horror building up inside of her. Carefully she descended the stairs and made her way out into the driveway, the sour taste of dread in the back of her throat.

The saddle was already beginning to dry out. Jake's clothes were heaped next to it alongside the water-marked safari boots. Nicola sank to her knees and buried her face in her hands. None of them were aware of Max's silent approach.

"For God's sake get up, Nicola. You're making an absolute fool of yourself in front of the servants." He turned and looked into his daughter's terrified eyes. "What on earth's the matter with you, Catherine? Pull yourself together!"

Luke, emboldened by the truth in front of him, intervened. "We have found a saddle in the lake, and also some clothes and boots. They are belonging to Bwana Jake."

"Nonsense! They could belong to anyone, and the saddle. Take these things down to the stables, Luke, lock them in one of the rooms. Do it now!"

Luke got into the driver's seat and drove towards the stables, his face creased with anxiety.

Max watched him go. Damn the bloody drought! He turned back to his wife and daughter. "Well, don't just stand there. I'm sure all this can be explained. Get back inside. It's far too hot to be out here." He watched them go inside before walking swiftly down to the stables.

Nicola put her arm around her daughter and squeezed her. "Come on, darling," she said, her voice breaking. "I'm sure everything can be explained."

"They're Jake's clothes, Mummy. Why didn't you say anything?" she demanded. "We have to go to the police and tell them what we've found, let them investigate. Why is Father always so angry with everyone and everything? Sometimes I really hate him!"

"Hush Cat. We can't be sure the clothes belong to Jake. Let's give it a few days then I'm sure Daddy will contact the police and do the right thing."

Chapter Forty-Three

Two days later Nicola sat at her desk writing a letter to her sister. Cat was lying on the sofa, reading. The thunder growled and boomed outside reverberating through the house. The air was thick and still as it waited for the storm to break. Luke had been right - it had only been a matter of days for the rains to arrive.

Cat yawned and closed her book. "It's so hot I can hardly keep my eyes open." She wandered over to the window. "It looks like an almighty storm is coming. Shall I ring for tea or is it too hot even for that?"

Nicola screwed the cap on her pen and looked up at her daughter. "Let's have tea."

The front door banged and they looked at each other, fear and apprehension mirrored in their faces.

Max strode into the sitting room and threw his hat on a chair. "There's a massive storm coming in the next hour. I've sent the workers home to the village before it breaks." He looked at his watch. "Time for a gin and tonic, I think. Anyone going to join me?"

Nicola shook her head. "A little early for that," she murmured, "we're going to have tea."

He shrugged his shoulders. "Please yourself. Catherine, tell Luke to bring me a drink."

Cat left the room abruptly, and he turned back to Nicola. "What are you looking so miserable about?" he hissed. "Still trying to work out what happened to your lover? I wouldn't bother if I were you. He's dead, one way or another. Good riddance, I say."

Luke came into the room with Max's drink followed by Cat. "Ah, thank you, Luke. I hope you made it a large one. Bring the bottle of gin and some more tonic will you?"

Cat sat down next to her mother and fiddled with the tassel on one of the cushions, aware of the tense atmosphere in the room, and the gathering storm.

"So how are you enjoying your holiday, Catherine?" he said absently. "Finding enough things to do? Maybe next holidays you should bring a friend out with you, eh? It might put a smile on your face for a change."

Cat hated it when he spoke to her like this. As if he was spoiling for yet another row and whether it was the atmosphere outside, or inside, she felt her temper beginning to rise. Luke set down the tea tray and withdrew.

"I don't think I will, Father. I don't think any of my friends would enjoy the atmosphere of this house. In fact I've decided to stay in England for the next term break, or maybe I'll go to the States and stay with Aunt Elizabeth."

She poured her mother tea and handed it to her. "It's no fun being here, you're always so angry and I don't enjoy the holidays anymore. I'm seventeen now and you can't force me to do anything," she said defiantly.

Max looked at her, the colour rising in his face. "I'll decide what you can and cannot do. Perhaps you should ask yourself why I'm angry all the time?"

A slash of lightning ripped through the garden, briefly lighting the rapidly darkening room, a loud crack of thunder followed. Cat jumped nervously.

"Alright," she said, "so why are you so angry all the time. Is it me? I've known since I was a little girl you didn't like me much, but I could never work out why."

Max narrowed his eyes. "It's not that I don't like you, Catherine, it's just that I don't know if I'm your father."

Nicola's cup clattered in the saucer as she leaned forward to put it on the tray. "Please Max," she whispered. "Please don't do this to us."

Cat looked at her parents, waiting for one of them to say something." I don't understand what you're saying - what do you mean about not knowing if you're my father?"

"Well I could be, it's true, but then again so could Jake Henderson. Who's to know? Your mother was having an affair with him for years, so you might be his little bastard. Why don't you ask her?"

Cat looked at her mother with disbelief. "Is this true, Mummy?"

Nicola sat up straight and looked into her daughter's shocked eyes. She took a deep breath; she had nothing more to lose. "Yes, it's true. I loved Jake, but you have my word he wasn't your father."

Cat smiled through her tears. "I loved him too..." She turned to her father.

"Did you kill Jake because Mummy loved him more than you? Did you dump his clothes and saddle in the lake?"

Max poured himself another copious drink. "Well now, that was for the police to find out and for you to work out. I might have killed him but then again, maybe I didn't."

Cat stared at her father. "It was you, wasn't it! That's why you locked his things in the stables, to hide them." Her voice rose accusatorily. "Anyone else would have called the police immediately..."

"Oh stop being so dramatic, Catherine. If you can't say anything sensible, get out of the bloody room."

Cat stood up, incensed at being dismissed. She snatched the keys to her jeep from the silver tray. "I tried to love you, Father, really I did, but the truth is, I don't even like you. But I did love Jake; he was more of a father to me than you ever were!"

Max laughed. "Well maybe we should have kept our first child and given you away instead. What do you think, Nicola?"

Cat turned to her mother, her face ashen. "You had another baby? Why didn't you tell me Mummy?"

Nicola turned to him furiously. "How could you! How could you do this to Cat? Why are you so intent on destroying everything around you?" She turned to her daughter, holding her arms out, her eyes full of tears.

"I'm sorry, darling, I didn't know how to..."

"I thought we were close, Mummy, close enough so you could tell me anything. How can you live with yourself and all your secrets? I hate both of you, and I'm never coming back to this house!"

Nicola stretched out her hand, to her. "Don't say that, Cat, please don't say things you may regret. Don't drive off with this storm coming, it's too dangerous. Please Cat!" she implored.

Luke, who had been standing outside the sitting room waiting to collect the tea tray, shouted out to her as she rushed past him nearly knocking him over.

"Little one, you must not go out into the storm, your mother is right, the rain has already started."

"Leave me alone Luke," she screamed hysterically, "I can look after myself! I don't need any of you anymore."

Luke watched Cat start the jeep and drive off. The vehicle fishtailed in the dust as she fought with the steering wheel. The lightning had become more frequent and the thunder cracked and rumbled over the house. Suddenly the rain came and within seconds had become torrential, bringing strong winds which whipped and tore through the trees.

Luke hesitated for a moment, then he returned to the kitchen for his raincoat, shrugging it on he ran towards the building where the other vehicles were parked. Snatching the keys from the board he jumped into the Land Rover, gunned the engine and set off in pursuit, the rain drumming unabated on the canvas roof.

Nicola turned from the window, her face white and drawn, her voice tight with panic. "Please go after her, Max, I'm frightened for her. She's not an experienced driver and it's treacherous out there. Please, I'm begging you - go after her!"

He laughed. "Send Luke. I've had far too much to drink and you're always telling me drinking and driving is dangerous. Not so? Catherine will probably head for the hide. She'll be safe enough there until this blows over, and before you send Luke after her, ask him to bring me some more ice and lemon will you?"

Terrified for the safety of her daughter Nicola made for the kitchen. Cookie looked up as she entered.

"Bad storm, Memsahib, very bad storm." Glumly he continued to chop an onion. "Luke has followed Miss Cat, he will find her and bring her home."

She looked up as another massive clap of thunder shook the house, and rattled the crockery on the shelves. "Please God," she whispered fervently, "don't take my daughter from me as well, please let her come home safely."

Nicola ran up the stairs to her bedroom and stood at the window, peering through the sheet of rain coming down like steel rods as it thundered over the gardens, breaking and bending the plants and flowers, the wind whipping the trees into a frenzy and snapping off heavy branches.

She sank onto the window seat, her eyes searching the rapidly darkening garden. "Please God," she whispered again, "don't punish me anymore. Please be a forgiving God and keep her safe."

Luke struggled to keep the Land Rover from sliding across the bush road as he strained his eyes trying to catch a glimpse of Cat's jeep. The rain hissed and spat at the windscreen as the wipers struggled to deal with the deluge.

Trees lay strewn across the bush, felled by the fury of the weather and for once he was grateful for the constant streaks of lightning which lit up the bush as he searched for her. The animals huddled together under trees, waiting for the storm to abate, their coats darkened by the rain. Monkeys clustered together as they clung to each other, and the branches of swaying trees.

Finally he reached the hide. Her jeep wasn't there but perhaps, he thought, it had broken down and she'd taken shelter. Leaving the engine running he pulled his raincoat over his head and ran along the muddy path and into the hide. It was deserted.

Suddenly he heard a roar and ran out onto the deck. He saw the huge river of water flood the waterhole, filling and covering it in minutes. In all his years out here in the bush he had never seen such a mighty storm and he was frightened by its intensity.

For three hours Luke searched the bush, his arms aching from trying to keep the vehicle upright, his eyes stinging and bloodshot by the constant searching in the dark night. Exhausted, he stopped the Land Rover and closed his tired eyes, resting his head in his arms on the steering wheel for a few moments, wondering which other direction he should go that he hadn't already searched.

He rubbed his eyes wearily, grateful that although it was still raining hard it had eased up and the wind had blown itself out. He put the vehicle into low gear and gingerly made his way through the detritus of the storm.

A brief flash of light caused him to change direction and as he rounded a bend on the treacherous muddy track he saw her stationery jeep, its lights piercing the dark bush and sky. The vehicle seemed empty. Puzzled he looked around for her then back at the jeep. The only sound was the rain pattering relentlessly on the roof of his vehicle. Turning the Land Rover around he turned the headlights onto her vehicle and saw the heavy tree lying across the bent and broken roof.

With trepidation he opened his door and walked towards it. Cat was lying across the passenger seat, her long blonde hair covering her face. "Little one," he called softly. "Are you sleeping? Can you hear me?"

"Luke," she whispered weakly. "I'm hurt, Luke."

He went around to the passenger door and tried to open it but the damage from the fallen tree made it impossible. He went back around to the driver's side and bent his head down. "I will have to get you out, little one. I will try not to hurt you. Can you sit up and hold Luke's arms. If you can do this I will pull you out."

He reached over and gently pushed her hair back from her face, his eyes filling with horror when he saw the injury to her head.

Carefully he pulled her from the car and wrapped his coat around her shivering body. "We will rest awhile, little one, and then I will take you home."

"Hold me tight, Luke, like you used to when I was little? I'm so sleepy..."

Luke held her in his arms and sank to the ground, leaning back on the Land Rover as he rocked her back and forth, crooning an African lullaby she had loved as a child.

"Take good care of her, won't you, Luke," she whispered, "tell her I'm sorry. Tell her how much I love her. Promise you'll never leave her. Promise me, Luke?"

"You can tell her this yourself, little one, when we get home," he said, his voice breaking.

His tears, and the rain, ran down his cheeks as he adjusted his coat around her and held her close.

"Luke?"

He bent his head as she whispered his name, his tears splashing on her wet and bloodied face.

"Luke is here, little one. You are safe now."

"I'm going away now. I loved Jake, just like Mummy did. I'm tired Luke..."

Mutely he nodded his head as she shivered once and then lay still in his arms; softly he spoke to her, his voice breaking again. "Goodbye, my little one. Go well to this other place. One day Luke will come and find you there."

The rain from the trees dripped onto his raincoat as he glanced up at the now clear night and the stars; then he looked down at the still body of the young girl lying in his arms.

He leaned his head back on the side of the vehicle, his shoulders heaving, giving into his grief at the loss of the child he had loved more than his own.

Nicola saw the lights of a Land Rover and stood up. She ran down the stairs, her daughter's name already on her lips. Pulling open the heavy doors she stopped, her knuckles white as she gripped the door.

Luke looked at her, unable to speak, holding Cat's body in his arms, the tears running unashamedly down his face.

Her screams ripped through the night as she ran towards him and sank to her knees in the thick mud, holding her arms out for her child. "Give her to me, Luke. Give her to me."

Nicola held her daughter close, brushing her hair back from her wet face and cupping her cheek in her hand. "It's alright, darling, mummy's here, you'll be alright. You're so cold, my darling. Luke, bring me a blanket, Cat's freezing."

Luke returned with a blanket and helped her wrap it around her daughter. He put his hand on her arm. "It is cold and wet out here, Miss Nicola. Let me take Cat and put her in your bed. She is too heavy for you to carry, let me do this."

With as much care as possible he wrested Cat away from her reluctant arms, then walked slowly into the house and up the staircase to Nicola's bedroom. When he returned he found her still on her knees staring sightlessly at the ground, her arms loose by her side, wet mud seeping through her clenched fists.

He helped her to her feet. "Go sit with your child, Miss Nicola, I will find Bwana Max and call for the doctor. I will bring you some brandy."

"She's dead, Luke," Nicola said dully. "My beloved little girl is dead. What good will a doctor do?"

Tika stood completely still under the tree, watching the house, his body black with wetness. Down each side of his dark head ran rivulets of water leaving a path like tears on his wrinkled face. Then he turned around and disappeared between the dripping trees.

Luke looked at Max with disgust, seeing him snoring in his chair in the sitting room, knowing there was no point in trying to wake him. He returned to the kitchen and poured a glass of brandy, placed it on a tray with a warm bowl of water, then made his way to the bedroom.

He lit the candles at each side of the bed then carefully washed Cat's face, taking special care to remove the blood. Nicola sat in the chair, her brandy untouched, staring blindly at her daughter, saying nothing. Then she stood up and lay down on the bed next to Cat, gathering her in her arms and whispering to her.

248

The next morning the storm had passed and as the light seeped into the bedroom Luke, who had spent the night watching over them, rose stiffly from his chair and left the room. Nicola still held her daughter.

He made coffee and took it through to Max who was sitting groggily where Luke had seen him the night before. "There has been a bad accident," he said bluntly. "Miss Cat is dead. We must call for the doctor to come here."

Max looked at him blearily, his eyes bloodshot, the colour draining from his face. "Dead," he said incredulously. "What happened?"

"I searched many hours for her before I found the jeep. A tree had fallen on it causing it to hit a big rock. Miss Cat was killed by hitting her head on the steering wheel."

Max looked around wildly. "Where is she? Where is the memsahib?"

"They are together in the bedroom. It is better you do not go there. It is better if you go and get the doctor for the certificate."

"Certificate?"

Luke looked at him contemptuously. "The certificate for the dead. Afterwards it is the funeral we must make."

Pushing Luke aside Max bounded up the stairs to the bedroom and pushed the door open. Walking to the bed he looked down at his daughter, and his eyes tightened with tears.

Nicola was lying on her back holding Cat's inert body in her arms, singing softly to her, staring blindly at the ceiling, unaware of his presence.

He ran his hands over his face, searching for words of comfort and finding none." I'm sorry, Nicola, I'm sorrier than you can imagine," he said grimly.

"I'm going into Nanyuki to fetch the doctor. There are things that need to be done. It's the least I can do," he mumbled.

Nicola closed her eyes and stroked Cat's hair, still singing softly. Max left closing the door after him.

Later in the afternoon the doctor, the hearse, the undertakers and the priest arrived at Mbabati. Luke tapped on the bedroom door and let himself in.

"Miss Nicola," he whispered, "the doctor is here to see you and Miss Cat. He is waiting downstairs with Bwana Max."

She turned to him and smiled. "It's alright Luke, Catherine is fine here with me. Just leave us alone will you?"

******

The priest waited at the side of the open grave, his robes moving languidly in the warm breeze, the flickering pages of the bible open and ready in his hands. He watched as the pallbearers, staff from the estate, came towards him, balancing the coffin on their shoulders. Nicola stumbled as she walked behind it, Luke, as always beside her, holding her arm to steady her. Max followed a little distance behind with the two grooms and Cookie.

The coffin was lowered into the ground, the rich red earth piled up next to it. The priest cleared his throat waiting for the child's mother to start the burial process but no-one moved. The only sound was the soft call of doves in the garden and the faint rustling of the leaves on the trees. The priest nodded to the undertakers, indicating they should proceed with the burial.

Suddenly he held up his hand.

At the gates of Mbabati the workers from the factory had gathered, and then as one their voices rose in perfect harmony as they sang their haunting goodbye to the girl they had watched growing up. They sang knowing her spirit would fly on the pure melody of their voices.

Nicola stared at the grave, her tears falling unabated, as she listened to the sound of their clear pure voices, aware only of Luke's firm grip on her elbow, but unaware of the tears on his own grief-stricken face as he wept unashamedly.

After the funeral Nicola stayed behind refusing to leave the graveyard. She sat on the iron bench and stared at her daughter's freshly covered grave, her lips moving as she spoke to her. Darkness descended over the house but still she didn't move.

Luke approached silently; he put the lit lamp down and wrapped a warm blanket around her thin shoulders. Sitting next to her he took her cold hands in his.

"Miss Nicola, you must say goodnight now and come back to the house. Miss Cat will be here tomorrow to talk to. She will be here every day now. She has come home."

Nicola, coming out of her reverie, looked at him her grief stricken face confused. "She doesn't like the dark, Luke, she was always frightened of it. She won't like it out here on her own."

"I have brought the lamp for her so she will not be afraid, and I will sit here through the night to comfort her. You must come back to the house now for food and sleep."

Nicola stood up, putting her hand on his shoulder to steady herself. "If she needs me you will come and wake me, won't you?"

He guided her back to the house before returning to the grave. Pulling his coat around him he settled down on the bench and closed his bloodshot eyes.

He sensed his old friend coming towards him. Tika caressed the freshly covered grave with his trunk, then lifted it high in the air as if he was searching for her. He touched Luke's face, as though wanting to share his grief; he stood for a long time with his old friend, then walked away into the dark shadows of the garden.

Chapter Forty-Four

Elizabeth

I have had many regrets in my life, but the biggest one, which led to the catastrophic events that ensued, was introducing my sister to Max Gray. I knew the first time I ever slept with him there was a violence and cruelty in him which was not apparent on the surface, but blatantly obvious between the sheets.

If I had known what an appalling influence he would have on our lives, and the lives of people he was yet to meet, I would have avoided him at all costs, but I didn't, and as he ingratiated himself into our lives he set the course for all of us, and the devastation which was to follow.

My sister's house was exquisite and I marvelled at how such a thing of beauty had been built in such a remote place.

Then there was Luke. I found him a cheerful and pleasant man who adored my sister and was fiercely protective of her. In the years that followed, Luke would play a large part in what happened at Mbabati, and this would leave him there alone, carrying the weight of a secret most of us would be unable to contemplate.

Over the following years I travelled to Kenya as often as my schedule would allow. My own career had a habit of stalling and stopping; being an actress was not an easy road and parts were hard to come by.

As for my own relationships with men, well, there were many, but no-one I would contemplate spending the rest of my life with. Why have just one man when there were so many of them out there? Yes, I admit, I accepted money from some of them in exchange for sleeping with them, (unlike my sister I'd blown my own trust fund, went through it like a hot knife through butter.)To be honest I just didn't have what it took to be a good actress, I had to be content with walk on parts, and I didn't have the talent - unlike Nicola who had it by the bucket load.

It was Jake who gave us the opportunity to talk on the phone every couple of weeks. Max had inherited the cottage down at the coast in a place called Watamu, and in the following years I would join Nicola and Cat there on their holidays - Max didn't know I was with them (no doubt too busy in town with his latest mistress). Cat, who seemed to dislike her father more than I did, never breathed a word to him.

I'll always remember those times at the coast. The days were spent lying around in the sun, reading or swimming in the tranquil warm sea. A local fisherman would come each morning and take our order for fish, lobster or prawns. Amos, the young African who looked after the cottage, would go to the local market for whatever else was needed. It was perfect.

Jake always joined us down there, much to the delight of Cat - and Nicola of course. He spent hours in the water teaching Cat to swim and playing with her, tossing her into the air, her squeals and laughter carrying to where we sat watching, sitting on the warm sand.

In the evening we would walk along the beach watching the setting sun, swinging Cat between us and watching her racing after crabs, dancing in the water or doing somersaults and cartwheels in the wet sand. Amos always built a bonfire on the beach at sunset, and after dinner we would sit around it talking and laughing.

Jake would strum his guitar and sing softly, with that lovely Irish lilt he had, the flames from the fire reflecting on his gorgeous face. He would spend those precious nights in Nicola's bed and leave at dawn, before Cat woke up.

One night, after Cat had gone to bed, I wandered out onto the beach and saw Jake and Nicola holding each other in the sea, their bodies one dark sleek shape, oblivious to everything. There was an enormous moon and I saw them clearly. The intensity and passion of their feelings for each other seemed to reverberate through the water.

I guess I've always been cynical about love. We've all done it, fallen in love, this is the one, happily ever after - then the debris when it all ends. Then, whoa, here comes another one and we fall in love with the whole idea of it all over again, and on it goes. I suppose it's all a dream really - this thing called love. But… but, Nicola and Jake's love was almost mystical. It seemed to me that they had always been moving towards each other.

I knew I would never come anywhere near finding something like that - but my sister and Jake did - nothing seemed to touch them, and their love for each other. It seemed to transcend everything. Those two loved each other, they really did. They lived for the moment, every second, when they could be together.

I knew Max was never going to let her go, so the relationship was thwarted from the beginning, and unless he dropped dead from a heart attack they were never going to get together. I was a little in love with Jake myself, but his love for Nicola was all consuming and I didn't stand a chance.

Cat didn't know her mother was once a famous pianist, even this had to be kept a secret. One slip from the child, perhaps telling a friend, would have brought the French media out in their droves, curious to see where she had ended up.

I began to see why my sister loved Kenya so much. To sit up in her music room and listen to the croaking frogs and insects, and sometimes the cruel laugh of the hyenas, or the throaty rasping calls of the lions, was a different world. Her music would carry on the balmy night air and I imagined the animals out there lifting their heads and listening spellbound and, of course, there was that bloody great elephant Tika who came to visit whenever he felt like it.

As soon as I heard the news about Cat's death I returned to Kenya to be with my sister. For Nicola, losing Jake had come as a tremendous shock, but to lose her beloved daughter as well was more than she was able to take, it devastated her.

I loved that child more than I thought possible...

Sorry. Just give me a moment will you.

Anyway as I was saying, Nicola was understandably inconsolable, so much so I wondered if she had contemplated taking her own life. I think the only thing that stopped her doing this was the fragile hope she'd always harboured that one day she would find the child she had given up for adoption - the child who was never far from her thoughts.

Every night she would go to Cat's grave and talk to her, and sometimes their old elephant friend, Tika, would appear as though he wanted to show her he understood her grief. I was scared stiff of him.

I asked her why she hadn't put Cat's name and dates on the headstone. It seemed a bit odd to me. She told me her daughter was ageless now and dates would make no difference to anything. She said she wouldn't be able to look at her daughter's name on a headstone because this would make her death too real. She had even removed every single photograph of Cat and put them away somewhere.

I think of Cat's grave now and wonder if the bush has reclaimed it. I try not to imagine what the years have done to the simple headstone, or if indeed it's still visible. So Nicola was right, you see. In the end nothing makes any difference; in a hundred years' time we'll all be dead and the ones who follow will not care who paid which price for what, or who was buried in a forgotten graveyard in the middle of nowhere. We're all forgotten eventually which makes you wonder what the whole point of our existence is really.

I stayed for a month, (Max wasn't happy about it but there was nothing he could do to stop me under the circumstances) trying to comfort Nicola, but she seemed to have gone somewhere far away from all of us, a place where she could be with her beloved Cat, and, of course, Jake. The emptiness I saw in her eyes frightened me.

I tried to persuade her to go to the hide with me, a place she had once loved, but she wouldn't go. The saddest thing of all was her refusal to play her magnificent piano.

I never heard her play again.

I left Mbabati and returned to the States. To be honest I couldn't bear the atmosphere of the house, it felt as though all the life had been sucked out of it. But the hardest thing of all was watching my sister, my gentle, wounded, broken sister, her once beautiful face now lined with unbearable grief. She barely spoke and spent hours in her bedroom just staring into the distance and, as far as I am concerned, she was never the same again. When I realised my presence was making little or no difference I reluctantly left.

I sometimes read about Jake Henderson in the newspapers. His work is much sought after now and the nature of his unexplained disappearance has added even more value. His masterpiece still hangs in Mbabati and is worth a small fortune, but in that abandoned house deep in the African bush it has probably been forgotten, its existence unknown.

Jake had produced the most beautiful book with his agent in New York. She sent me a copy. Going through the pages and seeing the unusual photographs with their classical music theme made me quite emotional. Cat really was a child of Africa and I suppose it was fitting she died there, it's what she would have wanted, but obviously not at the age of seventeen.

Fate is a cruel mistress and if I had been offered a part in a film and never returned to Mbabati things would have taken a completely different turn.

But let's go back to Nicola.

Chapter Forty-Five
MBABATI
1988

Nicola arranged the posy of white roses on Cat's grave; she would have been nineteen-years-old today. She brushed the dirt from her hands and wiped them on her trousers. "Happy Birthday, my darling," she whispered before turning and walking towards the stables.

Luke was waiting for her with the horses ready and saddled up, the rifle strapped to his horse. "I'm going to try for an impala today, Luke, but first I want to go down to the hide."

When they arrived there she dismounted and asked Luke to hold her horse. She unstrapped her saddlebag and removed a square tin containing her diary, Jake's letters and the photographs.

"It's best if this is never found again, Luke, and perhaps it's better if you don't know where I'm going to hide it. That way, should Bwana Max ask you, you can tell the truth and tell him you don't know."

He nodded. He knew precisely where she would hide the tin, and exactly what was in it.

Nicola raised the rifle and aimed at the young impala grazing slightly apart from the rest of the herd. At the sound of the shot the herd scattered in all directions. Luke smiled. He had taught her well and she had brought the animal down with a clean shot to the heart.

He strapped the still warm body onto his horse and they set off back to the house.

Max ate his dinner in silence, barely glancing at her. He had arrived back from Nairobi late in the afternoon. She could see he had been drinking and her heart sank. Since Cat died, his behaviour had become even more unpredictable.

She sighed and rang the bell for Luke, asking him to serve coffee in the sitting room. The evening stretched out endlessly in front of her and she wondered, as she had so often done, how she would get through the next hour or day, let alone the next year.

She picked up the two-day-old newspaper. It seemed life went on as usual all over the world, people making money, murders and missing children, politicians making promises they would never keep, earthquakes and so on.

An aircraft had exploded over a town somewhere in Scotland and she shuddered at the sheer wall of grief relatives would have to go through. Plucking up the courage she put the newspaper down and took a deep breath.

"I'm going away to spend some time with Elizabeth, I need to see her - I need to get away from here for a while," she said to him firmly.

He ran his fingers through his thinning hair. His bloodshot eyes looked unsteadily at her. "Don't be ridiculous, my dear, who do you think is going to pay for a trip to America, by sea, because of your ridiculous fear of flying? Not you, certainly, you haven't contributed a penny to anything for years now.

"Not the beautiful Nicola DuPont the world remembers, are you? What use are you to anyone anymore? You don't play the bloody piano, you don't talk, you don't do anything?"

"You can't hurt me anymore, Max," she said wearily. "I'm way beyond being hurt by what you say to me. I'm going whether you like it or not."

The speed at which he left his chair startled her. She stood up and reached for the poker. "Don't touch me, Max or I swear I'll use this."

"You don't have the guts. You never did have any guts if I recall, apart from taking a lover, but you couldn't even get that right, and look what happened to poor old Jake." He leaned against the fireplace and kicked at one of the burning logs.

"I killed him, of course, as you know, but even then you didn't have the guts to do anything about it, just sat and snivelled, too scared to go to the police.

"Do you know what Jake's final words were before I shot him? 'I love Nicola.' Yup, that's what he said. Just as well somebody loved you, because I never did. You were the means to an end that's all.

"Even our daughter hated you if I recall her final words before she drove off into the night. No, let me rephrase that - not our daughter, because I'm still not convinced she was mine; in fact, thinking about it I'm not even sure the little bastard we gave away was mine either." He snatched the poker from her hand and grabbed her by the throat.

"Don't fucking threaten me, Nicola, you're not going anywhere."

257

Luke reached silently into the gun cabinet by the sitting room door and withdrew a rifle. Max heard the soft click as Luke loaded it, and without releasing his hold on Nicola he turned around. "What the hell..."

"You must not harm her or I will kill you," Luke said evenly, the rifle pointing at Max's chest.

Max threw back his head and laughed, releasing his grasp on her throat and pushing her roughly aside. She stumbled backwards and lowered herself into the chair, her legs collapsing under her.

"Go away, Luke, this is none of your bloody business. Shoot me and they'll hang you."

"You must not harm her." Luke repeated, the rifle steady in his hands.

Max narrowed his eyes. "Put the bloody gun down and get back to the kitchen where you belong. This is my house, my wife, my land, now fuck off and bring me a drink. It's your job if I'm not mistaken?"

He smashed the poker against the fireplace and stormed out of the room, his rage unabated by the insolence of his servant. The front door slammed behind him and they heard the sound of the Land Rover crunching down the drive.

"You must go to the police, Miss Nicola," Lue murmured as he returned the rifle to the gun case. "He is a dangerous man and one day he will hurt you badly."

They both turned as they heard the Land Rover coming back. "Get out here, Luke," Max bellowed. "I need your help!"

"Do as he says," she whispered, "you mustn't make him any angrier. Go and see what he wants."

Nicola stood at the foot of the stairs and saw her husband and Luke carry the heavy planks upstairs. For the next hour the hammering nearly drove her out of her mind as she realised what he was doing.

Luke watched Max nailing the shutters of the windows together, the sweat running down his face and the shirt sticking to his back, before starting on the carved doors of the room. Mutely Luke passed him the long nails and helped him close up the music room. A single sheet of music fluttered briefly on top of the piano and then the room was plunged into darkness.

Chapter Forty-Six

Elizabeth folded the letter from her sister knowing she had to go to her. It wasn't what Nicola had said in her letter, it was what she hadn't said which caused her concern and now she feared for her sister's life. She replied immediately:

Hang in there, Nicola, don't do anything stupid. I'll come as soon as I can. Something must be done about Max, and his dangerous behaviour. I can't promise I'll stay with you indefinitely, but I'll stay as long as I can to give you my support, and hopefully get you back on your feet.

With all those guns around anything could happen, be very careful and don't antagonize him.

Elizabeth stirred her coffee and absently scratched a mosquito bite on her leg. She had been at Mbabati for two months, although to her it felt like two years. Max swung from being morose to despicable, and the silent meals in the dining room were intolerable.

She looked at her sister who was staring into the distance saying nothing, something which was beginning to irritate her.

"Look Nicola I haven't come all this way to sit in silence for hours on end, I don't seem to be making any difference here. You must decide what you're going to do and when. You have to leave him."

When Nicola didn't reply she lost her temper.

"How can you sit across the table from him knowing he killed Jake and, quite frankly, if he hadn't fought with Cat that terrible night she wouldn't have taken off in the storm." Elizabeth's voice tapered off as she saw Nicola's anger mount into fury.

She stood up, knocking over her coffee in the process. "Leave me alone, will you! Max will never let me go anywhere - you know that!"

Elizabeth smiled. Finally she had got a reaction out of her. "Where is he at the moment?"

"Luke said he went to the hide, though God knows why."

They looked at each other for a long time. She reached out for her sister's hand. "Shall we go for a ride...it will be lovely and cool down by the lake."

Max parked his car some distance from the hide and approached on foot. He'd searched the house for days trying to find her diary, which had to be destroyed now he had told her categorically he had killed Jake.

His bloodshot eyes darted around the deck and the small living area; there was no obvious sign of the diary. Putting down his rifle, he walked into the bedroom and searched around until he found it tucked behind the bed. "Got it, you bitch!" he muttered to himself.

Grabbing his rifle he strode purposefully from the hide towards his vehicle. Flicking through the pages of the diary he didn't see her standing there.

From where he stood at the water's edge, Luke saw her step from behind a thicket of bush, then, raising her rifle, she took careful aim and fired.

He watched her drop the rifle, then, walking quickly towards Max's still body, she bent down and snatched back the diary still clutched in his hand. Running back to her horse she mounted swiftly, and galloped away in the direction of the lake.

Luke squatted down next to Max, who was still alive although all colour had bleached from his face.

"Help me, Luke," he groaned, his face contorting with pain.

Luke looked down at his childhood friend feeling nothing.

"Which bitch shot me," Max said bitterly, "which bitch was it?"

Luke stood up and shook his head. "You did not help Bwana Jake, when you shot him. It is right you die the same way now."

Max closed his eyes briefly and then looked up into Luke's expressionless face; the blinding sun behind him burning his eyes.

Luke stood and glanced over his shoulder. "Tika is standing at the waterhole. I think he is waiting."

Seeing the terror in his old playmate's eyes he nodded. Hunkering down under a tree, he waited.

Max tried to sit up to pull himself towards the hide, but the pain in his chest forced him to collapse back and lie still. His fingers felt sticky and when he raised them as far as he was able to, he saw they were red with his own blood. His eyes opened wide as a shadow blotted out the sun overhead. He looked up at the massive shape towering over him.

Tika lowered his head and raised both ears. Max screamed in terror, his bowels exploding with panic. The elephant speared him through the stomach with his tusk and tossed him in the air like a rag doll. Moving to his prone and shattered body, he leaned forward and crushed him beneath the great weight of his head. Max's terrified screams echoed across the water and then there was silence.

Impassively Luke saw Tika run his trunk over the inert figure, before walking away, his feet sending up puffs of dust. He came over to Luke and searched his pockets for an orange, then he looped his trunk around his neck, as if in apology, and strolled off.

Luke looked down at the body for a few seconds and then, with difficulty, he pulled what was left of him into the back of the Land Rover. Retrieving Max's rifle he fired one shot into the air, then turned the vehicle and drove towards Nanyuki.

******

"Tell me exactly what happened," Inspector Groves instructed Luke, pulling a blank statement form towards him. He was visibly shaken after being shown what was left of the shattered body in the back of Luke's vehicle.

Luke perched on the chair opposite the policeman. "Bwana Max has had much sorrow these past years. His daughter was killed in the bad storm two years ago?"

John nodded, wondering how long it would take Luke to get to the point. "Yes, I remember." He hesitated, looking more closely at Luke. "I know you, don't I? I interviewed you about the Henderson case?"

"It is true, sir. I am Luke Adoyo."

Luke continued: "Bwana Max has spent many hours alone in the place they call the hide."

John tapped his pen on his teeth and studied Luke. "Why did no-one mention the hide when we were investigating the disappearance of Jake Henderson?"

Luke shook his head and shrugged.

"What happened today?"

"Bwana Max was drinking too much even this morning. After lunch he told us he was going to the hide and must not be disturbed."

"Was this unusual?" John interjected.

"Not so much after his daughter died. If he went to the hide we were told not to go there. This time we heard a gunshot."

261

"Who heard the gunshot?"

"Miss Nicola and Miss Elizabeth - she is the sister."

"Miss Nicola she asked me to go and see if Bwana Max was alright. He was dead, his rifle was beside him with a strong stick. From how Bwana Max is looking, I am thinking he is killing himself with his own gun - before the elephant came."

"You think he committed suicide and then was attacked by an elephant?"

He looked at the Inspector's face and saw his incredulous look. "He said it was good to have the flesh picked from the bones," he explained, "better than to be buried or burned. I am thinking he killed himself outside so the vultures would come."

"But why would an elephant attack a dead man, Mr Adoyo?"

"I cannot say what this elephant was thinking sir, I am only a servant and not wise in the way of elephants and what they are thinking."

John rubbed his eyes and pushed the completed statement towards him." Please read this, and make sure it's correct."

Luke looked blankly at the statement. "I cannot read sir."

"Alright, don't worry about it now. I want you to take me to the hide."

John followed behind Luke's Land Rover until it stopped. Luke got out and stood in front of what John thought was a pile of bushes. He looked up briefly and saw vultures spiralling on the thermals of the hot afternoon air.

"Why have we stopped here?"

"This is the hide sir."

He followed Luke down a short path. He looked around with interest at the basic furnishings and the deck overlooking the waterhole.

He walked around as Luke followed him. "I will show you where I found Bwana Max?"

John followed him out. He saw the large pool of dried blood and the thick cloud of buzzing flies about halfway between the entrance of the hide and Max's parked vehicle. He squatted down, his stomach soured and turned over at the sight of bits of the deceased's internal organs.

"You say the gun was lying next to him, Luke?"

"Yes sir. I am thinking he put the gun in his mouth and pulled the trigger."

"Unlikely with a rifle," John said dryly, pulling out a packet of cigarettes from his uniform pocket and lighting one gratefully.

"Perhaps he is using this stick sir," He nudged the stick he had placed there earlier, with his foot, "for shooting the rifle?"

John felt the sweat running down the back of his neck, and his mind went back to the Henderson case.

The hide was not only the perfect place for two lovers to meet undisturbed - but also the ideal place to commit a murder, he looked up again at the circling vultures; and an easy place to get rid of any evidence.

He walked back to Luke. "I'll need to take a statement from Mrs Gray and her sister. Please tell them to expect me tomorrow morning."

Chapter Forty-Seven

He looked up at the house and straightened his uniform as he approached the front door.

Luke showed him into the sitting room. "Mrs Gray?" She nodded briefly but didn't get up.

"Inspector John Groves, I'm not sure if you remember me?" He cleared his throat and removed his hat. "May I sit down?"

Again she nodded. "Your Mr Adoyo - Luke - came to the station yesterday and reported the death of your husband. He's convinced he committed suicide before he was crushed by an elephant," he said as delicately as possible. "As he's unable to read or write, I need you to read and countersign the statement on his behalf."

Fumbling for her glasses, she took it from him, read it, signed it, and handed it back.

"Yes, this is what Luke told me when he came back from the station yesterday."

"Did your husband display any suicidal tendencies?"

She had her hands calmly folded in her lap as she looked at him. "He was badly affected by the death of our daughter, Inspector Groves. There was an argument the day she died and he never forgave himself." She twisted her wedding ring around her finger.

"It's not difficult for me to understand he took his own life. I thought about doing this myself many times. Losing a child is unbearable, so yes, I do believe he was capable of taking his own life." She dabbed at her eyes with a small white handkerchief.

John studied her closely.

"There will be an autopsy on your husband. Not wishing to be crude there will be some difficulty in doing this, given the state of his body. We'll get forensics in Nairobi to examine the gun and check any fingerprints, although from what I can gather from Luke the family has four rifles and you all use them randomly."

He saw the question in her eyes. "What I'm saying is no particular gun was used exclusively by one person. If the examining doctor agrees it was suicide, I'll record your husband's death accordingly.

"You'll want to make the arrangements for your husband's funeral. I would imagine he'll be buried here on the estate?"

She nodded as she reached for a small silver bell and rang it.

"Luke will see you out, Inspector."

"Just one more thing, I'd like to speak to your sister," he looked down at his notepad. "Elizabeth. I understand she's staying here with you. I need her to read the statement and sign it off."

"I'm afraid that won't be possible, Elizabeth's in Nairobi at the moment. She wasn't here yesterday. Luke was busy in the wine cellar and didn't see her leave." She looked up as Luke entered the room. "You can ask him yourself."

She nodded at Luke. "I have a terrible headache; I'm going to lie down for a while. Please excuse me Inspector."

John drove off the estate winding down his window to let in what little breeze there was. Things were getting interesting. A murder and a suicide in the same area and in a time frame of just five years - a bit of a coincidence? He didn't believe in coincidences.

Chapter Forty-Eight

Nicola threw a handful of dirt on top of Max's coffin before turning to her daughter's grave and placing a bouquet of apricot roses on it. She had insisted his funeral be a private family affair, and had refused to let anyone other than the undertakers, the priest and Luke to attend. Elizabeth had vehemently refused to be present. Martin Shapiro had expressed his wish to attend but she had refused him as well.

******

It was three weeks after the funeral. Elizabeth lit a cigarette and looked out over the gardens; the smoke curled and hung in the breathless air. Nicola closed the book she had been reading.

"You seem restless, Lizzy. What are you thinking about?"

"All sorts of things… Luke in particular. His statement to the police was a work of art. I don't know how he came up with his story, but it was bloody good."

Nicola flinched. "I'll have to ask Luke what he saw… but I don't have the courage at the moment. He said the elephant was definitely Tika. He was always nervous around Max, as a calf, but what on earth made him attack like that?"

Elizabeth tossed her cigarette into the bushes watching the glowing tip arc and then fall in a shower of sparks. "Who knows what elephants think about; I'm more concerned about what the damn police Inspector is thinking. They hang people for murder here in Kenya."

Elizabeth lifted a hand to her neck, imagining the coolness, and the roughness, of the rope around it, trying not to imagine what the final moments might be like as fear slithered like an eel through her stomach.

She pulled herself together and continued, "It's too late to go to the police now. Max deserved what he got. He took his own life and was then attacked by an elephant." she said determinedly.

"No doubt the rest of the country will be discussing it over their pre-dinner drinks, handing gossip around with the potato chips, but there's no reason to think anyone will talk about murder. The gossip will die down and we can get on with the rest of our lives.

"Which brings me to my next question - what are you going to do with the rest of yours?"

Nicola looked at her helplessly. "Just like Max was, I'm tied to this house now. I've asked Martin to come here and go through his Will, and I'll have to change mine."

Elizabeth looked at her. "Yes, I've thought about this too. Who will inherit Mbabati when you go?"

"I thought I'd leave it to you, I know how much you love it." Nicola said, a wintry smile crossing her face.

Elizabeth looked at her sister aghast. "Yes, I do love the house, but I'd love it more if it was in the middle of Manhattan, not in the middle of the bloody bush, anyway it has to be passed down the line."

Nicola watched her sister knowing what she was going to say next. "You'll have to start searching for that child of yours."

******

Luke showed Martin Shapiro to his room and placed his overnight bag on the bed.

"Miss Nicola is sleeping, Bwana. You are early from Nairobi I think?"

"Yes, I thought it would take me a lot longer to drive here. The last time I was here was when Mr Gray senior died, so it was indeed many years ago. The roads haven't improved much, I have to say. Perhaps I could find somewhere to sort through all these papers?" He indicated his bulging briefcase. "When I was here last I think we used the room at the top of the house?"

Luke looked briefly up to the top floor. "It is not possible to use this room now. The dining-room has a big table for all this paper you are saying you have. It is summer now, I will serve dinner on the veranda tonight so these papers can stay here with no trouble."

"Excellent Luke. I remember you from my last visit; you were a young man then."

"Yes, Bwana, it is true. I was a young man then, the same age as Bwana Max. Winston ran the house, and now it is me who has this job," he said proudly. "Winston is dead now and Cookie has gone to his family in the village. There is only one groom for the horses and two gardeners. I am running the house for Miss Nicola."

267

"Good. I'll take a shower and then use the dining-room. Perhaps you'll let me know when Mrs Gray is available."

Martin showered and changed then made his way down the grand staircase. He stopped in front of the portrait. Impressed, he continued on his way to the dining-room and found Nicola waiting for him.

"The house, of course, is now yours," he said as he unpacked his briefcase on the table." It would have passed to your daughter, Catherine, had she survived you."

Nicola stood up and closed the door. "There was another child I have to tell you about..."

******

At six their meeting was over. "Let's go through to the sitting room, my sister will be joining us shortly, I want you to meet her."

As they walked through the entrance hall he commented on her portrait.

"An exceptional piece of work, if I may say so. His work is extremely valuable now, but I don't have it anywhere on the contents register of the house? I do have the Steinway listed though, perhaps you'd play for me after dinner?"

Nicola shook her head. "I'm afraid I can't. Max boarded up the music room some months before he died. Don't ask me to explain." She looked up at the staircase. "Elizabeth, there you are! Come and meet Martin."

Martin looked up and smiled broadly in surprise as she descended the stairs.

"I'm delighted to finally meet you Elizabeth," he said as he shook her outstretched hand. Still smiling and shaking his head, he followed them into the sitting room.

Chapter Forty-Nine

Martin Shapiro read the front page story, folding his paper he looked out over the city from his office window, thinking about his next move. Ben, the editor of the newspaper, and an old friend, had called him the day before to warn him about the article he had just read.

He told him that the police were considering re-visiting the Henderson case. Jake's parents, were insisting on this otherwise they would go to the American networks with their own suspicions. They found it inconceivable their son's body has never been found.

"Jake wasn't just an ordinary bloke," he told Martin. "If he had been, his parents wouldn't have much clout. They think going to the media might rekindle the public's interest in what happened to him, maybe produce other witnesses."

Martin had said nothing but listened with rising concern staring unseeingly at the traffic below his office window.

Ben told Martin that the article was leaning toward the fact that Max killed Jake over an alleged affair with his wife, and then killed himself. Hardly anyone the police had spoken to had believed Max would commit suicide. There was speculation Nicola might have been involved in the deaths of both her lover and her husband.

Martin drummed his fingers on his desk. The article had been well put together, raising more than enough questions for the police to re-open the case.

He reached for the phone and asked his secretary to call Inspector John Groves.

"John, Martin here. We must be due for a couple of rounds of golf. How does next weekend look?"

"Nice try, Martin," said John dryly, "I know what this call is about. You've read the morning papers right?"

"I understand you're taking another look at the Max Gray suicide?"

"Indeed we are. It's beginning to look more like murder."

"If the case is being investigated again I need to advise Nicola accordingly. You can't go swarming all over her property without the correct paperwork, or valid reasons to do so."

"We're well aware of what we can and cannot do, Martin," he said testily, "I can assure you it will be done by the book."

He phoned Nicola immediately. "You've nothing to worry about, Nicola," he told her, having explained the situation.

Martin cleared his throat and chose his next words as discreetly as possible. "Forgive me for asking you this, but it's important. Were you in a relationship with Jake?"

"Yes. We were lovers for many years. I loved him, I still love him."

"Do you think Max had anything to do with the disappearance of Jake?"

"Yes. But I've nothing to prove it was him, that's why I've never said anything to the police. If they had questioned him and let him go, well, I can't imagine what my life would have been like. He was unpredictable and violent and he would have punished me for the rest of what turned out to be, not many of his days."

Nicola put the phone down and walked out onto the veranda, seeing her ashen face Elizabeth stood up uneasily.

"What is it? You look as though you've seen a ghost! Here, have a cigarette."

Nicola repeated what Martin had told her as she puffed nervously on her cigarette. "I can't go through it all again, Lizzy, I just can't do this anymore. I have to tell the police about Jake. Tell them Max killed him..."

Elizabeth chewed on her thumb nervously. "We're in deep trouble, we have to do something."

"Maybe I should go away for a while..."

Elizabeth cut her short. "Oh, for God's sake don't you realize what a dangerous situation you're in? You might be implicated in two murders, Nicola! Of course you can't leave!"

Seeing the raw fear in her sister's face Elizabeth said. "Come on, let's have a stiff drink - yes, you as well. I want you to tell me everything you can remember about Jake and the lead up to his disappearance".

"I'm going to get Luke to repeat his story of what happened down at the hide; how much he saw. We need to make sure there are no holes in the story, it has to be, must be, utterly watertight.

"You'll have to let Amos go as soon as possible and close up the cottage in Watamu. He's the weakest link in the chain because he saw us all there every year. Groves mustn't get anywhere near him."

Chapter Fifty

Luke looked at the clock in the kitchen as he gutted the fish. The two sisters had been in the sitting room with the door closed for nearly three hours, and he was anxious to know what they might be talking about.

He placed the fish in the oven and wiped his hands on his apron. When he heard the bell he walked with trepidation towards the sitting room; not realizing that in the following hour he would become entangled in what was to be the end of the predictable life he had always known at Mbabati.

******

Three days later Luke stood on the steps with Elizabeth's suitcase at his feet. She took his hand in hers. He frowned at her. "You will not stay with your sister with all these troubles?"

She shook her head. "You'll take good care of her Luke, I need to go away for a while. But I will come back. My sister will be safe with you, she always has been. Goodbye Luke."

Silently he placed the case in the waiting car and watched the sisters as they drove away.

******

"By the way," Elizabeth said as they approached the outskirts of the city, "you said you wanted to go to church?"

Nicola pulled up outside of the church and turned off the engine. "Why don't you come in with me - I bet its years since you went to confession. Might be a good idea all things considered?"

Reluctantly Elizabeth got out of the Land Rover and they made their way up the steps and into the church.

She drew the curtain across the confessional and bent her head. "Forgive me, Father, for I have sinned ..." Father O'Neill crossed himself and prepared to hear her confession.

Over the following year Martin Shapiro had his work cut out for him trying to keep Nicola's name off the front pages of the newspapers in Kenya.

271

The police re-opened the case and once again made an intensive search of the Gray estate. On discovering the clothes and the watermarked saddle buried at the bottom of the cupboard in the stables, Inspector Groves, triumphantly, asked Nicola to accompany him to the station for further questioning.

She had looked at him haughtily. "I'm perfectly capable of driving myself to the police station, Inspector Groves. I have absolutely no intention of accompanying you in your police van, like a common criminal. How dare you ask me to do that!"

"Can you explain who these clothes belong to, Mrs Gray?" he asked her in the interview room, watching her intently.

Indifferently she had glanced at the saddle and clothes displayed on the table and shook her head. "I'm afraid not, Inspector. I've never seen them before in my life, or the saddle. I'm sure Ezekiel will be able to verify if the clothes and saddle belonged to his former employer. I suggest you ask him."

John narrowed his eyes. "We already have - they did. Were you intimately involved with Jake?" he asked her bluntly.

She shook her head.

"When did you last see him, can you remember?"

"I've told you all this, Inspector," she replied with exasperation, "the last time was at the airport when I was seeing my daughter off to school in England."

John waved a fly away in front of his face. "One thing puzzles me, Mrs Gray. Why didn't anyone mention there was a hide on the property, when we were searching for Jake Henderson?"

Flustered, she twisted her wedding ring around on her finger. "If I recall you were given a free hand to search the entire estate and we presumed you'd seen it."

Groves shook his head with disbelief. "Did you ever meet Jake there?"

"No, I did not," she said clasping her hands tightly in her lap.

He made some notes, then looked up at her." The discovery of Jake Henderson's clothing in your stables casts a different light on things.

"Perhaps Max found out about the affair and killed him. Then two years later, after a fight perhaps, you shot and killed your husband. Did you kill your husband, Mrs Gray?"

She looked at him, her heart thundering in her chest, trying to hide her fear at the direction the questions were now heading.

John looked at her steadily. "We have it on good authority, from our own elephant experts here in Kenya, that it's unlikely an elephant would attack a man who is already dead.

"Whoever fired the gun at your husband before he was attacked, is guilty of his murder. I have reason to believe this person is you."

She glared at him. "I didn't shoot my husband."

He snapped his notebook shut and stood up.

"Shall I see you in court, Inspector?" she said snatching up her bag, "because as far as I'm concerned you have little proof of the accusations you've made against me."

"I think I know exactly what happened, I just have to prove it, and I will.

"We've searched your holiday home in Watamu, with the correct warrant, of course. It seems your man Amos has left the property - but we'll find him."

John turned on his heel and left the room.

She drove back towards the house, then changing her mind, headed for the hide. Inspector Groves had come dangerously close to the truth and she wondered how much more she could take before he broke her down, and if poor old Luke would survive an interrogation such as the one Groves had put her through with such intensity and purpose. Amos was not a problem - he had returned to his family in Tanzania, well away from the long reach of Inspector Groves.

Chapter Fifty-One

Doggedly Inspector Groves had followed up any tenuous leads. The saddle and the clothes had been damning evidence, but he didn't have enough concrete proof to arrest her. He couldn't even prove Jake Henderson was dead, no body having been found, and now unlikely that it would be.

One day Nicola Gray would slip up and he would have her. Somewhere along the way she would make a mistake. It was a pity her sister Elizabeth had left the country in such a hurry before he could question her as well.

******

Exhausted by the endless questioning and searches of the property and the hide, she had stuck to her story, hoping after weeks and weeks of interrogation the police would eventually give up and leave her alone.

When that long awaited day finally arrived, and she felt the dust had settled, she made an appointment with her lawyer.

Martin ushered her into his cool office, then looked at her and frowned. "Have you had an accident, Nicola. What happened to your hand?"

She sat and smiled at him wanly. "I missed a step and grabbed the balustrade to stop myself falling and twisted my wrist. Nothing serious."

"What can I do for you? I expect you're immensely relieved the police investigation is well and truly over."

"It was nerve racking to say the least, but, as you say, it's all over now. I'm going away, back to Paris, I long to see it again; I need to get away for a few months.

"I want to leave instructions for the running of the estate and make some changes to my existing Will. I need to make sure Luke receives his salary regularly, and has enough money to keep the house going in my absence. I've let the rest of the staff go; the grooms took the horses with them."

Martin looked at her questioningly. "What other changes would you like to make?" He pulled his pad towards him and uncapped his pen.

When she had finished with the instructions for the estate, he looked up from his notes. "But what will you live on?"

"As you know I inherited a considerable amount of money when my mother died. It's in a trust for me in France. I've made arrangements to have this transferred to Kenya and paid into your company account, under my name. If I need money I'll let you know."

Martin made notes on the pad in front of him. "No problem with any of this. The item which has the greatest value in the house is your piano. I want to get it insured so someone needs to come out to the house and value it. Is the room still barricaded up?"

She picked at the bandage on her hand. "Yes, I'm going to leave it as it is, my piano will be quite safe, and Luke will be there to keep an eye on things."

He made another note. "You'll need to sign some papers with the instructions you've just given me."

She smiled. "I've been thinking about this for some time and I've drawn up a document myself, and signed it."

He narrowed his eyes, watching her closely as she reached for her handbag. She withdrew the document and placed it on his desk, standing up she held out her left hand to him. "Goodbye, Martin. I'll be in touch when I get back."

He watched her from his window as she got into her car. Uneasily he returned to his desk - something wasn't quite right.

He wondered when, and if, he would see her again.

Chapter Fifty-Two

She paced around the sitting room going through everything in her mind. The long isolated months at Mbabati with no company except for Luke, had been more than she'd been able to cope with.

Saying goodbye to him was going to be the hardest thing she would have to do.

He was tidying up the kitchen when she went through to see him. "I need you to do something for me Luke; I need you to find my diary?"

He looked at her puzzled. "It is hidden as you know, Miss Nicola, down at the hide. I will get it for you tomorrow."

She poured a glass of wine and stepped out into the gardens, wondering if Tika would come to say goodbye. She opened the gate to the graveyard and sat down on the bench.

"Hello Cat darling, Mummy's going away for a while but Luke will look after you 'til I come back."

She glanced at the lit lamp at the head of the grave. "I know how you hate sleeping in the dark, but Luke will come every evening and light your lamp so you won't be frightened.

"Now, I'm going to tell you a story - I know how much you love stories…"

When she had finished she knelt down and patted the grave. "Goodbye my darling Cat, I'm going home for a while now. I loved you very much, we all did, and still do. I hope Tika will come and visit you, I'm sure he will. I'll come back, I promise."

After breakfast she sat with the diary open on her knees looking through the letters to and from Jake. The words swam and blurred before her eyes. With tremulous hands she tied them up again with a piece of white ribbon. At the back of the diary she found the photographs: one of Jake which she put to one side, and one of Mbabati. The letters and the diary she replaced in the tin, and then rang the bell for Luke.

"I want you to take this back to the hide and bury it somewhere. Only you will know where it's hidden, it will be your secret."

When he had left she made her way up the stairs to her bedroom. She took a small trunk from the bottom of the wardrobe, and placed it on the bed with all the things she would be taking with her. Carefully she selected the photographs, the baby blanket and the silver framed photograph, and put them in the trunk. Finally she took the locket from around her neck and placed it on top of the blanket. Reaching into the bedside drawer she picked up the Tanzanite bowl checking Jake's ring was secure inside it; she packed it in the trunk and closed the lid.

She took a final look around the house, her eyes filling with tears at all the memories it held; closing the front door behind her she walked unsteadily to the car.

"You mustn't worry about your money, Luke," she said as they drove through the gates, "and you must take good care of the house until I come back."

"When *are* you coming back?" She heard the trepidation in his voice.

"I don't know Luke." She checked the time. "We must hurry, I don't want to miss the evening train to Mombasa, or the ship will leave without me tomorrow."

She watched Luke stow the trunk in her compartment; he stepped back onto the platform and looked at her. She took his hands in both of hers, her eyes filling with tears again.

"Goodbye, Luke."

He nodded his head mutely.

Looking out of the window she saw Luke's forlorn figure standing there alone on the platform, his arm raised in farewell, then the train rounded a bend and he was gone.

On the voyage to England she wrote to her sister:

The safest place for you is still the convent - what a brilliant idea it was. Who would think of looking for you there! I know it was only supposed to be a short term solution but you'll have to stay until it's safe for both of us to return. I wish I could tell you how long that will be but I have no idea, Groves will be after you for the rest of his days - he knows as well as we do that Max was murdered.

I've had a lot of time to think on this journey. I'll need to make money to live on and I don't want to leave any kind of paper trail by asking Martin to make regular transfers to me. He plays golf with the damn Inspector and he might let something slip.

"I'm thinking of getting a job entertaining passengers on a cruise ship. Moving from place to place seems the safer thing to do. No-one will recognize me now; I've taken care of that.

Chapter Fifty-Three
MBABATI 2008
Alex

A lex parked his car and turned off the ignition. Luke was waiting for him at the top of the steps.

On the journey back from Nairobi after his meeting with Martin, Alex had decided not to confront Luke with the facts he now had. The old man had carried the sisters' collective guilt for too many years. After all, Alex had been a stranger to him until a couple of weeks ago. Why should he trust him enough to tell the truth?

The first thing Alex wanted to do was study the photographs again.

"Your journey to Nairobi went well?" Luke asked politely.

"Indeed it did. May I have a beer Luke? I'll take it in the sitting room." He looked up at the portrait. "Hello, Nicola, I'm back."

Luke placed the beer and a glass on a tray and took it through to Alex. "You have found the man you are looking for?"

Alex took a long drink from his glass. Sighing with satisfaction, he wiped the cold foam from his lips with the back of his hand. "Yes, his name is Martin Shapiro; he's a lawyer. I think you met him many years ago when he came to talk business with Miss Nicola, after Max died?"

"It is possible, but hard for an old man to remember after all this time."

Alex let that one go. "Your money will still come to you every month, so no worries there. You'll be taken care of."

Luke, looking relieved, went back to the kitchen.

Picking up his glass of beer Alex went across the sitting room and stared at the photographs, remembering when he had asked Luke why there were no photographs of Elizabeth; Luke had replied - "*They are here, but you cannot see them.*"

Of course they were. He looked at the grandfather clock. Time for a shower and shave before dinner. As he reached the bottom of the stairs he looked up at Nicola. She stared coolly back as if challenging him to find out the rest of the story.

"I'm getting closer to finding out what made you run, but where did you really go Nicola?" he whispered.

Running a comb through his hair Alex reached for his sweater and pulled it over his head. Smoothing down his hair, he glanced out of the bedroom window and saw Luke heading in the direction of the graveyard. A few minutes later he reappeared and made his way back towards the kitchen.

Alex went through to the kitchen and helped himself to another beer from the fridge. Luke looked up, surprised. "If you ring the bell I will bring you this beer, Bwana Alex."

"No worries, Luke. You carry on with dinner; I'm going to take a walk around the garden." Sipping his beer Alex followed the path towards the graveyard.

A lit lamp stood at the head of what he now knew to be Cat's grave. Surely Luke hadn't been doing this each night since the young girl died over twenty-two years ago? Perhaps tonight was the anniversary of her death.

He hadn't noticed the light any other night since he had been here, but then again he hadn't been looking. He found it strangely peaceful, as he sat on the bench and studied the graves, with only the soft call of an owl to break the silence. Finishing his drink he made his way back to the house.

"Tonight is the French food," Luke told him as he served dinner. "This food was taught to me by Miss Nicola, there is much cream in it."

"Thanks Luke, it looks good. By the way, I took a walk to the graveyard before dinner. I saw you'd lit the lamp on Cat's grave. Is it the anniversary of her death today? She was the daughter of Nicola, wasn't she?"

Luke placed the lid back on the serving dish and carried it back to the sideboard. "Yes, she was the daughter. When Miss Nicola was here she would go to the grave at night and talk to her. Cat was frightened of the dark and so the lamp would be lit for her. Sometimes I sing her a lullaby so she knows I am there. I have done this also since Miss Nicola left. This was a promise I made."

Unexpectedly Alex felt his throat tighten with emotion. "Why is there no name on her grave, Luke, and no photographs of her around the house?"

The old man shrugged. "The ones who love Cat know where she is buried; no need for a name. No need for photographs."

Luke stared into the fire recalling the years now gone. "I was here the night Cat was born. They called her Catherine then. The night of the big storm my little one was lost out in the bush. I went to look for her.

"Cat always asked me to sing our African lullabies when she was small and could not sleep, or if she was frightened of the night. As she was dying I sang this song to her, she knew I was there with her and she was not afraid."

Alex, his food forgotten, looked at Luke as he told the story of Cat's death. He remembered seeing the rusting jeep with its buckled roof in the workshop.

"How was Miss Nicola after this?"

"Her heart was much troubled, her mind gone to another place. For many days after the funeral she did not leave the bed. I sat at the grave with the lamp watching over Cat. Tika came to say goodbye."

"Tika?"

"Tika was a small elephant found without its mother. Tika came to live here. Many years later he went back to his herd but came to visit sometimes. He has been here when you were playing the music upstairs. He is big but he is very quiet.

"You are not liking the French food with the cream?" He looked anxiously at Alex's untouched plate.

"I'm sorry, Luke, I was listening to your story." He turned back to his food as Luke left the room.

After dinner Alex made his way to the music room, profoundly touched by Luke's story. Selecting a tape he inserted it into the machine and sat back to listen to her play. Once or twice he went to the window to see if Tika had come to visit but only saw Luke huddled in his cloak, sitting on a bench with his eyes closed listening to her play.

******

The next day Alex spent a few hours writing up his notes, ready for the planned article on Mbabati. He'd decided to write it up in the house where the story began, rather than London; he longed to see Sophie and bring her up to date with everything.

281

In the kitchen he could hear Luke crooning softly to himself as he worked. Tonight he was going to try and get the old man to talk about the sisters.

Chapter Fifty-Four
Elizabeth

Knowing there was no alternative to the plan I had come up with Nicola had no choice but to go along with it.

We spent hours going over everything meticulously; there would be no room for error. One mistake, one wrong sentence, and it would all be over.

When we were younger our appearance would always provoke some kind of reaction.

We were identical twins you see. I was born twenty minutes after Nicola, so she was always my big sister.

On my first visit to Mbabati it amused me to see Luke, Cookie and Winston react when they first met me. I don't think they'd ever seen a set of identical twins. I would often catch them casting surreptitious glances at us, especially when we were together.

I wore my hair differently, short and spiky, and I wore loads of make-up, unlike Nicola who wore very little, but take off the make-up and our faces were identical.

Little Cat knew her mother had a twin sister and her mother had shown her photographs of the two of us when we were younger. I don't think she understood though, and this was why she reacted by bursting into tears when I first met her.

Apart from being identical we shared many other talents - including acting and music. Nicola dedicated herself to playing classical music and although I had had the same training I preferred the more modern stuff. So both of us were equally talented, except she had an absolute gift for it, whereas I had to work hard at it - even so, I wasn't bad. I was bloody good actually.

In the beginning Max had been amused. The idea of sleeping with two sisters who were identical appealed to him enormously - God knows what he was thinking when he made love to Nicola, and I often wondered if he pretended it was me lying there; I bet he often imagined having both of us in bed at the same time.

You're probably wondering why none of his friends ever realised we were twins? Well, they weren't bothered if his wife was at any of the parties I went to. They knew she didn't care for any kind of social life and that was that. What did they care? With the tons of make-up I wore I had a different sort of look. Martin Shapiro, the servants and Jake were the only ones who ever saw us together.

When Nicola went away to hide her pregnancy Max persuaded me to return from America and perform in the concerts he had committed her to. The five concerts it had been impossible to get out of without explaining that Nicola was pregnant.

He had thought of everything. A long blonde wig to hide my spiky dark hair, and because he was always in control of what Nicola wore to perform in, and how the lighting should be, he arranged for the single soft spotlight to be turned on only when I was seated. We fooled everyone.

I thought I would be able to save her career by impersonating her, but I made a complete and utter balls up of it. I suppose a couple of stiff drinks beforehand wasn't such a good idea. The press was brutal with their reviews; they might have been prepared to excuse the first performance, due to one thing or another, but after the fifth one they were baying for blood, and I was booed off stage.

Losing her baby and her professional life was a massive blow to Nicola and not a day went by when I didn't regret what I'd done. I was so ashamed of destroying her career that I never told her. But I vowed if she ever asked me to do anything for her, anything at all, I would be there for her.

When that fatal day arrived I leapt at the chance to make everything up to her.

I thought a year out of my life would be a small price to pay and I planned on making this my finest performance ever.

Little did I know it wouldn't be a year as I anticipated; it would be a part I would play for the rest of my wretched life.

So after Max's so-called suicide I stepped in. Nicola understood that if she was going to avoid a possible trial for murder, something I knew she'd never be able to handle, she would have to play her part as well.

Luke would be the hardest one to fool. If he suspected anything at all it wouldn't take the policeman Groves long to get it out of him, to trick him somehow.

I explained to Nicola that in order to pull the whole thing off she had to become me and I would become her. By some quirk of luck on this particular trip to Kenya, we had the same hairstyle - long and blonde, and without any make-up it would take a genius to work out which twin was which.

Swapping names was one thing but it had to be more. It meant swapping passports, which was not difficult when you think about it, and swapping characters, mannerisms, clothes, style and jewellery. And I finally got to wear a wedding ring - hers.

We practiced for hours. I was proud of Nicola because although she was terrified of the situation she found herself in, shooting Max down at the hide for a start, she played her part perfectly. On reflection it was a small role to play because she was going to leave the country at the first opportunity. I, on the other hand, would have to stay and go through any interrogations and a possible trial for murder.

We drove to Nairobi to catch Nicola's flight to London - the first and only flight she ever made - she was terrified at the thought of flying. Before she left she made her confession to the priest, which I wasn't at all happy about because I knew what her confession would be, and the less people who knew about what had really happened to Max, the better. But she was adamant. Always the good Catholic, my sister (apart from the affair with Jake that is) and already determined to play her new role she told the young priest, Father O'Neill, her name was Elizabeth.

The plan at this point was that she would go to London for a few months and, when the dust had settled, I'd meet her there. We'd swop identities again and she'd return to Kenya. I would go back to America.

I think if Nicola had known she would never return she would not have gone, despite the dire circumstances she found herself in. She loved her adopted country and her beloved house, and, of course, Cat was buried there.

When Nicola got back into the car she was calmer. The priest had suggested she go to a convent he knew of, in London. Fortunately, or maybe unfortunately, once she joined the order of the Daughters of the Lord, she never left it.

As I said, it was the finest performance of my rather unremarkable career, starting with Inspector Groves coming to the house to show me the statement Luke had made regarding Max's suicide. Little did he know Nicola was hiding upstairs. I thought I handled this well, although I had the distinct impression the handsome young inspector didn't like me much.

So on it went, with Inspector Groves relentlessly following every bloody lead he could get hold of in his search of the truth. When he found Jake's clothes and the saddle it was a bit of a shock, Nicola had forgotten to tell me where they were hidden. Well, our intrepid Inspector unearthed them and confronted me with what he thought would be the evidence he needed to convict me. I told him I'd never seen them before in my life, denied any affair with Jake and so on - of course I was telling the truth! But I could tell he didn't believe me...

Finally when he could prove nothing at all, he begrudgingly told me I was free to go, but he warned me that he would never close the case.

I hastily made my own plans to leave, but first I had to pay a visit to Nicola's attorney in Nairobi. She'd told me of her plans for the sisal business and I knew exactly what to say to him. This was going to be a bit tricky - to fool him.

When I first met Martin at the house I had exaggerated my American accent. Now I had to imitate Nicola's soft sexy voice with its slight French accent. But I pulled it off; after all I was an actress wasn't I?

So I arranged all this with Martin and, not knowing for sure when Nicola would be returning, I arranged for a monthly sum to be paid to Luke.

Martin wanted me to sign some papers as I anticipated he would, and I knew her signature would be different from mine. Martin was no fool and would have picked it up immediately, hence the story about spraining my wrist. Nicola, of course, had signed the document, I gave to him. So you see I was good - I'd thought of everything.

I re-checked all the photographs displayed in the sitting room, and removed the ones of Nicola and me together. I only left the individual ones with both of us wearing hats and sunglasses. If, at some point in the future, Inspector Groves decided to give the photographs a cursory glance he would never work out he was looking at both of us.

Luke took me to the station and as we drove down towards the entrance gates I looked back at the house slumbering in the afternoon sun.

I never saw it again.

At the station I said goodbye to Luke and I was about to turn and leave when he put his hand out and touched my arm. "Memsahib?"

With that one word he had told me he knew who I was.

I was struck dumb. How on earth had he worked it out and got it right?

Then he told me.

On the sea voyage to England I had a lot of time to think. I had to make another plan.

I was terrified Inspector Groves' tentacles would reach out and find my sister. If this happened he'd drag her back to Kenya and break her down until she told him the truth. She would be tried for murder and the Kenyan government would hang her.

I spent the next six years on cruise ships in Europe, and sang under a different name. I changed the colour of my eyes with contacts and wore a dark wig - just in case.

One day, by chance, I picked up a discarded magazine in the first class passenger lounge. Over and above expounding the delights of a safari in Kenya, there was an article on Max and Jake, and how the police were anxious to locate, and question, two sisters in connection with their murders. It was thought the sisters were in Europe somewhere.

After reading the article I knew our plan for Nicola to return to Mbabati was never going to happen. Groves was not going to give up until he had hunted her down.

I immediately applied to the shipping line for a different route, away from Europe, and my next cruise was to South Africa where I knew what I would have to do.

I left the ship in Cape Town and began my secret and reclusive life. If Groves should ever track me down there (now a possibility) he would assume I was Nicola, and if he searched my simple cottage he would find a trunk full of her things to prove it. He would drag me back to Kenya to be tried for a crime I didn't commit and it would be me who would be hanged.

Looking back now, I could have had a much easier life in Cape Town; after all, as Nicola, I only had to contact Martin for as much money as I wanted, but I thought it was too risky; it might leave a trail to where I was.

For twelve years I led a solitary life; I found a poorly paid job in a bookshop and eked a living out of that.

It was safer for me to have no friends, but the isolation of being so utterly alone often made me think of killing myself. I had lost everything in my bid to save my sister's life, but the hardest thing of all - I knew I would never see her again.

When the bookshop closed down I was too old to find another job and I ended up on the streets of Cape Town, clutching the bowl Jake had given to Nicola, and begging for money.

I thought of Nicola often, remembering our last brief meeting before I sailed for Cape Town. I told her then that neither of us could ever go back to Mbabati. She wept like a child at the thought of Luke there, quite alone, of the house she would have to abandon now - and she would never again be able to go and sit with Cat and talk to her every evening.

It was the last time we saw each other. It was unbearable. Even now it's the one thing that will bring me to my knees with overwhelming grief. I missed her terribly.

Chapter Fifty-Five
Alex
MBABATI

A lex studied the photographs in the sitting room. He had been looking at her all the time but hadn't realised the sisters were identical twins; any one of these photographs could be Elizabeth. He thought back to his conversation with Martin.

"When I met her I could hardly believe my eyes. I was standing at the bottom of the staircase with Nicola and looked up to see Elizabeth. They were mirror images of each other - it was uncanny.

The last time I saw Nicola was when she came to my office to drop off some documents and tell me she was going away. Before she said goodbye she begged me not to tell anyone she and Elizabeth were twins. I promised I wouldn't."

After dinner Luke brought the coffee through and placed it on the side table in the sitting room. Alex was looking at the photographs again, tapping his teeth with his nail.

Without turning he said. "I see Elizabeth now. I thought these photographs were one person but now I see there are two."

"Yes, they are the same face but two different sisters. When Miss Elizabeth first came to Mbabati her hair it is different to Miss Nicola, short like a boy, but the faces were the same face. I had never seen two white people with the same face before."

Alex turned around and smiled. "Did Elizabeth play the piano?"

Luke nodded enthusiastically. "Yes, both sisters play the piano but different music, but sometimes the same.

"May I bring you anything, Bwana Alex, before I clear the table in the dining room and say goodnight?"

He shook his head. "Good night Luke, I'll see you in the morning."

He and Sophie had opened the trunk in Cape Town, and found the packet of photographs, all of Nicola. Sophie's voice came back to him now: *"A bit obsessive, isn't it, to have all these photographs of yourself, including the one in the silver frame?"*

He whistled softly. Now he had it!

289

Elizabeth had been an actress; she'd taken Nicola's place and been thoroughly investigated over a period of nearly a year but the police had been unable to trip her up.

He grinned. Of course they'd been unable to trip her up because she'd been telling the truth; she'd never had an affair with Jake Henderson.

The trunk they had opened in the cottage and the things they found, *had* belonged to Nicola; they had been deliberately placed there by Elizabeth, to outwit the police should they come knocking on her door. She had gone to extraordinary lengths to protect her twin sister.

The woman who had died in his arms had been Elizabeth, protecting her sister to the sad and bitter end.

Alex walked out into the entrance hall and sat on the stairs, he looked up at her.

"It was you wasn't it Nicola - you killed Max."

******

The next morning he found Luke dusting the photographs in the sitting room. He looked up warily when he saw Alex sit down. "You are wanting something Bwana Alex?"

"No," he said smiling encouragingly. "I'd like to talk to you. Why don't you sit down for a minute?"

Luke perched on the corner of the chair, squeezing his duster anxiously.

"Miss Nicola killed her husband didn't she?"

Luke mopped his brow with the duster, and took a deep breath. "She shot him it is true, but Tika killed him. I was there, I saw this.

"Both sisters are dead, the police can do nothing."

"Alright, Luke, let's leave it at that. The letters and the diary you sent to the shop in London were for Miss Nicola, weren't they? You knew all the time this was where she was. How did you work it out?"

Luke twisted the duster between his hands. "At first there were only small things. Miss Elizabeth did not eat the same way. Also there was much wine with dinner, this Miss Nicola never did..."

Luke told him how he watched Elizabeth visit the grave every night, how she always smoked there before walking back through the gardens. "Then I knew the truth - the sisters with the same face had changed their names.

"When Miss Nicola was a small child she had a riding accident, when the weather was cold or wet, she always walked a different way as if her leg was hurting. Miss Elizabeth walked the same always and liked to smoke, Miss Nicola only sometimes."

Alex nodded his head. It would have been a dead give-away for someone as observant as Luke.

Luke frowned then took a deep breath. "Before Miss Nicola came to Mbabati there was another child, and this child she gave away. After the little one died there was no child left to love. I am thinking she went to London to look for this lost child."

The child, Alex thought, Martin would now be searching for.

Chapter Fifty-Six

Alex placed the pink roses he had picked from the garden on Cat's grave. He sat down and stared at the soft glow of the lamp, shaping the story he planned to write about Mbabati.

His thoughts were interrupted by a light rumble of thunder, puzzled he looked up at the crystal clear skies above him, dazzled by the majesty of the millions of stars; it didn't look as though a storm was coming tonight.

A dark shape emerged from the side of the graveyard and his heart begin to hammer in his chest. A bull elephant stood watching him, its enormous ears moving back and forth.

Dear God, he prayed silently, let this be the friendly fellow called Tika, and not some wild elephant with a bad temper.

He clutched the side of the bench, trying not to think about the way Max had died, as the elephant came closer. Feeling the soft touch of his trunk he opened his terrified eyes. Tika touched his face and lightly explored his body.

"Hello Tika, how are you, mate? Good to finally meet you," he croaked.

With another heavy rumble, Tika ran his trunk over the grave in greeting, then sauntered off into the night.

Shaking his head with disbelief Alex headed back to the house. Mbabati had had its fair share of grief over the years but it was the most magical place he'd ever been to. Meeting a fully grown elephant called Tika was something he would never forget.

Later, up in the music room, he selected another tape and pressed the play button then went to the window. Luke appeared from his room and came to sit on the bench to listen; within minutes Tika had appeared again, both of them looking up at the music room.

Alex ran his hand over the closed piano as he listened to her play and thought about his friend, Peter, the hotel manager in Cape Town. Of course the old "bag woman" as he had called her was Elizabeth, though why she had suddenly decided to play he had no idea. She had impressed Peter with the calibre of her playing, but he doubted she had been as superb as the pianist he was listening to now.

Idly he opened the lid of her seat and flicked through the pile of music inside, then he saw the hard corner of a book buried at the bottom of the box. Lifting it out, he went over to the hurricane lamp and sat down.

The photograph on the front caught his immediate attention. A grand piano sat beneath an acacia tree framed by a fiery sunset, to the right of the picture was the ghostly shape of an elephant. He looked at the title on the spine. *The Lost Child*. Intrigued, he opened it and caught his breath as he read the author's name - Jake Henderson. He turned the page and read the dedication:

"For Nicola DuPont whose gentle touch I came to love."

So Jake had made sure that by giving her full name, his enduring love for her would be recorded somewhere.

He turned the pages studying each photograph - they were magnificent. The child holding up her arms to the elephant could only be Cat with Tika. He recognized Luke, his proud young face looking into the distance and Nicola, in shadow, as she played in the room he was now in.

Under each photograph was the opening bar of a piece of classical music which Jake had married to the theme of the photograph shown. He turned the book over and studied the back cover.

The child was standing at the end of a jetty, the lake glittering in the sunlight. He could see the joy on her face as she held it up to the sun, her arms lifting in front of her saluting the elephant standing in the shallows of the lake. Jake had captured the might and magnificence of the elephant and the vulnerability, innocence, and joy of a young girl in the African bush.

Jake Henderson's love for the woman and the child in his book was deeply obvious; she had undoubtedly told him about the baby she had given away, hence the title of the book.

Alex went through the pages again, looking closely at the woman and child. It had been the same with the photographs in the sitting room, something... but he couldn't pin it down.

The next morning Luke noticed the book on the dining-room table as he cleared away the breakfast plates.

"I found this last night in Miss Nicola's music seat," he said to him. "The little girl," he turned the book over, "is Cat, right?"

Luke smiled. "Yes, she is Cat. Inside this book is a picture of me!" he said proudly, "And the elephant is Tika."

293

"Yes, I had the pleasure of meeting him last night; he scared the hell out of me!" Alex ran his hand over the book. "Wasn't it dangerous for Miss Nicola to put this book in the box? What if her husband had found it? Surely there would have been trouble for her."

"Very big trouble. Miss Elizabeth brought the book from America when she came after Cat died. Miss Nicola was afraid so I took the book and hid it in my house.

"So how did it get in the box if the music room was boarded up?"

"I myself placed it there when we cleaned the room last week. In this box was found the ring belonging to Bwana Jake. After Bwana Max killed him he took this ring and put it in the box for Miss Nicola to find."

Alex shook his head in disbelief. "Max killed him! But what did he do with the body?"

Luke looked into the distance. "He left him there for the hyena and vultures. No body left after this."

Alex felt his breakfast shift in his stomach. At one point he'd thought Nicola had maybe seen Jake after his disappearance but now it was clear - she'd never seen her lover again.

He looked at Luke's gentle face, wondering how he had coped with all the tragedy over the years.

He stood up and patted the old man's shoulder. "I have to go back to London and when I return I'd like to bring a good friend with me, her name is Sophie, and she owns the shop where Matthew delivered your parcel. I'd like her to see the house and meet you, if that's alright?"

Luke's hand trembled as he poured the coffee. "But perhaps you will not return?"

Alex assured him that we would.

"When you do this, I will give you the diaries and the letters of Miss Nicola."

Clever old bugger, Alex thought. That would guarantee he'd come back. Laughing he went upstairs to pack.

Chapter Fifty-Seven

LONDON 2008

It's an amazing story, Alex," Sophie said as they strolled through the park, "I think it's too good for just an article. You should write a book."

He reached for her hand. "That's what I'm going to do. I was thinking on the flight over about going to see Harry at the paper and asking him for six months off to write it."

"In Cape Town?"

"No, I want to go back to Mbabati, being in the house where everything happened seems right to me. Luke said he'd show me the diaries and letters.

"I want to approach a few publishers to see if there's a level of interest. I thought I'd write up a couple of chapters and take it from there."

Sophie let go of his hand and pulled her coat around her as the sun dipped behind a dark cloud. "I don't think I can bear months of not seeing you; not being able to phone or email you on a regular basis is too much for me, it's horrible having you so far away."

He saw she was on the verge of tears and put his arms around her. "I know, my darling, that's why I'd like you to come with me. I have to go back, book deal or no book deal. I promised Luke I would, and I told him I'd bring you with me."

"I'd love to see the house," she said looking up at him wistfully, "and I'd like to meet Luke." She wiped her eyes with the back of her hand. "But it always comes down to the same thing - the flipping shop, and finding someone to run it for me."

"Well, I'm sure you'll come up with something. I don't want to go back without you." Alex opened the umbrella against the rain and held it over her head.

"Will it be alright for us to stay at the house though?"

"I've cleared it with Martin. I dropped in to see him on my way to the airport and he didn't have a problem with it, he liked the idea of someone being there until he finds the elusive heir who'll inherit it.

"Come on, let's get out of this rain, find somewhere and grab a coffee."

Seated at a small table near the window they sipped their hot drinks. "There's something else I need to do," Alex said watching the rain snake down the window. "I need to see the scary Mother Superior again."

******

The Mother Superior eyed him warily. Alex Patterson was not going to give up until he had the whole truth - he was almost there, but not quite.

"I appreciate you coming back to see me Mr Patterson, and telling me of your visit to Kenya. After reading the diaries I was quite aware which sister I had living here, but it makes no difference now does it. Nicola needed protection from the outside world, despite her past, and this we gave her. May her dear soul rest in peace." She crossed herself quickly.

"I have something to ask you, Reverend Mother?"

She rolled her eyes at him. "Will you never be satisfied? You have the truth, what more can I give you?"

"I want to take Nicola back to Kenya, to Mbabati. Her child is buried on the estate and I'd like them to be together again."

"God is truly with you, Alex Patterson," she said dryly. "Nicola was specific about what she wanted after she died. Her ashes were not to be scattered in our Garden of Remembrance. She hoped one day someone would come for her and take her home, perhaps her sister Elizabeth."

"But why didn't you tell me this when I was here last time?" he said.

"You were not family, Mr Patterson, and even worse, you were a journalist after a story. But I admire your tenacity," she said grudgingly, "and you have spent a considerable amount of time trying to find Nicola, therefore I am prepared to give her to you on one condition."

He raised his eyebrows in question. "You have told me you plan to write the story of her life. If you'll give me your word the name of this convent will *not* be mentioned, I will let you take her home."

Alex looked at her with relief. "You have my word, Reverend Mother."

She stood up. "I'm sure your book will be a great success considering she was once such a famous pianist and her," she cleared

296

her throat as if searching for something appropriate to call Nicola's lover, "and her friend, an artist of some note I understand.

"When the book is published there will a great deal of media interest. The last thing I want here, in God's house, are hordes of photographers and reporters camped outside the gates with their intrusive cameras, ladders, and flashing lights. I trust you'll protect us here as we protected Nicola?"

"You have my word, once again, Reverent Mother."

"Very well. We have a death certificate, of course, but in the name of Elizabeth DuPont." A ghost of a smile crossed her lips. "I suppose all that's needed is for you to swop them around in order to satisfy the lawyer in Nairobi.

"They chose to use the same surname in order to confuse anyone who might wish to pursue them, the police in particular. All this, and more, will be revealed when you read the diaries.

"When you compare the dates on the death certificates you will see both sisters died in the same month, which is not uncommon with twins.

"When you've decided on your return date to Kenya you will let me know, and arrangements will be made for you to collect Nicola. Until such time, she will remain here with us."

He stood up and held out his hand which she took in both of hers. "What plan do you have for Elizabeth, Mr Patterson? I'm sure you have one."

"It might be more complicated and take a bit of time, but you're right. I plan to bring her from Cape Town and take her to back to Mbabati. The twins were close throughout their lives and had an unbreakable bond between them. I want them to be together again."

The Mother Superior watched him from her window as he strode towards the convent gates. The world might seem to be full of people whose only mission in life was to have money and power, but Alex Patterson was a man of compassion with a natural love for his fellow humans.

She wiped an unexpected tear from her eye. She would remember him in her prayers tonight.

Lying in bed together they went through the book, savouring the exquisite work of Jake Henderson. "He was a gorgeous looking man." Sophie said studying the photograph of him on the inside front cover.

"Not bad at all. Small wonder Nicola fell head over heels in love with him. What do you think of the shots of the little girl, Cat?"

"Beautiful child. She looks so wild and free in all her photographs. She must have been a happy little thing with the bush as her playground and an elephant for a best friend."

He yawned and closed the book. "Better get some sleep if I want to start on my chapters tomorrow, and I still have to clear things with Harry down at the newspaper. Come on, lights out."

Some moments later he sat bolt upright in bed and fumbled for the light switch. Sophie looked at him in surprise. "What?"

"That's it - I've got it! Both the sisters played classical piano, right?" She nodded.

"Those bad reviews in the press? It wasn't Nicola playing - it was Elizabeth, she was the one responsible for the demise of her sister's career.''

Sophie rubbed her eyes. "You think that's why she sacrificed the rest of her own life protecting Nicola from the police, to make up for what she'd done to her?"

"Absolutely. I'm putting my money on the fact that when Nicola fell pregnant she wasn't married to Max, a big scandal in those days, so he whistled up her twin sister and made her play whatever he had scheduled."

"But why?"

"Greed. Nicola was obviously making huge amounts of money and as her agent he would have been making it too. She was probably booked up years in advance and he couldn't get out of the contracts. My guess is that he bullied her into giving up her child and planned to get her back up on stage as if nothing had happened. But as we now know it didn't quite work out like that - her public crucified who they thought was Nicola - and that was the end of it all."

******

Over the coming weeks Alex finished his three chapters and went in search of a publisher. After being rejected by five of them he gloomily phoned his editor at the newspaper.

"Hey Harry, it's me, Alex. How about a pub lunch tomorrow, I need someone to tell me what a great writer I am."

Harry worked his way through his prawn sandwich as he read the first three chapters of the book. Brushing the crumbs off the pages he handed them back to him.

"It's good, damn good. I'm happy to give you six months off to finish it, as long as we can sign a contract giving the newspaper exclusive rights to publish what we want to take from it, and I want exclusive rights to print the first story about this before you're published. Okay? Put the story of your Zimbabwe farmers on the back burner. I think this is going to be a quite a story, a big one."

He drained his pint of beer and put it down on the bar. "You said you're finding it hard to find a publisher? They're an arrogant lot and it's difficult to get their attention, but I have some contacts. I'll make a few calls."

Alex let himself into the apartment and went through to the kitchen pleased with how the meeting had gone with Harry. Underneath the fridge magnet was a note.

Sweetheart, I have to rush to Paris. Mama is ill and has been taken to hospital. I've closed the shop as I couldn't find anyone to run it at such short notice. Should be back by the weekend. Hope you had some success today. I tried to call you on your mobile but it was off.
Love S

A lamp next to the bed cast a warm glow around the hospital room, the only sound the low hum of the machine behind her mother's head. Sophie bent and kissed her forehead. "I'm here, Mama," she said in French, "I came as soon as I could. Can you hear me?"

Her mother squeezed her hand and opened her eyes at the sound of her voice. "I'm sorry Sophie," she whispered, "I told them not to call you, not to bother you."

Sophie stroked her mother's silver hair, alarmed at her pallor. She had spoken to the doctor who told her that at seventy-eight one mustn't expect too much. Pneumonia in an older person could be dangerous.

"Sophie?"

"Yes, Mama, I'm still here."

"There is a small box in the table here…"

Sophie bent down and retrieved it, putting it on the bed next to her mother's hand. "Shall I open it for you?"

She nodded, her breath rasping in her chest.

Sophie pulled out a white toy rabbit and a delicate necklace. Attached to the thin chain was a small charm. "Is it for me, Mama, did you buy me a present?" She smiled through her tears.

"Come closer, *cheri.* The *petit* rabbit, and the necklace was given to me on the day after you were born."

"Why did you not give it to me then, Mama? Why wait until I'm nearly forty-five?"

Her mother ignored her questions and continued. "Shhh..Sophie, you must listen to me, it's important.

"So often I wanted to tell you this but always my courage failed me. You are more precious to me than you will ever know. I've loved you from the moment I looked into your little face when you were first placed in my arms."

Her mother reached for her hand and continued. "Papa and I were unable to have children of our own. We found you through a private agency in Paris. They sent us to Geneva, some months later, and told us there was a baby who would be ours."

She paused to catch her breath and continued painfully. "The mother of the child wished her daughter to be called Sophie, and asked for her to be brought up in Paris, she wanted her child to have the *petit* rabbit and the necklace you have in your hands." She ran a shaking finger down the side of the soft fur.

"I looked into your face and felt the pain of your mother, and I promised to do as she wished. It was a small thing to ask in return for such a beautiful child."

Sophie listened to her mother numbly. "But why did you not tell me I was adopted, Mama? I would still have loved you as much as I do now."

"Papa and I were sworn to secrecy, we signed papers to say we would never divulge the name of the real parents. That's why I could never tell you.

"I knew who your mother was. It was on the birth certificate. She was loved throughout France, and I understood why she had to give you away."

Sophie took her mother's hand and brought it to her lips. "I don't care who gave me away, you're the only mother I've ever had."

"Hush child and let me finish. Your mother was so young to be pregnant and perhaps she is still alive. After you were born nothing was heard from her again. Try to find her… let her see you again."

The doctor tapped Sophie on the shoulder and held a finger to his lips. Reluctantly she stood up, leaning over she kissed her mother. "I'll be back tomorrow Mama." Holding the necklace in her hand and the rabbit in the crook of her arm she left her mother to sleep.

******

The call from the hospital came through in the early hours of the morning. Grief stricken she phoned Alex who immediately booked a flight to Paris.

Now sitting at her mother's window she looked out over the city, watching the dappled sunlight on the pedestrians hurrying to work. Nothing has changed, she thought, life is going on, but Mama has gone. How can it ever be the same again? Her tears splashed down on the soft rabbit in her lap. Picking it up, she buried her face in its fur and gave into her grief, her raw cries echoing around the silent apartment.

******

Alex held Sophie as they buried her mother. The funeral was well attended by her many friends in the city and past students she had taught music. Sophie was inconsolable and still reeling from the shock of finding out she was adopted; she hadn't mentioned it to Alex, needing more time to absorb the information her dying mother had given her, and overwhelmed by the loss of her.

"My darling, there are certain things which have to been done now," Alex said firmly the following week. "The lawyer will be here shortly, we must start to sort things out. Your shop's been closed for over a week now, and I have to get back to London."

Sophie nodded numbly. Hearing a knock at the door Alex stood up and went to let the lawyer in.

"Mademoiselle, your mother's Will is straightforward. There are papers for you to sign, of course, and here," he handed her a large cream envelope, "are her personal papers which she always left with me."

Alex helped her sort her mother's apartment out. It had been rented furnished so little was left to pack up.

"Pick out what you would like to keep, my darling, and I'll arrange to have it shipped to London. Why not leave all the personal papers until we get home? You'll feel stronger then and more able to deal with things."

******

Alex put down the phone, a rush of excitement coursing through his veins. Four weeks after submitting the first chapters of his manuscript to the contact Harry had been in touch with, he had a deal. Forbes and Hunter, based in London, were keen to publish the finished manuscript.

Over dinner that evening they discussed the good news. Sophie was as excited as he was. "You'd better start planning the trip back, poor old Luke will think you, like the sisters, have deserted him."

"Did you ask Sally if she'd help with the shop?"

"She said she'd would, so I'll be coming with you!" She pushed her plate aside and stood up.

Alex's chair toppled backwards in his haste to wrap his arms around her. "My darling, you have no idea what this means to me, and to Luke, and it'll be good for you too, God I love you so much, you've no idea."

She held him tightly before disentangling herself from his arms. "I'd better start going through Mama's papers. I can't keep putting it off, and I need to get things sorted out before we leave."

"Good idea. You get stuck into that and I'll crack on with my manuscript."

Glancing up occasionally through the door in his study, he saw she seemed to be coping well with her task. Satisfied, he returned to his manuscript and was soon lost in his story.

"Alex! Oh God. Alex!"

He looked up startled at the sound of her stricken voice. She was leaning against the door as though it might prop her up. Her face was ashen and he leapt up in alarm.

"What is it? You're as white as a sheet. Sit down for a minute; I'll get you a brandy. You look as though you could do with one."

He put the glass of brandy on a small table in front of her. Wordlessly she handed him a piece of paper.

"It's my birth certificate."

He scanned it briefly, reached for her brandy and knocked it back in one gulp. He lowered himself into a chair, looking at the names of her parents in disbelief.

"This can't be. It's impossible! You didn't tell me you were adopted. Why didn't you tell me?"

"I didn't know myself until Mama told me when I saw her in hospital. The shock of losing her so suddenly wiped it from my mind. When we got back to London I decided it wouldn't make much difference. Telling you would have made it real and I already had too much to deal with."

"I'm having a hard time dealing with this myself. I can't believe it!" He looked down at the birth certificate as the ramifications of what he was seeing became apparent. "I just can't believe it," he repeated.

He stared at the certificate again. "I suppose it wasn't impossible really. Nicola's life was classical music and your mother was in the same world, a teacher of classical music. Nicola would have wanted it that way, maybe insisted on it as part of the adoption agreement. Even so..."

He knelt in front of her and took her icy hands in his. "We found her," he said, his voice breaking. "We found the lost child."

Chapter Fifty-Eight

Alex had called Martin in Nairobi the day after Sophie found the birth certificate.

"I hope you haven't got your agents scouring various countries for Nicola's daughter, because I've found her for you!"

There was silence from the other end of the phone, and then Martin spoke. "You never cease to amaze me, Alex. Notices are due to appear in various newspapers around the world next week. It's taken some weeks to tie up the estate, it was complex."

He paused for a moment. "When you came to see me and asked about the only surviving relative I didn't tell you if it was male or female, so how did you know what you were looking for?"

"It's a long story... Did Nicola tell you the name of the child she gave up for adoption?"

"She did, but she wasn't sure if the adopting parents would agree to call her by it. They were under no obligation to do so after all. You'll have to give me some irrefutable proof this person is Nicola's child."

"Don't worry, I have the birth certificate. So what did Nicola want her daughter to be called?"

"Sophie. It's here in the file."

"And Sophie she is, Martin. Oh, and something else I've been able to do - I plan to bring Nicola's ashes back to Kenya with me and, obviously, you need to meet her daughter."

"You went back to Cape Town?"

"No, the woman buried there is her sister, Elizabeth. Nicola spent the rest of her life in the convent in London. I'll tell you about it when we get to Nairobi."

******

The aircraft made an ungainly landing before making its way to the terminal building in Nairobi. Alex took her hand in his, brushing the hair back from her face he leaned over and kissed her forehead.

"Ready?" he asked her as the aircraft came to a hissing halt. She nodded apprehensively.

"As ready as I'll ever be. It's hard to believe we're bringing her home. I'm a bit overwhelmed by it all actually, but strangely excited to."

"That's my girl. Once we've cleared customs and immigration we need to go to the Cargo section and collect Nicola."

A suitably sombre Kenyan official handed Alex the sealed urn having checked the death and cremation certificates.

"Welcome home, Nicola. Welcome back to Kenya," he whispered as he reverently carried her back to Sophie waiting by their luggage.

******

Martin stood up as his secretary ushered in Sophie, Alex and Nicola. He watched Sophie, fascinated, as Alex filled him in on what had been happening and how he had worked things out.

Silently Martin studied the birth certificate. "I'm going to need more than this, Alex. We're talking about a substantial estate here and there'll be no room for error, no room at all."

He turned to her. "I'm sorry, Sophie, I don't wish to cast doubt on the fact you're Nicola Gray's daughter, that she was your mother. In fact I can see a similarity, the same eyes and hair colouring; even so I hope you understand my reasons for being cautious?"

She nodded, reaching for Alex's hand, finding it hard to believe the man in front of her had known her natural mother.

Alex handed Martin an envelope. "When we found out Sophie had been adopted, and found the birth certificate, we went back to Paris. Here are the original adoption papers."

******

Luke looked up when he heard the car at the gates of Mbabati and a smile spread over his face as he made his way as quickly as he could down the drive. Bwana Alex had returned, as he had promised.

Unlocking the padlock he opened the gates and let the car through, then closed them again.

Alex stopped the car and they climbed out. "Welcome, Bwana Alex, you have come back!" He turned happily towards Sophie, blinking his eyes rapidly with surprise.

305

Alex took Sophie's hand and put it in Luke's. "This is Miss Nicola's daughter, Sophie."

"Yes I see this now." He squeezed her hand lightly in both of his. "I am happy you have been found Miss Sophie..." his voice trailed off as he stared at her.

"Hop in the back, Luke. Let's show her the house."

Sophie looked up at Mbabati, overwhelmed by the sheer grandness of it, and her connection to it. Pulling up outside, Alex switched off the engine, and they got out.

Lifting the urn from the back of the vehicle he handed it to Luke. "This is for you, my friend."

With a puzzled frown Luke examined it. "This pot is for me? What is in this pot?"

Alex took it back and handed it to Sophie. He put his hands on the old man's shoulders. "Inside are the ashes of Miss Nicola which I have brought from London. She wished, after her death, to come back to Mbabati - to be with you both again. I think she would like to see her daughter now, don't you?"

The tears ran unchecked down Luke's face as he turned to Sophie and reached for the urn. "I shall take care of this, Bwana Alex. She will be safe with me, as she has always been." His voice faltered as he turned towards the graveyard holding her close to his chest.

"Come, Miss Nicola, come and see Cat, she has missed you very much, she will be happy you are home again. I am happy also, that you have come back to your house, and to old Luke."

Alex rubbed his eyes surreptitiously, then taking Sophie's hand, he led her up the steps and into her house.

******

Alex looked at her across the gleaming dining table; Sophie looked utterly exhausted by the events of the day.

"Take your time, my darling, it's a lot to take in. Tomorrow I'll leave you to walk around on your own. You've a lot to think about."

"Yes… Is this really all mine?"

"Yup. I can't get my head around it either."

Sophie hid a yawn with her hand. "The big question is do I want to live here permanently? It's a major move to make and I'm not

306

sure...I've never even thought about living in Africa. Phew! This is a huge decision to make, what about my shop?"

"Don't worry about that now, no rush to make any decision. After dinner I'll show you Nicola's music room. Hey, why don't you ring the bell," he raised his eyebrow, "the bell responsible for this whole fantastic story."

Her eyes filled with regret as she remembered the nun. "It's hard to believe I tried to give it to her when she came into the shop, and even harder to think I was looking at my own mother. Now I know why she wanted me to keep it.

"Remember I told you Sister Elizabeth, as I thought she was, asked me my name and how she looked so intently at me when I saw her in the shop? I wonder how she found me..."

"Things happen in life, my darling, which just can't be explained. I've read loads of stories about twins separated at birth, and then later in life find they've been living two blocks away from each other. The same with mothers who give up their children for adoption, some of them have an uncanny way of finding them again. It's all been documented over the years and no-one can explain why.

"My guess is Nicola, over the years, walked past your shop often, looking in the window just to catch a glimpse of you. I think, instinctively, she knew who you were and when you told her your name, well, then she knew for sure."

Luke brought a bottle of wine from the cellar and left it to cool in a gleaming silver ice bucket.

He cleared his throat. "In honour of Miss Nicola and her return to Mbabati, I have made the French cooking, which she taught me," he beamed self-consciously as he served them, "it is the veal with the mushrooms and much cream. Her favourite."

When they had finished eating Alex stood up and held his hand out to her. "I want to show you something."

They sat silently on the bench in the graveyard. The lamp at the top of Cat's grave gave off a soft glow. Next to it Luke had placed the urn.

Nicola had finally come home.

"To think I had a sister called Cat," Sophie whispered. Alex saw her making a conscious effort not to look at her father's, unkempt and neglected, grave.

Alex put his arms around her and held her, lost for a while in his own thoughts, Sophie interrupted them with her question. "How come Martin and Luke could see the similarity between Nicola and me, but you didn't pick it up?"

Alex thought for a moment. "It was the one thing that bugged me when I was looking at the photographs in the sitting room, there was something that I couldn't put my finger on. In my own defence I can only say that when I met who I thought was Nicola, she was in her mid-sixties and the portrait was painted when she was in her twenties." He cleared his throat. "Both Luke and Martin had known her for over twenty years so it was easier for them to spot the resemblance.

He stood up and held out his hand to her. "Let's go back to the house."

"And this," he said opening the top floor door with a flourish, "is the music room, Nicola's favourite place in the entire house. Magnificent, isn't it?"

Candlelight reflected off the deep mahogany wood of the piano. Sophie ran her hand across the top of it, then sat on Nicola's stool. Lifting the lid she ran her fingers over the ivory keys feeling the presence of the woman all around her, sensing her. Softly she began to play.

"I'd no idea you played the piano, Sophie?"

"Mmmm - you never asked. I didn't think it was important. My mother was a music teacher, so she insisted I learn," she grinned at him "and before you say anything I'm well aware I'm not in the same league as Nicola!"

He came up behind her and put his arms around her. "Afraid not, my darling, but you're not bad, not bad at all."

Chapter Fifty-Nine

Alex and Sophie sat around the dining room table as Martin went through the mound of paperwork necessary to transfer the estate into her name. She'd insisted Alex sit in on the meeting and he had not objected.

"It's going to take a couple of days to go through things," he had told her on the phone from his office in Nairobi. "I'd like to go right through the house and make sure we have everything on the inventory. For insurance purposes, now that the music room is open again, we should get someone out to check the Steinway and make sure it hasn't been damaged in any way by its twenty years of isolation."

Now he cleared his throat. "There's a safe in Max's old study on the ground floor, I have the key for it and the combination; Nicola, or as it turns out Elizabeth, left it with me the last time she came to my office.

"I'm not sure what's in it but whatever's there will need to go on the inventory. Then it's all yours, Sophie."

The sun was beginning to set as she signed the last document. Alex stood up and stretched. "Time for a drink I think, I'm sure we can all use one. I'll get Luke to bring out the drinks tray. Where would you like it, my darling? Veranda?"

She stifled a yawn. "Okay. I need some fresh air and a large gin and tonic! Are we done here now?"

Martin screwed the top onto his fountain pen and glanced down at the last document. "Yes, we're all done. Tomorrow you can open the safe or now if you like?"

She shook her head. "My head's spinning as it is. Tomorrow will be fine; right now I could murder that gin and tonic!"

******

The safe, in Max's old study, was recessed into the wall and hidden behind a large painting of a hunting scene, the hounds milling around the riders. Sophie followed Martin's instructions for the combination lock and turned the handle. The door swung open revealing several small boxes.

Sophie turned and looked over her shoulder, one eyebrow raised in question.

309

"Jewellery I would imagine," he remarked. "Let's have a look."

Carefully she carried the boxes out of the safe and placed them on the table. Martin unscrewed his pen and opened his pad in readiness.

"I'm sure Alex would like to be here, I'll go and call him, I'm sure he won't mind me interrupting his writing for half an hour."

A few minutes later they both came into the study. Sophie opened the first box and withdrew a triple strand pearl choker. She gasped. "This is the one Nicola was wearing in the portrait. It's gorgeous!"

One by one she went through the boxes. Half an hour later Martin put his glasses on and cleared his throat. "Right, let's check we have everything."

He went through the substantial list of jewellery. "Both happy with that?"

They nodded. Martin scribbled something on his notepad.

Alex put the jewellery back in the boxes and carried them back to the safe. As he put the last box in his hand brushed against an envelope. He pulled it out, looking at the name, written in an elegant hand.

Sophie.

Silently he handed it to her. She looked at him and laughed. "For me?"

"For you."

Not taking her eyes off him she sank into the chair. Putting on her glasses she looked down at the letter in her hand.

"How about some tea or coffee Martin?" Alex said diplomatically.

My beloved daughter, my beloved Sophie,

I write this letter to you with little or no hope you will ever read it. Tomorrow I leave this house and the country, both of which I have come to love dearly. I hope with all my heart that one day I will be able to return here.

I don't even know the name you have been given, but to me you will always be my little Sophie.

My dearest wish is that your life has been happy and you have been well loved, as I once was. Not one day has passed without me thinking of you, and praying for you.

310

I've missed so many precious moments; seeing your first smile, hearing you laugh, hearing your first words and most of all watching you grow up.

God has punished me for giving you away; he took my other darling daughter, Catherine, too. She is buried here on the estate - your sister. It will be impossibly hard to leave her here alone... without me. But Luke will take care of her and this brings me some comfort. He loved her as much as I did.

If by some miracle this letter should find its way to you, which I very much doubt, you will know I am now dead.

Mbabati belongs to you. Someone must know where you are, someone must be able to find you and bring you here? I'm sure Martin will do his best and search for you.

Once I had everything, too much perhaps, but I would give it all back if only I could have my two girls again, and the man I truly loved. But it is impossible.

One day I hope you will sit in the music room and play my piano - I never stopped loving you, or thinking about you, Sophie, not for one second.

My only prayer now is that one day God will forgive me enough to let me see you again - just once.

Mummy

Sophie folded the letter, which her mother had written in French to her. Through the words she felt the pain and sadness and her eyes filled unexpectedly.

God had been forgiving.

She shook the envelope and a black and white photograph slid out onto the table in front of her. Two sisters, identical twins, standing beside a piano, both of them laughing into the camera, their faces pressed together.

Sophie looked at it for a long time. Even she could not tell them apart.

Thoughtfully she put the letter and the photograph back in the envelope and left the study.

Chapter Sixty

Alex worked five hours a day on his manuscript, happy to let Sophie get to know her house and Luke. Sometimes he would watch them in the gardens as they talked and he knew, even though she had been shocked to find out she had been adopted, that she was curious about her mother, who she still insisted on calling Nicola.

He was pleased to see, after reading the letter addressed to her in the safe, she had taken to wearing the silver chain with the miniature piano charm. He also noticed that whenever she passed the portrait she paused and spent some time looking at her mother, sometimes sitting on the bottom step of the staircase just staring at her.

That evening, sitting outside, Sophie looked up at a sky stained with stars knowing she was seeing what her mother must have seen over the many years she had lived there. She reached for Alex's hand, comforted by its familiar shape and warmth.

"I feel I already know Nicola, but even so I want to know more. Luke has told me so many things about her life here, information you can use in your book. How's it coming along by the way?"

"Good, it's taking shape nicely. I'm waiting for Luke to give me Nicola's diary and letters, I'm not going to ask him, I'll wait for him to decide when the time is right.

"I thought I'd ask him to take us to the hide tomorrow, and see where they were buried for so many years. What do you think?"

Sophie looked at him and smiled. "Stroke of luck for you that I've given you permission to have your story about my family published - what if I'd said no?"

He threw a cushion at her. "You love me too much to refuse me anything."

He pulled her to her feet and gave her a lingering kiss. "Come on let's go to bed..."

Alex had been sensitive about how she would feel; after all, he had told her, it was now the story about her parents.

She had thought long and hard about it then made her decision. Nicola had been one of the finest pianists France had ever produced. It was time to tell the true story of what happened to her.

The next day Luke unwillingly agreed to show them where the hide was.

"We are here now Bwana Alex, you must stop the car." Luke reluctantly climbed out of the vehicle.

Sophie was the first one to adapt her eyes and see the soft shape hidden in the bush. Alex looked around curiously as Luke showed Sophie the overgrown path and the entrance to the hide. Inexplicably he shivered; the place had a seriously bad atmosphere.

Luke had obviously not been there for many years, except for the brief visit with Matthew to retrieve the letters and the diary, and the place was falling apart.

The outside deck had been eaten away by ants and other insects, as had the furniture inside. Birds nested in the collapsed thatch of the roof and rose up in alarm when they entered, their hardened droppings sprinkled on the floor. Lizards scuttled away from beneath their feet and a long green snake leapt off the broken deck and vanished into the thick bush.

Branches had broken off the tree in the bedroom and the collapsed bed was covered with dirt and leaves. The natural canopy created by the tree was now full of gaping holes. Tufts of stuffing from the darkly-stained mattress lay on the floor where small creatures and birds had torn into it to make their nests.

Sophie had also sensed the atmosphere at the hide and was anxious to leave it.

"You can feel something bad happened here, can't you, Alex?" she whispered nervously." The place is giving me the creeps." She turned towards Luke. "Are you ready to go Luke. I don't like it down here."

"Yes, Miss Sophie." He looked around fearfully, remembering the horrors that had happened there - the horrors only he had been witness to.

******

After dinner they sat outside with their coffee. Heat from the fire took the chill off the cool evening as they listened to the sounds of the night. Down in the lake the hippos grunted and guffawed, and somewhere far away a male lion throatily called his pride to hunt, his rasping call cutting through the darkened bush.

313

An elephant trumpeted and they looked at each other and smiled. Sophie had yet to meet Tika but Alex was sure he would come and visit when he sensed strangers in the house again.

Sophie watched the sparks from the fire as they crackled and spat up into the night. "I think we should pull the hide down. Burn what's left inside and let Mother Nature return it to its natural state. I don't think I ever want to go there again, do you?"

"No, apart from freaking me out the place is unsafe. I agree with you, it should be flattened and forgotten. But we'll need labour for that, which is sadly lacking at the moment.

He took a sip of his coffee. "You need to think about what you'd like to do with the grounds and outbuildings," he paused, "and the house. Maybe chat to Martin about it?"

She nodded and leaned back in the chair. "The piano needs tuning, and it might be an idea to get an expert to examine Nicola's portrait; there must be someone in Nairobi who could help - Martin will know. God knows how many bugs might have traversed its surface over the years."

She looked out over the blackness of the bush. "I love the portrait; Nicola seems to be watching me all the time. I think she's happy I'm here."

"Nothing would have made her happier. Ah, here comes Luke with what I hope is the diary and the letters."

Sophie looked up as he approached. "I didn't think I'd ever see those again!"

Luke held the diaries and letters out to Alex. "These are for you now, Bwana Alex, for reading. You will tell me if Miss Nicola is writing about old Luke sometimes?"

Alex held out his hands eagerly. "I thought there was just one diary Luke; you seem to have quite a few here."

"Miss Nicola had many diaries." He passed them to Alex. "She was writing many times of her life here in these books. I have kept them in my house for her. Hiding only this one. This one I sent with Matthew."

Sophie went up to the music room and played softly to herself. Alex went into the sitting room and started to read the letters and the diaries, he was soon lost in a long ago world. The hide then - this was where it had all happened... No wonder the place had spooked them out.

314

He would make sure his story would evoke a great deal of sympathy for Nicola, it was the least he could do for her - she'd suffered enough. But he was going to nail Max and expose him for the bastard he had been, and the pain he had put her through.

He rubbed the back of his neck and flexed his shoulders. Standing up to stretch, he saw Tika standing absolutely still as he listened to Sophie playing.

He took the stairs two at a time. "Sophie! He's come to visit. Tika's here. You have to come and meet him."

Holding hands they ran down the stairs and out into the grounds. Tika lifted his trunk and caught their scent. They sat on the garden bench and waited. Tika watched them, slowly moving closer. Sophie closed her eyes and took a deep breath - he was gigantic.

"Don't be frightened," Alex whispered, "he's big but he's as gentle as a kitten."

Tika ran his trunk over her body, lightly touching her face in greeting, a low rumble coming from the depths of his cavernous stomach. Tears ran down Sophie's cheeks and he moved his ears slowly as he felt the wetness of them.

She thought about all the people the old elephant had loved in his time: Nicola, Luke and Cat, and how he faithfully came to the house to see if any of them had come back.

Tika touched his trunk to Alex's neck in greeting, then rummaged slowly in his pocket looking for an orange. He snuffled with pleasure when he found one. He turned and walked silently through the grounds, heading for the graveyard.

"He knows Nicola is back," Sophie whispered, completely overwhelmed, her voice thick with emotion at her encounter with the magnificent beast.

Alex smiled at her tears and wiped them away with the cuff of his shirt. "I'm sure he does, that old elephant seems to figure everything out. I've been reading about him in her diary and how much they loved him.

"Nicola knew Max shot Tika's mother, Luke told her, and that's why he attacked him down at the hide. He must miss them. Not Max though."

In the early hours of the morning Alex closed the last diary and looked at Sophie lying asleep next to him. So often through the years Nicola had written about her daughter and wondered about her life, and where she was living. Her love for Jake had seared through the pages of the diary, his death had devastated her, as had her daughter's.

When Elizabeth had suggested they swap identities Nicola had the proof she had been searching for - her sister had played at those final disastrous recitals in Paris.

He turned out the light and put his arms around Sophie, his only tenuous connection to Nicola Gray; the woman who had fascinated him enough to write a book about her, a woman whom he had come to love, but not as much as he loved her daughter.

After Sophie had read the diaries, if she wanted to, and the love letters between Jake and her mother, he was going to suggest they burn them.

******

Sophie and Alex spent four months at Mbabati. Alex completed his manuscript and submitted it to his publisher.

Luke happily looked after them both and ran the house, aware changes were coming; he hoped he would be included in them, then chastised himself; he was too old, they would probably want a younger man in his place.

Sophie, Alex and Martin spent hours going through the house and the estate discussing various plans and ideas for its future.

Now Sophie waited until Luke had removed the dinner plates and brought the coffee tray to the sitting room.

"Before you leave, Luke, I wanted to tell you what we've decided about the future of the house."

"Yes, Miss Sophie," he said looking at her with apprehension.

She smiled at him putting her hand out to squeeze his reassuringly. "You've always been part of the family, a very big part, and we want you to stay on and continue to look after Mbabati, if you'd like to that is?"

"You will stay here, Miss Sophie?" he said, his voice faltering.

"I'll come and visit as often as I can, at least once every two months, until I decide what to do with my shop in London."

Luke's face fell and she continued hastily. "Alex will stay here and we'll need your help and guidance as always."

Luke glanced at Alex who was nodding at him encouragingly. He looked down at his feet to hide his emotions, he nodded solemnly at them before he left the room, overcome with the news that he still had a part to play in the future of Mbabati and that he was still needed and wanted.

Chapter Sixty-One
MBABATI 2011

They had been reluctant to even consider turning Mbabati into a country house for paying guests, but Martin had been persuasive. He'd told them that after paying the death duties and all the other expenses, there would still be a good amount of money left in the Estate. However it wouldn't last forever and they'd need some kind of cash flow to keep the place going.

Alex and Sophie had tentatively agreed, but were not convinced they wanted to open the house to the public. Martin had continued persuasively.

"Tourists still flock to Kenya despite the bad press we get sometimes; it would be a good source of revenue for you. There's plenty of land here and you could easily build yourselves a small property, perhaps overlooking the lake? With only eight bedrooms, you wouldn't be able to live here yourselves. Have a think about it."

They had discussed it for days and finally agreed Martin was right, although neither of them knew anything about running a country house or organizing rangers to take guests on game drives.

"We'll have to hire someone to manage the place for us, Sophie. I'm more than happy to oversee things," Alex told her, "I love it here, but running it as a hotel, a game lodge, is something I've no experience of. The manager would have to be single as well. We can't have children running all over the place, not at the rates we plan to charge."

Sophie gave this some thought, and grinned at him. "There are loads of game lodges in Kenya - all we need to do is put the word out and poach the best. They'll be queuing around the block given the history of the place; Mbabati opening up again is a big story in Nairobi.

"Wait a minute…what about Bruce?"

"Bruce?"

"Yes, the guy who ran the game lodge we stayed at in South Africa? He said he would give anything to come back to East Africa! He'd be perfect…and he has a link to this place. Let's get hold of him - offer him the job."

Alex slowed his pace so Luke could keep up with him as they headed towards the graveyard. The scaffolding had been removed from the newly-painted house, the rich apricot tone reflecting in the late afternoon sun. The shutters were freshly painted and the roof re-tiled. He stopped to have a few words with the foreman and the architect before continuing on with Luke.

The head gardener waved to them before turning back to his team of men who had transformed the gardens, and brought them back to their former glory. Fine sprays of water clicked and arched over the lawns, keeping them green and lush. Birdsong echoed through the gardens as brightly coloured birds swooped and bathed in the cool spray. The formal rose gardens exuded a heavy scent from the nodding pink, white and yellow roses, the bushes bending slightly from the weight of the flowers.

In the paddocks the horses lifted their heads from their grazing and watched Luke and Alex as they walked past. The stables had been rebuilt, the dazzling white paint contrasting with the dark green doors of each stable.

The stately old Jaguar had been meticulously restored and parked in front of the garage. The safari vehicle and the three Land Rovers had also been restored and were neatly lined up inside the building. Cat's damaged jeep had been discreetly removed.

Opening the gate to the graveyard, Alex looked around. There were three new graves now, each with a simple headstone: Nicola Gray, Elizabeth DuPont and Jake Henderson. All three graves were as far away from Max's as had been possible.

It had taken a great deal of time and legal paperwork to have Elizabeth exhumed and flown back to Kenya, but with Martin's dogged help, and a sizeable amount of money from the estate, they had achieved it.

After discussions with Luke and Sophie it was decided to bury Jake's ring next to Nicola's grave and erect a simple headstone in his memory. Max's grave had been cleared of the vicious roots with their deep tentacles and the headstone cleaned of the lichen which had clung to it for so many years. Luke's reluctance to clean up the grave had been transparently apparent.

"It has to be done," Alex had explained reasonably, "whatever happened doesn't change the fact the estate belonged to the Gray family. People will be coming from all over the world to see the graves. It must to be done, old man, I'm sorry."

Cat's grave was unchanged; the headstone remained blank, as Nicola had wanted it to be.

Satisfied with the neatly arranged graveyard, they left.

All eight bedrooms in the house had been refurbished to a high standard, the plumbing in the bathrooms modernized. In the music room the Steinway Concert Grand stood alone in all its glory, now cordoned off with barrier posts and gold rope. Although the house now had electricity the music room remained as Nicola had wanted it - lit only by candles.

On the wall above the fireplace was a large blown-up photograph, in black and white, of Elizabeth DuPont, a cigarette held between her fingers, the smoke drifting upwards as she gazed unseeingly out of the window at the African bush.

The telephone company had installed telephones in each bedroom and access to the internet was available in Max's old study. The sitting room, dining-room and study had been cosmetically restored but left much as it was when Nicola had lived there, with the original prints on the wall and the photographs still displayed; two more framed photographs had been added, one was of Jake, the one Alex and Sophie had found in Elizabeth's trunk in Cape Town, and the other of Cat. Sophie had found the packet of photographs of her sister, at the back of a cupboard. She had chosen one of her as a young woman of seventeen, perhaps the last photograph ever taken of her.

Nicola's portrait hung on the wall just as it had always done.

The kitchen had been modernized and the old gas stove removed, replaced with a modern cooker. Additional cupboards had been built to house new crockery and cooking pots.

The hide had been dismantled and no longer existed; the bush had claimed it back. All that remained was the old tree which had grown in the bedroom, and the waterhole, where the animals came again to drink.

Sophie flew out to Kenya every month and was as excited as Alex about the restoration and plans for the house.

"It's looking stunning, isn't it!" she exclaimed as he showed her the finished house. "So now the house is ready, and your book is about to be published, I think we're good to go, don't you?"

"Just about. Luke needs a little more time to train up the junior chefs he's taken on, but his housekeeping staff are in place, and the gardeners and grooms.

"I've managed to poach the general manager from the Norfolk for a month, before Bruce gets here to take over. He's bringing two waiters who were made redundant - I think we can train them to be butlers.

She nodded approvingly as he continued. "Bruce is insisting on building an airstrip and buying a plane to ferry the guests in - and I think he's right, no long trips on bumpy roads, no grumpy guests - we fly them from Nairobi straight into paradise!"

******

Harry called him from London. "We're ready to roll Alex. I thought we'd do a review of your book, making it a bit of a taster for the full article to follow a week later. I'm going to email it to you - see what you think."

Alex printed it out and read it intently. It was perfect. A poignant love story - with all the right ingredients. Woven throughout the article was the story of two sisters, identical twins, who had chosen different paths to protect each other, and who were only reunited again in death at an extraordinary house in the middle of the African bush - the house called Mbabati.

He emailed it through to Sophie. "You realize our lives are about to change forever, my darling. When the media, especially the French media, read the review there will be a stampede to get to Mbabati, and a week later the full article comes out. The place will be swarming with reporters who want to see where all this happened. After that we'll be inundated with bookings from all over the world, guests will want to come and stay here, to re-live the love story. Just like they did when the movie *Out of Africa* came out - people came in their droves.

"I'm not sure poor old Luke will be able to handle all the attention after being here on his own for twenty years, but he seems quite excited at being part of it all."

Sitting at a pavement cafe on the Upper East Side in New York City, Susan Cohen bit into her bagel as she read through the arts column in the British newspaper, *The Telegraph*. Sipping her coffee she picked up the magazine and flicked through it. A headline caught her eye: *The Lost Child.*

Abandoning her half eaten bagel, she paid the bill and raced back to her apartment. She had to get on the first flight to Nairobi, but first she needed to speak to Alex Patterson. The article had given the phone number of Mbabati. Checking the time difference she picked up the telephone.

"I saw the review of your book in *The Telegraph* - about Mbabati? Am I pronouncing it right? I need to come and see you as soon as possible."

Alex frowned down the phone. It hadn't stopped ringing since the review had come out. "I'm afraid it won't be possible, Ms. Cohen. The house is fully booked up for months..."

Susan interrupted him. "Honey, I can't wait for a bed to free up, this is real important. It's about Jake Henderson; I was his agent. He left me a document. It's to do with the book he produced, *The Lost Child*. I think someone in the family needs to take a look at it."

Alex sat bolt upright in his chair, excitement surging through his body. "Forgive me, Ms. Cohen, but how do I know you're not another reporter? Just about every person I've spoken to so far has claimed some kind of link to the house, and the people who once lived here."

Again she interrupted him. "In the house, the name of which I can't pronounce, there's a painting. It's a portrait of Nicola Gray, she's wearing a long blue gown and seated next to a piano. It was painted by Jake. The portrait wasn't mentioned in the article, but Jake showed me a photograph of it. He told me it was one of his finest pieces. I have to see it. Must be worth a fortune in today's market."

She was telling the truth. There had been no mention of the portrait in the book review. Alex didn't hesitate. "Let me know your flight details and I'll pick you up at the airport."

Now, three days later, Susan stood in front of the portrait and studied it silently. "This is one of his best, if not the best. Would you consider selling it, Alex? I can get you a good price."

"It's not for sale I'm afraid. It belongs to Nicola's daughter. She inherited everything here including the portrait." He looked at his watch. "We've prepared the guest room for you at our place. I've a

322

press conference in an hour, with the French media, so I have to stay here, but Sophie's expecting you."

"I'd like to sit and look at Jake's portrait for a while longer, and I could murder a martini after the flight and drive out here. Was that a road we drove on or a sidewalk?"

Alex smiled at the small, energetic woman dressed head to toe in black. He picked up a small bell from the reception table and rang it. "The butler will mix it for you. I'll take you down to the house in fifteen minutes."

Alex drove her down to their newly built house on the lake, introduced her to Sophie, and left them to it.

Susan looked out over the lake whilst Sophie mixed her another martini. A pod of hippo was cavorting near the shore grunting and belly laughing. "Honey, are those beasts likely to wander into the house?"

Sophie laughed at the nervousness in the American woman's voice. "You're quite safe, they only come out onto land at night when they browse; they're just playing and having fun at the moment."

She handed Susan her drink. "You have a document you wanted to show me?"

"Yeah. Jake left it with me when he returned to Kenya. I never saw him again." Unexpectedly tears came to her eyes, and she swiped them away abruptly.

"I loved working with him, he was charming and amusing and gorgeous as well. I sure was upset when he disappeared. I thought he might pop up one day at my office and explain things, but he never did..."

She took a gulp of her martini and continued, "He told me about the book he wanted to produce and how many copies he wanted printed - just twenty. Three were to go to Nicola's sister in the States, the rest I was to hold until he gave further instructions. Of course, not seeing him again, I just kept the document, not knowing what to do with it. I read the review about Alex's book - I had to come and see you."

She put her glass down on the table. "But one thing bothers me. He told me Nicola's daughter was called Cat. There were photographs of her in the book playing with an elephant. Did you change your name?"

323

"No, my name is Sophie. Cat died, she's buried here on the estate. There's a memorial to Jake as well. I can show you later if you like?"

Susan reached for her drink and shuddered. "No thanks, honey, I don't do dead people. Gives me the creeps going around a graveyard. Gimme live ones any day. More money in it. So if Cat is dead, who are you?"

"I'm the so-called lost child. The one Nicola gave up for adoption."

"Okay, so that makes sense now. Jake always liked to plan ahead. In the document he only refers to Nicola's daughter, clever of him. He told me about Nicola losing a child and I thought she'd miscarried. Didn't figure it had been given up for adoption."

She nudged the olive in her drink with her finger then sucked it. "He was hedging his bets leaving the rights to her 'daughter'. If Cat had lived she would be the beneficiary but as she's dead that leaves you, right?" She handed over the document and waited for Sophie to read it.

"Jake left all the rights to publish his book to you, and the film rights, should there be an interest in them. When Alex's book comes out there's going to be huge interest in Jake's work and it will include the book, *The Lost Child*. I have the only existing copies in New York, all signed by him.

"But this document gives you the right to reprint - honey, this is real big. People will want a copy. You could sell millions of them. I told him this when he was alive but he wouldn't listen. He wanted to protect the woman he loved, your Mom. He was crazy about her."

Sophie kept silent; this was a lot to take in.

"I know plenty of people," Susan went on, "who'd be interested in producing a film about these two lovers and what happened to them. I'm good at what I do, honey, and I'm happy to be your agent... for the usual fee, of course," she said modestly, "I'll get the best deal for you. What do you think?" She took another deep swallow of her drink and looked at Sophie.

Sophie took off her glasses and folded the document; she put it down on the table, aware of the look of expectation in the other woman's face. Already her mind was on the two other projects close to her heart. The royalties from reprinting the book, and maybe even a film, would give her the funds she needed.

Susan was eyeing her beadily.

Sophie cleared her throat. "Should we decide to reprint Jake's book, and perhaps if someone takes an interest in making a film about them, I'd be more than happy for you to be our agent, given your history with Jake."

Susan rubbed her hands together with delight.

Sophie imagined dollar signs in the woman's eyes and smiled.

"Sure thing. I guess I'll have another martini and hit the sack. It's a long way to come from the States, but I think it's been worthwhile. By the way, that bloody great elephant the kid was playing with in the book, is it still around? Do you think he might come snooping around this here house tonight, waving his trunk and looking for people to sniff?"

Sophie threw back her head and laughed. "We haven't seen Tika for months; I suppose he doesn't like all the noise of the building going on around the estate. Would you like to meet Luke?"

"Is he another elephant, honey? We have enough wild people in New York. Like dead people, I don't do wild animals either, so no thanks to that as well."

Sophie laughed again. "Luke is an elderly African; he's lived at Mbabati for over fifty years. He knew Jake well."

"Nah, thanks again. I can't even pronounce the name of the house and sure as hell won't be able to understand a word he's saying. I need to get back to New York, honey, there's work to do, money to be made."

"I know Jake drew up this separate document," she held it up to Susan, "but what happened to his other things?"

"His parents came to New York to see me and we agreed I would sell all his art which was on display in various galleries around the world. The place he had in Kenya belonged to his folks and I guess they probably sold it; if I recall it was called Leopard's Leaves or something. They told me they never wanted to go back to Kenya. Their only son had never been found and the country just held bad memories for them. I guess I can understand that."

She looked out over the lake watching the hippo. "Maybe he was killed by a wild animal or something. To this day no-one knows what happened to him. It's a real mystery, but what can we do. We have to go on, don't we honey?"

325

She gave a cavernous yawn and stood up. "I'm looking forward to reading Alex's book, get him to FedEx me a copy will you? See you in the morning."

Sophie watched her retreating back. She didn't think Susan would enjoy the book which would tell her the truth about how Jake had died.

******

Their game of golf over, Martin Shapiro and Inspector John Groves were sharing a drink at the empty club bar. "So you can finally close your case, John. Both sisters are indeed back at Mbabati, but not in any state to be questioned again."

John narrowed his eyes. "Thanks for letting me know, you certainly took your time about it."

"Sorry about that, but I was overseas for a couple of months and then became involved with the changes at Mbabati, and the legal ramifications needed for the various projects Alex and Sophie want set up. I've been busy."

John stared into his empty glass. Nicola Gray - the one that got away.

He had been out of the country when Penny had called about a man called Alex Patterson who was asking a lot of questions and staying at Mbabati. By the time he returned to the country, keen to find out more about Patterson and what he was up to, the man had returned to London.

Martin drained his drink and stood up to leave. "Oh, by the way, John," he said casually, "you did know Nicola had a sister, didn't you?"

"Of course I bloody knew, but I never met her. Did you?"

"As a matter of fact I did. They were identical twins. Impossible to tell apart. I brought you *The Sunday Telegraph*, it arrived by courier this morning, hot off the press.

"There's a cracking good article about them in it. I think you might enjoy the book as well - I had to sign it off so I've read it. Those twins have made you famous John."

He threw down the newspaper and chuckling, he left the room.

John glared at his retreating back, then stared gloomily into the depths of his glass, deep in thought. The last piece of his puzzle had

326

fallen into place. Ordering another glass of whisky he raised his glass in salute to the two sisters. "So," he said to the empty room, "as it turns out I did meet you both after all. Well I'm buggered...

"Clever girls. Very clever indeed." He finished his drink in one gulp, snatched up the newspaper and stumped out of the club

Chapter Sixty-Two

Mbabati Country House was booked up four years in advance. Alex's book *The House Called Mbabati* hit The New York Times bestseller list within weeks and sold millions worldwide.

Jake Henderson's book, *The Lost Child*, sold out in days and the publishers ordered a massive reprint in time for Christmas.

Susan Cohen was busy cutting deals with the rights to the film and had decided to auction them off to the highest bidder. The press was already speculating who would play the leading roles of Nicola and Jake.

Sophie's shop had tripled in value and when she was made an offer she couldn't refuse she sold it.

"Instead of imagining other people's past through their things," she told Alex, "I found my own through theirs."

She gave up her life in London and went to live with Alex in Kenya, and together they ran the estate and the projects they had been able to set up from the millions they had made from the book sales, and would make from the film rights.

At some distance from the house they had set up an orphanage for abandoned elephants, they called it The Tika Foundation.

In the village where Luke had lived as a small child, houses had been built for the influx of workers, and staff, now employed by the Mbabati estate. A school and clinic were built for the villagers in and around the area, and was named Luke's Legacy in his honour. They had tried to persuade Luke to let them build him a new house but he had stubbornly refused, preferring his old round thatched home.

Alex and Sophie made a generous donation to the Mother Superior and her convent The Daughters of the Lord. Alex sent her a copy of his book and included a short note.

"As promised there's no mention of your convent and I hope our annual donation will go towards helping other women who have lost their way in life. Nicola and Elizabeth are finally together again and are buried here at Mbabati.

The diary and letters which led us to you, have been destroyed. I realize now, having read Nicola's diary yourself, that you knew Sophie was the child she gave up for adoption, and when you saw her at the convent you noticed the resemblance to her mother.

Sophie inherited Mbabati and she is here with me now. We were married quietly in Mombasa with only Luke and our lawyer, present. Luke proudly gave her away. We re-named the beach house 'Cat's Cottage' in memory of the daughter Nicola lost and the daughter I found.

Mr and Mrs Patterson put in place an annual cancer research fund in memory of the two sisters.

The French press, as predicted, went wild when the true story of Nicola DuPont was published. Old records were digitally reproduced and shot to the top of the charts where they stayed for months. In her honour they named a concert hall in Paris after her.

Luke became a legend in his own right and guests would ask for him by name when they made their bookings at Mbabati. Although now in his mid-seventies he still showed the guests around the house and grounds, telling his story in his own unique way. Visitors and guests were not allowed into the graveyard, but were able to see the headstones from behind the railings.

Each evening, before dinner, the butler would set up the sound system in the music room and the house would fill with the sound of Nicola playing her piano. Guests would listen enchanted, trying to imagine what life had been like when she had lived, loved and played there.

Every evening, Alex, Sophie and Luke would make their way to the graveyard. Luke would light the old rusting lamp at the head of Cat's grave and the three of them would sit for a while lost in their own private thoughts.

Tika was never seen again.

If you enjoyed reading this book and would like to share that enjoyment with others, then please take the time to visit the place where you made your purchase and write a review.

Reviews are a great way to spread the word about worthy authors and will help them be rewarded for their hard work.

You can also visit Samantha's Author Page on Amazon to find out more about her life and passions.

Also by Samantha Ford:

The Zanzibar Affair: A Novel Out of Africa

A letter found in an old chest on the island of Zanzibar finally reveals the secret of Kate Hope's glamorous, but anguished past, and the reason for her sudden and unexplained disappearance.

Ten year's previously Kate's lover and business partner, Adam Hamilton, tormented by a terrifying secret he is willing to risk everything for, brutally ends his relationship with Kate.

A woman is found murdered in a remote part of Kenya bringing Tom Fletcher back to East Africa to unravel the web of mystery and intrigue surrounding Kate, the woman he loves but has not seen for over twenty years.

In Zanzibar, Tom meets Kate's daughter Molly. With her help he pieces together the last years of her mother's life and his extraordinary connection to it.

A page turning novel of love, passion, betrayal and death, with an unforgettable cast of characters, set against the spectacular backdrop of East and Southern Africa, New York and France.

Printed in Great Britain
by Amazon

67776517R00196